Bone Grove
Merchant

EMBERWILDE

Obsidian

Lyre

WHITEWATER

Whitewater

Valakut

Roserun

Akashra

THE
BAKU SANDS

ELANTA

reestone

SETSUHA

SHEN SHE

Blackthorne

The Bone
Grove

THE BONE GROVE

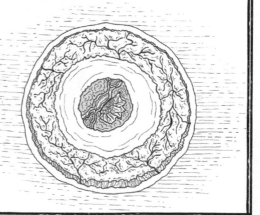

Bone Grove Merchant

BOOK TWO OF FATESPINNER

S.K. AETHERPHOXX

First Printing: April 2018
Second Printing: December 2018

Thoughtweft Publishing
281 Moubray Rd.
Kelowna, British Columbia, v1v 1v2
www.thoughtweft.com

Cover Art by Daniel Kamarudin
Cover Designer/Interior Typesetter: Stephen Ikesaka
Copy Editor: Stephanie Appleby
Map Artist: Robyn Hiebert

ISBN
Paperback: 978-0-9952112-3-0
Hardcover: 978-0-9952112-4-7
E-Book: 978-0-9952112-5-4

This one's for you dad. I don't thank you enough for the support you've given, but I want you to know you're always loved and appreciated.

MY INSTRUMENTS

You believed, and I became

Sundee Bruce
Nina Bournival
Matt "Rufus" Fuller
Colleen Glendinning
Keith Ikesaka
Sarah Kloos

REFERENCES

CHARACTERS

Ashissa: *(Ah-she-sah)* A pure blooded serpentine Shén Shé representing her neighboring realm in search of power through knowledge. She is arguably one of the best enchanters in the world, revered for her mystical aptitude and feared for her race's innately venomous virulence.

Agathuxusen, The Ravenmane: *(Eh-guh-thuk-su-sen)* Origin unknown, he is a massive lion-folk from the southern deserts known as the Baku Sands. Standing taller and broader than a normal Baku, with a mane of jet black fur, he readily wields highly volatile liquid fire which he uses to melt all in his way—flesh, bone, and stone alike. An Instrument of Ivory, he obeys her every command in exchange for his fearsome power.

Azel Katmin: The Blue Wolf Swordsong. A master of dual-weapons serving as a Moth.

Blackrock: The only man to escape the Blackrock prison, he is an Orbweaver on a mission of vengeance.

Carver: Captain of the *Last Breath*, pirate leader of the Fleet of Sunken Links.

Casamir Waylander: Son and eldest child of Elder Waylander, he is to be the heir to their name and legacy. However, Casamir struggles with finding his own identity outside of his family's tradition of becoming a Moth of the Realm.

Dawry: Pirate captain of the *Countess*.

Diana Laurellen: Geomantic soothsayer of the Moths, she is a psychic who glimpses into the future.

Djagatt: *(Juh-gat)* A Daggermouth Baku from the southernmost cliffs of the Baku Sands, he serves as first mate on the *Windborn Chance*.

Elder Waylander: Head of the Waylander family and leader of an elite organization of warriors and assassins known as the Moths. Oathbound to King Liam Whitewater.

Fenwight: *(Fen-wite)* A magical creature born from the earth and stone of the Setsuha. Resembling a massive wolf of mottled fur and moss, their cloudy eyes are blind to anything that does not touch the ground. These spirit wolves travel by melding in and out of trees anywhere within their territory.

Fever: A sultry and seductive assassin from Emberwilde, she is a broken mind that loves to create chaos. Aptly named for the poison-induced fever her victims endure before death, she is a highly hunted criminal of Emberwilde. Now an Instrument of Ivory, she summons serpents of ichor and shadow from her black diamond bangles.

Howlpack Shade: A highly skilled hunter, tracker, and assassin, Shade is the Alpha of a group of warriors known as the Howlpack. He is the Instrument of Howlpack Sentinel Avelie and traverses the realm to silently execute those who threaten its future.

Howlpack Sentinel Avelie: The second of the Fates, Howlpack Sentinel Avelie is the guardian of the Weave.

Illy the Flux: The third of the Fates, Illy the Flux observes the fatespinners—predicting the future and calculating the necessary changes to make it better.

Ivory the Unwoven: The forlorn Fate, Ivory the Unwoven was once maestro to the deaths of the fatespinners and their cycle of life energy. She has renounced her role as the fourth Fate and now seeks to destroy the Weave and bring free will back to the people of Elanta.

Jury: An Orbweaver gatekeeper who manages cult affairs from the village of Roserun.

Katya Waylander: Daughter and youngest child of Elder Waylander, she is a gifted healer and alchemist studying in the city of Lyre. Excelling at her studies and spiritual growth at a rate far more impressive than Casamir.

Lau Lau: A young, free-spirited psychic pirate who can read minds and hear treasure. She is a founding member of the Bone Grove Merchants and assists with navigation on the *Windborn Chance*.

Liam Whitewater: Also known as the 'Whitewater Leviathan', he is the last of a race of giants that once ruled the mountains. When his adopted human father, Leomund Whitewater, led an army into the mountains to destroy the leviathans, Liam was taken as an infant and raised to be the next king. He rules his people with fairness and grace, gaining the praises of the common folk and the scorn of the noble blooded.

Lilia: A General of the Bastion Nine. She is a noble highborn from Clan Firefly, an elite group of assassins that hunt Elanta's most dangerous criminals. Unlike most Fireflies, she wields two swords, one of which belonged to her brother—a former Bastion.

Me'landris Eiliona: Draconian mate to Savrae-Lyth and father of Whisper, he disappeared after the Dragon War and hasn't been seen since.

Nuith: *(New-eeth)* The second oldest of the elders, she is named after the dusk, and is often teased for her constant fussing over tradition and safety. A perfectionist at heart, she mothers the other elders to ensure they remain vigilant in their duties.

Ogra: A large dragon, formerly the leader of the honey shrikes before he was cast into the Overworld and twisted by its essence, he is now one of the four Chitin Kings. He seeks to conquer Elanta.

Oona Kismet: Captain of the *Windborn Chance*, pirate leader of the Bone Grove Merchants, and master swordsman on the run from the Phoenix Queen and her military.

Origin Progenitus: The first of the Fates, Origin Progenitus hatches a new fatespinner whenever a creature with a soul is born.

The Phoenix Queen/the malikeh: From the Palace of Roiling Cinders, with its ancient architecture built into the side of an active volcano in the middle of the city of Obsidian, she rules over all Emberwilde. Few have gazed upon her, but all fear her cunning, intellect, and wrath, leading and empowering her realm with strong militaristic efficiency.

Phori: A highly decorated General from Clan Salamander. She is one of the few warriors skilled with the exotic two-bladed staff and holds a coveted seat in the Bastion Nine. An Instrument of Ivory, she has the power to manipulate the density of objects she touches.

The Ram: A General of the Bastion Nine and member of Clan Ram with a penchant for rules and tradition.

Rowan Bastet: Though a foreigner to Whitewater, his proof of loyalty and skill earned him a place among the Moths, serving as Elder Waylander's closest friend and ally.

Salem Eventide: A subtle streak of violet sheen through his dark hair, though hardly noticeable in contrast to the vibrant emerald green of his eyes. Marked for death by the Fates, he carries with him the power of the Queen of Drakes. A power long thought lost.

Savrae-Lyth: *(Suh-vray-lith)* The Queen of Drakes and ruler of Setsuha, she tore her own heart from her chest to end the Dragon War. Her power currently resides within Salem Eventide.

Selva: *(Sel-vah)* Fenwight friend, companion, and guardian of Vaexa since he was a puppy.

Vaexa est'alara: *(Vay-ksa ess-ta-lah-rah)* Youngest of the Setsuhan elders, her name translates to 'White Diamond Dove'. Unlike other Setsuhans, which are made flesh from hard stone, she was sculpted from soft selenite. The high resonance has made her sensitive, both emotionally and physically, and has instilled in her a desperation for freedom and adventure beyond the mountain to which she is bound.

Vaughn Cross: A young, brilliant man, made chancellor of the King's Court, he is a prodigy that governs the economic development of Whitewater. He thinks himself above all others, excluding Salem Eventide, with whom he competes fiercely to prove he is the best.

Venetta Valentina: Arguably the strongest Moth serving under Elder Waylander; she is also known as 'battle-mad' for her cold convictions and ruthlessness. Fastened to her back, wrapped in white silks and violet sigils, is a sword as tall as she.

Victor Fairchild: Treasurer of the King's Court, he is a man of high standard and expensive taste. Every bit of wealth traverses his logs as he accounts for the realm's expenses and income.

Whisper: Orphaned in infancy and left in the mountainous seclusion of the Monastery of the Eternity Ring, strength and vengeance were once her only callings before her tragic death. Feared for her capacity and willingness for destruction, she is a legendary mercenary on the lips of mortals, but now maybe something more.

Wrath: A monstrously large creature known as a leviathan, he is clad head to toe in obsidian armor. An Instrument of unstoppable force at the command of Ivory, the Unwoven.

Yoru: An elantan velvetine—a talking, not-talking, cat, not-cat.

WHITEWATER

Whitewater is the central realm of the world. At its northern and southernmost points, it is greeted by the shores of the ocean, while other realms border its eastern and western ranges. Temperate forests of pine and bittersweet grove scatter across the ridges of green grass and gray stone, up until the snow dusted forests of the north.

EMBERWILDE

The westernmost realm of the world, it only borders Whitewater to the east and the Baku Sands to the south. Glistening ocean crashes at the base of sheer rock faces to its west and north, cooling their otherwise arid climate. Basic military training is a rite of passage for both men and women, rich and poor, and begins in their youth. When basic rank is achieved, a single white feather is woven into their hair. This signifies they are a true citizen of the realm and have earned their right to liberty. As rank progresses, new feathers are added or colors are changed to reflect their new status.

SETSUHA, THE REALM OF THE SNOW LEAF

The Realm of the Snow Leaf is a massive mountain that borders Whitewater's north-eastern influence. There is ocean to the north and east, the temperate tundra of Whitewater to the west, and the humid jungles of the serpentine Shén Shé to the south. Their freshwater rainforests and pristine rivers have been guarded from outsiders for thousands of years by illusions, enchantments, and the supernatural evolution of its flora and fauna. Nearly everything has developed some form of carnivorous nature that prevents trespassers from invading their lush realm.

THE WEAVE

A separate plane of existence created and inhabited by the Fates as a safe haven for their fatespinners, where destiny is woven, watched, and altered to create the most favorable outcome in their eyes.

SHÉN SHÉ, THE REALM OF THE GOD SNAKE

A small realm to the east of Whitewater and south of Setsuha; a consuming maze of jungle and sheer, vine laden mountains. The snake-like humanoids and aberrations that inhabit it have an unquenchable thirst for knowledge and a penchant for enlightenment. They can be incredibly dangerous, but are otherwise very spiritual. Their cunning and monstrous nature, however, keeps them untrusted in the eyes of their human neighbors.

THE BAKU SANDS

A large peninsula to the south of Emberwilde, its deserts stretch far out into the ocean. Home to several different tribes of lion-folk creatures known as Baku, their individual territories are often fiercely guarded.

THE BONE GROVE

An island heavily protected by the elements and home to the Bone Grove Merchants. The heart of the island is surrounded by three dangerous trials: The Fear, The Dance, and The Shallowdeep.

0

PROLOGUE

Death can be a sinking stone. A descent into a cold, numbing darkness that consumes you from all sides. It can be a plunge into fading ripples, quickly forgotten, onto a riverbed, quickly lost. An envelope of lonesome quietude that only a crushing lack of resolve could conjure. This, of course, is not the fate of everyone in death, an eternity of solitude amidst the forlorn, but this was Whisper's death. For some reason she could remember it clearly.

She could taste the heat as golden arcs of electricity turned her flesh to cinder, feel the wash of light as it blinded her brilliant cobalt blue eyes, and smell the acrid smoke as lightning surged across her face and turned her raven hair to ash—an agony so fierce, yet it filled her final moments with frigid emptiness.

For a brief moment she remembered the day she lost her mother and father. Though she was only an infant, she could recall the soft wool blanket in which she was wrapped and the way the light glistened off her father's tears—somehow she could not bring herself to remember his eyes. Almost as though she had never once seen them before their tragic separation. It was a room of crisp, cool air that quickly soured with her mother's blood as it soaked into the long sleeves of a man who wore the shadows like a cloak. His power radiated with a force so incredible that it smothered her into unconsciousness and left her to awaken in the arms of a monk, deep within the mountains of the eastern arid realm known as Emberwilde. How she got there, who she was, and who had taken her family from her were the only three questions with which she burdened herself to answer.

Though she wasn't coherent enough to realize it until she was older, she was what the people of the world called a 'mistborn'—a child born too close to the misty borders that surround their world like a dome. Deformed in the womb by exposure to the unknown energies that exist in the mysterious beyond. Opalescent scales grew across the left side of her face, the pupils of her eyes stretched into demonic slits, and her left arm, armored with jagged plates, grew three large claws. She was only a child, wanting to be a woman, destined to be an exile.

Her memories skipped nearly two decades as she breezed past every lesson of combat and quill. Lessons the monks desperately hoped would hone her mind and ease her inner tempests. Though many of the monks dedicated their lives to becoming enlightened, a state of spiritual awakening that allowed a person to manipulate certain energies, it quickly became apparent her mistborn traits gifted her with innate power. By the age of five she shattered her first stone. Seven, she made her first tornado. It was only by age twelve, when she blew her first jet of orange flame, that the monks truly began to question their safety. For eighteen years, deep in the sanctuary of the Monastery of the Eternity Ring, she studied and trained. Eagerly awaiting the day she could find out who took her family and tear his head from his shoulders. Blood was her calling and vengeance was all her heart knew—until she ventured to Emberwilde's eastern neighbor, the realm of Whitewater. That was where she met him.

He was her window into the truths of the world, her distraction from the ruination in her soul. With every word he brought understanding and with every laugh came peace. Even in their darkest hour, watching his secrets tear his soul asunder at the lip of a bottle, the more she learned of him, the more she learned of herself.

He was Salem Eventide. Honored and revered as the Voice of the King, yet marked for death by the Fates governing the known world.

She didn't know if he was still alive. In the confines of her mind, as an assassin of the Fates took her life in a battle of lightning and flame, she pleaded with the Fates to spare him their wrath. It was her very first moment of sheer selflessness in a lifetime of survivor's instincts, imploring silently that her spilled blood be enough. Whether or not her plea was heard was something she would never know—perhaps that was the hardest part. The golden lightning washed agony over the body she'd worn weary, but nothing could compare to the breaking of a heart she just learned to use.

Reaching for the light as you sink into darkness.
Calling voicelessly to ears that will never hear.
Death can be a sinking stone—cold, lonesome, and hopelessly heavy.

Whisper's awakening was like that of a blindfolded sip of wine. Musty, bold undertones crept across her palate while a heavy bouquet of oak and spices tingled her sense of smell. Slowly, she began to feel her body rock in all directions, like the gentle swirling of a glass.

"Get the cap'n," sounded the stern voice of a man who probably looked as much a weasel as he sounded. "She's wakin' up."

Heavy footsteps strode across wooden floorboards to open a door, which flooded her with the resounding chaos from beyond—loud voices, water, and the banging of metal all mixed with creaking wood in the near distance. Though she could not yet bring herself to open her eyes, she began to feel she was aboard a ship. The hull moaned in drawls as she wondered how she managed it. Her fingertips crawled along what felt like a thin cotton blanket, and though it pained her, it was remarkably tolerable considering the nature of her 'death'.

Before long, the scrunching of leather and cloth accompanied the jingle of keys and coin as someone entered the room.

"She's healin' quick," spoke a boldly accented voice. He could have been from Emberwilde, but she couldn't be certain without seeing the red tinge of his eyes. "Half 'er burns are gone. Even 'er hair is growin' back fast."

"Aye, sir," the weasel replied.

With great force of will her eyes began to open. Even the dim ambiance of the room was blinding. At first, everything was a collage of blurry shapes and colors, but as her vision cleared she began to recognize the crisp edges of cargo tethered to splintered walls. By the smell of it, they were carrying dried spices of some potent variety.

The weasel's crooked features made him look as daft as he sounded, meeting her eyes with his and grinning something terrible. "She'll fetch a fine price, Cap'n."

The man to whom he was speaking was dressed in rough brown leathers, worn to near uselessness. She figured it made him either poor or sentimental, perhaps both. Regardless, he seemed to hold the unwavering respect of his crew. Hung at his side was a sabre, dull and chipped with incredible neglect—one would be bludgeoned to death long before bleeding.

As the captain scoured her gristly, he quickly soured as his eyes adjusted to the darkness of the room. "'er hair was growin' blond when we found 'er." He was nearly as confused as he was disappointed, "and the silver in 'er eyes is gone."

Nervously, the weasel approached her and pried her eye open further. Though his features were jaded, crass, and ruthless, she could both see and feel his fear as he frantically searched her iris. He then tilted her head and examined her hair. It was short, still growing back from being burnt away, but was impressively long considering it had only been days. "How's it possible? Her eyes' gone blue now and 'er hair's turned black."

"Fates!" The captain slammed his fist against the top of a crate, taking pause to wallow in his unforeseen misfortune. "I told Carver she's a dove with silver eyes. Now she's a blue-eyed raven."

The weasel swallowed hard, knowing full well how Carver earned his name. "'er burns are healin' fast. If she doesn't scar she'll be a beaut. Maybe he'll overlook it if we give 'er cheap-like."

"Well, she's enlightened at least." The captain crossed his arms and contemplated the fate of the frail woman before him, playing with the idea that giving her away would keep Carver from hanging him from his ankles and skinning him alive. "The only way she could be healin' so quick." He dared imagine a deal gone wrong. Carver had a terrifying reputation of flaying those he couldn't bring himself to trust. Enough moral turpitude to strangle any chance of a conscience and plenty of coin to employ some of the realm's finest psychopaths. Dealing with him was as risky as it was profitable.

The weasel looked back into her weary eyes with absent minded hope and, as his train of thought trailed, Whisper groaned and shakily lifted her hand to the collar of his shirt.

"What's she tryin' t'say?" The captain gestured for the weasel to allow her fragile, burnt fingertips to draw him closer.

The blanket slowly rose as she took in the briny air of the open door and closed her eyes to hone her focus. The room felt still in the solitude of her mind, quelling the motion of the ship, staunching the rancid smell of sour fruit upon the weasel, and silencing the bustle of the crew and water beyond. It was a stillness wound in anticipation as she licked her cracked lips and winced.

Everyone fell completely still, as if to defy any urge to make a sound that would interfere with what labored words she could be trying to muster, until, bursting through the tension like thunder, her head snapped forward and crashed into the weasel's crooked face. He dropped to his knees, barely clinging to consciousness as the room melted and flexed. With an exhaustion that caused her arm to tremble she strained to keep her grip and pulled him close once more. She plunged her forehead into him a second time, which filled the room with the sickly crunching of cartilage and bone as his face collapsed inward. Broken teeth skipped along the wood, followed by the gushing of warm blood and matter. Only then did she release her grip and allow him to fall.

Her body sunk, rife with disappointment over how the man's head had not burst beneath her initial ferocity—a testament to her abysmal decrease in strength. Over her last three years as a mercenary she had crushed a multitude of human skulls, but this was the first time it took more than one try, and the first it hurt her to do so. The warm, dull throbbing of her forehead resonated down through her neck and she cringed as she coped with the pain for the very first time.

The captain's footsteps slowly crossed the floor toward her, heavy with intent. Laboriously, she opened her eyes only to see the rusty guard of the captain's sword moments before it struck her face and hurled her back into complete darkness.

Though her arm fell limp the captain's nerves had yet to rest as he covered his mouth to contend with the stench of blood, stool, and piss on the mangled corpse at his feet. This frail woman, whom only days prior was nearly unrecognizable, had healed half her wounds and somehow found the strength to murder a member of his crew from the comfort of her bed. He cautiously looked her over and nodded to himself. An enlightened woman with a spirit as strong as hers might just be enough to keep him in Carver's good books.

Thousands of years ago, four powerful and ageless mortals sought to govern the world of Elanta. Each of them conspired to specialize in one aspect and together they worked to create and manage the world's ideal destiny. This grand aspiration began with the creation of the Weave, a separate plane of existence where they could watch the mortal realm in peace. As these four became more and more influential the believers of Elanta grew to know them as the Fates.

The first of the Fates is Origin Progenitus, who hones his power into that of tangible representation. Whenever a creature with a soul is born, a tiny spider called a fatespinner hatches from a nest that rests along his hunched back. The fatespinner then enters the Weave with a near infinite number of other fatespinners, spinning a line of silk to represent its creature's timeline. When two strands connect in the massive web it is called a waypoint and represents a change in that creature's destiny based on the influences of another. Some people live lives of massive influence—their fatespinners weave huge clusters of waypoints in a bustling and seemingly chaotic knot of white threads. While others live lives of isolation—connecting to only a few waypoints as they have little impact on the world around them. Manifesting tangible timelines was an unimaginable feat that took its toll on Origin's body, turning him old and frail as he feeds the nest on his back with the power of his soul.

The second Fate is Howlpack Sentinel Avelie. Charged with protecting the Weave at all costs, her focus of power makes her, arguably, the strongest creature in known existence. Though she began her role as a human woman, her training and dedication to the art of destruction began to change her form to best reflect the carnal instincts within her heart and soul—a massive bipedal wolf. Her hair twisted into thick black fur, her face elongated to allow for rows of razor sharp teeth, and she grew long claws sharper and stronger than steel. No creature of power dared go searching for the Weave, knowing full well that her incredible senses were as inescapable as her jaws.

The third Fate is Illy the Flux. Though Origin Progenitus was the father of time and Howlpack Sentinel Avelie was a force most feared, Illy was the Fate to whom the people would call out to in life—whether it be in gratitude or a plea. Illy harnesses the powers of omniscience and perceptive precognition, allowing her to watch every fatespinner at once, calculate its timeline, and predict its future waypoints. She tirelessly supervises the Weave to determine which fatespinners must be manipulated to keep Elanta from destroying itself and every outcome, both boon and demise, is presumed to be her will—almost always accepted as the greater good.

The fourth and final Fate was Ivory the Unwoven, who later became known as the Forlorn. Ivory was the harbinger of death, orchestrating the transition between when a fatespinner dies and reincarnates. When a creature dies and its fatespinner falls from the Weave, Ivory deconstructed the energy and cycled it back into Origin Progenitus so that he could construct a new fatespinner when needed. While Illy was whom the people would call for the tribulations of life, Ivory was the name on their lips in the clutches of death. Some would beg for more time, some would pray in resolution, but all would die at her will as she ferried their soul into their next life. She was a pivotal part in the cycle of life and death until she denounced the Weave and disappeared, leaving the remaining Fates to struggle with filling her role.

Origin Progenitus was already using the bulk of his power to sustain his nest and Howlpack Sentinel Avelie's role was too crucial to take attention from, especially with a rogue Fate in the aether. This left Illy the Flux to divide her attention between watching the Weave and balancing the entire cycle of life and death.

Two decades passed since Ivory, the Forlorn, entered into the mists that border the mortal realm of Elanta, and now she has returned—with an army of demons and occultists in tow.

Mossy stone stairs led several stories to the flattened top of a pyramid altar, where five roughly hewn stalagmites towered high in a circle. Glowing blue arcs of lightning slowly crawled across the hazy violet sky as mystical glyphs churned above. This was the Weave, isolated on a plane where time was an abstract concept the laws of nature barely abided by.

Each of the five towering stalagmites that circled at the peak represented a realm within Elanta—the world of mortal man. Dense clusters of web interlaced between them to create a mass that was nearly impenetrable—except for the Setsuha stone, which had hardly any strands connected to it at all and created an opening into the center. Very few fatespinners ever travelled to Setsuha and most immediately met their end. Every creature within the realm of Setsuha was created and sustained by the mountain itself, making it impossible for Origin Progenitus to forge a fatespinner. For millennia the stone stood almost completely bare, but Illy would always face it in case someone had the audacity to enter.

Illy was an elegant woman who adorned herself in the same silks she watched. The ghostly translucent fabric hung weightlessly off her delicate frame, her clouded eyes seemed to stare into nothing, and her long wispy white hair waved as though the air were fluid. She would stand in the center of the Weave itself, each strand of hair stretching outward to touch a line of the fatespinners' silk, allowing her to see, feel, hear, and experience the vast multitude of timelines simultaneously. For any normal enlightened human, scrying even a single fatespinner would be both overwhelming and dangerous, but for her it was second nature.

From the outside of the mass, Origin Progenitus and Howlpack Sentinel Avelie approached the final steps, stopping at the pinnacle and watching Illy from beyond the Setsuha stone. Despite their roles as Fates, they were forbidden from entering the heart of the Weave—just as Illy was forbidden from leaving it.

Origin's knees rattled as he reached the top, just loud enough to be heard over the crackling of new fatespinners hatching from the nest upon his back. The tiny spiders crawled along his skin and leapt to the Weave, carried through the air by strands of silk that seemed to catch the breeze.

Avelie sneered and rolled her eyes. She knew why he was as weak and frail as he was. Each Fate had a vassal of power known as an Instrument—a mortal of their choosing they bestowed power upon and used to complete tasks in Elanta. This allowed them to focus on their role in the Weave, but also subjected them to 'feedback'—a painful surge of desynchronizing energy that occurs when their Instrument is slain. Such was the ail with Origin, and Avelie had no sympathy for the weak or gravely overestimated.

Both Whisper and Salem were worrisome variables to the Fates because they somehow possessed no fatespinner. When the decision was made to execute them, Origin's Instrument was responsible for bringing Salem to his end. His Instrument was the esteemed Lady Rhoswan Gray, who turned out to be far too sentimental for the assassination he charged her with. She showed weakness, Salem took her life and escaped, while Origin suffered a feedback surge that nearly crippled his already tired body. He would recover in time, but for now he was barely holding on.

Avelie's Instrument, the Legendary Dragon Slayer known as Howlpack Shade, fared only marginally better in his mission, barely surviving his altercation with Whisper. Had he not poisoned her from the start he may not have succeeded in striking her down with an arrow of pure lightning. Her charred body thrown into the river and sent to sea, quickly forgotten.

The world was not short on perils, the greatest of which was the reappearance of the Forlorn Fate, Ivory. Descending from her exile to the Overworld with an army of cultists and demons she was creating a massive wake in Elanta. The remaining Fates were struggling to manage the chaos. Ivory razed a whole city by reducing it to diamond sand, prepared unimaginably monstrous forces in the safety of the mist, and captured an ancient artifact so powerful that even the breaking of its seal washed the world with a golden energy that continued to linger in some spots.

Illy expressed worry as clusters of fatespinners grew listless. They were confused, unable to feel their creature's soul and thereby unable to spin their destiny. It was a phenomenon she experienced only recently, after the artifacts seal was broken and the mists of the Overworld rained down upon Elanta. She theorized that the properties of the mist shrouded the cultists from her omniscience, and worse yet, it made it impossible for her to find Ivory or her Instruments. In a world where knowledge was power she was gravely uninformed and supremely vulnerable.

A strand of Illy's hair gently touched Lady Rhoswan's timeline, where she could relive the memory of Salem Eventide telling her that Ivory was responsible for the world's current tribulations. She was quick to remove herself from the memory before re-living Rhoswan's untimely demise. It had happened once, and never again.

"You wanted to tell us what is going on," Origin crooked his neck as a spider crawled across his ear. "It is true, that Ivory has returned?"

Illy nodded gently. "I wanted to be sure before telling you. She also has many Instruments. Four, it seems."

Avelie and Origin were perplexed. Having enough power for more than one was unheard of, but four seemed impossible.

"At least." Her strands of hair travelled to a large knot of silk on the Whitewater stone, where no fatespinners seemed to be weaving—the former city of Lyre. It was once a great city before Ivory and her Instruments invaded—now a lifeless desert of diamond sand. "There have been many sightings to confirm."

Avelie smiled at the idea that Ivory was foolhardy enough to weaken herself so badly, though if Ivory were able to harness the full power of the artifact she stole she would easily return to full strength—perhaps even stronger.

Origin cackled. "Four Instruments? Impossible. Even if we had the strength to have more than one at a time it would be suicide to spread one's self so thin."

"We choose one vassal because we require the bulk of our power to sustain the Weave," Illy reminded them. "Ivory does not have that responsibility anymore, leaving her with power to spare. We shouldn't underestimate her."

"What do we do then?" Avelie asked.

Illy drew her attention to a cluster of dazed fatespinners on the Emberwilde Stone. "My inability to see Ivory puts us at a big disadvantage. Howlpack Shade should use his abilities to track her down while my Instrument will seek to unveil her plan."

Origin immediately interjected. "What about Salem Eventide?" Rhoswan Gray lost her life at his hand and he wanted retribution.

Illy tried to calm him with the confidence of her voice. "His lack of a fatespinner is a problem, but he is not our biggest anymore. He will be dealt with, I assure you, but in priority. We have little time now. The demons in the mist won't remain there forever, and their appetites are voracious."

1

HOWLPACK SHADE AND THE BLACKTHORNE HUNT

The heavy crash of wood and clay echoed through the empty halls and chambers of the late Lady Rhoswan's famous redwood pagoda. Cool morning mist danced above the still waters of her pond and weightlessly lingered around the stone lanterns that decorated the property. Normally, maids delicately wandered the grounds and tended to their chores, but since her recent death, everything had grown solemn and ghostly.

Another loud crash resounded through the upper floor as a man clad in rugged leathers and hide struck an elegant rosewood bedside table with such ferocity the legs buckled beneath it. His teeth ground behind his bristled cheeks as pain surged up his hand and arm, both wrapped in bloody cotton. He was Howlpack Shade, Instrument of Howlpack Sentinel Avelie, and though he suffered significant injury while fighting Whisper in the groves of Freestone the pain was of little consequence when venting his frustrations.

He brushed his long black hair from his face and looked to the bed, upon which lay the body of Rhoswan Gray. Her pristine figure was carefully cradled in exquisite silks. White to match the mysterious purity of her hair, red to memorialize her sultry spirit.

"I didn't think you cared," growled a voice from behind him.

Though it was supernaturally deep, it had a second voice layered upon it—lighter and more effeminate.

Shade immediately recognized it and bowed to a knee. In the corner of his eye, a massive creature strode forth and stood before him. Long black fur coated her tall muscular frame as she stood on two paws as a large bipedal wolf. He could feel the blood red gaze of her eyes through the top of his skull as they peered down her long snout. Howlpack Sentinel Avelie, second of the Fates and guardian of the Weave.

"Forgive me, I hadn't noticed your arrival." Under most circumstances, when a Fate transcended into the mortal world to speak with their Instrument, time would slow to a stop. This time was no different, but there was little natural movement within Rhoswan's pagoda to allow him to notice the phenomena.

Avelie turned to the corpse of Lady Rhoswan with feral eyes. "It was foolish of Origin to ask her to kill Salem Eventide," she growled. "His strength was his mind and his weakness was combat. We should have had you slit his throat and leave the simple minded mistborn girl for her to ensnare."

"It was personal. She was close to Salem and felt that..."

"Felt?" she sneered as she slowly dragged her claws along the wood of the nearest wall. "We are at war."

Shade hung his head and stared shamefully at his knee.

"As we speak, Ivory is amassing an army of both monsters and men. Blood and bone will be the foundation of this confrontation, and sentiment will be our undoing."

"My apologies. The Lady Rhoswan was ordered by Origin to execute Eventide. I would have interjected if I felt it was my place," he feebly defended.

Avelie tilted her head back and scowled. "Origin is an idiot. He knows nothing of getting things done. He makes a fatespinner the moment a soul is born, but leaves it for me to guard, Illy to lead, and Ivory to kill. He knows only of immediate necessity and nothing of foresight."

"You're right. I should have relieved Rhoswan of her duty."

Avelie wrapped her claws around the dome of his skull and

pulled his head back to meet her eyes. Though she seemed fearsome in intent, there was pause to lead him to believe otherwise. "Yes," she began. "You have erred, but so have I. I should have beaten some sense into Origin from the beginning. This tragedy is his mistake and our mess." She released her grip and gazed out the window across the groves of burnt peach trees.

"Shall I hunt Eventide?"

Avelie growled. "I would like nothing more than to have you track him down before his own volition throws more knots in the fabric of time."

Shade bowed his head once more. "Are you worried Ivory will seek to recruit him?"

"There are many things that worry me, but what matters is whether or not it worries Illy," Avelie began. "We rely so heavily on the Weave for information that a man like Eventide, who has no fatespinner, is essentially invisible. Used properly he could be very dangerous. This leads me to ask a question of you I truly wish I didn't need."

"Anything."

"I don't have access to the heart of the Weave and therefore cannot see or interpret the many webs of fatespinners as Illy can. However, my connection to you grants me a very limited view of you and your interactions. As you were fighting the mistborn girl I noticed I could not sense her spirit."

"What does that mean?"

"It means that she too, has no fatespinner. Both Whisper and Salem are abominations of the Weave, invisible to our sight and impervious to our influence. Whisper was very, very powerful, so I imagine you understand how dire our situation could be."

"Of course," he agreed, "but Whisper is dead. Only Salem remains."

"I need to be sure." She labored with the need for reassurance, wishing she could trust his success without question. "I have never had reason to doubt you, but I have to ask if you are absolutely certain you killed Whisper."

Shade wanted to be offended, but a part beyond his pride knew that their situation was becoming increasingly dire. His Fate had every right to need absolution. "I stood over her charred corpse. She was not breathing and had no heartbeat." He recalled the battle's conclusion clearly. The acrid smell of flesh turned ash, the glistening beauty of lightning kissed earth turned glass, the continued defiance in her eyes. His heart skipped a beat. "Her... eyes, though."

Avelie lowered her massive maw to peer directly into the dark of his pupils. "What of them?"

"They did not burn." He wanted to assure her it was nothing, but in a world where the impossible was becoming continuously challenged, even he had his doubts.

"What do you mean?" Her concern was growing, making Shade nervous.

"Her whole body was burnt beyond recognition, but her eyes remained pristine." He had slain many powerful creatures in his lifetime, but he had never seen that before. Usually the intensity of his favorite attack would cause the fluid within the eyes to boil and burst. "What does it mean?"

Avelie turned to gaze out into the grove. "I don't know. Where is the body now?"

"She was a true warrior, I had my wolves give her a warrior's memorial."

"You sent her body to sea?" She sneered. Though it was an entirely understandable tribute it was unfortunate to no longer have the body to be sure she was indeed dead.

Shade nodded and withdrew a small ledger from a pouch at his side. "I have sent some of my wolves south along the river to Blackthorne in the event Eventide tries to find the mistborn girl's body before it floats to open water. I will send word for them to collect her body if they can." He shakily fumbled with the wounds of his hands while opening the bindings on the ledger. "I found this." With weary fingertips he managed to open it to the last written page, midway through. "Rhoswan, by order of Origin Progenitus, was carefully documenting Eventide's movements and business transactions. According to this, not only does he have property and status in Whitewater, he is also welcome within the borders of the

Realm of the Snow Leaf. If he isn't found in Blackthorne, it's likely he will either flee to the capital or eastwards."

Avelie's gaze snapped back to his, growling as she pondered. "Yes…" she began. "The Snow Leaf is nearly impenetrable for anyone uninvited. It would be the safest place for him to hide, though Whitewater would be more comfortable."

"Where should I go?" Shade asked.

Avelie pondered a moment. "Illy's Instrument, Elder Waylander, will be told to go to the Whitewater capital, assuming he isn't already there. Illy is whispering to the fatespinner of King Liam Whitewater to incept Waylander's promotion to Judiciar as we speak. From his new role we will have him watch the city for Eventide."

"I will make the journey to Setsuha immediately," he replied. "My injuries should be manageable by the time I reach their borders."

"No," she began. "I have made you this world's greatest hunter, but the realm of Setsuha is an entity unto itself. It has evolved countless dangers to keep itself cleansed of foreigners. Every shadow has eyes, every wind carries words, and every living thing, be it plant or animal, would try to devour you. Salem's death isn't worth the risk, and if he retreats to Setsuha it is very unlikely Ivory would find him anyways."

Shade nodded. Tracking Salem was important, but if he was receiving different orders they had to be crucial.

"You will travel south to Blackthorne in search of the mistborn's body. After that go to Whitewater and rendezvous with Waylander. Eventide has proven he can kill an Instrument, and if your wolves found him in Blackthorne they might already be dead. If he travels to the capital it may take both of you to ensure his death."

"Of course, my Fate." Shade bowed, wincing as a wound opened a little.

"Ivory's demons of the Overworld grow stronger beyond the mist. Though they haven't moved on the capital yet you will be deep in enemy territory, tread very softly. The city center is lost to the mist and the Whitewater Leviathan has ordered the bulk of his military to enforce martial law, treating any suspicious activity with extreme prejudice. The citizens are being relocated by district, but it is a process as slow as it is organized. Tensions are very high. You will encounter little or no support if confronted."

"And if I find Ivory?"

Avelie's blood-red eyes narrowed. "Call my name and I will deal with her."

In the narrow streets between hovels of splintered wood and thatch, a figure clad in thick brown wolf's fur cut through a dense fog. The moisture in the air smothered the street lanterns. Though the weather did the small village no justice by sequestering it in a miasma of faded color and damp cold, this was the lovely village of Blackthorne—plum groves south of Freestone and birthplace of the legendary Lady Rhoswan. Even through the haze the delicate silhouette of weeping branches adorned with blossoms of dark pink and violet graced the senses with an aromatic sweetness that caressed the palate and calmed the mind. Though Blackthorne was much smaller than Freestone, its sweeping landscape of rivers, knolls, and plum trees made it no less awe-striking, and served as one of the last villages before the stony southern shores of the world.

With footsteps far lighter than one would imagine the cloaked figure strode silently past the occasional townsfolk, examining each with intensity from beneath the wolf skin cowl over his head. This fog was not like that of the tragedy in Freestone or Whitewater, where the mist of the Overworld brought forth demons of despicable origin. This was a common fog that formed from the warm groves and the cool ocean breezes, and therefore the people here were simple and calm, tending their wares in peace. Though most had seen foreigners clad in pelts, none had ever seen one of such size. None were courageous enough to ask questions. Nervous eyes watched him closely as they gave him a wide berth, which allowed him to stride the streets and hills unhindered. With a near weightless turn he disappeared between two buildings.

The wolf gracefully bounded up the wall and perched on the rooftop, peering downward at a small hovel across the road.

It appeared to be abandoned, but he and the other wolves of the Howlpack had tracked Salem Eventide here, after he fled Freestone. In the wake of Rhoswan's murder, the Howlpack had strict orders to find and kill him for his crime. Raising a hand, the wolf signalled to two others at street level and they each entered an alley on either side of their target. If Eventide was hiding within, he was not to escape.

The fog hung in the air as the people of the street began to thin, but movement within had yet to be spotted. The wolf on the rooftop tried to adjust his footing when he noticed he couldn't move.

"What are we looking for?" whispered a curious voice behind him.

The wolf struggled to speak but could only move his eyes, shifting them back and forth in their sockets.

"Ah, good. You cannot speak." A man sat beside the wolf and examined the contents of a foldable tin he held in his hand—within were a variety of needles. "I was worried I would miss your nerves through the pelt."

The wolf could feel it now, a radiating numbness centered at the base of his neck and along his spine from the length of steel that was inserted between his vertebrae. The man next to him wore a traditional military peacoat and a violet scarf, meeting his gaze with brilliantly sharp emerald eyes. The muted color of the fog sequestered the violet sheen in his dark, messy hair, but from the scent there was no mistaking that this was Salem Eventide, Voice of the King.

"There are two more of you, correct?" Salem asked, though he knew the wolf could not speak. Instead, he focused on the dilation of the wolf's eyes. "Ah, as I thought. Thank you." He opened the lapels of the pelt and began to sift through the wolf's equipment, disarming him of his blades and opening each satchel on his belt and harness. "I suppose I should go take a look," he said, opening a small bottle of what appeared to be antivenom and smelling it to confirm. It was almost floral, playing to the sweeter notes. Salem stood and brushed himself off before removing the needle in the wolf's neck. "If you experience any light headedness or shortness of breath, that is just your heart stopping."

The wolf collapsed and silently writhed, clutching at his chest as he watched his mark disappear over the ledge. He tried desperately to call to his brothers, but could find no air. The light began to fade and all he could feel was the cool thatch against his forehead before everything went dark.

Salem spied on the hovel from across the street, approaching a horse tethered to a rail. He gently examined the saddle and untied the lead, spotting a wolf in the corner of his eye. He appeared to be peeking through the slats of wood that barred the windows.

The wolf quietly walked to the next window and tried to look through. Old, moist planks nailed it shut from the inside, but there were small openings that looked into the emptiness within. He could catch Eventide's lingering scent, but something acrid began to overwhelm his sensitive sense of smell.

"Anything of interest in there?" Salem asked.

The wolf turned to see Salem perched on a crate with a small clay wine cup in hand, which he gently placed on the wood before clasping his hands. Cautiously, the wolf looked to each side and drew a dagger from his belt.

"Is there any way I can convince you to not kill me?" Salem asked pleasantly.

The wolf sneered. "This isn't a negotiation."

Salem nodded and gestured to the cup. "And that is not wine."

The cup burst in a loud flash of blinding white light that rung the wolf's senses and sent the horse into a fit of hysteria. The wolf rubbed his eyes with the back of his arm and tried to quell his double vision, only to have it center on the faint glimmer of a filament draped around his neck. It immediately pulled taut by the fleeing horse and tore him off his feet, dragging him by the throat down the alley. He raised his blade to cut the line, but was struck by the corner of the building, breaking his shoulder, tightening the line even further, and leaving him to kick and struggle fruitlessly as he disappeared into the fog of the streets.

From the other alley the last wolf heard the commotion. Shutters and doors opened as people curiously searched for the source of the noise and those who actually witnessed it stood frozen and perplexed as they stared off into the fog. The wolf walked toward the street and as he turned the corner a man placed a palm over his mouth, gently pushing him back.

"Shhh," Salem whispered as he pressed the wolf against the wall. He watched intently as the wolf's eyes rolled back into his sockets and fell unconscious. Salem removed the row of thin needles he had placed at the base of the wolf's jaw, and as the body fell limp Salem relieved him of his pelt and swung it over his shoulders. With a pull of the cowl he shaded his eyes and disappeared into the fog, leaving in his wake only the silent aftermath of creeping cataclysm.

2

THE WINDBORN CHANCE

With the salty sea winds came the gentle spattering of water as the hull of the *Windborn Chance* cut through the waves with ease. Marbled wood of amber sheen glided through the vast stretch of navy and white—seemingly endless, if not for the wall of foreboding mist that marked the edge of the world far, far in the distance. Though the sea seemed empty, many merchant ships frequented the southern coasts that stretched from the far western realm of Emberwilde, down past the southern Baku Sands, and along the southernmost point of Whitewater. It was rare to see a ship any further east along the jungles of Shén Shé and unheard of further north from there—the realm of the Snow Leaf was renown for its monstrous creatures and no one dared the crystal waters that teased the living mountain's borders.

The warmer southern water was an important route of trade between the three largest realms of the world—Emberwilde for its ore, precious stones, and exotic fruit; Whitewater for its wine, produce, textiles, and dyes; and the Baku Sands for... sand. Though it was their only resource, they had plenty of it, and the prospect of getting things in return for something so useless helped civilize the coastal tribes enough to grant safe passage for most merchants—so long as they were carrying spices or cured meats. Lion-folk cared little for most luxuries and even less for fruits and vegetables.

With such frequent merchant traffic came the ever-present danger of pirates. One of the most notorious of which, was Carver. While most pirates would raid a ship only for its cargo, this was not his style. Carver would bind the entire crew together, from one man's ankles to another man's wrists, with the last man tethered to the bow, and loot the ship only moments before scuttling the vessel. Beneath the tranquil waters, dozens of sunken ships littered the seabed, each with a chain of corpses to mark Carver's victory. It was these abominable actions toward seafarers that inspired him to call his growing armada The Fleet of Sunken Links, whose ships flew flags of black shackles backed in red.

The *Windborn Chance* was no such ship. With light, shimmering junk sails of brilliant red and a long and slender frame she was one of the easiest to spot, but the hardest to catch. Traits her captain took into consideration when associating her with the free spirit of the wind itself, immortalized in the glorious figurehead of a woman in light robes with her hair in the wind. Handcrafted by one of the finest woodcarvers money could buy, it was designed to be a reflection of his soul—light, free, elusive.

Seated with his back to the stern rails, the captain lounged on the deck with his tricorne tipped over his eyes. A long, slender pipe of briar and red oak wafted curls of light smoke from between his lips, while he crossed his arms beneath a heavy black coat that draped across his chest like a blanket—thick silver buckles clinked with the gentle sway of the ship. Though it seemed he was sleeping, the crew knew full well he was aware of every action and every word. A fearful respect that kept them at the tip of an invisible cutlass.

Standing at the helm was Djagatt. A broad Baku, whose lion-folk physiology had him shadow even their largest crewman. Small bells of black steel jingled on a series of hoops pierced along both of his ears. His fur was a mottled off-white, contrasted with the occasional stripe of rich brown that shimmered when the light hit it just right. Though tribal distinctions were easy for the Baku to notice, most humans would never know he was a Daggermouth. Born from a small tribe dwindling on the southernmost cliffs of the Baku Sands, they had been slowly pushed further and further south by the rapid expansion of Blademane territory. Most Daggermouth males were born without manes, which made them a lesser species in the eyes of the other Baku tribes.

"Much further, Captain?" Djagatt growled.

"Ask the girl." The captain barely moved a muscle.

Far to the bow stood a young girl of twelve, whose sandy brown hair danced in the ocean breeze. With arms outstretched and eyes closed, she basked in the feeling of flight as the *Windborn Chance* soared across the glistening stretch of pristine water. A living spirit of innocence and wind that even the figurehead could envy.

"Lau Lau!" called the Daggermouth, "How much further?"

"Still a ways yet, kitten!" she replied, letting the wind carry her voice to the bells of the Daggermouth's ears.

Djagatt sighed and shook his head.

The captain smirked beneath the shade of his hat. "She does it because she knows it bothers you. We all know that under the claws, teeth, and primal hunter's instincts you're just a fluffy pussycat in need of a scratch. Lighten up, Djagatt. It's funny."

Her voice carried on the wind once more. "Tell Kissy one hour, maybe two!"

Captain Kismet slowly pulled the pipe from his lips and used the stem to tip his hat, just enough to spy her evilly from beneath the brim. Ever since she was old enough to speak she had found several names with which to test his patience. They were only endearing when she was younger.

"You're right, Captain," Djagatt smiled—the fur of his snout scrunched and bone white fangs curved over his lower lips. Nearly a snarl were it not for elation in his orange eyes. "It is funny."

Kismet slowly stood and stretched his arms, squinting in the light of the day. He gave his coat a brisk wave and slung it over his shoulders, resting one hand on the hilt of his sword, and the other on the brim of his hat. He looked out over the rails of the helm and upon his crew. The newer recruits seemed tickled by the nickname while the seasoned veterans appeared to know better.

"For those of you new to the *Windborn Chance*, every single one of you is replaceable. She is not," he declared. "Minor concessions are my prerogative to make, but Fates help any one of you should I ever hear anything less than Captain Kismet cross your lips." He casually leaned on the rail and began tapping the burnt remnants from his pipe. "These sails are my eyes, the walls are my ears, and this sword," he waved open the corner of his coat to draw attention to the longsword sheath at his waist—rich bois de rose with brilliant silver and ornate ruby inlay, "my judgment." He turned his back to them and began filling his pipe. "Back to work."

Djagatt watched as Kismet lit a length of tinder in the flame of a lantern they never let die and used it to ignite the contents of his pipe. "Lau Lau's senses are getting weaker as she grows older," Djagatt declared quietly. "Perhaps we shouldn't give her so much responsibility."

Kismet exhaled a thick stream of smoke and stood at Djagatt's side. "You're not wrong," he began. "Her range has gotten much shorter, but she'll still be useful to have around when negotiating. There's strength in knowing people and no one knows people better."

Djagatt nodded, the bells in his ears jingled lightly. "We've been traveling for a while now, though. Do you think she's right this time? That there really is a treasure calling out to her?"

Kismet nodded softly. "Yes, I feel it too. Something valuable. Something lost."

"It sounds like she's rubbing off on you."

The glistening of the waves shimmered in the dark of Kismet's eyes. "These waters run through my veins, they are a part of me. There's something out there, Djagatt. It's in my waters, I feel it."

"What do you think we'll find this time? Another chest? A map? Jewels, maybe."

"I don't know." Kismet was losing himself in the distance. "We are but simple silk merchants just looking for an adventure, right?"

Whisper's second awakening was much less a glass of wine and more of a hangover. Dull throbbing pain radiated across her head and neck in a way she had never felt before. Within the confines of the room a pair of voices could be heard talking to each other, though she wasn't yet coherent enough to understand. As she shifted beneath her sheets, the soft clinking of chains caught her ear, giving her pause as she noticed the weight of irons clamped around her wrists. Wearily, she opened her eyes and gazed at the shackles, nearly confused. The length of chain didn't seem very restrictive and having been in much worse situations she was oddly comfortable with it. So long as her captors assumed she was helpless she had the advantage.

"Well, well. 'wake again," the captain of the ship said from the other end of the room. Restrained or not, he'd seen what she could do and wanted nothing of it.

Whisper licked her lips as she contended with the dryness of her mouth. Slowly, she turned her head and looked him over with eyes half open. "Who are you?"

"I'm Capt'n Dawry, and you're on my ship, the *Countess*," he replied. "Curious'r, is who you are."

She hadn't noticed at first but there were two other men seated in the room as well, hugging the shadows as they cautiously observed. "What's it matter to you?"

Dawry chuckled sternly at her spirit. "Found you half dead, we did, days ago. You were floatin' toward the edge a the world, wrapped in the largest damned wolf skin I ever laid me eyes on."

The mention of the wolf pelt brought back the memory of her battle with Howlpack Shade. Her defeat lingered on her tongue with the metallic tinge of blood. "Why bother saving me?" She proceeded to scour the room once more, looking for something perhaps she hadn't seen the first time she woke up. Surely enough, the large pelt laid wrapped up on a crate.

"I needed t'ask what this is." Dawry reached beneath the collar of his shirt and pulled out a large ruby charm on a length of chain. She immediately recognized it as the one her father gifted to her before his death, and though she hadn't the strength to express it she was furious that Dawry had taken it from her. "Looks expensive and I couldn't help wonder it might have some story I need hearin' before

I sell it."

"Give—it—back," she labored angrily.

He simply ignored her and continued to gaze into the facets of the elegant gem. "The craft is fancy, I say. It's no trinket." He slid it back under his shirt and crossed his arms. "Seems more than a fair price. Ye'know, for saving yer life."

Whisper sighed and collected her thoughts. "You aren't actually a spice merchant, are you?" No one she interacted with so far seemed educated enough for any legitimate trade.

The two other men chuckled at the idea.

She smacked her lips once more, looking over the crates of the room with nonchalance. "For a pirate, you sure have taken great care in keeping this room dry to transport your goods. Not a level of detail I would have figured for a man of your profession. It's premium cargo, on a beautiful ship." She tilted her head toward him and placed her index finger to her thumb. "Should burn quickly." Whisper placed the circle of her fingertips to her lips and exhaled, intent on washing the room over with glorious red fire. Yet nothing happened. Stunned, she slowly took a deep breath and tried once more. Nothing.

"What're you doin'?" Dawry asked, nearly as confused as she was.

"I—I'm not—" she wasn't clear on how to answer. Ever since she was a child, she had always been able to breath fire, but now she could feel the absence of power. "It's nothing." Exhausted as she was, she was a warrior. Perhaps even one of the world's finest. She had a long list of ways to kill a man from shackled supine and harnessing the elements was more flourish than necessity. "I'm just thirsty. It has my mind hazy."

Dawry eyed her suspiciously, unhappy with the idea of him or any one of his men approaching her. "Too bad."

Whisper rolled her eyes. "Come now. Whoever this Carver person is that you intend to sell me to, I'm sure he's not going to want some frail, weak, sickly woman. That's a poor reflection on you." She lifted her right hand enough to remind them she was chained down, smiling at the realization she was handling the situation much more like Salem than her old self—calm, calculated, and a little sassy. Mind you, had she thought she had the strength she would have torn the chains from the floor and sent the ship to the bottom of the ocean by now, regardless of whether or not she'd go with it.

The captain looked to the two men, the faintest hint of curiosity laid behind the cold of his eyes. He gestured to the closest one, flicking his head toward her. The man swallowed hard and apprehensively stood. He retrieved a polished steel tankard from atop a crate they used as a table; old dishes and worn cards laid strewn across its surface.

"Oh, you poor thing," Whisper goaded softly.

The man carefully scooped water from a small barrel. "Me?"

"Yes." She spied him carefully, her innate predatory instincts slowly intermixed with Salem's penchant for psychological warfare. "You must know why I'm shackled down. Clearly, he's willing to risk your life and that makes you the most expendable person in this room. Perhaps even this whole ship."

The man briefly made nervous eye contact with Dawry.

"Don't listen to 'er," the captain interjected. "She's just tryin' to get in yer head."

"I was in the weasel's head too," she smiled, "I believe that's what killed him."

With unsettled steps, the man approached with the tankard outstretched, intent on being no closer than necessary.

Whisper shakily lifted her hand and reached for it, her fingertips gently slid along the foremost edges of the cup. As she nearly wrapped her hand around, she snapped forward and grabbed his wrist, sharply staggering him inward. As his instincts implored him to use his other hand to pry himself free, she flicked the sheet around his head and cinched him down toward her. Blinded within the muffled darkness the man desperately clawed at the fabric in hopes of unravelling it from his face, dropping the tankard, and slipping into a panic.

The room, once awkward and still, turned chaotic with the blood red procession of vicious strikes as she repeatedly drove her knee into the side of his head. In a matter of moments the white of the cotton was soaked—sticky globs of crimson dripped through the fabric and stained the wraps around her chest. Once the body became entirely lifeless, she struck him one last time for good measure and dropped his corpse alongside the bed.

Though the other man looked mortified the captain seemed to fight a gleam of admiration by suppressing a smirk in the corner of his lips.

Whisper casually leaned over the edge to collect the fallen tankard. "Fates. I seem to have spilled my water." She shook the tankard side to side, indicating she wanted them to refill it.

Dawry playfully looked to the remaining man, who raised his hands and vigorously shook his head. "Quite a show," the captain admitted. "Usin' the sheet to bring'em close."

"I'm just warming up," she replied, placing the cup to her lips and drinking what little water remained. "A little more rest and I'll be ready to murder the rest of your crew in my sleep." She looked to the captain as though she had an epiphany. "Or you could just surrender now."

Dawry chuckled. "You'd spare me and me crew, that right?"

"Fates no. Your crew, perhaps, but you," she held the tankard out and pointed a finger at him, "I will reclaim my charm by tearing that chain straight through your neck."

Dawry's smile slowly faded. "I think tighter shackles er'n'order."

"Yes. Restrain me more, that will save you." Her voice, rife with sarcasm, trailed off at the end of her sentence as she caught her reflection in the surface of the tankards polished steel. Immediately, she brought it closer and adjusted the angle to better use the light.

In the faint sheen of the cup the first thing she noticed was her eyes—round, brilliant. And normal. She raised her left hand to the side of her face only to feel the supple softness of her skin beneath her fingertips. It was then that it struck her hardest. Fingertips? Outstretched before her she gazed upon the smooth skin and five fingers of her left hand. Time seemed to stop and all other presence faded as the entirety of her focus fell upon her lack of mistborn mutations. Not a single jagged ridge jutted from her arm, not a single opalescent scale shimmered along the left side of her face. Somehow, her three claws had become a normal human hand, and her eyes— as spectacular a cobalt blue as they had ever been, but completely devoid of the slit pupils for which she had gained the most renown.

Dawry watched her curiously, pondering to himself as to what bewilderment had enthralled her.

"What is—how did—" No words could pay justice to the feeling of disbelief as she could feel her heart conflict between joy and displacement. Ever since she learned she was an abomination, she both hated and owned herself. Now that, by some strange feat, she was normal, a part of her felt as though she had lost what little identity she once had. What new life could she live now? How hard would she have to work to keep her fearsome reputation? And Salem— what would Salem think? She dared blush at the idea when a rush of dread washed away all her wonder. The innate power within her, the gifts that came from her mistborn traits, they were all gone. She had associated the weakness with her recovery, but now that she was aware she could feel the abysmal lack of power. Her vision was no longer telescopic or accelerated, she could create neither wind nor flame, and her strength—her glorious strength—lost in her sudden normalcy.

As the picture became clearer, so did the signs she hadn't noticed. The dull throbbing of her first headache, the cumbersome weight of her shackles. Everything had changed and for the first time in her life her anger and confidence couldn't sequester her nerves. She knew she was in serious trouble.

3

ROIL, THE ELECTRIC BLOSSOMS OF FREESTONE

Envied Emerald to the East. The words continued to perplex Salem. In the soft wash of low lantern light, seated on the rotting floorboards of a home long since abandoned, he scoured each poorly written verse knowing that this unusual text surely had some relevance to the assassination of his old friend, Grove. As one of Whitewater's most talented enchanters, Grove's death was tragic. Leaving in his legacy several hand written codexes of sigils, wards, and information near priceless to a man of the mystic arts.

Page by page Salem couldn't help but feel that this unusual volume of nonsense, found at the side of Grove's rotting corpse, had some deep significance to either his passing or something greater. Though written in his hand, it was unlike anything Grove had ever written before. It was sloppy, confusing, and ill informed, lacking both consistency and accuracy.

He referred to another sheet of parchment pressed between the pages, a note left by Whisper. Before their separation at the hands of Lady Rhoswan and Howlpack Shade, she had used her incredible eyesight to recognize and make note of the several letters and words within the text that stood out, namely because their edges were supernaturally crisp and defined. Tried as he did, there were a near infinite number of combinations for the random letters, and assembling a message was impossible.

The disappearance of Whisper weighed his heart, the hunt of the Howlpack weighed his head, and the momentary reprieve he would allow himself to solve the mystery of this book was the only peace he could find as of late.

'She is still alive,' whispered a soft, yet powerful voice. 'It is very, very faint, but I can feel her out there.'

"My queen?" Salem replied, drawing his attention from the pages at his fingertips.

In a ghostly dance of roiling electric light, the room shifted into a projection of Freestone's peach groves. Blossoms danced through the air on slowed time and graced him with the sweet aroma they once had. Standing barefoot in the grass was a tall, slender Setsuhan woman— sharp almond eyes, delicate physique, and beautiful feathers instead of hair. Her plumage was long and brilliantly golden, cascading atop a cloak of vibrant colored feathers that trailed far behind her. Surrounding the narrow pupils of her eyes was the draconian sheen of a silver blossom that stretched across irises of brilliant scarlet, sharply contrasting the glorious pink and white blooms in the ocean of trees in the phantom grove. The iris blossom was the universal tell of a female dragon and was the only feature impossible to change when they shapeshifted between forms. Crafty dragons could cast illusions that would temporarily conceal their telling eyes, but such techniques were rarely used. Dragons were as proud as they were powerful.

This illusion was the first Salem had experienced and he slowly dropped the book to his lap, letting his senses take in every lick of static that flicked from the edges of the leaves. "What is happening?"

She looked around curiously, equally intrigued. 'I'm not sure.' Gazing down at her gown of white silk, the edges of her delicate frame danced in the distorted reality. 'It must be a residual effect of Lady Rhoswan's enchantment.'

Salem quickly stood and bowed before her, revering in her presence. It had been twenty years since Savrae-Lyth tore her heart from her own chest to end the Dragon War, secretly storing her power within Salem's body until her heir was strong enough to accept it and assume her role as the new Queen of Drakes. Salem willingly accepted this quest and was fully aware of her consciousness stirring within him, but had never been able to contact her until Lady Rhoswan tried to kill him. When Rhoswan locked him inside his mind, it was the first time he and his queen were able to speak, and now as a side effect of her unusual enchantment it seemed that a pathway was forged, allowing his two identities to converse unfettered.

'Finally,' Savrae-Lyth sung sweetly as she took a deep breath, as though the false aroma and illusory grove were a freedom she had coveted for so long. 'What a fortunate advantage we have.'

The wealth of information he now had access to was formidable and he nervously looked around the static projection of the room wondering how suspicious he must look talking to himself.

'I am a manifestation of our combined consciousness. No one else can see or hear me.' Her smile was brimming with power and grace.

"But people can see and hear me." 'Can you hear me if I do not speak?' Salem wanted to be sure he didn't have to risk an audible conversation.

Savrae-Lyth laughed. She had been a playful soul when she was alive, but the joy of projecting herself back into the world was incredibly exciting. 'Yes, I can hear you.' She pointed to the book. 'Grove's codex. It occupies your subconscious often. Have you made progress in deciphering it?'

Salem drew his attention back to the rough leatherbound text in his hands. "No. The cover is barely blemished, the spine is rigid, and the contents are made of paper instead of parchment or vellum," he began. "This book is relatively new, written perhaps while Grove was held captive by the Orbweavers. It is for this reason I believe it holds some degree of significance. Some important message he knew I would find after his death."

Savrae-Lyth slowly stepped to his side and leaned over the pages, examining them carefully. He could smell the crisp clean air of Setsuha's highest peaks along her collarbone. 'There is a very strong enchantment over this codex.' With gentle hands, she carefully traced her fingertips along the surface. 'Made to be both powerful and subtle.'

"I must determine a way to remove it. Perhaps there is a key at Grove's stead I overlooked."

'It's possible, but returning to Freestone would be foolish. Especially since Grove's stead is the epicenter of that energy anomaly. Assuming you survived the Howlpack, I'm not sure how you'd fare with the demons.'

A false breeze drifted across the electric grass, reminding him of the peace in simpler days—the wealth of the Scarlet Ribbon Estate and the fulfilment of his journey with Whisper.

"My queen, I am rife with angst." Salem's voice grew solemn as he closed the book and set it aside. "I am at no loss for options, and I dare say I am feeling overwhelmed. My heart wishes to pursue Whisper to ensure she is safe, my mind tells me to return to Whitewater and help prepare the king and his realm for the wake of Ivory's ruination, yet my instincts tell me I can do neither so long as I do not contend with Howlpack Shade and his hunt for my head."

'Howlpack Shade will be very distracted with recent events. This may be the safest time for us to make a run for the capital. When Whisper finds her bearings, Whitewater will be one of the first places she will look for you. I dare say that things will only get tougher from here.' Savrae-Lyth looked off into the illusory distance, as though she were sensing something far away. 'As a result of you once being a Setsuhan, you have no fatespinner. Origin Progenitus only knew of your existence through your contact with Rhoswan Gray, but Ivory was not privy. When she finds out about you and Whisper, and I'm certain she will eventually, she may try to force you to her cause.'

"Ivory is a woman of leverage," Salem replied. "She would not pass up an opportunity to recruit two of the only people in the world undetectable to the Fates she wishes to war. In fact, I expect it."

Savrae-Lyth tilted her head curiously. 'You would consider an alliance with Ivory?'

"It depends on the nature of the deal," he stated with calculated undertone. "With everything that is happening it may be prudent to declare a side. Deflect any attention we may incur while we try to finish the plan you and I began so many years ago."

As the Fates knew it thus far, this was a war between the Weave and Ivory for control of Elanta. All other politics beneath the surface were unknown to Salem, but he was certain Ivory was wise enough to have reasons for taking such dramatic actions—assuming her journey into the mist hadn't driven her mad. As a man of extreme convictions himself he was open to hearing her side before vilifying her completely, after all, the remaining Fates were trying to kill him so how good could they be?

What the Fates, current or forlorn, did not yet know was that Salem and Savrae-Lyth intended to free the Immaculate Artisan, Shiori Etrielle. The presumed creator of the world, artisan of the three most powerful artifacts known to mankind, and closest ally to the dragons before their tragic extermination. Shiori Etrielle was a legend nearly lost, and the best friend of Savrae-Lyth in life. In Shiori's prime thousands of years ago, the four Fates served beneath her, until she was betrayed for control of Elanta. Shiori believed that faith in Elanta was a necessary part of their growth, choosing objectivity over interposition. However, the Fates agreed that the races of Elanta were too young and inexperienced to be trusted, and to prevent their own self-ruination an influence was needed to preserve the world in the grand scheme. It was within this conflict of interests that the four Fates rallied to overthrow Shiori. The Fates, then, were still young and inexperienced, lacking the cumulative power to guarantee her death. United, they imprisoned her. Now, after Shiori's name had been wiped from nearly every text and memory, the Queen of Drakes, Savrae-Lyth, had finally collected enough power to enact a scheme with Salem Eventide to release her. Unbeknownst to Whisper, and fortunately the Fates as well, her role in this plan was pivotal. Should they manage to succeed in freeing the Immaculate Artisan the balance of the world would shift back to that of its original creator, and the Fates and their Weave would be wiped from existence at the hands of her righteous vengeance.

'It is crucial we find Whisper soon, but she can handle herself for now,' Savrae-Lyth assured him. 'The Fates believe she is dead and Ivory doesn't even know of her existence. For now, our priority should be escaping the hunt of Howlpack Shade, as we can't afford to inadvertently lead them to her.'

"I agree." Salem wrapped the book in soft cloth and tucked it into a satchel. "I have no plan as of yet, which is discomforting at best, but I am certain something will arise so long as I stay a step or two ahead of him."

'It is important you know that the **Queen's Gaze** technique will not work on Howlpack Shade.' The draconian eye technique she developed in her prime would paralyze anyone unfortunate enough to be gazed upon with oppressive intent. As the Queen of Drakes and single most evolved dragon in known history the technique was one exclusive to herself. Having her power sealed within his body allowed him to recreate lesser versions of her skills with great effort. 'When I designed the **Queen's Gaze**, I used fear as the base emotion through which to instigate full body paralysis. The technique forces energy into the victim's subconscious and triggers a replication of the same emotional effect. Although it easily worked on the Lady Rhoswan, Howlpack Shade is entirely incapable of feeling any degree of fear as a result of his Instrumentation.'

"Thank you," he pondered. "I am certain I will devise something effective."

'I dare say we do not have the strength to confront him on even ground,' she warned.

Salem stood and slung the wolf's pelt around his shoulders, pulling the cowl below his eyes. "Confrontation comes in many forms, all of which I never do on even ground."

4

CARVER'S LAST BREATH

Blinded by the light of day, Whisper squinted. Her wrists churned within the confines of iron manacles—flecks of rust and sharp notches bestowed superficial cuts. A thin trickle of blood trailed down her palms and although it was slightly discomforting she couldn't help but overwhelm herself with the new sensation of having soft flesh instead of scales. Long had she accepted her lack of symmetry and now that she had lost her mistborn identity she could bask in the details a normal person couldn't appreciate—wearing normal clothing, for example.

She was bedridden for days after awakening from what she was certain was death and this was the first time she had tried walking since. Step by step her knees shook as they fought to keep balance with the gentle sway of the *Countess*. The feeling of muscle fatigue was exciting enough that she enjoyed the experience, but was troublesome enough that she finally understood why some people complained as often as they did.

Though just blurs and silhouettes at first, the bustling crew slowly came into focus as she was escorted from the hold and set foot on deck. While most took pause, nearly all soured. She was used to the judgement, but it was almost always for her mistborn mutations.

This particular attention must have been because she mercilessly claimed the lives of two of their comrades, in which case she was familiar with that form of judgement as well. She smiled to herself— better to be feared for your actions than your looks.

To the starboard of the *Countess* another set of sails towered high into the sky, black as the night was dark. The ship to which they belonged was nearly twice the size, with dark letters scrawled across the stern that read *Last Breath*. Approaching from across a steep plank that stretched between both decks was a surprisingly pleasant looking elderly man dressed in a tailored gray suit. Round, thin-rimmed spectacles sat on the bridge of his nose, giving him a distinguished look. Hardly who she expected to see leaving a ship with such a cruel name, but from what she could see of the *Last Breath*, the ship was actually quite fancy. The four large men that followed him fit her imagination much better, mercenaries as grisly and battle worn as good mercenaries came.

"Welcome 'board the *Countess*, Carver," Dawry bowed.

The pleasant man squinted as he smiled and curiously observed every aspect of the ship. "This is a quaint vessel you have," he chimed as he rapped a knuckle against the grain of the mast. Whisper could tell his movements seemed a bit stiff.

"Thank you." By reputation alone Dawry knew Carver loved needless violence and the nicer his mood became the more afraid everyone else should be. He couldn't help but worry that Carver's interest in the *Countess* might inspire him to take it for himself.

"So—" Carver outstretched both of his arms and placed his hands on Whisper's shoulders as though he were adorning her with pride and reverence. From this close his smile seemed so cute, the wrinkled delight of an innocent old man. "You must be the silver eyed dove I was promised."

Whisper knew she wasn't what he was expecting and chose to remain silent on the matter. Hearing Dawry plea for his life would feel so wonderful and she didn't want to sour the moment.

Carver seemed surprisingly genuine as he tilted his head back and looked down the bridge of his nose. He examined her forehead, running his thumb along a bruise she didn't know she had. "Are you in pain?"

Whisper couldn't help but smile at the sensation. "Actually, I am!" She quickly realized joy wasn't the appropriate response.

Carver gently tapped his palm on her cheek and smiled a wrinkly, condescending smile. "Not quite right, are you?" He turned and chuckled, looking over his mercenaries who sneered a laugh out of sheer obligation.

It was one thing to assume she was weak, but it was something entirely different to assume she was dumb. If only they knew who she was, they wouldn't have dared leave the safety of their ship. The fact that he stood as closely as he did assured her he was not informed of her recent murders. Whisper remained silent and cut him down with fearless eyes—eyes that seemed to have forgotten she wasn't strong enough to break her bindings and crush his skull if he demeaned her again.

"Captain Dawry," Carver addressed him playfully. "Perhaps you should have at least tried to dye her hair, instead of assuming I was an idiot."

"I can explain—" The bitter tinge of fear was palpable in the mix of salty air. "When we found 'er, she really did have blond hair and silver eyes. She just... changed."

Carver gently pat Whisper's cheek again, as though to ease the violence in her eyes and show her he wasn't afraid. "No offense, my dear, but I have many ravens. Your blue eyes are but a minor perk." He then turned his attention back to Dawry. "Tell me, Captain, how do you imagine this will end?"

"I knew you'd be cross, sir, s'why I want to give 'er to you free of charge as a token of me apology."

Carver walked over to Dawry and placed his hand around the back of his neck, pulling him to his face and holding him firmly. "Now, this is very embarrassing for me, which I like to believe is terrifying for you. Having me come all this way to buy a gem, only to gift me a stone."

"I—she, the girl had this on 'er." He withdrew the ruby charm from beneath his leathers and lowered it into Carver's open hand.

"Ahhhhh." Carver winked at him. "This unfavorable situation has become... better, at least." He held it up to the sky and admired the many red facets wrapped in the spiralling strands of platinum. "Yes. This is acceptable."

Dawry sighed a breath of sheer relief, only then noticing he had been holding it in the first place.

Carver continued to admire the charm, turning it side to side to take in all it had to offer. "Castrate him."

Immediately, two of his mercenaries stepped forward. The first clutched Dawry by the collar of his vestments while the other withdrew a short, curved blade.

"No, no, no! Wait!" he pleaded as he was dragged across the weathered deck of the *Countess* along his heels. "Don't do this, I beg you!"

"I find your tribute worthy of your life, but not my trust. If I am to give you a second chance I'll need assurance your will is broken." Dawry's cries lingered as the two men carried him away. "And you..." his attention turned back to Whisper's defiant gaze. "There are many ways to break the will of a woman."

The rage within her began to peak and moments before she could no longer contain herself a voice shouted from the crow's nest of the *Last Breath*. "Captain!" it called. "There is a ship in the distance!"

Carver turned to the two remaining men he had boarded with. "Do we have space in the hold if we intercept the incoming ship?"

"Yes sir," one replied.

Carver nodded, pleased, and made a circular hand signal to convey his command to intercept. He met Whisper's eyes once more. "What would happen to my reputation if I went a full day without filling a man's lungs with water?"

Dawry's cries for help reached their peak as his screams resonated through the nerves of the crew, shaken to the core.

"Sir..." the crow's nest called, "it's coming straight for us and incredibly fast!"

Carver made another hand signal.

"No sir, not military. I think it's the *Windborn Chance!*"

Though the mercenaries seemed unfazed, Carver's smile vanished for the first time since boarding. "Damn."

"Captain." Djagatt woke Kismet from another nap at the helm. "Two ships ahead."

Kismet groaned and stretched, clambering to a stand only to flop over the railing and peer ahead from under the rim of his hat. "Who?"

"Lau Lau! Who are they?" Djagatt's voice roared across the deck to the bow where the young girl continued to feel the winds with eyes wide shut.

"The *Countess*... and the *Last Breath*," she called back.

Djagatt immediately seemed nervous. "The *Last Breath*... Carver is pretty far out of his waters." His sharp, feline eyes turned back to Kismet, who was carelessly grooming beneath his nails.

"He thinks they're all his waters."

"What should we do?"

"We run blue," Kismet replied as though it were the obvious answer.

The bells and rings jingled in his ears as Djagatt shook his head and apprehensively complied. "We run blue!" he called out to the deckhands.

Two of the crewmen immediately fetched a large blue flag from a chest at the base of the mast and began to hoist it up a rope to the top. "Running blue, sir!"

There weren't many ways for ships to communicate with one another, but the most common was to signal each vessel with flags of different colors and designs. The *Windborn Chance* was no stranger to using the blue flag, warning other ships that they meant no harm, so long as they surrendered a portion of their cargo.

"Is this such a good idea, Captain? Won't blue just aggravate him? Maybe we should be more diplomatic when dealing with someone so strong willed."

"The *Last Breath* is a ship out of her waters, we treat her like any other. As for Carver, he's a man of method." Kismet tilted his head back and forth to stretch his neck. "Do you know the weakness of a man of method?"

"No."

"Himself, Djagatt. Anger is the greatest poison of the rational mind."

"Is that why you're always irrational?" Djagatt smiled.

Kismet laughed under his breath. "It's why I'm never angry."

"Blue? That pompous fool," Carver growled. "He'd have me surrender." His hands gently trembled in clenched fists. "He means to belittle me in front of my crew."

The two mercenaries returned to the group, wiping clean the curved blade that dripped with Dawry's blood. "Why don't we just kill him when he boards?" The blood lust stirred in the dark of their eyes, something Whisper found deeply nostalgic.

"Idiot," she spoke aloud, using her fearlessness as a blinder to confuse the much larger men. They looked over her with both offense and bewilderment, unaware of what to say. "If he thought you could handle him he wouldn't be afraid in the first place, would he?"

Carver turned to her and paused, as though he were about to interject. Though his eyes stayed affixed to hers she could sense he was beginning to overwhelm himself with the many plans and ideas rushing through his head. Forcibly, his demeanor slowly relaxed enough to speak with affirmation over emotion. "The raven is right. This wouldn't be a problem if I thought any of you were a match."

The four mercenaries looked to each other, some less offended than others. "You're joking," the largest retorted. "I've slit the throats of every man who got in my way. Even a few who didn't."

"Your hubris is exactly what a man like Kismet preys upon," Carver snapped. "You may be the best money can buy, but you fail to realize that there exists talent no coin can purchase."

"You would have us flee with our tails between our legs?"

"Believe me, if I thought we could outrun the *Windborn Chance* I would not hesitate for a second. Our only option is to comply and make him pay dearly in the future." Carver took a moment to collect his thoughts. "Take the raven and get back on the ship."

Disgusted, the large mercenary simply waved his hand and walked away, leaving Whisper behind for the others to escort.

Cold steel clanged against itself as Djagatt carefully slid each of his claws into a pair of bladed gauntlets fitted for his hand. Back home on the southernmost cliffs of the Baku Sands, tooth and claw were highly formidable weapons of tribal war, but while the Blademanes, Long Claws, Haineko, and Daggermouths slaughtered each other flesh on flesh, the rest of the world had evolved more ingenious means of killing one another. Humans forged steel and experimented with alchemy, the dragons perfected their eye techniques, and the Shén Shé mastered enchantments. All but the Baku developed tools for war, but while the realms sought new methods to take lives the Baku honed their survivability. Senses, instincts, cunning, and dexterity grew evermore formidable with every new generation, and only the Salamanders of Emberwilde had really taken the time to notice—the Phoenix Queen's southern house of border militia responsible for keeping the Baku raiders at bay.

The secret strengths of the Baku were not lost on Kismet. He had travelled the world, both land and sea, and attested that there was no better vessel of death than a Baku well equipped. Built like assassins, raised like warriors, and wrought with archaic tradition. It was the perfect underestimation, and Kismet never missed an opportunity to be underestimated. This mysterious admiration was one of the main reasons he jumped at the chance to convince Djagatt to join his crew as his first mate and took the liberty of having the pair of bladed gauntlets crafted just for him.

Djagatt locked the second gauntlet around his other wrist and flexed his claws. The light glistened menacingly along the curvature of the razor edges. Protruding from the back of the gauntlets was a series of jagged, comb like daggers. As lethal and intimidating as they looked they were actually sword breakers, designed to capture a blade and snap it with a twist of the wrist.

Kismet puffed gray smoke from his pipe and revelled in the Daggermouth's pride. "They're still holding up well."

Djagatt's narrow eyes continued to admire the blades. "A weapon like this could make me a pride leader, though some would call it cheating."

Kismet sighed and looked out across the water. "What manner of life is that, do you think?"

Djagatt paused to gaze upon the crests of the waves as well, seeing the world through the same eyes as his captain. "A dull one, sir."

Kismet nodded as he took it all in. "You'll be guarding Lau Lau when we board."

The bells jingled as Djagatt turned to meet Kismet's eyes with concern, but was hindered by the shade of the tricorne. "Is it wise to bring her aboard the *Last Breath*? Carver is not like the others."

"That's precisely why she needs to come." Kismet pulled the pipe from his mouth and used the stem to push up the tip of his hat. "He wouldn't risk being so far from the safety of his fleet if there wasn't something valuable, and I need her to tell me what it is so I don't let him sail away with it."

"I understand. What is the plan?"

"Carver is too clever to try to strong arm us. He will likely allow us to board, let us take what we please, and send us on our merry without fuss." Kismet continued to smoke from the briar.

"Why make him angry by running blue?"

Kismet rested his hand on the hilt of his sword and leaned against the rail of the helm. "I plan to enrage his mercenaries by making Carver tighten their leashes."

"I don't understand."

"I assume Carver will give us no troubles, but I can't promise there isn't a chance of an ambush. If I can stir his dogs by stirring him, I can goad them into attacking me head on."

"It seems like you're just trying to pick a fight."

"No, no... I'm trying to get them to pick a fight," Kismet chuckled. "Besides, how many mercenaries could he have possibly brought with him? Three? Four maybe?"

"Eight," Lau Lau yelled from the bow. In her mind she could hear every word of their conversation.

Djagatt eyed Kismet carefully for a reaction, but received only silence.

"...It's still a good plan," Kismet shrugged.

"It's suicide."

Kismet lazily shrugged and returned the pipe to his lips. "Meh."

5

SCARLET CHARM

Though the common perception of the pirate life was one of filth and malnutrition, Carver seemed to have a much more refined taste for the *Last Breath*—flagship of his fleet, the Sunken Links. The soft, pale glow of delicate runes illuminated the narrow yet rich redwood corridors within the hull of the *Last Breath*. The rattling of Whisper's irons muffled against the rows of decorative tapestries that hung in even intervals until her escort of two mercenaries approached a door.

As the mercenary ahead of her withdrew a ring of long keys, she carefully sized them both up. The one ahead was lithe, and though it seemed like he was unarmed she was certain he was skilled with something discreet—short blades, poisons, garrots, or hand to hand combat. There was a chance the bulk of his skill was with enchantments, which was far more dangerous a weapon in her current state. Not knowing what she needed to be cautious of seemed to stir a very curious blend of nerves and excitement.

The mercenary to her back was a far more ideal target—broad, slow, and stupid, with a large falchion harnessed to his back. The long, curved edge of the heavy blade would be nearly impossible to wield in the narrow confines of the corridor, assuming he could find the room to draw it in the first place. Regardless, he would be no match for her speed.

The hinges moaned as the door opened and the broad mercenary behind her gruffly pushed her forward. The room was, surprisingly, an elegant guest's chamber. Warm blankets and crisp cotton sheets stretched across a bed next to a stand with a single drawer. Along the furthest wall was a cabinet and at the base of the bed sat a heavy chest to lock away important belongings. Natural light poured in through a porthole far too small to fit through, which caused the ornate runes of light to dim until it was dark enough.

"You'll stay here until Carver is ready to talk to you," the lithe said.

Whisper stepped into the middle of the room and turned toward them. "You're locking me in here?"

The broad sneered heavily. "Got somewhere to be?"

"Oh no, this is much better than the *Countess*," she confessed, "but if the door will be locked anyways, could I have the shackles removed?"

"Absolutely not," the lithe replied as he instinctively tapped his pocket to ensure his keys were still there.

"Of course..." Whisper's eyes narrowed as a sinister smile crept up the corners of her lips. "That would make it too easy." She quickly grabbed the handle of the drawer and pulled it from the stand, arcing it hard and smashing it against the bridge of the lithe's nose.

The broad stood dumbfounded as the drawer's contents scattered amidst the scraps of wood—parchment, ink, and books. His instincts kicked in as he looked at the lithe's crooked nose, soaked in blood, but he couldn't react before he felt the nauseating pain of her knee as it crushed his genitals into his pelvic bone, felling him prone where he began to dry heave.

The lithe turned back toward her, drawing a short blade from his leathers with one hand and tracing a glyph of green light in the air with the other.

Damn. Fine luck she was having today.

In a blinding flash, the glyph burst toward her and struck her shoulder as she twisted to avoid being hit in the chest. Immediately, the glyph branded against her skin and made her whole arm numb.

Though she had never experienced this enchantment before she was aware of its existence. It was a mark that would temporarily disallow motor function, essentially paralyzing someone while keeping them fully conscious and aware—a mark that had as much practical application as it did sinister. In the realm of Whitewater, such an enchantment was as forbidden as chthonomancy or necromancy, and any practitioner using one would be punished with the removal of his hands. Had the glyph successfully branded her chest she would have been completely incapable of moving.

Whisper wasted no time and strafed wide to take advantage of the lithe's teary eyes, a tactical advantage from the breaking of his nose. The distance closed remarkably fast, but his reflexes were well honed. For every strike she could muster with her working arm he had just enough wits to either block or dodge. The more she was defied the more she realized his inability to see properly was not truly as much of an advantage as she had thought, but served only to balance out her own impairment.

The weight of her dead arm greatly hindered her accuracy and the lithe seized an opportunity to graze her with his blade, nearly driving it deep into her collarbone. Much to his surprise, the room tumbled once over as she snatched his wrist and swept his legs, sending him hard to the floorboards.

The broad mercenary slowly clambered back to his feet, pale with discomfort, only to have Whisper crouch and thrust her fist up between his legs. The pain resonated across every inch of his body and buckled him once more, leaving him barely conscious as saliva oozed from his open mouth.

Whisper turned in time to narrowly avoid the edge of the lithe's blade, to which she answered with another strike to his broken nose. The pain staggered him and in a moment of near weightlessness he struck the floor again. He tried to maneuver himself back onto his feet but quickly realized his arm was locked in place. Through the misty haze of tears that swelled in his eyes he saw Whisper upon him, with her leg entwined around his arm in such a way that she could immobilize him without the need for hands.

In the corner of her eye the broad wearily reached up to his shoulder to grab the hilt of his sword. Though he was severely weakened and disoriented she couldn't risk being struck with the weight of such a blade and quickly reorganized her priorities. With a swift twist she dislocated the shoulder of the lithe and snatched the blade from his hand, plunging the cold steel deep into the armpit of the broad. The massive man roared in pain as he curled to kneel, clutching the hilt of the dagger and building the nerve to tear it from such tender flesh. Whisper, rife with anxiety over silencing him before the others on the quarterdeck could hear him bellow, scooped a book from the floor, shoved the corner into the soft of his throat, and used her knee to drive it in with all her might. The broad's loud cries quickly drowned in a gurgling desperation of collapsed cartilage, and as the terror in his eyes began to roll backward he plummeted to the floor in a pool of his own blood.

The lithe met the cold ferocity and bloodlust in her eyes as she dropped the book and heaved the large falchion from its harness. He immediately ran for the door. The weight of the sword was far greater than Whisper could effectively wield without her unnatural strength, especially with only one hand, and instead she chose to clutch the hilt and spin her whole body. The air around her began to hum as the sweeping blade picked up speed.

The lithe escaped the room and slammed the door shut, but he knew he had to do more to ensure she couldn't pursue. He took a deep breath, focused, and began to draw a ward across the surface of the door to ensure she could never escape and roam the boat freely. As wispy white strands of energy were quickly drawn into an enchantment that would seal the door in place, the thrum of the spinning blade within the room quickly came to a stop, and all went dark.

"Carver, good sir." Kismet smiled sharply beneath the brim of his hat, being sure to scan every shadow as he stepped aboard the *Last Breath*. There was almost a hundred crew on deck at the ready, well armed but likely moderately skilled at best. Evenly spaced along each railing were heavy shoulder-mount crossbows mounted on swivels, pairs of cylindrical bolt drivers for breaking masts with chain shot, and at the bow and stern of each side were large ballistaes with a passive load of barbed harpoons and rope—to easily ensnare boats and reel them in for looting. As he boarded he noticed a few enchantments on the hull as well, likely something to assist with boarding or ramming but he couldn't be sure. "You should have told me you were visiting my waters, I could have welcomed you more warmly. Fruit basket perhaps? You look like a fruit basket kind of guy."

Carver folded his hands patiently and cut him down with entertained eyes, rich with confidence and ego-centrism. "Oh," he began, "Did we accidently enter the Bone Grove? We must have gotten turned around, new navigator and whatnot."

Kismet chuckled at Carver's insolence. "You know full well if I ever made an excuse like that in *your* territory you'd make me eat my hat, right before sinking me to the bottom of the ocean."

"Perhaps. I'll be the first to admit I can be rash at times."

"Well, let's hope the day never comes," Kismet smiled. "I like my hat, and the water's cold."

Behind Carver stood four mercenaries, one to each side, with two casually observing from the base of the nearest mast. Violence and anxiety wound through the look in their eyes as they sized up both Kismet and Djagatt.

"What do you want, Oona?" Carver asked sharply.

Djagatt sidestepped slightly to better shield Lau Lau.

"Are we on a first name basis already?" Kismet replied. "Kismet will do just fine."

"Oona..." Carver goaded. "It's a girls name, isn't it?"

"You can call my sword a spoon too, if you wish, but it won't make you bleed less."

Though Carver was not used to being on the defensive he knew that, despite what it looked like, he was at a disadvantage. Even though his ship was much larger and he had more men at his disposal, Kismet's swordplay was unmatched and the *Windborn Chance* was known for her tricks. Carver forcefully swallowed his pride enough to bow his head slightly. "Of course, where were my manners?"

Kismet cracked his neck to express his irritation and Djagatt couldn't help but notice the captain's plan to aggravate Carver wasn't quite going as intended. "Let's get straight to it then." Kismet turned to Lau Lau and gestured for her to speak.

The young girl curtsied nervously and cleared her throat. "The *Last Breath* is a modified frigate of three masts and fourteen sails. The primary hold has almost one and a half tonnes of cargo. There is a standard crew of three hundred, a prize crew of twenty five, and eight mercenaries—four on the deck, two in the cabin, and two within the ship."

"What kind of cargo?" Kismet asked her.

"Silk, salt, spice, ivory, and iron."

"Anything in the cabin of value?" Kismet began to narrow his search.

Lau Lau focused silently for a moment. "Jewels. Gold. One large chest."

Carver hadn't expected the presence of a psychic and nervously began to grind his teeth.

"I can be kind," Kismet began. "I would like half of your jewels and the choice of one type of cargo for my troubles, and then you may travel home. Quicker, even, because you'll be lighter."

"No honor amongst pirates then?"

"Pirate? Good sir, I am but a humble merchant deciding what wares he will carry today. I prefer to think of this as a business exchange." Kismet's eyes looked beyond Carver to catch the challenging grit of one of the mercenaries. "Tell your dog to walk away before our business gets personal."

Carver resentfully waived at the mercenary. "Back off." If they were going to chance killing Kismet doing it head on was not the best idea.

The mercenary continued to glare menacingly at the exchange. "I will not."

"You should," Kismet replied. "Your owner may be pompous, but he is no fool."

"He is not my owner," the mercenary growled.

Kismet delighted in the goading, knowing full well that if

he could make an example of one of them he could potentially demoralize the remaining mercenaries. Apprehensions would be his advantage should they muster the nerve to ambush him later. "Oh, my apologies. I assumed that because you couldn't make decisions for yourself—"

Carver grabbed the leather harness that crossed the mercenary's chest and glared at him fiercely. "You may not fear him but you should fear me. Fate's help you should you disobey, because I will make you rue to your very last breath."

"Fine," he sneered as he shrugged away Carver's grip and proceeded to turn around.

"Impressive," Kismet quipped. "Do you castrate your hired help as well, or was he just born without them?"

The flux of rage was a palpable force that stopped the mercenary in his tracks. The other three postured as their muscles wound, ready to react in the event things escalated. The mercenary quickly clutched the handle of his sword and tried to pull it from its sheath when his hand weightlessly rose with the force of his draw. In his grasp he held the handle of his weapon, but the blade was sheared at the guard and remained in the sheath.

"Your eyes are slow," Kismet's voice resounded cleverly as the brim of his hat concealed his eyes, but left a curling smile on each side of the pipe between his teeth. The ocean breeze ruffled the loose sleeves and buckles of the coat over his shoulders as he held a scarlet blade outstretched. It was a magnificent instrument of death the length of a long sword but made entirely of deep red honeycomb stone. The wind whistled as it wove through hollow hexagons that reinforced the construction of the middle of the blade, and the light seemed to dance inside the resin-like material.

The mercenary stared blankly at the broken sword in his hand, angry and perplexed—the only one not focused on Kismet's extravagant artifact. Kismet had named her The Scarlet Charm and even though Djagatt and Lau Lau knew to expect the draw, it was almost too fast and lethally precise to comprehend. A deathly silence befell the crew as breaths held anticipation over what would unfold next, until Carver interjected.

"Fine. Half the jewels and a single piece of cargo," Carver nervously stepped between the two with hands lifted and open. "Forgive his insolence, I assure you he will be punished."

All eyes watched the unusual blade as Kismet slid it back into its scabbard, a rich bois de rose with silver accents, ruby inlay, and a set of small gears. As the blade entered the gears began to turn and once the sword was fully sheathed it clicked. Kismet pushed a tiny lever with his thumb, which lifted a silver bar that ran along the bottom of the scabbard.

Carver curiously spied the scabbard uncertain as to what feature it was outfitted with. All he was certain of was that it was not at all ordinary. "Allow them passage. No one is to interfere with my business." His address carried to the ears of his crew and mercenaries, who cautiously relayed the message to the two in the captain's chamber. "I request you claim your goods and take your leave, Captain."

Kismet smiled at Djagatt. "Well then, what should we take? I'm a fan of the silks myself. Easier to roll around on in the thrill of sweet victory."

Lau Lau, vacant and flighty, tilted her head as her pupils dilated. "The woman."

Kismet looked around with an air of confusion. "I'm not bringing Carver, if that's what you mean."

"The woman in the ship. Red hands, red heart. Roiling, coiling, tempest of the world, last of her kind. Alone, angry, lost, in love. She is the treasure."

"What by fate is she rambling about?" Kismet scowled. "The jewels aren't the treasure?"

"No..." her voice trailed as her mind sunk further. "The woman in the ship. She is why we're here."

"If I may," smiled Carver, "The woman is to be sold into slavery and is thereby cargo. You may take her if you wish, but she counts as your one selection."

Kismet soured with the idea of forfeiting goods for a single slave. Manipulating all transactions so he may never have to go back on his word was a skill of great pride. If she truly was cargo and the *treasure*

Lau Lau had him sail so far to attain then he was bound by his own code not to renegotiate. "Fine," he sighed. "Make sure your lackeys inside don't attack me."

"They won't," Lau Lau replied. "They are both dead."

"What?" Carver seemed genuinely surprised.

Lau Lau's eyes grew solemn. "Hearts filled with fear, they died in silent screams. No shackles will tame her ire. You were fools to try."

The crew of the *Last Breath* fell into a ghostly silence that slowly grew awkward. Kismet crossed his arms and settled into the stillness. "She grows on you, doesn't she?"

6

THE HEIRESS OF HOUSE EILIONA

The door to the inner levels of the *Last Breath* swung heavily as Kismet cautiously peered down the flight of steps that led to the soft, rune-lit hallway of rich wood and silk curtains. With a tilt of his head he gestured for Djagatt to handle the exchange of jewels while he searched for the woman Lau Lau continued to spin strange mysticisms over. He quietly approached the lower landing and saw a man leaning against the furthest door, using the whole of his body to keep it closed.

"You there," Kismet said as he strode the hall on soft heels. "What are you doing?"

Though his voice was clear, the man made no attempt to move or communicate, and as Kismet drew closer he was struck with the metallic tinge of dark blood as it pooled from beneath the door. Upon closer examination, the man was certainly dead—impaled upright by a massive blade that protruded from the other side.

Kismet grabbed the corpse by the collar and pulled him free of the blade. The body collapsed in the corner. Cautiously he turned the iron latch slowly and proceeded inward.

"Anyone in here?" he called softly. The door groaned as it revealed the body of the large mercenary strewn awkwardly across the floor, his eyes wide open. "Anyone... else?" The floorboards creaked with every step as he entered the room, maneuvering around the splintered wood and personal effects that were littered about.

He crouched beside the body and examined it, turning his head from side to side as though inspecting from different angles might somehow reveal the cause of death. The corpse was definitely fresh—sticky blood still oozed from its open mouth. There were no signs of recent defensive wounds and the only telling mark was a small red blotch across his throat. Whatever happened to this one seemed far quicker and less dramatic than the one he found against the door.

Kismet stood and looked the room over once more, oblivious to the slow and silent figure that lowered itself from above the door's frame behind him.

The pads of Whisper'sfeet gently touched the ground while she clutched her shackles taut, as not to have the chains jingle in her approach. Just as she had hoped, the paralysis of her arm had faded, yet her thirst for blood was prevalent as she stalked her new prey.

Kismet sighed as he pondered what had happened and where the woman had gone. He would need the help of Lau Lau if he were to locate her on the ship, assuming she hadn't been killed and dragged off to 'who knows where'. Before he could finish his thought, a strand of iron links swung over his head and attempted to cinch around his throat. If not for his reflexes, it would have worked. Before the links managed to tighten, he cupped his hand and wrist along the side of his neck to prevent his circulation from being completely cut off, creating a small space for his trachea as well. As he struggled he felt his assailant's full weight as a pair of legs wrapped around his stomach and squeezed his diaphragm, laboring his breaths.

With her elbows dug into his shoulder blades for leverage Whisper torqued the chain, rife with the intent to take his head clean off, but his defensive technique was precise enough to ensure she would have to work for her kill. Nonetheless, she enjoyed the struggle and, without some clever thinking on his part, he would soon weaken and she would claim her victory.

Kismet quickly took his sword by the sheath and slid the hilt and guard through the space between the chain and his throat. As carefully as he could, he pressed the base of the blade against the chain and padded his fingertips for the small trigger bar of silver near the top of the sheath. Once found and firmly pressed the sword shot out with remarkable force, cutting through the chain as though it were hot wax and striking the ceiling above them.

Whisper fell backward and sprung from her hands onto her feet. Her severed chains dangled from the shackles on her wrists. The sword of scarlet glass landed at the far end of the room and she couldn't help but appreciate the inherently beautiful hexagons that resided within it. Who knew that such a sword existed, cutting through iron with such ease. Her eyes turned to the sheath, with its unique clockworks and trigger. Being able to fire the blade dramatically increased both the force and speed of the initial draw in combat. Her heart began to race as a smile crept across her lips. This opponent was both dangerous and clever, and she was awash with the thrill of pitting her skill against him.

Kismet coughed violently as he applied pressure to the side of his neck. Blood trickled through his fingertips from a scratch of the sword's guard. "That was low, even for a pirate..." He turned to his aggressor with a glint of fire in his eyes and froze. This was no mercenary, but a young, beautiful woman of rags and iron.

Whisper's raven hair had quickly grown in her recovery aboard the *Countess* and began to cascade down the sides of her face and over her shoulders—the fantastically brilliant cobalt blue of her eyes pierced through the veil and glimmered in the light.

"Good afternoon, milady." He tipped his hat to her and gave a sly smile.

"Pick up your sword," she demanded as her shoulders began to drop. An unreasonable ire churned within her eyes as she elated with the thought of battle, especially now that her hands were free.

"Oh love," he chuckled, "you don't want to put a sword in my hand. You may have heard of me, I am the legendary..."

"Okay," Whisper dashed in for the clinch and violently twisted him to the side, thrusting her knee into his ribcage. The glorious sound of air rushing from his lungs empowered her and with one solid kick to the stomach he flew off his feet and tumbled into the hallway.

"Wait..." he wheezed as he clambered to his hands and knees with the help of the sheath he somehow still held, "I'm..."

"Legendary?" She clutched him by his collar and slammed him into the wall, his face flushing red as she cinched it taut around his bleeding throat. "I heard you the first time."

He wedged the sheath between her arms and twisted, breaking her grip. The rush of blood to his head made him reel and before he could muster a block she pulled his tricorne down over his face and struck him hard through the hat. Blinded, he could sense the world spinning as his ears rang.

"It this all you've got?" she roared, thrusting her forehead into his face just as he pulled his hat away. Though she didn't hear the satisfying crunch of cartilage collapsing beneath her ferocity it was definitely solid, snapping his head back and bringing him to a knee.

"By fate—" he cursed as he cupped his face. It immediately went dark once more as Whisper pulled his coat over his head and wrapped the sleeves across his face, trapping one of his hands against his eye.

Whisper wound back and hurled another knee to the struggling bundle. The difference in martial skill was laughable and were she not having fun with her ingenuity she would have tossed him aside and walked away in disappointment. Instead, she leapt in the air and wrapped her legs beneath his arm and around his head, locking him into an awkward triangle as she fell to her back and flexed.

The heavy boarskin was suffocating, pressure was building behind his eyes, and Kismet tried desperately not to panic as he could feel blood stream down his face. He could tell she was wrapped around him somehow because it felt like his head was about to burst, but her weight led him to believe she was on the ground. If he could land one good hit with the sheath he stood a chance at breaking her onslaught and gaining positional advantage. He slid the sheath through his hand so the weight of the gears and trigger were at the tip and swung it desperately in the vicinity of her head. Not to his surprise, she blocked it. Or he hit her and she didn't flinch, honestly he couldn't tell.

She had him where she wanted him and she could feel his strength wane. Even armed his swings became more and more confused, and soon hs energy waned, dropping his weight onto her legs as he fought to remain conscious.

"Whisper! Stop!" cried a young voice.

Whisper turned to the base of the stairs, where a young girl stood with eyes of pure sadness. *Who is this? How does she know my name?* Whisper's mind was a momentary flood of questions and distraction until the solid crack of silver and clockwork struck her beneath the jaw and all went dark.

Kismet collapsed upon her as she lost consciousness and in a crippled haze he rolled onto his back, coughing desperately.

"Kissy! What did you do?" Lau Lau scolded as she rushed to Whisper's side.

With aching weariness he clumsily freed himself from his coat and gasped for air.

Djagatt's heavy steps rattled the floorboards as he approached.

Kismet's eyes swam in their sockets like lazy fish as he looked up to the Baku that towered over him. "Be honest Djagatt," he gurgled, "how bad is it?"

The bells on the Baku's rings jingled as he cringed. Green and violet bruises had swollen around Kismet's eyes, one of which had burst a vessel and looked a sickly red and yellow. Thick streams of blood flowed from his nose, mouth, and throat, though they seemed superficial enough to staunch without worry. "It's bad, sir," he replied, "but you'll live."

"Good thing I was here to rescue this poor, defenceless damsel in distress."

Lau Lau knelt by Whisper's side and gently placed a hand upon her head. "She is Whisper, daughter of Me'landris and Savrae-Lyth. Lost heiress of house Eiliona."

Kismet's eyes widened as he mustered the strength to turn to the unconscious woman beside him. "You're joking..."

7

FOXES AND WOLVES: SALEM EVENTIDE VS. HOWLPACK SHADE

Since the wolves tracked him to Blackthorne, the idea of staying within the town much longer was uncomfortable at best. Especially since he was eager to get back to the city of Whitewater. Under the hooded cloak of borrowed wolf's fur not only had he been unhindered in his journey so far, but when he inquired about purchasing a horse for his travels he was fearfully offered an impressive discount—one he imagined couldn't be beaten even if they knew he was the Voice of the King.

Taking the main road into Whitewater would be foolish. Fortunately there were other routes that would get him there with less attention, the shortest of which led up through the mountains and curved along the coastline like the spine of the realm. Taking the route would get him to Whitewater in less than a week, but the narrow roads and fickle weather made it riskier than most. However, there would be no bandits and the idea of a journey uninterrupted was one worth the danger.

The first few days passed with cautious monotony and the cool mountain air was growing clearer and crisper as he neared the tallest stony peaks of Whitewater's south. They were nothing compared to the frigid northern cliffs, but the view was astounding nonetheless.

Salem sat on a ledge of stone that precariously reached outward, dangling his feet as he let his horse rest back at the trail. His breath took to the air like ghostly gossamer clouds before disappearing against the vast forest at the base of the mountain, breaking only at the endless stretch of ocean blue beyond. The magnitude of water and height of his perch gave the illusion he was not far from it, but he knew it was at least a two days ride. From his altitude he could barely see the small volcanic islands scattered closer to the mist, but specks of merchant ships could be spotted if he focused hard enough. Merchants were less likely to travel Whitewater's southern coast unless they were bringing goods to Blackthorne. Any further east and they would pass through Shén Shé, and then into Setsuha. Though the Shén Shé were very welcoming to boats, sailors seldom risked getting that close to Setsuha, whose depths were rumored to have unfathomable terrors.

'It reminds me of home,' sung Savrae-Lyth's sweet voice as her visage appeared beside him—ghostly, lightning kissed peach petals drifted past them as the projection brought Freestone with her. Her long cloak of vibrant feathers draped down the sides of the peak in a flowing cascade of greens, reds, yellows, blues, and violets, and her golden plumage shimmered with opulence in the natural light.

"It does look like Setsuha." It had been almost a year since Salem last visited, but it was under the mantle of economic transaction; straight to the heart and out with the goods with no sightseeing. A view like this reminded him of Setsuha's sacred mountain peaks and it had been about twenty years since he last gazed from them. He squinted as he noticed a black spot in the far distance. Three ships clustered together, one of them spectacularly large for a merchant vessel. Though ships wouldn't normally spark his interest, there was something innately curious about it. A ship that large had to be a flagship and one this far out could be none other than the *Last Breath*. The second ship was of average size, but the third was low to the water and built for speed—its beautiful red junk sails could be seen even at this distance. There was no doubt it was the *Windborn Chance* and the two flagships of Elanta's greatest rival fleets side by side meant something violent was brewing—and where there was violence, often there was Whisper.

'Did you notice the forest below?' Savrae-Lyth pointed down to the miles of trees that blanketed the base of the mountain. 'There.'

Salem broke his focus from the ships. Though he couldn't tell at first, there was a stretch of trees that ran like a ribbon along the landscape, taller and more robust than the rest. "Very unusual that a length of environment could be so different than its immediate surroundings, and for such a long distance." The ribbon of vitality ran along the base of the mountain for as far east and west as he could see.

'I'll take a closer look,' she said as she lifted some of the feathered fabric of her cloak and wrapped it across her face and body. She tilted forward and plummeted from the peak. The train of feathers waved in the wind, twisting around her as she picked up speed in her thousand-foot dive. Her cloak burst open into two pairs of iridescent wings, revealing her true draconian form of glistening opalescent scales. A brilliant, flaming halo of gold and blue wrapped around the dragon's eyes—the iconic trait of, what once was, the world's only halo drake.

Salem watched in awe as she soared with such grace. Even as a spirit her wings instinctively shifted with the winds and it reminded him of a time since lost. Watching her glide along the cliffs of Setsuha in her prime, commanding both fear and reverence at once.

Savrae-Lyth scoured the forest canopy from afar and began to return to the ledge. As she neared her size became much more apparent, dwarfing Salem as he sat in wait. She breezed past him overhead, tingling his sixth sense with static, like lightning moments before it strikes. Her four wings wrapped around her body and shifted back into her flowing cloak. Slowly, her lovely Setsuhan form floated back down to him with her halo of fire still wrapped around her eyes. With a pull of her hand, as though discarding a mask, the flames dissipated to reveal her crimson irises once more.

'There is a great energy coming from beneath the forest. It seems to be filling it with vitality,' she explained.

Salem didn't respond and instead closed his eyes and took a deep breath of the mountain air, teased with the phantom aroma of Freestone and electric aura that coursed across his skin. A gentle breeze arose and brushed his face, as though the mountain knew the peace he was feeling in that moment.

Savrae-Lyth's eyes softened as she smiled, and she, too, took a deep breath—head turned to the sky, eyes closed. Life gives only a few moments like these, the wise never waste them.

The canopy of deep green conifers cast shifting shadows, swaying lazily to a song of carnal discord that lurked in the nettles of the forest floor. Warm smears of blood and fresh earth lingered from the corpse of a stag, bones spying through savaged flesh.

A large, muscular creature of thick brown fur hunched over the kill, hoarding it to itself and feasting on every inch. Wet lips smacked between grumbled breaths and the cracking of bone in its jaws warned the birds nothing was going to waste. A murder of ravens taunted from above, impatiently waiting for the creature to slow its pace and leave the eyes for them to pluck, assuming it would get its fill before then. Just in case, they slowly built the nerve to approach, growing more and more daring with each noisy mouthful of carrion. The creature raised its thick, bony head and roared to warn them of his menace. A roar so deep and vengeful it shook the air and commanded the raven's complete silence, if only for a few moments. The caws took to the air once more, fearful and irritated, angry and scornful, until everything went quiet. Each one turned to peer cautiously into the foliage below them, and even the feasting beast stopped its gruesome decadence. The creature rose onto its hind legs and flexed its long claws, ready to ruthlessly defend its prize.

A man slowly breached the trees as he approached, the ferns and thorns bowed in his presence and swayed from his path. His hood of soft hide cast shadows above the bristle of his jaw, but the ravens knew full well he was scouring them with dark eyes. They shuffled nervously in silence, scattered above like little black sentinels ready to flee at a moment's notice. The man looked to the large creature, whose feral eyes and territorial posture quickly shifted into that of fear and reverence. It dropped down to its front paws and hung its head low—terrified eyes surrendered beneath its bony brow as it whimpered and cautiously backed away.

With every step, the earth was quiet. With every breath, the air was still. Even the laws of nature knew to bow to the legendary dragon slayer, Howlpack Shade, and as he passed the fallen stag he watched the predators and scavengers of the realm cower in his presence. As swiftly as he had come, he disappeared into the trees beyond, leaving in his wake a bounty of food with little will to eat.

The air began to thin as a breeze rustled the trees and Shade stopped. He raised his head to the sky and breathed deeply, reading the wind's secrets. There was something... curious. It was well off his path, but something he had to see to believe. He broke from his route and hurried through the foliage, jogging tirelessly until the canopy began to thin with the altitude and, through a break in the trees, far up on a mountain nearly a mile out stood a horse tethered to a sapling.

He crouched and sniffed the air once more, drawing the bow from his back and nocking an arrow of deep red fletching. The warped wood, reed, and antler groaned as he drew it back and slowly exhaled, stilling the beat of his own heart for an impossible shot.

Savrae-Lyth gracefully followed Salem as he left the peak and began his return to the trail. *'What will you do once we reach Whitewater?'*

"I will have to meet with the king before anything else. He is the only one I can trust at the moment."

The Queen of Drakes nodded. *'The Orbweavers have proven to be capable of incredible deception and resource. You determined that agent Dask was a spy, but he certainly wouldn't be the only one.'*

"When Whisper and I sent a raven to warn the king of Dask's betrayal, it was only shortly after that the golden surge of energy from Lyre struck Freestone. I am afraid we must assume the raven did not survive the flight to Whitewater and that Dask is still operating freely within the city."

'Excellent point,' she replied, 'but whether or not he is still an agent of the realm, know that all Orbweaver informants will see you as an immediate threat upon arrival.'

Salem sighed. "I know, but my unexpected return will yield a major advantage. So long as I act quickly I should be able to stay a step ahead."

'What advantage is that?'

Salem could see the horse as he descended the shale, sliding a few meters at a time with perfect balance. "I suspect they began to make their move on the capital as soon as Whisper and I left, and in comfort breeds carelessness. There will certainly be new evidence of their movement and I will simply have to expose the spies before they kill me."

Savrae-Lyth laughed lightly. 'It's ironic to think this is our safest option—running from the Howlpack by hiding in the belly of another beast.'

"If I can survive long enough to reunite with Whisper then the Orbweavers will be of little concern." Salem broke a small smile as he remembered Whisper's sass, which quickly left as something sparked across his instincts. His reflexes heightened, slowing his surroundings to a fraction of real time. Trees barely turned with the wind, bits of shale barely shifted beneath his feet.

'Dodge left,' Savrae-Lyth said.

In the half heartbeat he had to act he flinched left, narrowly avoiding something that whistled past his chest and shaved a button from his coat. The object struck the shale and shattered, leaving only the broken shaft and red fletching of an arrow amongst the stones.

It was a powerful shot—improbable precision from an impossible distance, which meant only one thing. Howlpack Shade.

Shade winced as he flexed his arm, a thin streak of crimson on white cloth slowly spread as he tore open one of his wounds. Though he had healed significantly since his fight with Whisper, she left him with some grievous injuries that were healing far slower than he was used to.

He clenched his teeth and drew another arrow, stilling his heart once more as he watched Salem scurry to his horse. He gently exhaled along the shaft, illuminating ghostly enchantments that delicately danced like vapor. For any mortal man a shot from this range would be unfathomable, but he was no mere mortal. He was a master of the hunt, the Alpha of the Howlpack, and an Instrument of the Fates, capable of incredible, impossible feats. So long as he could see his target, his arrow would carry solely on the winds of his intent.

He let loose the arrow, which barely skimmed the back of Salem's neck as he flinched again. Somehow the Voice of the King had incredible reflexes. If he were to land a decisive blow he would have to get creative.

Shade watched as his prey mounted the horse and began to dash, disappearing into the trees. He quickly sprinted in pursuit along the base of the mountain, leaping, bounding, and tumbling through the terrain's evergreens. Salem Eventide would not get away so easily.

'*How did he find us?*' Savrae-Lyth's voice sounded in his mind.

'*I am more concerned with how to lose him,*' Salem replied silently.

'*Surely the horse is faster. If we keep this pace the distance will broaden.*'

'*No one knows the forests of Whitewater better than Howlpack Shade,*' Salem thought. '*Trust me, the distance will not open.*'

The trail began to curve along a cliff face before briefly opening to a magnificent view of the valley below.

'*The horse!*' She warned sharply the moment they cleared the last tree, but it was impossible to veer the steed with such little time and an arrow burrowed deep into its shoulder. It immediately collapsed into a tumbling mass of stiff flesh and dirt, hurling Salem from the saddle. As he flew through the air Savrae-Lyth warned him of Shade's second arrow, perfectly predicting his path. In mid air it was impossible to dodge, but with absolutely perfect timing and technique he *could* survive. Salem flicked his open palm against the front of the arrow and slapped it off course, and while he felt it breeze past him the sudden friction tore a strip of flesh from his hand.

He struck the ground incredibly hard and even though he managed to tumble the brunt of the impact, his head still rung. It was disheartening how precise Shade was with his bow, predicting his exact position with an arrow that had at least five seconds of flight before impact. He was also getting clever with his shots, and traveling the mountain road was far too risky. Salem scrambled to the base of a large tree to catch his breath.

'*What are we going to do?*' Savrae-Lyth asked. She was familiar with Shade's skill as a hunter, having lost many great dragons to his bow and steel during the war, but she had never met him herself.

Salem panted and wiped the blood from his palm on the pelt around his shoulders. "I don't know," he said aloud.

'*You said 'don't' instead of 'do not',*' she said, surprised. '*Did you know that you only use contractions when you are under extreme duress?*'

"Now isn't the time."

'*There it is again.*'

Salem took a handful of dirt and rubbed it into his wound to help it clot, rolling his eyes as the pain stung more than he anticipated. His breathing began to slow and he attempted to collect his thoughts. "Okay. We will have to go into the valley."

'*But Shade is in the valley. That seems unwise.*'

"It is definitely stupid, but right now he has a clear line of sight. If we go to his level then the forest will force him to close the distance."

'*What if we jumped?*' she said as though her suggestion wasn't suicide, appearing beside him to gauge his reaction.

Salem knew they were hundreds of feet up, but chanced a quick glance at the ledge to humor her. "What is the drop like?"

The halo of golden blue flame wrapped around her head to conceal her eyes once more as she used her static aura to precisely map her surroundings. '*Long, but not sheer—four hundred and twelve feet. Angle of declination is seventy-nine degrees. Howlpack Shade is approximately one mile from the base, giving us about six and a half minutes before he reaches our point of impact depending on his stamina, which I imagine is phenomenal.*' She removed her halo and peered down the cliff face.

'The fall will be fast, tricky, and very dangerous, but it can be survived. Probably.'

"It sounds insane," he replied, unimpressed.

Salem could feel her smiling as she spoke. 'That's why he'll never see it coming.'

Shade remained perfectly still, bow drawn, waiting for any sign of movement. From a distance it almost looked like his trick shot had worked, striking at Salem while in the air to limit his range of escape, but something didn't feel right. Salem's body fell too clean, leading him to believe he somehow deflected it. The idea alone was riddled with doubt, but if the Fates wanted this man dead as badly as they did, he was certain to have some incredible tricks up his sleeves.

Blood trickled from his wounds as the binding cloth along his arm became oversaturated. He pushed himself much further than he should have, but Salem was prey too important to lose. He began to lower his bow to rest when he caught Salem leaping from the ledge of the trail, free falling until his feet struck earth and he began to slide down along the mountain face. The absurdity and recklessness perplexed him, wasting a precious second before he raised his bow to take another shot. Salem's descent was too fast to time and he let fly an arrow he knew would miss the moment he committed. Surely enough, the arrow struck the stone well after Salem disappeared beyond the treetops. Shade ground his teeth and burst into the trees, cursing beneath his breath as he raced to find where Salem landed.

It was a hard run navigating the dense terrain, but with his grace and endurance he managed to traverse the mile with minor delay. Unfortunately, all he found was a pile of broken branches, stripped bark, and loose stones. Much to his surprise there was no body, but if the day had proven anything thus far it was that this hunt would not end swiftly.

Shade lifted his nose to the sky and immediately caught the powerful scent of wolf's fur and fresh blood. It filled his senses with musk and iron, showing him the exact path Salem took as he fled his landing. Shade quickly pursued and the trail began to mix with the clean, crisp scent of fresh water. Before long, he reached a wide river that began to rush the further he travelled along its bank. The scent of blood was no longer increasing and as he reached the stronger rapids he began to understand why. Far down the river, disappearing around a bend into the valley, was Salem, curled in the pelt to fight the icy water and clutching a large branch that surrendered to the current.

Shade stopped to think of where the river would lead him. If he cut through the trees he was likely to catch up to him quicker, presuming Salem continued to ride the rapids. There was a small risk of losing the trail, but the scent of blood and musk was too strong to dissuade him. He quickly began to give chase, leaping across the stretch of water and disappearing into the trees on the other side—leaving only the spatter of his open wounds as proof of his presence.

Salem thought Shade would never leave as he frigidly watched from beneath the roiling caps of churning water. He waited a few more minutes to be sure he was gone before removing the heavy river stone from his chest and floating back to the surface. In his teeth he held a hollow reed, spitting it from his lips once he no longer needed it to breathe.

The water was incredibly cold and he struggled to pull himself onto the bank, shivering as he chilled to the bone. He reached for the root of a tree to help pull himself out, noticing the three acupuncture needles he'd placed in his wrist, relieved they were still there.

Static took to the air and the visage of Savrae-Lyth appeared before him as he crawled onto the shore. She crouched to look at the needles in his wrist. *'You stopped the bleeding in your palm.'*

Salem rested face down in the dirt. "Yes," he labored. "For Shade to have tracked us so well I had to assume smell was the strongest of his senses. I needed him to hone his focus on the bloodied pelt, making him oblivious to the traces of my natural scent or staunched wound."

'How did you know he wouldn't notice the pelt was tied to the branch, though?'

Salem chuckled. "Have you ever fired a bow?"

She tilted her head slightly, curious of the connection. 'I have not.'

"Well," he said, shakily climbing to his knees and scooping handfuls of dirt to rub over his body, "good archers use vision to aim, but a master such as Shade uses instinct. A communion between body and bow that lets the arrow tell the mind when it is ready to fly. Shade's eyesight is simply normal, perhaps even muted by his sense of smell, but his instincts are indisputable." He looked around to gather his bearings while continuing to cover himself with earth. "We will have to cross the mountain at some point, but we can travel from here for now."

Savrae-Lyth looked up to the mountain curiously. 'Why do we need to cross it? Couldn't we follow it to Whitewater?'

"We are going to Roserun."

'Roserun? The fencer's haven? Why would we go there?'

"From the cliffs I noticed the *Last Breath* and *Windborn Chance*, and it occurred to me that if Whisper was found at sea the pirates would surely know. Roserun would be the best place for information."

'Opiate merchants, slave traders, and sellswords. This is actually a worse idea.'

"Shade is expecting me to go to Whitewater and finding Whisper is our top priority. Roserun is the best option at this point. Fortunately, now that we know Shade is hunting with scent we can take precautions. The raw environment will suffice until it is safe to build a fire, then I can create something more potent." He carefully stood and grabbed a cluster of pine needles, rubbing them into the fabric of his coat. "Until then, we must make haste. Shade will not be fooled for long and will certainly not make light of my trickery."

8

NO HONOR AMONGST THIEVES, WAR THE SUNKEN LINKS

Whisper dangled helplessly over Djagatt's shoulder as he, Lau Lau, and Kismet approached the main deck of the *Last Breath*.

"Now that I'm injured and Djagatt is encumbered, there is a higher chance Carver will try to attack us," Kismet warned Lau Lau before breaching the daylight. "Is our crew ready?"

Lau Lau's pupils dilated as she seemed to temporarily step out of her body, visualizing a handful of crewmen below deck on the *Windborn Chance*, laughing amongst themselves and wringing their dark cottons, drenched with ocean water. "Yes, they're ready."

"Good." Kismet rolled his aching shoulders and adjusted his sheath and harness, just in case. "We will go straight to the *Windborn Chance*, and you will remain behind me at all times. Understood?"

Lau Lau nodded and held the base of Kismet's shouldered coat.

Kismet nodded back and turned to exit the stairwell. Fortunately, at first glance, the crew and mercenaries hadn't repositioned themselves in their absence. A good sign that their intentions were still to allow them passage. However, Carver's expression grew lighter as the bruising hidden beneath the shadows of Kismet's tricorne became more apparent.

Carver's eyes seemed to assess Kismet's injuries as they approached the starboard of the ship. "Run into some trouble, old friend?"

Kismet smiled. "Fell down the stairs. Very embarrassing."

"I see." Carver gave a look to his mercenaries, making Kismet uncomfortable.

Lau Lau tugged at his coat. "Kissy," she whispered.

Kismet stopped at Carver and gestured for Djagatt to continue to the boarding plank connecting their ships. "As always, it's been a pleasure doing business with you."

"Kissy," Lau Lau whispered once more, "his necklace."

Kismet drew his attention to the chain that barely glinted as it hid beneath Carver's collar. "Let me see it."

Carver laughed. "Absolutely not, you've taken your bargained share already."

Kismet's head swayed as he begrudgingly agreed and tilted back toward Lau Lau. "Why do I need the necklace?"

"Because it belongs to Whisper."

"Is there a better reason?"

Lau Lau looked around cautiously, uncomfortable with what she had to say aloud. "Kissy," she tried to pull him closer so she could be as quiet as possible, "it's an Etrielle artifact."

Carver either heard her or was superb at reading lips, either way he stepped backward and signalled to his mercenaries, who drew their weapons and began encroaching.

Kismet sighed heavily as he spied their approach—cautious, slow, and nearing his lethal range. Were he in better condition and without the burden of his ward, he wouldn't be at all worried about the engagement, but as it stood his attention was divided in many different ways.

"Kill him!" Carver commanded.

Kismet's hand swiftly met the Scarlet Charm and in a crimson blur the blade split Carver's shirt to reveal the glimmering ruby charm beneath. With an abrupt strike he grabbed the charm and pulled him close to use him as a shield.

Carver raised his hands to ease his crew as the flat of the Scarlet Charm rested on his shoulder. He could feel the edge of the honeycomb stone, so sharp the simple idea that it neared his skin was enough to convince him it was already splitting. "Now Oona, how do you think this will turn out?" The mercenaries were keeping at bay, for now, but many of the crewmen shouldered the heavy crossbows and swivelled them in his direction.

"You'd never risk your own life for a small chance at mine," Kismet said, tugging the charm and chain to guide Carver backward, toward the boarding plank. "Even with all these men, you have to know your odds aren't great."

Carver chuckled. "You presume they are aiming at you."

Kismet could feel Lau Lau tighten her grip on his coat, overwhelmed with the number of murderous eyes she could feel upon her. With a small turn he better placed his body between the starboard swivels and her. Deflecting shots directed at himself wouldn't be too difficult, but predicting Lau Lau's flinches would make protecting her from an onslaught of bolts much more difficult.

Carver felt them reach the boarding plank and was assisted onto it. "Leave the Etrielle with me and you have my word I will let your little psychic leave alive."

"Sorry Carver, she calls the shots and she wants the charm. Besides, it's like you said, she's psychic. If she thinks we'll get away with it then who am I to argue."

The boarding plank was no more than three feet wide, and due to the difference in height between their two ships the incline was quite steep.

"You do realize that if you kill me you'll spark a war with the Sunken Links."

Kismet stopped on the rail of the *Windborn Chance* and eyed the barbed harpoon ballistae that adjusted its aim for his ship. "I have a feeling we're well past that. And if I do kill you, you'll be awake, armed, and looking me in the eyes." He cut the chain from his neck and swung the blade at their feet, cutting the plank. Kismet balanced on the rail of his ship and gleefully watched as Carver plummeted into the ocean below.

"Kissy!"

Kismet continued to watch Carver until he splashed, flourishing his blade to deflect three bolts from the *Last Breath* without raising his head. "Get below deck, Lau Lau."

As she began to run he followed, cutting down a slew of bolts that whistled through the air around them. "Djagatt!" he yelled. "Get us to her stern!"

The Baku quickly ran to the helm, passing Lau Lau as she fled to the safety of the lower deck. "Booms! Sails!" he roared to the crew, who had taken cover. "Now!"

The men burst from hiding and quickly began preparing the *Windborn Chance* for travel. Though Kismet continued to deflect the brunt of the targeted attacks, one by one crewmen began to fall to the iron rain.

"Ballistae, sir!" Djagatt called. They had begun to pull to the *Last Breath*'s stern but were not clear of the harpoon.

Kismet strode the stairs to the upper helm and faced the ballistae, sheathing the Scarlet Charm and locking back the hammer of the sheath. The four arms of the massive bow strained with the pressure, snapping open upon its release. Wind whistled through barbs of iron and malice as it streaked toward him and only once he could feel the breeze of impending death did he choose to strike. He clutched the trigger, drawing the Scarlet Charm with all her speed and grace, and in a dazzling flash of golden sparks he split the iron shaft straight down the middle. Each half burst outward from a wave of sonic force that rippled in the air, missing Kismet to each side and skipping along the deck. The broken iron tumbled to a halt against the rails, a molten red faded as the sudden cut began to cool in the ocean air.

Kismet slowly exhaled, relaxing his arm and gliding the blade along the sheath until the tip found home. He was no stranger to the dangers of meeting such a force head on, but no matter how many times he emerged victorious the fear he felt in the moment never seemed to wane. He liked to believe that the reality of death in failure honed his focus into dire necessity. With trembling fingers he adjusted his tricorne to shade his eyes once more and reached into his lapel for his pipe.

"We're clear to their stern, sir," Djagatt said, noticing the heavy crossbow swivels had locks to prevent them from turning too far in one direction. The only weapon that could reach them now was the ballistae, but they would be out of range long before it was reloaded.

Kismet walked to the front rail of the helm and pulled a rod from the hanging lantern, using the fiery red tip to light his pipe as he looked over the bodies strewn across the deck. He counted nine dead, with five more injured.

"We made off okay," Djagatt stated, mentally weighing their haul over their losses. "We've fared far worse for far less."

Kismet said nothing, instead filling his lungs with the soothing smoke as he focused on slowing his racing heart. He withdrew the ruby Etrielle and held it to the light. Glimmering within the gem was a symbol, one he could only assume was the mark of Shiori Etrielle. "We crossed iron with Carver, took the heiress of house Eiliona, and stole an Etrielle artifact." He turned around and walked to the stern's railing, where he sat and rested against the wood. "There is far more danger to come."

The crew of the *Last Breath* hoisted Carver from the water with a rope, bringing him to deck soaked and smouldering with rage. "What are you waiting for? Hard starboard, dammit! Bring us broadside and get a harpoon in her!"

"Sir," the helmsman said nervously, "The rudder is jammed. We can't turn."

Carver was speechless, glaring menacingly at the fear in his crew's eyes as they dared to step back. "How?"

"Some of Kismet's crew must have sabotaged it during negotiations."

Carver's eye twitched as he ground his teeth and looked up to the men in the crow's nest. "This is your fault!" He pointed a finger at them, to which they seemed to cower. "Get your sorry asses in the water and fix my ship!"

The men of the crow's nest hurried from their post and began to descend the mast.

Carver placed his hand on the helmsman's shoulder and pulled him close to speak directly into his ear. "Send word to our friends in

Orbweaver, I want the price for their absolute best." Together they looked at the men who had descended the mast and were preparing to enter the water. "Once the rudder is fixed, set sail for Roserun, and if you let them back on my boat I'll leave you behind in their place," he whispered.

"Aye, sir."

Carver turned to the rest of the crew, making sure to meet the eyes of each of his mercenaries. "The Sunken Links are going to war!"

9

ELUDING THE WOLF

It wasn't long before Howlpack Shade picked up the stronger tones of blood and musk from his prey. He could hear the water rushing in the near distance and began his approach, striding through the trees with ease. The white caps roiled and spat as the water churned over the riverbed, and through an opening in the trees on the bank he could see the mottled brown of wolf's fur—soaked and slave to the current. Shade breached the treeline and bounded on the rocks, drawing his bow and taking aim, but something was wrong. Now that he closed the distance the pelt had much less girth than he first thought. He let his arrow fly, pinning the pelt into the driftwood with a loud crack—the sound alone was enough to mark the foolery.

Shade ground his teeth beneath the bristle of his jaw, dropping his arms in defeat. Such a simple trick, he was ashamed to have fallen for it. Behind closed eyes he recollected the Lady Rhoswan, and though they had always been at odds with one another he couldn't help but feel he owed her vengeance for what Eventide had done. Now, graced with the opportunity to please his Fate and pay tribute to his fallen comrade he produced only failure.

His bow creaked beneath his grip and he howled—a deep, angry cry that echoed throughout the valley. Birds fled the trees, animals made for their burrows, and even the river's roar seemed to mute beneath the hunt master's rage. The gods and spirits of the woods were fearsome and fickle, but even they knew to bow in the presence of an Instrument scorned.

Shade took a deep breath and centered himself, taking in the mist of the water and filling his lungs with a forced peace and acceptance. Eventide would be seeking safety in Whitewater, but there was a long distance yet to travel. There would be many opportunities to catch him and even if Eventide somehow eluded him the whole way Elder Waylander would be waiting for him on the inside.

Shade placed his bow onto his back and began to head west, toward the capital city. Eventide's noose was tightening and though air continued to fill his lungs it would not for long. He was certain of it.

Night fell and the alpine air began to form thin veins of ice along the edges of the trees. Though the temperature wouldn't drop enough to pose a hazard, Salem clung to the glowing coals of his small fire as though his life depended on it. It was a hard trek to the forest along the coast by foot, but now that he and Shade were separated by a mountain range he could afford to rest.

Above the fire a small pot of water bubbled, to which he began adding anything he could find. Dirt, leaves, branches, moss, and needles, all placed in the water by the handful.

The tingle of electricity tickled his skin as Freestone's fragrance appeared—even through the strong earthy scents of the brew.

'What are you doing?' Savrae-Lyth's sweet voice asked.

"I am creating an olfactory camouflage specific to the region." Salem stirred the concoction with an evergreen branch. "The boiling water will strip out the oils and I will skim them from the surface. It should make it almost impossible for Shade to track me by scent."

'Very interesting,' she said as she crouched by the fire. As a projection she didn't need the heat, but the adoration of flame was a drawing force in any form. 'Such innovations are foreign in Setsuha.'

Salem chuckled. "That is because dragons hunt with their eyes and were rarely ever prey themselves."

She knew that, but she enjoyed being able to converse now that her spirit was free to wander his vicinity. *'I have never been to Roserun before. Tell me more about it.'*

The fire crackled as Salem added more wood, and the embers danced like fireflies before fading into fluffy ash. "Roserun was once a small fishing village, hugging the rocky waters of Fool's Cove."

The Queen of Drakes laughed. *'An unusual name.'*

"Yet, an accurate one. Beneath the surface of the water, jutting up from the ocean floor, there are sharp stones and reefs. Massive shoals take refuge in the rocks but it is very hazardous for boats to navigate. Many vessels have sunk, drawing more fish to sanctuary and, in turn, more sailors to ruin."

'How did it become a pirate haven? I would think that access by ship would be preferred.'

"In Roserun there grows a flower called a widow's bloom. It is a lovely red blossom that thrives along the rocks. When sailors would disappear at sea, the widows would burn the flower's resin as incense to calm the oceans ire and open their minds to the spirit realm—one last goodbye to their loved ones. What they did not realize was that the resulting sense of calm and visions were not that of the ocean spirit, but the hallucinogenic nature of the smoke itself. It was not until a geomancer from Lyre visited Roserun to map Fool's Cove that the widow's bloom was discovered to be a narcotic.

"After that, it was only a matter of time before the smugglers caught wind and moved to monopolize, forcing most the fishermen out and cultivating the widow's bloom in mass. The limited accessibility by sea protects Roserun from Emberwilde's armada and the narrow mountain range keep Whitewater's military at a distance. Beyond the reach of the realms, Roserun became the best place for pirates to shore and fence their goods while restocking their supplies. The indulgence in the widow's bloom became as common as liquor and thusly earned the name 'rumrose'."

'Do you think people will know who you are? I imagine a representative of the King's Court would be a welcome target for ransom.'

"They would know me by reputation, but it is very likely no one knows what I look like. Regardless, once we arrive I will procure a cloak to be safe." Salem used a branch to lift the handle of the small pot and remove it from the flame, placing it onto the dirt. Once the liquid cooled he could harvest the oils, but until then all he could do was rest.

10

FOOL'S COVE, THE HIDDEN TEETH OF ROSERUN

Thick tails of smoke coiled from Kismet's pipe, a slow and lazy waltz that wafted over the seemingly open waters of Fool's Cove. Curtains of red rumrose blossoms coated the rocks along the inlet, where children carefully tended for their taskmasters.

Anchored at the mouth were several ships, many of which belonged to Carver's fleet. Smaller shore boats, weighed down with plunder, carefully navigated from their larger vessels to Roserun for trade. The *Windborn Chance* was narrow enough to enter the hidden teeth without the need to disembark onto a smaller boat, but not without a great memory and nerves of honeycomb stone.

Kismet caught himself biting the stem of his pipe as he watched the darker shades of jagged reef pass below them. It was a captain's duty to know the waters, and that he did, but having a psychic aboard made everything much easier. Standing at the bow where the ocean wind was sweetest, Lau Lau would hold her arm either left or right and Djagatt would steer accordingly. Together they would effortlessly weave through the hidden stones and sunken ships of Elanta to safely dock in Roserun. Kismet watched as others spied them nervously from shore, waiting to hear the thunderous tearing of their hull on stone and holding their breaths until the ship cleared the reefs. Even though many had seen him weave through time-and-time again it was always a nervous wonder.

Kismet peered down the sunken mast of a ship below the surface, its rotting wood laden with mussels and algae, descending into the unforgiving darkness below. Surely enough, the *Windborn Chance* maneuvered past her last hidden stone and everyone sighed a breath of relief.

"Are you okay, Kissy?" Lau Lau chimed politely as she stepped down from the bow.

He knew she knew he wasn't and wondered why she would even bother asking if she already had the answer. "Djagatt, this will be a short visit."

Djagatt nodded, his rings and bells jingled. Usually they would take their time negotiating a fair price for their wares, but if the captain wanted a swift conclusion they would have to accept whatever offers they received. Fortunately, Daggermouth Baku were intimidating and it was unlikely anyone would have the nerve to gouge them.

"Carver won't be far behind us. I'd like to be gone before he arrives."

The ship slowed as the crew hurled ropes to the harbor hands and prepared a boarding plank.

"Sir," Djagatt said as Kismet prepared to disembark, "the dead?"

"Store the bodies below deck. It'll smell, but they belong in the Bone Grove."

"Aye, sir." Djagatt turned his attention back to the remaining crew and waved his hand, signaling that it was time to begin removing cargo from the ship.

Kismet strode down the plank, Lau Lau's little footsteps heard in tow.

"What are you doing, Kissy?" Her voice was meek with worry.

Kismet adjusted the pipe between his lips and continued toward land. "You know exactly what I'm doing."

"You shouldn't. Whisper is a person."

"We aren't keeping her. She needs to go home and we need to get paid."

"We don't sell people," she pouted. He refused to turn and see her disapproval, but he could tell she was cross.

"This isn't slavery," he replied, "We aren't sending her somewhere she doesn't already want to be. I'm simply making sure that the people who want her back reward us for our part in her return."

"So it's a ransom."

The crunch of stone and earth beneath his feet was surprisingly welcome. There was only one road through Roserun and most of the shanties and posts lined its edges up until it ascended into the mountains. The buildings were all crafted from rustic, ocean kissed wood, moist with moss and worn with character. Most were unmarked, as anyone visiting Roserun had a connection of some sort and didn't need guidance, but the larger buildings had signs of rotting wood and faded script. Lau Lau had been here many times before and she knew exactly where Kismet was headed first.

His boots sounded heavy as he climbed the stairs to an older building, blanched by time. A piece of wood, cracked with the weather, creaked as it swayed back and forth on rusty iron hinges— the bleeding paint of a red flower barely noticeable. He unlatched the door and pushed it open, releasing a plethora of scents into the world.

This was one of her favorite stops in Roserun, the Apothecary— ever curious about what unusual things were sealed within the many vials, bottles, and jars that lined the walls. The furthest wall had many narrow drawers, and she followed as Kismet ignored the wares and nodded to the keeper. The man was old, with features more weathered than the shop itself. On his nose he wore a pair of smudgy round spectacles, through which he peered down as he looked over the wall of tiny drawers. Eventually he chose one and withdrew a satchel of cured leather. He opened the flap and sniffed the aroma of the contents, then lifted it to Kismet. Kismet palmed him a bar of silver, indulged in the peppery bouquet, and accepted the satchel. In continued silence he turned to exit.

Lau Lau could smell the fragrance of dried rumrose as he passed and bowed politely to the shopkeeper before trailing behind. Only once they exited the quietude of the store did she begin to speak. "We shouldn't demand money from the King of Whitewater for Whisper's return."

Kismet slid the satchel into the chest pocket of his coat. "I can't give in to every bleeding heart and warm ideal. I've spilled far more blood, sweat, and tears than necessary, and since you won't let me keep the Etrielle I'll need compensation from somewhere." He removed the pipe from his lips and tapped the contents loose, spilling them into the street. "If it were just blood and sweat, maybe, but tears, Lau Lau. It's the tears that are expensive."

She could feel the deeper, quieter part of his heart aching behind the humor, but as the leader of his fleet he had a responsibility to his crew and that involved a lot of coin. There was no point in changing his mind about the ransom, if she did she would only be hurting him and his business. Something continued to discourage her from letting him send word though. "We should take her in person."

Kismet laughed. "We're pirates! The idea of traveling inland is bad enough, but to walk into the capital and make demands of the king, face to face? That'll never end well."

"I think powerful people are looking for her, Kissy." There was an escalating worry in her voice that hid tears behind her eyes. "Dangerous people."

He stopped and placed a hand on her shoulder to ease her spirit and raised the tip of his hat with the stem of his pipe. Beyond the purple and green of his bruises, through eyes swollen half shut, she could sense his compassion. "No matter what happens, I'll always protect you. You're the First Mate, don't forget."

She sniffed and wiped away a tear with her sleeve. "Djagatt is the First Mate."

Kismet shrugged. "That's only because he's tall enough to see over the helm. He knows you're the boss."

"I sense something bad coming and I don't know how to avoid it."

He cupped the back of her head and half hugged her against his chest. "Hardship is our calling, but perseverance is our legacy." He could feel her breath shudder as she sobbed. "We only have to run faster than Djagatt."

She mustered a small laugh between tears and pulled away,

punching him in the arm for even joking about such a thing.

Her little fists hurt much more than anticipated but he turned his wince into an awkward grin. "Striking a wounded elder. That's mean." He pointed his pipe at her. "You're mean."

A smile was finally beginning to peek through. "Maybe you should stop letting girls beat you up."

Kismet placed his hand on top of her head and ruffled her hair. She wasn't wrong. Whisper caused a lot of damage, though he liked to believe if he had been either willing or prepared he would have fared much better. "In my defence, that girl's insane," he jested lightly. "I feel bad for her pursuers."

"She killed a man with his own horse, you know."

He turned his head and spied her curiously from the corner of his eye. "I... believe you."

Hinges groaned loudly as the door to one of Roserun's oldest buildings slowly swung open.

"Good evening, Kismet," said a man, clean cut and seemingly out of place for the backwater town. He stood patiently behind a counter of wood and stone. The man turned his warm eyes to Lau Lau and tipped his head. "Milady."

Lau Lau smiled and bowed, though she did not reply. Her reputation as a psychic had spread through all of Roserun's channels and Kismet preferred if she remained silent while she was off the *Windborn Chance*. This made her presence very uncomfortable for most, but there were a few enlightened mortals who believed they could shield their mind by using enchantments. Lau Lau could feel the sigil of energy behind his ear, but would never tell him she was too powerful for it to have any effect.

"What does the wind bring, Jury?" Kismet pulled the tip of his hat further down to ensure his wounds couldn't be seen. Rumors creep like ivy, and everyone knows ivy exploits the cracks.

Jury folded his hands with intrigue and leaned toward them, smiling as the secrets within him were tugging at their chains.

Tattooed upon his wrist was a black spider with a red kris on its back—the iconic brand of Orbweavers willing to show the world their affiliation. Many Orbweavers operated in secret, so the brands were few and far apart, but Jury had no need to hide in Roserun. If anything, his connection to Orbweaver made his favor an asset. "The very face of Elanta is on the verge of a massive change."

"Really?" Kismet placed his hand on the counter, the sound of silver slid against the stone beneath his palm. "How so?"

Jury nodded, pleased. "Ivory, the Unwoven, has returned to our realm and brought forth an army of demons. Orbweaver is preparing to rise."

Kismet hid his surprise well. Very few people knew Lau Lau's ability was subject to distance, so this was the first he heard of Ivory and her demons. "Come now, Jury. I keep company with one of the world's greatest psychics. If you want to impress me I'll need a little more."

"Of course." Jury tried to balance a line between choosing something they might not know, but not something they should pay more for. "Anything bottled from the Scarlet Ribbon Estate is going to triple in value, at least."

"Interesting," Kismet said. He had a few bottles of wine and brandy stashed back in the Bone Grove, as well as a single bottle of the legendary dremaera. "Why is that?"

"The Lady Rhoswan was assassinated and the whole estate was seized by the realm."

"Didn't she have a partner?"

"Salem Eventide is missing. He and his mistborn vanished that very night and the king fears they're dead. I've heard that Howlpack Shade and his wolves were in Freestone when it happened."

"The dragon slayer..." Kismet clearly didn't like the news and it made the urgency of getting rid of Whisper palpable. "I have a message I need to send to Liam Whitewater."

"The king?" Jury seemed impressed and excited to hear what the message was. He reached below his counter and pulled out paper, ink, and a quill. "Raven, messenger, or enchantment?"

Kismet reached into the pocket of the coat upon his shoulders and withdrew two more thin bars of silver. "Enchantment, but suspend it. I'm not ready to send it yet."

"Of course," Jury replied, accepting the bars and inspecting their quality. He quietly approved and passed the quill.

Kismet thought a moment, scrawled his message onto the paper, and signed it with his full name and title. If the king were to use enchantment to reply he would need the details to ensure it didn't get sent to some other Kismet in Elanta. Jury peeked from the silver. He would eventually read it anyways, but his curiosity couldn't be helped.

"Oh, this..." Jury began as Kismet slid the paper back to him, "this is brilliant." He leaned in with a smile, whispering over the countertop as though the room were full of eager ears. "You have the king's mistborn? Here?"

"Not here, but yes, I have her. And he'll pay well to have her returned."

"Indeed he will," Jury leaned back and folded the paper in half, "but have you considered selling her to the Orbweavers?"

"This isn't a sale. I'm just negotiating her release."

"A fine line between selling rights and selling freedom, but I understand." Jury drew a sigil across the paper that quietly blazed a dark energy. "Same as always, just submerge the paper in water and the message will be delivered." The dark energy consumed the ink on the page until nothing was left, and he handed the blank paper back to Kismet. "Your secret is safe with me."

"We both know that's a lie. You'll probably tell your friends in Orbweaver or whoever pays you enough."

Jury shrugged. Everyone's information had a price, even Kismet's.

Kismet adjusted the coat on his shoulders and prepared to leave. "I only expect one thing from you, Jury. If someone wants to know my business, don't give it cheap."

Jury agreed silently, but caught himself staring pensively at the bars of silver before him. As they opened the door to leave he spoke. "Wait."

Kismet and Lau Lau stopped in the doorway, the breeze from the ocean beckoned sweetly for his return.

Jury seemed to be struggling. His eyes shifted, his lips pursed, and his fingers began to fidget. "I have one more thing I want to tell you. Free of charge."

Kismet didn't reply, but instead turned his head so the shadows from his tricorne would cast intrigue upon his face.

"Hours ago, I received an enchanted message from Carver. He wants to hire our best to help him attack the Bone Grove."

"He's asked before and the Orbweavers always said no. Two fleets using Roserun as sanctuary is far more profitable than one."

"You're right, but this time he's offered a substantial amount of money. Too much to say no to." Jury knew he wasn't supposed to be sharing this information with Kismet, but as the words fell from his chest he seemed to become more and more relieved.

"You're risking a lot by warning me. Why?"

"The Bone Grove Merchants have been very good to us. You respect boundaries, pay fair prices, and trade exceptional goods. If Carver took over it would only be a matter of time before he tries to force his way around here. I'd rather prepare for one war, not two."

Kismet gave a slight nod and looked to Lau Lau, whose eyes seemed flush with fear. He turned back to Jury. "The Bone Grove is impenetrable."

"Yes, but the Orbweavers have been harnessing the power of Ivory's demons as they prepare for war. They will send one demon and an Orbweaver rider to test their affinity in combat. I don't know if it will be enough, but they feel confident the Bone Grove will fall."

"Forgive my ignorance, but that hardly seems formidable."

Jury turned pale. "They aren't sending just any Orbweaver, Kismet. Carver has paid enough to hire Blackrock."

The room fell quiet, where even the wind that once playfully whispered his name disappeared and left him feeling a bitter foreboding. Ivory and her army, Howlpack Shade and his wolves, Blackrock and his demon mount—it was becoming easy to see why Lau Lau couldn't tell where the danger was coming from. Kismet nodded silently to Jury and took his leave, letting the weight of the door close itself.

"We have to get back to the *Windborn Chance*," Kismet said, wasting no time as his pace hastened.

Lau Lau scurried behind him when something brushed the back of her mind. It was a strange static that tickled her neck and briefly made her sense an orchard of peach trees. She stopped and looked out into the mountains.

Kismet quickly noticed she had fallen behind, but as he was about to call out to her he noticed the intensity of her focus and turned to look at the mountain as well. He could see nothing. "What is it?"

The static wreaked havoc on her senses and until Kismet spoke she had begun to believe she was standing in the middle of a fragrant grove. She squinted and shook her head to clear the illusion, seeing the white wash of Roserun and smelling the salty ocean shore again. "I'm not sure, but something is coming to Roserun." She felt like it was a person, but the power had an air of insubstantiality to it. As powerful as it was, she couldn't feel the twisted sickness of malice or hatred she had grown accustomed to on the fringe of Carver's territory.

"We have to go."

"They're looking for Whisper," she said softly.

"You remember everyone is trying to kill her..."

"This is different. This is love."

"Then some plan to kill her slower. Let's go." Kismet looked around nervously. Carver always had someone from his fleet in port, but it was unlikely anyone was informed of the upcoming siege on the Bone Grove yet. Nonetheless, his hand rested on the hilt of the Scarlet Charm to ease his spirit.

"They're a day or two away but this person is very strong, Kissy. Maybe they'll help us."

"Until they realize we're holding her for ransom."

For a young girl overwhelmed with the voices and emotions of others everywhere she went, she was capable of remarkable clarity and foresight. "This Blackrock person, as soon as his name was mentioned I could feel the fear and torment he creates."

Kismet shifted uncomfortably. "Many people fear him."

"I don't feel it from people," she said, turning to look at him. "I feel it from you. You know him, personally. You knew him before he was Blackrock, and you're scared of him."

"We have a rule Lau Lau," Kismet said sternly. He didn't care whose mind she read so long as it wasn't his and he had made his law very clear.

"Kissy, it's okay to be scared. This person wants to help Whisper, which helps us. We should try to get a message to them."

Kismet knew this was an argument he was going to lose, mostly because he knew she was right and he didn't have the time or energy to fight her on it. If there was any chance that someone could help them in their situation it was a chance worth taking, and if this person truly loved Whisper there was plenty of reason to help them fight—after all, she was about to be in more danger than ever. "Fine," he surrendered, "but we don't have the time to wait."

Lau Lau held out her hand. "Silver, please."

Kismet was too concerned with time to argue that a whole bar was far too much for whatever she planned and silently pulled one from his coat.

She quickly took it and dashed back up to Jury's, running up the stairs and storming into the shop. Moments later she emerged with a sumi, the block of solid black ink and sinew stained her fingertips. She turned to Jury's door and began to scrawl an unusual symbol upon it.

Kismet and Jury both approached to watch.

"You're okay with this?" Kismet asked as he tried to read Jury's reaction. Much to his surprise, Jury seemed entertained.

"She paid me," he replied. "Besides, it'll wash off in time."

Kismet nodded. Perhaps a bar of silver was the perfect price to deliver a message and deface someone's property. "What language is that?" It was a symbol he had never seen before, but it had a tribal elegance to it.

"I don't know," Lau Lau replied.

Even Jury shrugged as he tried to determine if it was an enchantment of sort. "What does it mean?"

"I don't know," she said again, "but it means something to someone, and when they come please give them my message."

11

TRUTH IN SILENCE

The red blossoms of Roserun were a welcome sight from the top of the mountain trail and the relief couldn't have come a moment too soon. Salem stopped to catch his breath and gaze upon the sparkle of ocean below. His feet had been aching since his near death experience with Howlpack Shade and no matter how much lamb's ear foliage he lined his boots with the blisters persisted. Finally, he was about to descend into his destination, where hopefully a bed and hot bath awaited.

Anchored outside of Fool's Cove was a massive ship of dark wood and black sails, where large flat bottom barges travelled back and forth with cargo, skimming above the hidden teeth that lurked below the surface. From the distance he couldn't see the flag on the mast, but any sane, fate-fearing soul knew she was the *Last Breath*.

Salem smiled. No one really wanted to be in the presence of Carver and his fleet, but if anyone knew what was going on out there in the vast blue it was him. Perhaps it was the hope that he was one step closer to Whisper, perhaps it was the fatigue of walking through a mountain pass without food, water, or rest, but seeing the *Last Breath* and sprawl of rumrose lifted a weight from his shoulders. The sense of impending danger eluded him, though compared to being prey to the Fates a pirate cove seemed a trivial concern.

As he neared the buildings, blanched by light and warped with the salty ocean air, the desperation within him began to take over. The pain in his joints, the emptiness of his stomach, the dryness of his mouth—the closer he neared sanctuary the faster his body began to fall apart, held together only by sheer will and necessity. He was almost there, after days of gruelling focus and physical strain, only to unravel and risk collapsing on the outskirts. He ground his teeth, trembled with labored breaths, and fought the laziness of his eyes as they tried to drift into the back of his head. With every ounce of strength he had, he staggered to a rain barrel heavy with water and submerged his whole head. It was icy cold, and just the kick he needed to force him to his senses.

Onlookers watched curiously as he ruffled the water from his hair and staggered onward, too unkempt for a noble, too well dressed for a drunkard. Keeping his hair damp and dark would better hide his violet sheen. It was unlikely anyone here would recognize him, but it was far better to be safe than sorry. He continued to stagger into town, frustrated with how few signs there were. He had never been to Roserun before and wasn't quite sure how to find a place to rest, if there even was one.

Loud, obnoxious commotion sounded from closer to the harbor—the ill tune of a drunken ballad carried on salty wind. From the distance it looked to be one of the larger buildings, better maintained than the rest. If there was a warm bed anywhere, it sounded like the place.

Salem began making his way toward it when Savrae-Lyth whispered in his ear. '*Wait.*'

He stopped, reeling ever so slightly as he looked around.

'*There, the door to that shop.*'

A mark of black ink stained the white wood, bringing the haze of his mind to a moment of brisk clarity. It was a language he hadn't seen in decades—draconian. Salem crossed the road and climbed the steps to inspect it closer, rubbing the mark with his hand and sniffing its edges. It had only been there a day or two at most.

The door swung open, nearly startling him as he peered on

foolishly. Jury curiously looked him over and noticed his interest in the mark. "Can I help you?"

"This mark," Salem began, "who put this here?"

"Do you know what it says?" Jury asked. The mystery had been testing his patience since Lau Lau drew it.

"I do. It says 'Freestone'."

Jury smiled, relieved. "Then I have a message for you." He walked inside the shop, leaving the door open for Salem to enter, and slid open a drawer behind the counter. From it he withdrew a piece of paper, placed it on the surface, and slid it toward him.

Salem couldn't hide his confusion. "Someone left this for me?" He wanted to believe it was Whisper. He picked the paper from the counter and read its only two words—Bone Grove.

'It's Whisper, she's there,' Savrae-Lyth said with confidence.

Salem was a bittersweet mixture of relieved and irritated—pleased to know Whisper was alive, but the thought of how much further he needed to go before finding her was exhausting. "How can I get to the Bone Grove?"

Jury adjusted his posture and quietly contemplated. Through the open door he could see the black sails of the *Last Breath*. "I may know of a ship that's going there."

Wispy strands of steam curled and vanished in the fall of dusk's cool air, carrying with it the aromatic scent of peppermint, lavender, and clove. A bath of hot water slowly seeped between the wooden slats of an old banded tub, but Salem didn't care—it enveloped him up to his neck and soothed every aching muscle. It was an opportunity to tend his minor wounds and rejuvenate, for night was beginning to fall and he was past due for another brazenly foolish exploit. He needed transportation to the Bone Grove, but unfortunately the only ship in port that was going there was the *Last Breath*. Jury refrained from mentioning Carver's motive, but Salem was well aware of the friction between fleets and knew it couldn't end peacefully. Nonetheless, it was his only chance. As the last of the cargo is loaded from the barge he would wear the darkness like a cloak and sneak aboard the one and only ship in all Elanta on which no man in their right mind would stow away. Until then, he had every intention of letting his body rest.

Somehow the tragic idea of failure was still incomprehensible. Perhaps, if he really focused, he could muster the doubt of his next adventure, but every time he closed his eyes he could see Whisper's face so clearly. He would see her again. It wasn't hope, but fact, and neither Shade nor Carver could convince him otherwise.

He rested his head along the rim, droplets of water trickled from his hair onto the floorboards. The rich, soothing scents filled his lungs while a strange force pressed within his chest. Heavy yet beautiful, weakening yet inspiring. It wrapped around his heart like a vine of bramble and rose.

'Are you alright?' Savrae-Lyth asked through the silence.

Salem opened his eyes and stared up at the ceiling. The flicker of candlelight cast shadows across the wooden beams and listless cobwebs. For the first time in as long as he could remember his mind was a blank canvas, taking in the beauty and mystery of dancing light and nothing more. "It's so... quiet."

'There are truths found solely in silence.'

Salem's eyes closed as he took a deep breath, sinking further into the water. "What truth does silence bear?"

'With truth comes perspective, therefore it is different for everyone.'

With each passing breath he focused on the dark behind his eyes—the blank void, the absence of thought. Much to his elation his mind was completely silent, free from the calculations, insights, and observations that plagued him in sobriety. In the silence of thought he began to feel it—the shallow breaths of a taut chest. It was a feeling he had never experienced before, powerful enough that it brought him confusion, yet subtle enough he wouldn't have noticed were his mind not completely quiet. Was this his truth in silence— this strange anxiety that brewed inexplicably within him?

"What is this feeling?" he asked. His brow furrowed; confusion was very infrequent.

'You are a child of Setsuha, carved from soft stone and given life by the *winds of the mountain, but ever since you stored my power within yourself and ventured beyond your borders I think you have been developing draconian emotions,'* she replied.

"Draconian emotions?" Just saying it aloud made him nervous and he reflected on who he was before the Dragon War. He was very different now. Many of the changes were subtle and thereby unnoticed, but there was one emotion that stood at the forefront of his mind—his intent to kill. The Setsuha were a peaceful race and feelings of rage and vengeance were extremely rare, especially to the resolve of taking a life, yet he took Rhoswan's with only minor turmoil. Even when confronting the wolves in Blackthorne, killing two of them was completely unnecessary. His resolve was growing ever stronger, and what began as a calculated plan to find Whisper was evolving into something much more passionate. It was no longer a rescue, but a reunion. No longer a mission, but a purpose. "Is this why I have grown so daring? Are draconian emotions the root of this aching ferocity I cannot control?"

He could hear her smile in her voice. *'What you see as daring is passion, and what you feel as aching ferocity is love. Neither of which can be controlled.'*

His eyes slowly opened to gaze back upon the ceiling. "Love?" he wondered. Crafted from the earth, Setsuhans experienced strong platonic bonds of companionship and union but the concept of amorous love was not a part of their culture. In his journey throughout Elanta he learned much about the concept, but never experienced it. A part of him was doubtful that was actually what he was feeling, but he also knew to trust Savrae-Lyth's judgement and wisdom. "Is love supposed to ache?"

'Love, at its very core, will always ache, for in quietude a heart will always yearn. It is within this vulnerability that we see our most fragile beauty.'

"Do I love Whisper?"

'Love can only be felt, manifesting from the aether between two souls. It will squeeze your heart, fog your mind, and turn everything you know upside down.'

Salem shook his head. "It sounds awful."

'On the contrary,' she said, 'love is a most beautiful confusion.'

12

WHISPER ON THE WINDBORN, THE TEMPEST IN CLEAR SKIES

Through lazy eyelids the blur of light slowly coaxed Whisper out of her slumber. Even before moving she could feel the dull pain radiating from the strike she took to the side of the head. The sensation of a headache was nauseatingly new and she was beginning to develop a bit of empathy for those she'd placed in such a state. Her head rolled as she licked her lips, her palate bone dry with dehydration, and she nearly began to rise when she stopped. Something weighed upon her chest, and she peered down her nose to see what it was.

Sharp green eyes surrounded by fluffy black fur stared back at her, half opened and completely content with remaining where it was. The slow rumble of purring resonated through her chest as it began to knead the blanket with its little claws.

Whisper's head rose to better focus, finally recognizing it was a cat, pitch as the night was dark. The cat's eyes closed while she continued to purr, and Whisper was overwhelmed with the urge to remain completely still. Somehow she was trapped beneath this animal, enslaved by its peacefulness. She lay motionless, watching as the cat rested its head and curled into a ball—she was in trouble. Fortunately, as she imagined a way to carefully displace the furry burden without waking it, the door to her room opened and a young girl walked in with a carafe of white clay.

The girl smiled and brushed some of her sandy brown hair behind her ear. She wore a simple cotton shirt with flaring sleeves that waved as she approached, placing the carafe alongside the bed and sitting next to her. She reached out and began to pet the cat, curling her fingertips into its cheeks. "Yoru told me you were awake. She thought you would be thirsty."

Whisper looked at the girl and then the cat. She raised her head once more and looked the room over, but there was no one else present. "Yoru?"

"Yes," the girl replied sweetly. "She's been watching over you."

"...The cat?"

The girl gave a strange smile, as though Whisper had just said something amusingly stupid. Either Yoru wasn't the cat or the cat wasn't a cat, she couldn't tell where she erred. The young girl carefully scooped her hands beneath the ball of fur and lifted it from Whisper's chest, placing it gently on her lap. "I'm Lau Lau, and this little one is Yoru."

"I see," Whisper replied as she sat up and reached for the carafe. The clay had the same rough texture as her old jug and she was momentarily surprised to see it was water instead of wine. Whisper placed the clay to her lips and began to drink, refusing to stop until she consumed every last drop. It felt as though it were days since she last quenched her thirst, and even when the carafe was empty she longed for more. She sighed in brief relief and placed the kiln-set clay back beside the bed. "You said Yoru told you I was awake."

"Yes." Lau Lau smiled down to the bundle of black fur and scratched behind its ear.

"Is the cat psychic?"

"No, she's an elantan velvetine."

Whisper didn't know what that meant. She was certain it was some fancy breed of cat and made no effort to hide her confusion, but as her head began to clear she remembered seeing the girl before she lost consciousness, again. "You called my name earlier. Do I know you?"

"No, but almost everyone's heard of your adventures." Lau Lau leaned in with a curious smile. "Is it true you beat a man to death with his own horse?"

Whisper rubbed her eyes. Somehow this was going to be her most defining accomplishment and she was beginning to think she should just embrace it. "Yes." She then remembered her mistborn mutations were gone and stopped to look at her hand. Everything was gone—scales, strength, claws. She still worried it was just a dream, no matter how many times she had awoken.

"Your power isn't gone," Lau Lau said, trying to reassure her. "Your body is just going through a change. It's preparing itself to grow stronger."

"How do you know that?"

"I just... know lots of things," Lau Lau replied.

"Seems that's the only company I keep." Whisper rolled her shoulder and stretched her neck, assessing her environment. It was a small, humble room of moaning wood that rocked gently on the waves. Whatever ship she was on now was smaller than the last two, but what mattered most was that she wasn't shackled. She looked at Lau Lau. This child was awfully well informed and could apparently speak with cats, but she wasn't ready to assume the girl was a psychic. Psychics were very rare in Elanta and it was more likely she was an enlightened with a skill for communing with nature. "This isn't the *Last Breath*. Where are we?"

Lau Lau seemed excited to answer the question, brimming with pride. "You are aboard the *Windborn Chance*, legendary flagship of the Bone Grove Merchants."

Whisper shrugged. She had never heard of them before and seemed to only care that she wasn't their prisoner. Or, at least, it didn't seem like it.

Lau Lau's shoulders dropped with disappointment, but she quickly perked back up. "Let me show you around."

Whisper stretched her legs, a walk would do her good. She nodded and slid out from under the covers, noticing she was dressed in a long frilly nightgown. She stared at it blankly, unsure if she was more offended by the attire itself or how she'd gotten into it.

"I found some clothes for you. Between what we had in cargo

and what I found in Roserun you should be comfortable." Lau Lau directed Whisper's attention to a chest at the foot of the bed. "In there." She placed Yoru on the ground and stood. "I'll meet you in the hall when you're dressed."

The door closed and Whisper crouched before the chest, opening the heavy iron latch and lifting the lid. Before her, atop an assortment of folded garments, was her father's charm. The glint of the ruby surrounded by a swirl of silver nearly brought her to tears, and as she quickly clutched it to her chest she could smell the gentle breeze of lavender Salem had made her notice. She was awash with relief, breathing in the sweet floral scent that reminded her of her father's last smile. Only then did it occur to her that she wasn't angry, but sad. Dying had changed her perspective on what was important and what was not, and she felt her need for vengeance lift enough to let her mourn. She knew the rage was still lurking in the shadows of her resolve, but for now it was biding its time and waiting for the right moment to make itself known.

She released the clasp on the chain and reached behind her head to fasten it around her neck, pulling her hair up from under it—it was surprisingly long, longer than it should be for the time that had passed. She carelessly ruffled it back and noticed it was also changing color. She held a bundle of it in her hand and examined it closely, what was once a shortcut of raven black now hung past her shoulder with very subtle tones of crimson. Everything was changing.

Lau Lau patiently waited in the hall as Yoru sat regally at her feet. "She doesn't know anything about her lineage."

Yoru looked up to her with its sharp eyes.

"No, I feel like there's someone else she needs to hear it from. Someone with more answers than me," Lau Lau replied in the silence.

Yoru squinted and looked down the hall.

"Me too! Do you think her eyes will change also? I've always wanted to see the blossom lacunae." Lau Lau's face became dreamy as she imagined the beauty of draconian eyes.

Yoru began to lick her paw and hook it behind her ear, her little pink tongue lapping silently.

"You're right, she does have the same color eyes as her father.

Could you imagine if she also developed his eye technique?" The awe was overwhelming and a smile stretched excitedly from ear to ear.

The latch to the room opened with a click and Whisper emerged. Both Lau Lau and Yoru gazed upon her with a reverence that made Whisper defensively suspicious. "What are you looking at?" she huffed. It was the first time she had ever worn anything the monastery hadn't provided her with, and a part of her worried she looked foolish.

"You're amazing!" Lau Lau smiled, bringing her hands to her face with glee. Whisper chose a white swashbuckler's shirt with a slight ruffle of fabric, accenting the low sweeping collar. The ruby charm glinted as it pressed against her chest. Across her stomach was a navy and silver corset, its black lacing blended softly. Over that she wore a long coat of soft black leather, collar upturned tall enough to brush her jaw. A silver chain stretched from one shoulder to the next, draping a half cloak of gray wolf's fur down her left side. Her pants were black boar skin, held up with a belt of brown leather and tucked at the calves into tall, soft boots of dark hide.

Yoru began to purr, to which Lau Lau replied. "You're absolutely right."

Whisper was willing enough to accept the cat was somehow part of the conversation, regardless of whether or not it was just in the young girl's imagination. "Right about what?"

"Yoru says you need a hat to keep your hair back in the wind."

Whisper had never worn a hat before. In fact, the half cloak was the most 'accessory' she had ever worn. A hat, at least, was functional, whereas she was beginning to realize the fur had no imagined use whatsoever—why would someone keep only half of their body warm? She quickly reconsidered her decision to try it and unfastened it from her shoulder. "Everything... fits."

"Yes," Lau Lau said, pleased. "I made sure everything was the right size and in a style I knew you would appreciate. Tighter at the waist to prevent catching, loose in the shoulders to keep your flexibility and speed, and minimal fabric with forgiving flexibility in the legs to maintain your dexterity when grappling."

Whisper looked over the outfit with a new appreciation. As she donned it, each of Lau Lau's criteria came to mind and rung true to Whisper's preference. However, the heel had a bit of lift and felt too feminine to be shameless. Knowing that the outfit was 'perfectly selected' left her feeling unusual, preferring the inconceivability of coincidence. "And the boots?"

"They just look great," Lau Lau smiled, "and think of how much it'll hurt when you kick someone with the buckle."

Whisper tilted her foot out and nodded. It certainly was a solid buckle.

Kismet sat against the rail of the helm as he always did, losing himself in the cool ocean breeze as it washed across his skin. He removed the tricorne from his head and placed it on his lap, running his hand through his dark hair. The ocean's daylight brought out the finite details Kismet always liked to shroud—the hazel sheen bounded across hair and waved like water, and the crimson hues that made his dark eyes glow like freshly blown glass. His head slowly rocked with the ship, creating dancing wisps of smoke that trailed from his pipe to the ceiling of mist far, far above. The embers of his rumrose were beginning to fade, but the careless haze of weightlessness continued to wrap around him. He had been consumed with worry since hearing he may be confronted by Blackrock and doubled his dose, sending him from functional to useless in a matter of minutes. Deep down he knew the threat still existed, but in the open air and comfort of his seaworthy home he couldn't have cared less.

Djagatt leaned against the wheel and watched Kismet from the corner of his eye. The wind brushed his fur of off-white and brown stripes like plains of sweet grass bowing to the breeze, and the bells of black steel jingled along the hoops in his ears. This was the worst he had seen Kismet in a long time and he was beginning to worry. He was aware that the Fleet of Sunken Links was likely to seek revenge on the Bone Grove Merchants, but the Bone Grove itself was impenetrable. The *Windborn Chance* was the first ship to ever survive the journey inside and since then only those entrusted with its secrets and skilled enough to sail them had ever joined them on the inside. Since resupplying in Roserun, things had become more tense than expected.

"Captain, is there something I should know?" Djagatt asked. Despite Kismet's incoherent condition he knew that while he was under the effects of the rumrose it was actually more likely he would get the truth.

Kismet sighed. "Have I ever told you about the vaults of Emberwilde?"

Kismet had actually gone out of his way to avoid mentioning anything about Emberwilde in the past. "No, sir."

"Grand. Beautiful. Elaborate." He slowly waved his hand as though he were painting in gossamer. "It's all so stupid. Anywhere else in Elanta, when someone wants to lock away their wealth they do it privately. Hidden, concealed—a secret, so no one can steal it. But in Emberwilde, the rich build elaborate vaults for everyone to see. It's a symbol of status and wealth, challenging others with who has better locks and bigger balls."

Djagatt's initial thought was that it was foolish, but there were merits to having a vault out in the open. "Emberwilde has a huge military. Breaking into a vault sounds more difficult if everyone can see it."

"That it is," Kismet replied. "It leaves the wealthy lots of confidence to flaunt their money to those less fortunate. Before I met you, I attempted such a vault."

"Really?" Djagatt perked with intrigue.

"I was young and brash, but I was good. I chose one so fortified, so feared, that it took me years to properly scout and infiltrate the grounds. Can you imagine—wealth and fame in one fell swoop? It was a perfect mark, but I couldn't do it alone. I had a partner, a friend, who shared the same ideal." Kismet smiled as he reminisced of his youth. "Our names were going to shake Elanta to its very core, breaking into a vault so impenetrable that no one dared to even consider it. Fates, many didn't even know the vault existed."

"Did you know what was inside?"

Kismet laughed and then faded into a mournful silence. "I had my suspicions, but in truth we had no idea. It could have been empty for all we truly knew, but it was worth the risk. Many people spent so much coin building their elaborate vault that they had nothing left to store within it, but what we wanted most was the fame. To let the world know nothing was out of our grasp if we wanted it."

Kismet's current fame was impressive, but exclusive to the fleets and armadas. There was something subtle that led Djagatt to believe Kismet was still hiding something, or at least disguising the truth. "You failed?"

Kismet shook his head in disbelief. "Actually, no. We did it." He sighed heavily. "But even with all the years of planning, all the suspicions I had conjured of its contents, nothing could have prepared us for what we found inside."

"What was inside?"

Kismet looked at Djagatt, brimming with sobering tragedy. "Neither wealth nor fame was behind that door," he began, "but the burden of a dark, monstrous secret. There were alarm sigils in the vault we weren't expecting. Like the guards, wards, locks, and doors of honeycomb stone weren't enough. We had mere moments in the vault before we were ambushed and I was presented with an impossible choice." He reached up toward the sky, as though he were trying to dip his hands into the mist itself. "My partner begged me to run, but I was drawn into the darkness, electing to reach out and claim something that did not belong to me—something that should not belong to anyone. In my weakness we were overrun, and in our struggle to escape an opening presented itself. It forced me to make a decision. They swarmed my partner, and in their struggle I had an opportunity to either drop what I held and help him escape or flee with my prize."

Kismet took the pipe from his lips and tapped the ash loose, sprinkling it to the wind. "I think you know what I did." He placed the empty pipe back into his mouth. "They captured him, tortured him, twisted him—and when they were done they put him in Emberwilde's cruelest prison, the Blackrock. Cells of untamed iron suspended over a volcano, with latches to release the floor from beneath them at any time. No one knows when the floor to their cell will open. Sometimes it never does, but what would start as fear of death would eventually turn into desperation as the heat from the volcano peeled them away layer by layer. Eventually, everyone begs for the floor to fall."

The tribes in the Baku Sands had many cruel methods of torture, only one of which sounded as bad as the Blackrock. Djagatt chose to say nothing.

"I tried to find a way to rescue him, but there was nothing I could do. Then a proposition came. Officials of the realm got a message to me, promising they would release my partner's floor and give him death if I were to return what I took from the vault. Surrender wasn't even required, they only demanded the treasure be returned, but I still couldn't do it. I chose to let him suffer, chose to let him burn. And then the unthinkable happened—he escaped. Who knows, maybe they even let him go in hopes he'd hunt me down. Either way, he was the very first in history and he massacred every last guard in the process. He consumed the Blackrock whole and with it its name."

"And now you think he hunts you?"

"Wouldn't you?"

"It's been many, many years, Captain."

"Yes," Kismet placed the tricorne back on his head and pulled it over his eyes, "but now he knows where I am."

Beautiful sigils of white light ghostly illuminated the inner corridors of the *Windborn Chance*, growing brighter as they neared and dimmer as they passed. Whisper was familiar with such cantrips from the halls of Whitewater, but didn't expect to see the application this far away from civilization. The use of oil lanterns on ships was probably common practice on lesser vessels, but on a ship as finely crafted as this it made sense there would be some luxuries. The wood was a dark, rich red that glinted of golden knots at the perfect angle. There was neither a chip nor scratch that she could spot and even the halls were pristine enough to eat from.

Yoru and Lau Lau took the lead and guided her to the hold, where the fragrance of perfume and spice still lingered from the cargo sold in Roserun. All that remained in the vast space were several crates of corked bottles, preserves, barrels of water, and a row of bodies wrapped in fine silk.

Whisper looked over the bottles and watched as Lau Lau bowed her head to the deceased. "Who were they?"

"Friends," she said softly, "Carver killed them when we were protecting you."

Whisper's eye twitched and Yoru's instincts warned it to recede. "They died protecting *you*," she said sharply, lifting one of the bottles from the crate to look at the label, "Or your Captain, or your ship, or their pride." She roughly placed the bottle back, jangling the glass within the crate. "No trades their life for mine."

Lau Lau looked as though she was about to cry, but as her voice grew meek it somehow became sharper as well, "Except your mother."

Whisper slowly rose, turning to face Lau Lau with a growing menace. Her chest wound tight and her head dropped to crush her with vicious intent beneath her brow. "What did you say?" she growled.

Lau Lau swallowed hard as she fought a tremble, the air somehow pricking her skin with thousands of tiny needles. Her vision began to shake in the pressure of the room as Whisper's hair wafted in a phantom breeze. It seemed Whisper was too blinded by her growing rage to notice the effect she was having. "What I mean is... your mother loved you so much she died to keep you safe. I wasn't trying to make you angry."

"Don't pretend you know anything about her." The glass bottles began to rattle in their crates as her vision narrowed.

Lau Lau could see Whisper's pupils begin to stretch and she hung her head to avoid staring into them. "But... I'm psychic. I only know because you know."

Whisper sneered. "A psychic, maybe, but I'm not an idiot. I know you're also a scheming little pirate."

"We're merchants!" Lau Lau raised her voice in defiance before realizing her argument wouldn't help her credibility. "We just... trade the goods we get from others."

"It's naïve to call it anything other than plunder." Whisper's hair began to turn blood red as it gently roiled.

Lau Lau curled her arms into her chest and began to cry, bowing her face into her hands. "I'm so sorry."

Something deep within Whisper saw the crying child and, in turn, she saw herself. A vulnerable innocence she had long since left at the steps of the monastery when she chose to seek vengeance for her family. She remembered being the same age as Lau Lau, crying in solitude in the gardens, letting the rain soak her clothes and chill her to the bone. Whisper's rage slowly receded and with it so did her physical transformations. Her hair slowly returned to a mixture of raven and cardinal and her pupils rounded. Her sympathy only ran so deep, but it was enough to quell the tempest she was becoming. Whisper turned her back to the sobbing child and walked to the doorway. "Mention my mother again and I will put this whole boat on the bottom of the ocean."

13

KISMET'S DARK SONG

The fall of darkness settled like a veil—delicate and thin, with cool air that cut to the skin even through the stillness. A handful of Carver's men strode the docks as they hauled cargo to the last barge destined for the *Last Breath*, their heavy breaths took to the night in wispy clouds before fading to the black water around them.

Salem walked the road with purpose, casually adjusting the cuffs of his freshly laundered coat while he studied the bodies that paced ahead. Fortunately, most of Carver's men had already returned to the ship with the previous boats, leaving this final supply run scant. As he neared the base of the dock he could feel Savrae-Lyth's tension in the back of his mind, quieted only when he hid behind a stack of crates.

He paused a moment to take a deep breath, exhaling his tensions and preparing himself for a short but dangerous walk. Once he was ready, he stepped out from the cover and continued onward, gliding silently across the wooden planks toward the largest of the crewmen, whose back was turned as he lifted a large box of supplies. Salem approached, uncomfortably close, and stopped directly behind him, posturing his shoulders to match. The man adjusted his grip on the corners and turned to look behind, but as his shoulders shifted so did Salem's, keeping him directly in the crewman's blind spot. The crewman spied only the stretch of lantern lit darkness and nothing more. He returned his attention toward the barge and began walking.

Salem shifted back, mimicking the crewman perfectly—every change in weight, every step upon the boards, he was but a shadow striding over the water. Another crewman emerged from the darkness ahead, rolling his shoulder as the burdens of the night were taking their toll. As the new set of eyes approached, Salem quietly paced himself to the right to keep his mark between them, crouching lower to ensure he remained obscured from both of their visions simultaneously. As his mark's attention drew to the other in passing, Salem silently spun in front and crouched beneath the carried crate, carefully matching pace with the crewman to ensure the supplies continued to provide cover.

In the near distance he could see the barge with a single man fastening cargo, and he spun as low as he could to return to the larger crewman's back. The two men briefly spoke to one another while the crate was exchanged, and as they both turned to go their separate ways Salem spun once more, keeping to both of their backs as he quietly boarded the barge.

Salem patiently waited in the shadows for an opportunity to sneak into a crate and used his free time sizing them up. Many were too small to fit in and most of the barrels would be filled with water, liquor, or salt, but the larger crates were a gamble. He sniffed the air, narrowing the scent of cheese, pork, coffee, and hardtack to three of the crates, while another gave no hints. If he were to remain hidden aboard the *Last Breath* as long as possible he would need a crate less likely to be accessed.

'*What is in that last crate?*' he asked in the back of his mind. He was avoiding the use of Savrae-Lyth's all-seeing aura just in case someone else was sensitive enough to feel the static, but with such a limited window to obtain cover he had to take his chances with the one man on the barge.

The tingle of lightning kissed petals briefly flickered across his skin before disappearing, fortunately the crewman hadn't noticed. '*Canvas, rope, and wood,*' she replied.

The lone crewman disembarked the barge to untie the anchors and ready for their departure, giving Salem a very narrow opportunity to sneak across the deck and slip beneath the lid of the last crate. His body landed atop rough canvas and coils of rope, within which he wiggled until he made a trench deep enough for his body so the lid could close flush. Fortune smiled upon him. Not only had he found a crate of replacement sail, but the wooden slats created gaps wide enough for him to peer outside without being noticed.

His vision was limited, but Savrae-Lyth could see everything if absolutely necessary. Chances were very good that Carver had someone in his employ that could sense energy, so he was restricted to his own two eyes unless it was an emergency.

He listened carefully as the three crewmen brought their last crates and supplies aboard. Ropes wound taut, nets were adjusted, and anchor iron rattled as everything was fastened down. Then, a new sound met his ears. Heavy footsteps approached from the dock, the wood squealing loudly beneath the weight. Salem's crate shook as the person boarded and the barge's buoyancy was put to the test. He tried to catch a glimpse through the slats when someone massive walked in front of him, briefly blocking all light.

'Do you want me to see who it is?' Savrae-Lyth asked.

'No,' Salem replied, 'we will find out soon enough.'

He felt the barge disembark and watched solemnly as the lights of Roserun began to fade into the distance. The sound of the oars upon the water was somehow peaceful—his own calm before the storm he so willingly approached. He would be out in the middle of the ocean with nowhere to escape, making every silent move a precious one.

Before long, the crewmen began to holler to one another as they approached the flagship. The barge shook as it gently bumped against the hull of the *Last Breath* and thick ropes flopped upon the deck from above. Salem watched as one of the crewmen fastened the rope to an anchor in the corner of the barge. He could only assume the other four corners were receiving one as well. The crewmen yelled once more and the loud sound of cranks followed suit. The ropes snapped taut and the platform began to lift from the pontoons of the barge itself, leaving behind a single crewman to oar the skeleton boat back to Roserun.

Salem hadn't journeyed on many ships before and, even when he had, they were nothing of this calibre. He peered wondrously outward as he was lifted higher, the wind gently swaying the platform so he could span the deck of the *Last Breath*. It was incredible. Over a hundred people worked tirelessly in tandem, each with the militaristic loyalty and diligence in their eyes that he'd expect from a ship of such reputation. Every man in his place, every task followed through, every result triple checked. For a man of such meticulous nature it was perfect, his curiosity and intrigue overpowered the dire nature of his situation.

The cargo abruptly stopped its ascent, swinging gently as it suspended midway to the mast and prepared to lower. Salem strained his eyes downward through the slats to see a dark gap in the deck, an abyss into the belly of the *Last Breath* where light and hope dared not tread. The shadows began to stretch toward him as he neared and once he passed the deck itself there was only the faint glow of sigil light to cast ominous silhouettes into his imagination. Below him, several orbs glistened in the luminescence—pale yellow with the faintest glimmer of red. As he neared the end of his descent a horror betook him. These were not the ghostly glow of any mere item, but six demon kissed eyes with long slit pupils that watched him carefully as his hiding place rumbled to a stop within the hold.

Salem dared not move as the citron eyes continued to affix upon him. The creature was massively long, taking up nearly half of the ship's hold as it lay tethered to the floorboards, though its body was almost indiscernible in the darkness. He had a perfect view of its face though; its narrow snout and thorny head was bound tightly. It continued to stare into Salem's eyes, as though it were unsure of his presence and waited for any flicker of life to confirm its suspicions. Neither moved, each barely breathing, until Savrae-Lyth whispered in the back of Salem's mind. *'I don't believe it... a honey shrike.'*

The creature roared as best it could and began to fight its restraints, twisting and writhing against the leather and iron for the slightest weakness to give it reign. It was almost as though it could hear Savrae-Lyth in Salem's mind and its eyes grew feral as it strained to reach him. Fortunately, its fetters were holding, for now.

Whisper sat on her bed and gently spun her father's charm between her fingers. The scent of lavender was prominent and it somehow made her solemn about how she reacted to Lau Lau. It was hard to confront how much of herself she saw in the child and it made her wonder what her father would think of her reaction. She felt ashamed. Lau Lau had met her with kindness and in return Whisper called her a scheming brat and almost sunk the ship. Although as the history of Whisper's temper went, this was actually very restrained.

Whisper flexed her fingers. Her mistborn mutations were gone along with her immediate power, but there was something big churning within her somewhere. She could feel it course beneath her skin, hardening her veins and honing her senses, but the moment she would notice its presence it would vanish. It was as though her power was a creature living within her, slithering through her body and hiding every time she became aware of it. It didn't want to be found and so far boiling her blood with rage was the only way to force it to surface and make it show its teeth.

Whisper sighed, Salem's name mournfully riding her breath. She missed him and realized it was yet another emotion she wasn't familiar with. Having lost her parents when she was an infant, she'd always thought the emptiness within her was what missing someone meant, but she was beginning to understand loss has many complex layers. Though she mourned her parent's absence and roiled with vengeance for it, the more she thought about her relationship with Salem the more she realized she didn't know her family well enough to truly *miss* them at all. She didn't know if her father would have given her words of wisdom in her days of confusion or if her mother would have taught her a woman's etiquette to prepare her for the social norms of Elanta. Though she loved them because they were her family, she couldn't even know whether or not they were good people. What she did know was that whenever Salem was around, she understood herself more than she ever had in the monastery. He brought her peace and clarity when all she saw was red, showing her that she was not bound to seeking identity when she could forge it herself. She couldn't help but feel Salem could explain what was happening to her—show her how to catch her fleeting power, explain why her mutations disappear and reappear, and push her to apologize to Lau Lau even though being humble was the last thing she wanted.

She was a mess. A chaos she only truly realized after Salem showed her she had a greater potential if she focused. She missed him. The adventure just wasn't the same without.

There was a knock at the door and before she could answer it opened to reveal a man with a dark jacket draped over his shoulders and a tricorne that shaded his face.

"I didn't say you could enter," Whisper said sharply.

"Your words are weightless on my ship." Kismet entered the room and pulled a chair to the edge of the bed, sitting in it and leaning toward her with an air of aggression. "The knock was a formality, not a request. Best not mix the two up." In his hand he held another black tricorne and hung it from the back of the chair. He pulled his pipe from his lips and lifted the edge of his hat with the stem. "My name is Oona Kismet, Captain of the *Windborn Chance* and leader of the Bone Grove Merchants."

"I see," she replied, noticing his wounds and remembering him from the *Last Breath*, right before she almost killed him. "Sorry about your face... and your name."

He ignored her quip and gestured to the ghastly purple that stretched around his bloody eye. "This? It's not my first fight, certainly not my last."

"It sounds like you're used to losing."

Kismet chuckled lightly. Under other circumstances he would have found her attitude more amusing, but a fearsome anger stirred within him. "I'm not here to talk about me."

Whisper nodded. "I don't know what to tell you, I barely know anything about myself."

"I'm not here to talk about you either."

Whisper tilted her head slightly, confused. "You're not?"

Kismet leaned in and though he spoke with a calm tone his eyes growled volumes on how much rage he was forcing down. "We aren't much different, you and I."

"Because we're both women?"

"Because we're both monsters," he said. "Neither of us is worthy of the bounty life has given us."

"For someone with a psychic you seem blind to how few bounties life has actually given me," she sneered.

"You're oblivious and ungracious. That just proves how undeserving you are. But you know who *is* worthy? The one shining light monsters like us have, to remind us of our fleeting humanity? Lau Lau." The chair creaked as he leaned a little closer. "You yearn to spill my blood? Fine. You want to send my boat to crushing depths? Try. But if you ever threaten Lau Lau again, know that I will rain upon you with a wrath you could only wish was nightmare."

Whisper's instinct was to argue. To laugh in his face at the idea that he could bring her harm, but she couldn't do it. There was a beautiful intensity in his eyes she had never seen before: love. Not the sweet nectar of poetry or soft strokes of a brush, but the dark songs that threw men upon blades with purpose. This man wouldn't just die for this child—he'd suffer. Whisper envied him. To love something with that much selfless ferocity would be a bittersweet undoing.

"Have I made myself clear?" Kismet said.

She couldn't avert her eyes from the red hue of his irises and nodded silently.

"Good." Kismet reached over his shoulder and lifted the leather tricorne from the chair, placing it on the bed before her. "I'm told you need a hat."

Whisper stared at it. Even still, she was being graced with perplexing hospitality. She reached out to touch its edges, soft and supple with stories of sunken riches and open waters. "Thank you," she said quietly.

"It's not me you owe gratitude," Kismet said as he stood and walked to the door, "I would have left you on the *Last Breath* and been on my merry." He exited the room, closing the door behind him and leaving her to the sullen quietude.

Whisper gently thumbed the leather of the hat. She knew she would have left him to Carver's will if the roles were reversed and yet now she had new clothing, a soft bed, and her own hat. Kismet was right, she didn't deserve the bounties life gave her, but she was beginning to feel like she could earn them.

14

THE HONEY SHRIKE HERESY

The low, deep breaths of the beast before Salem rumbled like shifting stone. It had been hours since the hold was sealed and the *Last Breath* set its heading for the Bone Grove. The gentle rocking of the ship seemed to ease the creature with its nautical lullaby of creaking wood. Salem wasn't about to take chances and continued to observe in silence.

'Do you think it's safe to speak now?' Savrae-Lyth said.

The creature's eyes narrowed upon Salem through the gap of the slats, but chose to no longer fight its bindings. For many, this would be a sign of submission, but it could not fool Salem. He could see the ferocity in its eyes and almost hear the calculations it quietly considered. This creature was patient, and where there was patience there was intellect.

'As safe as can be, considering,' Salem replied in his mind. *'Earlier, you called it a honey shrike.'*

'Yes.'

'Forgive me, my queen, but I do not recall learning of such a creature.' It wasn't often that Salem didn't know something and his curiosity had been almost unbearable since they departed.

'And well you should not have. The Fates erased all knowledge of their

existence after the shrikes fell from the draconian court. The Setsuhan's were never told of this tragedy and only the dragons could remember, as we have no fatespinners.'

'They fell from the draconian court?' he pondered. 'Then honey shrikes are dragons?'

'Indeed. Or, at least, they used to be. There was once a dragon named Ogra, and he was their leader. The honey shrikes were a small and delicate species, but more beautiful than anything you could imagine. Ogra and the honey shrikes were adored by Elantans for their grace and were once the feature on Elantan currency, but Ogra grew tired of sharing that adoration with other such beautiful things, like the breeze of the ocean or the scent of the rain, and soon the praise of the people wasn't enough.'

When Salem joined the High Council of Whitewater he had the honor of acting as the Voice of the King in the scholarly city of Lyre. There, in the vault of the great library, he once saw a collection of valuable coins that featured a beautiful feathered dragon, whose plumage was struck with different colored gemstone depending on the value.

Savrae-Lyth continued as Salem reminisced. 'Driven by vanity, Ogra developed an eye technique to further enhance his features, making him the largest and most magnificent of them all. With his new technique, the feathers upon his wings shimmered with colors the eyes of mankind could not comprehend and, as a result, any mortal who gazed upon him was driven mad and withered away in a state of all-consuming enamor.'

Salem tried his best to imagine it, seeing something so beautiful you'd allow yourself to be consumed. He was far too logical to understand. 'So Ogra took the lives of his worshipers?'

'Not just his worshippers,' she replied, 'but anyone who chanced a gaze. Man, woman, and child alike. It was the largest massacre of humanity Elanta had ever known and both the council of dragons and the Fates could not stand idly. The Fates erased all memory of Ogra's transgressions from Elanta while the draconian court captured Ogra and tried him, sentencing him to exile in the Overworld and demanding the removal of his eyes.'

'Why not execute him?' Salem asked.

'Because the honey shrikes made a plea and the court chose to hear it. If we spared the life of Ogra, the whole tribe would accept exile and join him in the Overworld, but if we lay him to the blade they threatened a most gruesome revolution. We needed to rid Elanta of the honey shrikes and chose to avoid the bloodshed of their vengeance, so Ogra's eyes were pulled from his head and the whole tribe advanced into the mist.'

Salem looked upon the creature once more; it continued to watch him carefully with its six eyes of emblazoned amber. It didn't look very beautiful. Graceful perhaps, but there wasn't a shimmering feather upon its body to give to its reputation. 'You are certain this was a honey shrike?'

'Without a doubt,' she said. 'The mist of the Overworld corrupts in many ways, but nothing can change a dragon's eyes. Our bodies may become twisted, our minds may succumb to the poisons of our virtues, but our eyes... they are the source of our power and are therefore inextinguishable.'

The lights of the room began to brighten as a door to the hold could be heard opening. Salem shifted within the crate to see if he could spot anyone, but the honey shrike remained affixed upon him. Heavy footsteps approached, heavier than any normal mortal, and before long the broad shoulders of a large man came into view. He stood tall, very tall, with scars that coursed across his shirtless frame. These were not the straight, ordered scars of steel or braided leather, but serpentine coils that wound like rivers of pink flesh that could only be forged in fire. They travelled across his chest and back, stretched up along his neck, and ended at the top of his head where hair once grew.

The honey shrike began to grow restless in his presence, wriggling against its restraints and growling with its throat.

The man stood before the honey shrike and looked upon it curiously. "What's wrong?"

The honey shrike growled again, uttering something guttural through the bindings of its maw.

'This is very bad,' Salem began. 'I think they can communicate.'

The man took a knee and began to unfasten the binding along the maw.

'It will tell him we're here,' Savrae-Lyth said, concern weighed upon her words.

Salem closed his eyes and focused on everything he knew about the room and its contents—the number of crates, the distance to the door, the size of the honey shrike, the rocking of the ship. Anything and everything could be useful, no matter how trivial. Then, it occurred to him. *'It does not see me. It sees you.'*

'Me?' Savrae-Lyth replied.

'You are both dragons. In fact, you were once its queen. It has not been reacting to my thoughts in solitude, but the moment you begin to speak it is as though it can hear your voice.'

He could feel her thinking. *'I suppose it makes sense, that a bond between dragons cannot truly be broken.'*

'You must manifest and draw its attention away from me so that I can escape the hold.'

'Done.' The electric roil of phantom peach petals took to the air, bringing with it the scent of Freestone and Savrae-Lyth in her beautiful Setsuhan form.

The honey shrike began to fight hard against the restraints, nearly taking the man's hand as he unfastened the last of the maw straps. "Fates, what's gotten into you?" The honey shrike growled and clicked with its throat as all six of its eyes followed Savrae-Lyth away from the crate of sail and rope.

"The Queen of Drakes?" the man said in jovial disbelief, "I doubt that." He proceeded to look off into the darkness nonetheless.

Savrae-Lyth walked to the far corner of the hold and began to speak. *'Look what has become of you.'*

Enraged growls filled the air, bringing with it the concern of anyone who heard. Even the shrike's handler was beginning to wonder.

'You chose to follow Ogra and walked into the Overworld of your own accord. You cannot blame me for placing judgement on your leader, you may only blame yourself for sharing it.'

The honey shrike began to calm, though its breaths remained aggravated. "The sea does you no favors by filling your head with ghosts," the man said, fed up with the dragon's rebellion. He reached for the maw strap to bind it once more, but the shrike twisted and flailed in resistance. The man grabbed one of the shrike's horns and forced it to meet his eyes. "You will be still," he commanded sternly.

The shrike immediately surrendered, its eyes shifting with what almost looked like fear. "Good," the man said as he began to fasten the restraint. "I was beginning to think we had a problem."

Savrae-Lyth approached the honey shrike with a light of sorrow glowing behind her eyes. She could sense Salem had escaped the room and needed only to end her manifestation to return to him. *'I am sorry for your suffering.'* She outstretched her hand to place it on its snout when she was struck with an overwhelming vision—a massive, eyeless dragon upon a mountain of bone with skin that ruffled with the wings of hundreds of honey shrikes, perched upon him like leathery feathers before taking flight and blotting the sky with an onslaught of living darkness.

Savrae-Lyth broke her manifestation to escape the reality of the vision and snapped back into Salem's mind. He immediately felt overwhelmed, though he knew the feeling was not his own. His heavy breaths filled his new, dark hiding place until he paced his lungs and collected his wits. *'What happened?'* he asked.

'Ogra,' Savrae-Lyth began, *'he has returned.'*

15

THE DAGGERMOUTH RITE OF PASSAGE

Whisper could hear the sound of clacking wood as she approached the stairs to exit the lower quarters of the *Windborn Chance*. It was a familiar sound, though it was many years since she last heard it. The last time was in the stone gardens of the Monastery of the Eternity Ring where she was adopted and educated by the monks, deep in the mountains of Emberwilde. It brought forth a nostalgia she couldn't deny and where normally she would look back on her life there and scowl, this time she felt guilty—for not being thankful, for dishonoring their principles, and for being a colossal pain in the ass.

She ascended the stairs, placed her new hat upon her head, and opened the door to the daylight and salty winds of the deck. There she saw Kismet and Lau Lau facing one another, each with a wooden sword in their hands. By the sound, Kismet was giving a lesson. Things were awkward between the three of them since Whisper's unwinding and Kismet's dark song, and everyone watched in silence to see who would be first to speak.

Whisper took a deep breath and stepped to the deck, tipping her hat down in hopes it would hide her shame and humility. "Lau Lau," she began, "I owe you an apology for my actions." Whisper walked to the child with a forced confidence and a lump in her throat. "I'm sorry."

Kismet gave a slight nod as he watched them, but Lau Lau said nothing. He tucked his wooden sword under his arm, withdrew his pipe from his coat, and began to fill it with rumrose. "She apologized to you Lau Lau." Once his pipe was full he walked to the stairs of the helm and reached up toward Djagatt, who was ready to hand him a sliver of flame from the lantern. "What do you say?"

Lau Lau's sandy hair waved in the wind and she tucked it behind her ears with her free hand. "Whisper," she said as she raised her sword, "I challenge you."

Kismet broke into a smoky cough and nearly blew the embers from his pipe. "No," he said in stern surprise, "You say 'I forgive you'."

"Coin is the currency of the Bone Grove Merchants," Lau Lau said near-fearlessly, "but an adversary of worth buys Whisper's respect."

"You're a neophyte, Lau Lau," Kismet said.

"Then I will lose," she replied, "but I will lose trying."

Kismet looked up to Djagatt, who leaned against the wheel and watched in curious entertainment. "Djagatt, say something."

"I think it's a good idea," he replied.

Kismet opened his arms in disbelief. "Say something else..."

The bells on Djagatt's ears jingled as he shrugged. "In my tribe, combat is a Daggermouth rite of passage. This will be good for her. It will make her stronger."

"Don't be foolish," he scowled, "This isn't—"

Whisper raised a hand to Kismet while staring deep into Lau Lau's nervous, yet courageous eyes. "I accept."

Kismet was speechless, knowing full well that even if he stopped them from fighting today they would simply do it behind his back another. With great hesitation he pulled the sword from under his arm and placed the handle in Whisper's palm. "I trust you will remember my words."

"Don't kill the girl," Whisper replied sharply, "I remember."

"No... I said don't *hurt* the girl."

"How's she going to learn not to challenge people she can't beat?"

Kismet let Whisper take the sword from his grip and watched with concern as they walked to an open space on the deck. "Don't hurt her," he warned.

"You heard the cat-thing, it's a rite of passage," Whisper said as she looked back at Kismet. "Bruises are like medals of valor."

"None."

She bobbed her head and winked above a clever smile. "Just a few."

The merchants of the *Windborn Chance* firmly held their posts, but couldn't help pausing to chance a glance as their child psychic and fellow Bone Grove Merchant, Lau Lau, prepared to cross wooden blades with the infamous mistborn mercenary of Whitewater, Whisper. Though most of them easily made their predictions of the outcome, no one knew how much restraint Whisper could truly hold in combat, leaving the duration of the match a mystery.

The boat gently rocked in the wind as each combatant slid their foot back and swayed, becoming one with both ocean and blade. Whisper watched Lau Lau's eyes, but studied her form in her peripheral. For the child's height, armed with a sword that was too long for her, she had a remarkably good opening form. More remarkable still, Whisper recognized it. This wasn't just any blade form, but the same she knew from the Monastery—Red Quill. It was the blade-bearing sister form to her own unarmed style, the Phoenix Pinion. Whisper never mastered Red Quill, preferring to pour her efforts into perfecting Phoenix Pinion instead, but she did have an advanced understanding of the technique and its origin. The form was the primary foundation taught to the soldiers of Emberwilde because of its strong, balanced fundamentals and demanding footwork. Many of the world's greatest swordsmen boast mastering Red Quill before anything else, as the core reflexive techniques balanced out the weaknesses of many other sword styles.

Whisper struck first, pressing forward and snapping with two quick cuts. Much to her surprise, Lau Lau shifted her feet backward and parried both strikes with ease. They each stepped to their left and exchanged twice more.

Kismet took a deep breath of his rumrose, failing to blink as he studied them both. It was obvious Whisper wasn't trying to win yet, but rather, she was testing Lau Lau's defensive technique and footwork. So far Lau Lau was reacting perfectly, but with an opponent such as Whisper this was still her battle to lose.

The crack of wood sung through the air with greater frequency as Whisper's combinations struck faster and harder, forcing the child to dodge the occasional swing instead of parry. Despite her growing efforts she still couldn't land a blow. Whisper stepped in and feinted a low swing, twisting the blade and snapping it down to strike the child's shoulder, but much to her surprise Lau Lau quickly parried it and countered with a swing that nearly clipped the tip of Whisper's new hat.

Kismet smiled around the pipe in his teeth. It was a beautiful counterstrike and if Whisper's sharp reflexes hadn't pulled her head back it would have been decisive. So far, Whisper was the aggressor and the merchants held their breaths the moment Lau Lau began to push back.

'That was close,' Whisper thought to herself as she slid back to re-establish her distance. Their swords cracked several more times as they took turns engaging and defending, and Whisper contemplated which of her advantages would best yield results. She had been holding back since the beginning, but Lau Lau's defence was forcing her to re-evaluate her strategy. Whisper had four potential advantages with which to exploit victory—reach, strength, speed, and experience. So far, any strike swung with intent was dodged, leading her to believe Lau Lau could recognize when she couldn't afford to parry. Any strike exploiting the difference in reach was quickly nulled with Lau Lau's impeccable footwork and any burst of speed met just enough technique to parry, though it always seemed close. All that was left to try was experience. Whatever that meant.

Whisper switched to defence and calmly parried as Lau Lau pressed forward with an onslaught. As impeccable as the child's defence was, her offence was easy to read. Whisper felt immediately enlightened with a revelation—'Easy to read...' She pulled her new tricorne down to shroud her eyes, making it almost impossible to see anything but their legs.

Lau Lau swung wildly for Whisper's collar and at the very moment before contact Whisper saw the wooden blade and parried, countering with a straight kick that buried itself so deep into Lau Lau's stomach the child nearly vomited as she tumbled backward into the mast. The merchants gasped as the thump of her tiny body rattle the deck and Kismet quickly postured to move in.

"Not yet," Djagatt said from the helm.

Kismet looked pained to spectate and angry to endure, but refrained from interfering.

Lau Lau keeled over and heaved, strands of saliva falling from her lips as she fought to catch her breath.

"I figured you out," Whisper said with a smile. "All this time I was treating you like a child when I should have been treating you like a psychic."

Kismet crossed his arms. He knew she'd figure it out sooner or later, he just wished she hadn't struck Lau Lau so hard.

"Your defence was almost impenetrable when I was the aggressor because you could read my every move the moment I planned it."

"How... did you win?" Lau Lau said between labored breaths.

"Simple," Kismet interrupted, "by limiting her vision she forced herself to counterstrike with pure reflex, leaving you with nothing to read. Something you don't yet know, because it only comes with experience."

Lau Lau struggled to stand when Whisper outstretched her hand to help.

"I treated you like a naïve child and I almost lost because of it," Whisper admitted. "You're much more than you seem and I was wrong not to see it."

Lau Lau took Whisper's hand and stood. Still reeling from the blow, she braced her other hand against the mast to keep balance.

"There is still someone who claims to be more than they seem, though, and I wish to see it." Whisper flicked Lau Lau's sword from the ground to her hand and threw it at Kismet.

Neither a buckle on his coat nor hair on his head moved as he caught the sword and tilted to shade his eyes. "What's the meaning of this?"

"I owe you a fair fight," Whisper said as she raised her sword and pointed it at him. "You claim to be legendary, but I can't respect your title until I've tested it."

The merchants of the *Windborn Chance* fell deathly still as they fearfully watched their captain. Even the bells of Djagatt refused to sound in anticipation of his response.

From beneath the shadows of Kismet's tricorne curled a smile, rumrose smoke drifting lazily through his teeth.

16

THE SMILE OF A SWORD MASTER

Lau Lau sat at the helm of the *Windborn Chance* with Djagatt, lacing her arms and legs through the gaps in the rail and nursing the bruising of her stomach. Her skin was already beginning to turn purple and before long it would spread across her whole chest like a sickly tapestry of unmitigated defeat. Even as the boat rocked in the wind she winced, but as she watched Whisper and Kismet approach the center of the deck, wooden swords in hand, her pain was quickly fleeting.

Whisper smiled, a sinister gleam appearing in the corner of her eyes. Whether she was awash with confidence she would win or excited for the opportunity to fight a worthy opponent, the fact that she was smiling at all meant she had no idea what she was getting into.

In their travels and adventures, Lau Lau saw Kismet perform miraculous acts with a blade. Well before he was captain of the *Windborn Chance* she and Kismet were vagabonds, always challenging masters for coin, always fleeing the armies of Emberwilde for a crime he would not let her know. Even from reading the soldiers that pursued them, all she knew was that it had something to do with the vault of someone very influential, the theft of something incredibly valuable, and the betrayal of the man she only knew as Blackrock. That was the original crime, at least. The further they ran the harder the realm pursued and eventually Kismet was forced to take a stand. A fang unit of fifty soldiers, two lieutenants, a captain, and a war general all slept to the Scarlet Charm that day and the decision was made that so long as their feet remained on Emberwilde soil they would never be free.

With her psychic abilities she could effortlessly read a person's surface thoughts and emotions, which they used to their advantage when negotiating passage on a rented ship, but to delve into memories required focus and intent. The more she practiced, she soon realized that objects were just as capable of having memories as people were, and with her new ability they discovered their first stash of lost treasure in a sunken ship, south of the Baku Sands. Suddenly, they were wealthy enough to build their own ship, the *Windborn Chance*, they were famous enough to begin their own fleet, and elusive enough to send a message to Emberwilde that the Bone Grove Merchants could never be caught.

Since learning she could pry secrets with focus, she knew if she tried hard enough she would be able to glean the memories from the darkest parts of Kismet's past, but honor and respect always won against her curiosity. They had an agreement, she and he. He would always defend her liberty if she never took his away, and defend her he had. Psychics were incredibly rare and the danger of kidnapping was ever-present. She was there when Kismet slew Emberwilde's fang of soldiers, smelled the blood of countless mercenaries hired to steal her by force, and heard the deafening silence when he slew the Blademane alpha in combat while defending the Daggermouth's trade agreement with the Bone Grove.

She saw him cut a man clean through as though he were parchment, split a pipe in twain while still in the teeth of his adversary, and shave a man's eyelashes with a single, sudden swipe. He was the greatest swordsman she had ever seen, and she had seen many, but there was one man many argued was better. He disappeared after the Dragon War, never to be seen again. A legend in the whispers of mankind, he was said to be so attuned to sharpened steel that swords would stretch from the earth like bamboo, begging to be wielded. Tried as she did, Lau Lau couldn't sense this man, so she was certain he was dead, but Kismet never lost hope. His greatest ambition, his greatest dream, was to pit his skill against the mythic swordsman and see who was victorious, the champion of Wind and Water or the bamboo's swordsong.

Whisper raised her sword, slid back her foot, and exhaled slowly, waiting for the pirate captain to do the same. Instead, Kismet stood with his sword down, presumably watching her from beneath the brim of his hat. Curls of smoke continued to rise from his pipe. He didn't appear to be ready, but he also didn't appear to be trying either. With a whistle of wind, Whisper closed the distance and opened with a slash meant for his throat. In the mere half second it took for her to swing, her hand went completely numb and she made no contact. She shifted her weight to swing the wooden blade back, but the sword was no longer there. She looked down at her empty palm, perplexed, flicking her wrist to make the tingling stop.

"That wasn't a bad first try," Kismet said, amused, his sword still down by his side. In his free hand was Whisper's sword, held aloft so she could take it back. "One more time?" The merchants laughed, though most of them weren't sharp enough to see how he came to disarm her so swiftly.

The corner of Whisper's eye twitched as she snatched the sword back. She had no idea how he did it, but she wasn't going to let it happen again. With both hands, she clutched the handle and swung again. Kismet gently drifted aside, placed his hand between her arms, and twisted to break her grip. She felt her other hand go numb this time, followed by a throbbing pain that surged across her ribs. She saw it, briefly, the flash of her own sword snapping across her breastbone. Empty handed once more, she clutched at her chest and took a deep breath. It stung, but it was trivial compared to the pain she endured before.

"Using two hands was smart, but your own arms betray you."

Kismet flipped her sword around, offered her the handle, and smiled cleverly. "One more time? I have yet to raise my own sword."

Her teeth ground as the corner of her lip turned into a faint sneer. It wasn't the match she thought it would be and he certainly wasn't being a sport about it. Forcefully, she pulled the sword from his hand while the merchants chuckled at her humbling. She didn't like it. Kismet's prepared defences were far too good for her to land a hit, let alone keep her weapon, so she decided to test his offence and hope her reflexes were good enough to counter. "Come at me, then."

Kismet smiled and took a deep breath of his pipe, the soft crackling of embers filled his ears as smoke poured from his nose and lips. With astonishing speed he sidestepped and thrust in, testing her footwork to see if she could keep up. She barely managed to turn and raise her sword in time to parry, but at the moment of contact he shifted his grip and slid the handle above her guard, striking her hard in the face. Her world spun with the impact and the numbness struck her hand once more before she fell to the ground.

Kismet held both swords again, but this time a warm pain surged up his hand. He looked down to inspect it—a thin stream of warm blood slowly dripped from his knuckles. Striking Whisper's face was akin to hitting stone and his flesh was feeling the full effects. From under the shadow of his tricorne he continued to examine the wound, confused as to how such a soft looking face could inflict so much damage when struck.

"Hitting pretty hard for a friendly match," Whisper said as she stood. A stream of blood trickled from under the shadow of her new hat.

"I think I owe you a few," Kismet replied with a smile. "How did you put it? How's she going to learn not to challenge people she can't beat?"

Whisper tilted each ear to her shoulder, cracking her neck and knuckles. "You'll bleed before we're done."

"You couldn't cut a loaf of bread with a honeycomb blade and a running start." He outstretched Whisper's sword for her to take, but instead she slid a foot back and raised a single open palm.

"Keep it," she said, "You're going to need them both."

17

SWORD AND FIST: KISMET VS. WHISPER

Whisper had a playful vengeance brewing in her cobalt blue eyes. Slowly, she flexed her fingers to loosen the joints and focused on her breathing, piercing Kismet with harrowing intent.

"You lost, Whisper." Kismet's joy in victory was fleeting. He still held a wooden sword in each hand, but kept them both down by his sides. "Best you get over it."

"I lost as a swordsman," she began, "but that's not what I'm known for, is it?"

Kismet had a very competitive spirit when it came to testing his mettle and she was succeeding at making his flawless victory seem hollow. "I suppose it isn't."

"A new challenge, then. I'll use my best weapons and you use yours. Master versus master."

Kismet chuckled. "You mean you'll be unarmed and I'll have a sword?"

"Two swords," she replied.

He shook his head and looked at the wooden sword in each hand. He never raised a blade to someone unarmed before and the advantage would sway to his favor significantly, but Whisper was certainly not *defenceless* by any means. "Okay, but..." The moment he agreed she appeared in front of him, narrowly missing a strike to his jaw as he leaned back. The wind of her palm tickled the end of his nose and nearly knocked his hat off his head. Both blades took to the air as he twirled them, pushing her back to a safer distance before resetting his stance. "That was a bit sneaky," he said as he adjusted the grip of his pipe between his teeth.

"All your talking leaves you open."

Kismet responded with a flurry of swings, but much to his surprise Whisper was managing to evade each one, albeit barely. She was fast, he couldn't deny that, but the further he pushed her the closer each strike came to sealing his victory. A tip grazed her corset and just as he thought he was about to land a decisive blow she clapped her hands over the flat of the blade, twisting the sword in his grip and producing an opportunity for her to close. She stepped in and struck him in the liver, nearly dropping his pipe from his teeth as he fought the urge to vomit. At so close a range the full potential of his lethality was smothered, but he was not helpless. He tried to slide back to re-establish his advantage of distance when she firmly stepped on his foot, holding him in place. The surprise threw him off balance and she struck him again, forcing the breath from his lips as her fist sunk below his breastbone.

Kismet switched the grip on his swords so they ran down his forearms, creating a tighter arc for closer combat, and swung sharply for her throat.

Whisper nearly failed to raise her guard in time and kicked him backward to the foremast, the sword grazed the collar of her coat. She expected him to be weak in closer ranges, but she overestimated how much the advantage would truly give. Along the bow of the ship were rows of belaying pins holding coils of rope. She wrapped her hands around two and pulled them from the pin rail, holding them close like a pair of wooden daggers.

Kismet caught his breath and readied himself, noticing the weapons she now held.

Whisper dashed in, deflecting his blades with her own. She swung for his head, striking the foremast behind him as he weaved to the side and countered by thrusting his head into the bridge of her nose.

Kismet's eyes widened as he staggered from the impact, ringing his senses much more than it should have. His vision quickly re-centered and he saw Whisper's eyes begin to narrow, while a strange crosswind arose and caused the sails to fall dead. A dark rage was building and the tingle of electricity across his skin hummed a foreboding.

She approached him with undeniable malevolence, striking with such force that the belaying pin gouged the foremast as he narrowly escaped. Clearly she did not like being struck in the face and as she began to spiral into a rage she could not control the danger became more and more present.

Kismet evaded another flurry and struck her across the jaw with a handle, hoping it would knock her out. It did not. In fact, her head barely flinched as his knuckles cracked from the impact.

Whisper's vision began to tunnel on him as the beast that lurked in her blood began to stir, and within her chest she could feel something she hadn't felt in what seemed like ages—her breath. She pressed her thumb and index together and raised her hand to her lips, breathing deeply the rising ocean air that now beckoned for Kismet's blood.

Kismet wasn't sure what she was doing, but as he watched her dark hair turn crimson he knew he had to get out of the way. With her exhale, a jet of brilliant orange flame roared from her lips, washing over the deck with destructive magnificence. Damp rope smoldered, black char stretched across the foremast, and the foresail was immediately set aflame. Kismet rolled out of the way, but as he strafed around her she followed him, spreading her breath of fire and wrath across the rest of the bow. Merchants leapt overboard to the safety of the water, some with eyebrows, some without, but before her flame could reach the main sail Kismet swung both swords with all his might, splintering them to flinders across her face.

Whisper's fire ceased as she briefly reeled. Her hair was now completely red, root to tip, and her pupils stretched into full draconian slits.

Kismet gambled on his strike rendering her unconscious, but now both of his swords were broken and he was utterly defenceless to her carnage. In the mere blink of an eye, leaving him no time to react, she grabbed him by the throat, raised him off his feet and plunged him through the deck. He struck the floor of the lower level in a daze—numbing pain danced from his toes to a head that felt full of water. His vision twirled as he tried to regain his bearings. He lay in a tangled bed of thick rope and he realized how truly fortunate he was. A few feet further and he would have struck the anchor winch, which would have either crippled or killed him.

Whisper stood at the hole in the deck, her silhouette a dark cloud against the sky with glowing blue eyes. Perhaps death would have been more fortunate. She leapt down to him and scooped him by the collar, throwing him up against the ceiling and back down to the floor.

The stem of Kismet's pipe cracked, but he refused to let it fall from his lips. At this point, the rumrose was the only thing keeping his body together. She clutched his throat and lifted him into the air, holding her free hand to her lips once more and taking a deep breath inward as she prepared to turn him to ash. His face slowly turned purple as his eyes wandered and in one last effort he blew sharply into his pipe, bursting cinders from the end and scattering them into her eyes. Whisper dropped him from her grip and rubbed the tiny coals from her eyes. Through a squinted haze she saw Kismet with a mallet in hand. He had a look about him, as though he wanted to say something clever, but the disjointed gloss of his eyes seemed to remind him he had about as much time as he did energy.

Kismet swung the mallet and struck open the heavy iron latch that held fast the anchor line, dropping the anchor from the side of the ship and snapping taut the tangled rope around her feet. She was pulled to the ground and dragged toward the anchor winch, forced to drag her fingertips in the floorboards to prevent her legs from becoming wound and broken in the iron. She slowed herself to a stop and burrowed her fingers into the floor to reinforce her grip.

Kismet crouched as he tried to catch his breath, rubbing his neck and throat to make sure nothing was bleeding. "Looks like I win."

Whisper growled through her teeth and stared him down as she began to pull herself along the floor. Inch by inch she began to reel the anchor back, piercing the floorboards with her hands.

"Lau Lau, hard to starboard. Trim the rear sails," he said as though Lau Lau were standing next to him. Suddenly, the sails caught the crosswinds and the *Windborn Chance* began to move again.

Whisper's arms strained as the ocean pulled at the anchor and even with her tremendous strength she could no longer pull herself to safety. She looked back to assess her situation, but all was dire without Kismet's help. If her arms couldn't hold, the anchor would pull her through the winch and crush her legs, maybe more.

Kismet sat down next to the winch and leaned against the wall, fishing through his jacket with trembling hands for his pouch of rumrose.

Whisper roared with anger as her defeat began to settle in, and as the humility began to overcome her rage the dark of her hair began to spread across the vibrant red strands like ink on fresh parchment. Her pupils slowly returned to normal as the creature hidden within her surrendered, taking with it her supernatural strength. The anchor pried her fingers from the floorboards and quickly pulled her toward the winch.

Kismet took his pipe from his lips and examined the crack, casually closing the iron latch he used to open the anchor winch. The teeth of the gears grabbed the iron and the rope abruptly stopped, Whisper's feet mere inches from it. She hurriedly kicked her feet free of the rope and rolled to safety, staring up through the hole in the ceiling with an awe that almost led Kismet to believe she was unaware of what she had done.

"I... don't know what to say," she began. She wanted a fight, but in her desire for a challenge this was not an outcome she thought possible. She always wielded her rage as a weapon, but her increasing lack of control and growing strength was beginning to worry her, as though some other consciousness or force within her was taking over her body and all she could do was watch. So far, Kismet and his merchants had given her nothing short of good grace and she couldn't afford a relapse, especially in the middle of the ocean. "Your ship..."

Kismet began to fill his pipe with rumrose, his shaking hands spilled flecks of the dried flower on his lap. "She can be fixed, though I can't say she's seen worse." The bustle of merchants putting out fires and reeling men back on board could be heard above.

"I'm a danger to your crew. I'm a danger to Lau Lau."

"Everyone gets a little crazy when they're punched in the face." Kismet looked around for something to light his pipe with, but the nearest lantern was on the other side of the room and he weighed whether the pain of moving was worth it. "A hazard you are, but a hazard we'll need come very soon."

She didn't want to say it aloud, but her apprehension wasn't that of fear, it was of joy. The power coursing through her, the heat of her flames, the feeling of slowed time that made her reflexes and speed so overwhelming—she absolutely loved it and the more her desire grew to wield it, the more risk she knew she would bring to those that didn't deserve it. "I don't know if I want to lose control again."

"Unfortunately for you, you're insane," Kismet began, "and I'll need that pointed in the right direction. I'll punch you in the face again if I have to."

18

THE VELVETINE'S MARK

The corridors within the *Last Breath* were narrow and difficult to navigate without being seen, but in the still of the night, Salem made his way to a hall in disarray. Splintered boards along the wall regaled him with volumes of ruination, while torn silk banners whispered the stillness of discord. At the end of the hall was a door, barred and sealed with irons. While many would have turned heel, his curiosity called out—he had to know what was inside and no mundane lock could keep him from it.

Salem removed the pouch of needles from his lapel and quickly picked the door free, sliding into the shadows before anyone noticed. The scent of blood still lingered in this room, even though it had clearly been cleaned. Splinters of wood still hid in the floorboards, a dark stain pooled along one of the walls and the door itself was boarded to cover a grievous tear. Something terrible happened here, recently, and it had Whisper's name written all over it.

Salem crouched and plucked a splinter from the floor, matching it to a side table with a missing drawer. Someone had been struck hard, and given the dark stain of old blood he was pretty sure it wasn't Whisper. He smiled to himself, chuckling under his breath. He was pleased so see she was still her feisty self.

Salem ran his hands through his hair, greasy and unkempt from the tribulations of his journey, and caught the scent of eggs and beans from the galley below. His stomach immediately growled.

'How much further?' Savrae-Lyth whispered.

He wished he knew, but he had no idea where the Bone Grove actually resided. In Whitewater, he didn't have a lot of naval experience and, though his geography was very good, the Bone Grove was only discovered in the last ten years or so. Even then, it was too small and inconsequential to be a matter of the Realm.

All Salem could think about was food. It was days since he had a real meal, but he would most certainly be caught if he tried to make his way to the galley. Sooner or later he would have to venture from relative safety to forage, but until then he had no intention of exploring the ship any further.

'That looks like Shén Shé,' Savrae-Lyth said curiously, filling him with the need to look out the porthole.

In the far distance was land, where dense jungle stretched along the coast for as far as he could see. They definitely weren't in Whitewater anymore and he was surprised to see they had gone the opposite direction he anticipated. Much of the pirate traffic happened along Emberwilde and the Baku Sands, so it stood to reason that their port of call would be close to their territory. If they were truly passing Shén Shé, then they had travelled much further from civilization, deeper into the untamed wilds.

Here, the waters were dangerous. Unlike the dangers of the west, where fleets of bloodthirsty pirates roamed and plundered, here in the east monsters lurked below the crests and waves. While pirates sought wealth and often left survivors, the creatures of the deep could not be bargained with, hungering evermore and taking what they want at any cost.

The waters of Shén Shé were known to have its creatures of nightmare, but it was relatively safe so long as one gave berth to the reefs. The idea was counterintuitive. Inexperienced sailors would hug the shores, feeling safer with land in sight and believing that deeper waters meant bigger creatures, but Shén Shé was unlike any other realm, especially since it bordered the carnivorous realm of

Setsuha. Fortunately for them, whomever was navigating the *Last Breath* was no amateur and they were well away from the churning caps of hidden stone and teeth.

'*The Bone Grove must be in Shén Shé. Perhaps that's why you've never heard of its location,*' Savrae-Lyth suggested.

It was plausible. Whitewater was at peace with the Shén Shé, but had no ambassadors within the borders. Any information regarding the realm was proprietary unless the Shén Shé deemed it inconsequential. If this was the location of the Bone Grove, it was likely Whitewater would never be told, but tugging at the back of Salem's mind was the only alternative he could imagine and he didn't like it. There was only one other place in the east secluded enough that the Bone Grove could exist in secret.

'*What if the Bone Grove is in Setsuha?*'

'*Fates,*' Salem replied, '*I hope not.*'

Whisper dropped her end of replacement sail on the deck of the *Windborn Chance*, sweat trickling down her brow. The fatigue of such menial labor was still foreign to her and it opened her mind to the fragility of the human race. It frustrated her. As joyful as she was to have her mistborn traits disappear, she missed the strength and endurance. Despite her constant vilification, life was somehow easier then. She looked across the deck and watched the merchants as they repaired the damage she had caused—even the young Lau Lau was helping where she could.

Kismet sat against the upper rails of the helm, presumably watching from beneath the shadow of his hat. Curls of thick smoke rose from his pipe. He had been smoking constantly since their altercation. It was probably because of the pain. Even though he defeated her, she wounded him badly yet again, and she was beginning to wonder why her welcome hadn't yet expired.

"Lau Lau," Whisper called to the child, who stopped what she was doing. Despite the events of the day, her young eyes were still vibrant and joyful, cleansed by the cool ocean breeze.

Lau Lau approached with a smile and bowed her little head.

"Why are you taking me to the Bone Grove?" Whisper asked.

"You don't want to come?" Lau Lau was cute, but it was clear she was deflecting.

"There are a half dozen ports you could have left me at if your intention was to let me go. Instead, you clothe me, call me friend, and sail me out to the middle of the ocean to a place people aren't even sure exists."

Lau Lau stumbled with Whisper's deduction, fidgeting with her hands while her eyes flicked to Kismet. "We're trying to protect you, Whisper," she said sheepishly. "Carver and the Orbweavers are hunting us now. The Bone Grove is the safest place to be."

"Just drop me off then." Whisper waved her hand to the nearest spec of land in the distance. "If my presence is putting everyone else in danger then put me on a beach and let them try to chase me."

"It's not that simple," Lau Lau replied.

Whisper's voice slowly grew louder as the agitation settled in. "Explain it, then."

From atop the helm, Kismet's voice boomed. "Coin, you cretin!" He rose and leaned over the rail, swinging the pipe in his hand as he gestured her toward the hole in the deck. "You think all this comes from warm hearts and whims? Fact is, the moment we saved you from Carver you've owed us a debt, a growing one at that, and I expect to be compensated."

"That's it then? I'm just a ransom."

"Look around you," Kismet growled, "I have a boat that's dead in the water, half a crew in the hold waiting to be buried, the other half hoping the risk is worth it, and a whole ocean that's getting narrower by the second as Carver and the Orbweavers close in. We were marked the moment we brought you aboard and now we're stuck with you until this mess resolves."

Whisper laughed loudly. "You're stupid, even for a pirate. No one in their right mind is going to pay you for my release. They might pay you to keep me, though."

Yoru approached and sat on the deck, judging her with sharp yellow eyes beneath her brow of pitch fur.

"And this damned cat!" Whisper just wanted more things to yell at. "Why does it always look like it knows something I don't?"

"She's not a cat," Lau Lau whined sadly.

"*Elantan velvetine.* Just a fancy name for *cat.*"

Lau Lau's voice was soft and meek, politely chiming from Whisper's peripheral. "Yoru wants to propose an agreement between you and Kissy."

Whisper didn't even know how to react.

"Kissy has a powerful enemy named Blackrock..."

"Lau Lau!" Kismet objected sharply. The young child simply raised her hand to stop him.

Lau Lau continued to parlay Yoru's message. "Blackrock is the biggest threat the Bone Grove Merchants have yet to face, but with your help we can beat him."

As absurd as it felt, Whisper crossed her arms and listened intently.

"Yoru proposes that the Bone Grove Merchants will give you hearth and home and in return you will slay Blackrock."

Whisper shrugged. "That's all I have to do? Kill someone?" A sinister smile crept in the corner of her lips as her eyes shifted back to Kismet. "That's currency I can work with."

Lau Lau and Yoru turned their attention to Kismet. "What do you think of this agreement?"

Kismet had nothing to lose. In fact, it was going more or less exactly how he expected it to. By using Whisper to kill Blackrock and continuing the plan to negotiate a ransom, he could protect the Bone Grove and get paid at the same time. "Fine," he replied sharply, masking his satisfaction with the irritation he felt over Whisper's attitude.

Lau Lau cleared her throat. "There is... one more thing. You said no one would care about your release, but Yoru and I want you to know that while we were in Roserun, there was someone looking for you."

"Is that so?" There was something in the velvetine's eyes that continued to unnerve her.

"Yes, someone with incredible power. Fate's willing, they will find you in the Bone Grove." Lau Lau recollected the intensity of the aura she sensed in Roserun. "When I first sensed it I smelled fragrant blossoms. It was beautiful."

There was only one person she could think of that would be looking for her and the blossoms immediately reminded her of Freestone. "Salem? He's alive?"

Lau Lau shook her head. "I don't know. Is Salem powerful?"

Whisper expressed disappointment as she recalled how quick he was to protect his face. "Not at all. Clever, but soft."

"Sorry Whisper. It's probably not him."

Whisper looked out across the water and wondered. Someone from Freestone. Someone powerful. The only person that came to mind was Howlpack Shade and her blood began to boil with the thought of a rematch. She was close to defeating him the first time and if she hadn't been wounded by his lackeys before he showed she might have slayed her first Instrument.

"Howpack Shade?" Lau Lau said curiously. "The Instrument of the Fates?"

Whisper nodded as she focused on her breathing. She had lost control of her inner beast too much already and the idea of tearing Shade's head from his shoulders was beginning to turn her vision red.

Lau Lau seemed confused. "But the Instruments are good, aren't they? They're the figureheads of balance."

Whisper smiled sharply. "Then it's only fair if *I* kill *him* this time."

"Lau Lau," Kismet called as he descended the stairs, two wooden swords in his hand. "This conversation is over and it's time for practice."

The young child bowed to Whisper and hurried to Kismet's side, accepting one of the swords.

Something in Whisper felt displaced and the gentle nudging of something at her leg commanded her attention. Yoru weaved between her legs, butting her fuzzy forehead into her ankles before sitting and staring up at her.

"Can I help you?" Whisper knew full well she wasn't going to get an answer.

The velvetine gave a long blink and turned her head toward

Kismet. Whether it was projection or coincidence, Whisper instantly knew what it was.

"Kismet," Whisper called as she approached him. She was all riled up from the argument and bowed her head to hide the anger in her eyes. "Teach me the art of the sword."

Kismet turned his back to her and tilted his head to spy over his shoulder, the buckles of his coats swayed in the wind. "Why, by Wind and Water, should I?"

Whisper rose, meeting him with cold ferocity. "Because I'm tired of lifting sails and your cat wants me to kill someone."

19

IVORY AND HER INSTRUMENTS

Ivory, the Forlorn, was a being of unspeakable beauty, whose unfathomably blue eyes devour every spec of surrounding color, transforming a vibrant reality into a mere scale of grays. The pupils of her eyes were the silhouettes of black spiders, set upon a white web that stretched across the depth of her irises. Upon her head she adorned a delicate crown of pure white ivory, beneath which her long raven hair cascaded and trailed behind her. Darkness wrapped around her throat like a collar, stretching into a spider's web that crossed her collarbone into a gown of roiling shadow—the base frayed and waved listlessly over a cloud of white mist that concealed her feet. Around her left wrist she wore Shiori's First Wish, a bangle of platinum wings that held a large, sparkling diamond.

She gazed upon the bangle with adoration, basking in the infinite power of wealth it promised—as all first wishes did. She gently placed her hand against the rough stone walls of her temporary home, a large cave deep in the heart of the underground 'city', Sabanexus. White crystalline tendrils crept from the bangle and slowly turned the damp, dismal rock into that of gleaming gemstone. Though the First Wish was capable of changing any material into any other wealth, she had grown to love the purity of diamond. Something so precious, pure, and solid formed from the intense hostile environments of natural law. It expressed herself in entirety. Beauty through perseverance, resolution through experience. How extreme pressure can create indestructible clarity for those who can endure.

The crystalline tendrils consumed the stone until every inch became that of pristine diamond. She took a moment to bask in it. In her right hand she held a scroll tube of pure platinum, emblazoned with ancient sigils. A smile stretched across her lips as her fingers traced the lines and she slowed her breath to calm her anxiety. Within this tube was the answer she sought for decades, after a thousand years of curiosity. An answer she betrayed her kin and brought forth an army of demons for. It was the only written recipe for one of the greatest draconian creations, honeycomb stone—more importantly it would show her how to destroy it.

Shiori Etreille, the Immaculate Artisan, made three incredible artifacts of power known as Shiori's Three Wishes, and before the Fate's imprisoned her she divided and hid them. The First Wish, that of wealth, Ivory discovered during her self-exile to the Overworld, but the Second Wish, that of power, was sealed in the indestructible honeycomb stone and buried in the frozen mountains of Whitewater's north. At the time the tundra was a desolate, uninhabitable landscape, but as humanity began to sprawl for mineral resources, and technology increased survivability, the bastion city of Lyre was founded and the Second Wish was eventually discovered.

With the help of her Instruments, Ivory was now in possession of the Second Wish, but even with her great power she was incapable of freeing the artifact. Honeycomb stone was an alchemical resin created by the dragons, named aptly for the hexagonal setting technique they would use to ensure maximum structural integrity. It was very rare, valuable, and came in a variety of different colors. The recipe was exclusive knowledge to only the most powerful dragons allied to Savrae-Lyth, and though it seemed completely indestructible they made certain to give it a weakness only they knew about, just in case their recipe was ever used against them. Fortunately it never was, but as pressure began to build on dragonkind and the war was beginning to brew, Savrae-Lyth cast the recipe into the Overworld so none could wield its benefits without the dragons.

She tilted the tube on its side and gleefully watched as she turned the top into coarse diamond sand, the multitude of tiny gemstones fell to the floor like glittering rain. She carefully reached in and withdrew a roll of tan leather, disintegrating the rest of the tube and rolling the leather open. The draconian text was exciting to see, each letter and symbol burnt into the hide with some form of acid or fire. Her thin smile grew larger as she combed over the recipe, astounded by the complexity of the technique. Several rare ingredients, very specific enchantment conditions, and many temperature ranges for melting, casting, and setting. As she continued to read, her smile began to fade and worry clouded the intense joy in her eyes. Her head began to shake in disbelief and upon reaching the last of the text she hurled the scroll to the floor. The room was a chamber of absolute silence while she stared into the facets of the diamond wall. This was the answer she had been searching for, the answer she weighed with Elanta's liberation, but it wasn't the answer she wanted. The power she would attain by having the Second Wish was worth a quest for the improbable, but this. This was almost ironically impossible.

FEVER, THE LOVELY PSYCHOPATH

Sultry blue eyes surrounded by long golden curls of hair gazed downward into a bowl of water while the glossy sheen of scarred flesh gazed back. Plagued with both anger and shame, the lovely psychopath Fever could not yet tear her eyes from her reflection.

As she took the city of Lyre to secure the Second Wish for Ivory she confronted the Shén Shé pureblood, Ashissa, who scarred her face with an acid trap. Unable to mend the wound, Ivory instead cast an enchantment that concealed it to those unaware of its presence, but Fever hated looking at it herself. Not only was it a blight upon her vanity, but it served to constantly remind her that she suffered a sacrifice to a cause she didn't really care for.

Before she was an Instrument she was a skilled assassin. She didn't need to accept Ivory's power because she already had power of her own—the power to take or spare life without bias, the ability to strike fear in the hearts of anyone even hearing her name. As far as Fever was concerned she was also a free woman. The idea that the Fates were in control of her destiny had little substance, making Ivory's grand scheme to restore free will to the people a boring ideal. At first she convinced herself she accepted the instrumentation because it would be fun, bringing gods to their knees and giving her more strength to terrorize Elanta with. The more she focused on blaming everyone but herself she began to determine she was blackmailed. Forced to accept the role by the Emberwilde Brigadier General, Phori, who captured her and threatened her with judgement for her crimes if she didn't comply.

Bitter were the many voices in her head, but there were still a few that argued for the appreciation of Ivory's grace. Though Fever made a very big sacrifice, Ivory went out of her way to apologize and do her best to make amends. The enchantment concealing the blight of her face was a far cry from perfect, but it was as close as she was ever going to get.

The abhorrent visage of her scarred skin and the clouding of one of her crystal clear eyes tore her soul asunder and in an outburst of frustration she swept the bowl from the table at which she sat. Clay shards shattered against the roughly hewn walls of stone. Blighted, she stared menacingly into the glowing flame of a lone candle. The dance of welcoming warmth and destructive potential slowly hypnotized the voices within her, bringing the noise to something much more manageable.

It had been over a week since she came to Sabanexus, the secret underground lair of the Leviathans, nestled in the dark caverns far below the surface of *who knew where*. The only exit she saw thus far was a single, massive hole in the ceiling of the main cave, through which a tornado of swirling golden energy and mist touched down—the same as she had seen in Valakut before she travelled to Lyre. From the mew of her cold, damp walls she would watch with fearful curiosity as chitinous monsters amassed in droves from the mysterious beyond. Most were then branded with glyphs from the hundreds of cultists that resided in the depths with her. When she first arrived, the cultists were only using one glyph, which they called 'mind-shackle'. Apparently, it was a means of connecting and enthralling the creatures so they could be organized into formations and used as mounts. Since then, she saw several new glyphs being used in their arsenal. One was created to help the creatures breathe the air with greater ease, while others reinforced their chitin plates.

Lost in the radiance of flame, the room grew darker, until it was all she could see.

"Fever!" called a voice.

The rare silence in her head was quickly interrupted, reopening the floodgate of voices within that called to her rage. Instinctually, a serpent of dripping ichor and shadow stretched from the black diamonds of her bangles and wrapped around the throat of her disruptor.

Lifted from the ground, toes scraping at the stone, the heavy black robes of a cultist flailed as he clawed to free himself. "Please..." he wheezed.

"What do you want?" she flared angrily, turning her head to cover the side of her face with her hair. She knew he couldn't see her scars through the enchantment, but her vanity was far too encompassing to find solace.

He struggled desperately as the pressure in his head continued to build, mustering just enough air to force a single word from his lungs. "Ivory..."

Fever knew what it was—a summoning. When she first arrived to Sabanexus she saw four monstrous creatures exit the tornado of mist. The cultists referred to them as the Four Chitin Kings of the Overworld and to her knowledge they were the most powerful and fearsome creatures of their demonic realm—much like the four Fates to Elanta. Recently, Ivory had gone to meet them and now it was time to discuss the next chapter of her ideal.

With the cultist's growing panic came Fever's joy. She tilted her head and a thin smile crept across the deep red of her lips. "Thank you," she sung sweetly as the smoky tongue of her shadowed serpent teased behind his ear. Filled with slow torturous intent, the serpent buried its fangs into his neck and then released him.

The cultist collapsed to his knees and coughed uncontrollably as his body begged for air. After a short moment of relief, he lifted his head and froze as the venom took effect.

Fever revelled in the constriction of his pupils and basked in the faint trembling in each breath. With strained fingers he lifted his shaking hands to his head and clutched his hair in massive clumps. As the room peaked in the horror of his silence, a storm of shrill terror finally befell the resonance of the chamber as he screamed at the top of his lungs.

Fever slowly closed her eyes as his cries echoed and her head began to sway as though she were listening to divine orchestration. She breathed deeply his anguish and lovingly indulged in the peace it brought her. Finally, the voices in her head quieted to a whisper and she hummed softly to the chords of ruination.

PHORI, SALAMANDER OF THE BASTION NINE

Massive black glass spires towered in uniform from the side of an active volcano, a magnificence that could be seen in the distance, long before arrival. Though Phori had much further to travel before arriving at the Palace of Roiling Cinder, she could now see the orange lines of flame and power that trickled in archaic sigils across its glossy surface. The palace was home to the malikeh of Emberwilde, also known as the Phoenix Queen—the immortal ruler of the realm of Emberwilde for the last thousand years. Proven to be impervious to death, the Phoenix Queen was possibly the only person who actually knew how and when the Palace of Roiling Cinder was created, as it stood tall long before her reign. It was a unique form of architecture that tapped directly into the thermal energy of the volcano, and by using a series of enchantments it would channel its destructive force into a multitude of functions—atmospheric control, fortification, light, and wards. Though many sages perused the great obsidian halls, no one truly knew of its origin, but the Phoenix Queen once stated it was the former home of Shiori Etrielle, the Immaculate Artisan. Other than the extremely advanced techniques used to create it there was never any proof of such grand presumption.

Nestled at its base, preceding the black gates that guarded the path to the palace was the city of Obsidian. True to its name, buildings of black glass stretched across the rocky terrain, as uniform and precise as its army was disciplined. Though there were many artisans, scholars, and people of various trades, every single citizen was required to hold a military rank, making it one of the most uncontested places in the world, second only to the mountain of Setsuha where even the vegetation was lethal.

Seated along the edge of a narrow path high atop one of Emberwilde's many treacherous cliffs, Phori rested against a boulder and looked out over the endless stretch of forest. Her hair draped over the pitch sheen of her armor, accenting the brilliant glass beads she had woven into her many thin braids. In her hair was also a long, violet feather, which marked her rank as a Brigadier General, and she carefully preened it as she looked over the sword and sheath she laid on her lap. Tassels were awarded like medals, and she had many— the bundles of red silk strands stretched across the sheath of black and gold. From the sheath also hung her clan crest, the mark of the Salamander. The Salamanders were responsible for protecting the southern borders from the Baku, but now that she was heading north she was temporarily clanless. She dropped her hand to the shaft of her double-bladed staff, which leaned in the crook of her neck and shoulder. Her fingertips traced the multitude of engravings as she began to lose herself in deep contemplation.

The thin, warm wind carried her mind back to the last meeting with her Fate, Ivory—awash in the vibrant shade of her eyes when she would steal the color from the world. Though it had been nearly a week, the anxiety of her mission still wound in her chest. Never once had she thought she would be graced with an opportunity to be the General of an army of Obsidian, and yet somehow Ivory managed to make it happen. A testament to the rumor that the whispering of Fates can do almost anything. It was years since her last visit to Obsidian, and with but a few, albeit major accomplishments of which to speak she couldn't help but wonder if the rest of the war council would meet her with disdain. She was, of course, the product of advantage and supernatural favoritism. Including herself, there were nine enlightened war generals of Emberwilde known as the Bastion Nine. Each earned their rank through countless years of training, enlightenment, loyalty, skill, and sacrifice, and the privilege of leading one of the queen's nine armies was the highest of honors.

Unfortunately for her, reception was the least of her worries. Not only was she walking into a room of the most experienced war minds of her time, she was expected to convince them to surrender the city of Valakut to the demons in the mist and remain combat neutral during the ensuing war. According to Ivory, it was a necessary evil that would ensure their advantage when striking against the Fates and the Weave, but it was all hearsay. The mere anticipation of their resistance strained her to no end and she dared fathom how she could convince them to lay down arms to a cause she was only just beginning to believe in. Recently, she received word from Ivory that the Orbweavers were in the process of obtaining something of leverage to ensure the Phoenix Queen's cooperation, but neglected to mention what it was.

The conundrum of Ivory's plot was continually perplexing. She understood the rewards of taking destiny out of the hands of the Fates and giving true freedom back to the people, but at what price? Ivory meant to strike the other Fates with the utmost of force and use the chaos as a blinder, but a war between gods was bound to litter the world with the unfathomable casualties of mortal men. How many lives would it take before it simply wasn't worth it anymore? If protocols were met, the city of Valakut would be ordered to evacuate to the outskirts, but she needed more than just faith to convince the war council not to march a legion into the mist to reclaim it.

As the air began to cool with the coming eve, Phori began to realize how much time had passed in the turmoil of her mind. The tips of the trees far below her overlook resided in cool, matte stillness, reminding her that time was of the essence. With a division that tired her both inside and out, she slowly clambered to her feet, harnessing her staff to her back and reattaching her sword to her hip. Another day, perhaps two, and she would be on the sacred streets of Obsidian—then would be her truest test of mental fortitude.

WRATH AND RAVENMANE

The honeycomb stone entombment stood just six feet tall and was about three feet wide on all sides. The ambient torchlight flickered against the thousands of translucent hexagonal facets and twisted with the large fissure that stretched from top to middle. When the Shén Shé pureblood, Ashissa, broke the powerful ward that surrounded the stone in Lyre, the massive release of energy caused the stone to crack. It was the first and only report in known history where someone caused damage to the draconian resin, but even with an explosion large enough to blanket the whole world it still wasn't enough to break it completely. The crack was only a few inches at its widest and for days the leviathans of Sabanexus were taking turns showing their might by trying to widen it further, but with no results.

The honeycomb stone had since been moved to another, private, chamber where only Ivory and her Instruments were permitted. It was a safeguard in the event the Chitin Kings decided to break their alliance and claim it for themselves. A potential outcome Ivory gleaned from the tensions in her meeting with them. Whether the kings acted the moment they felt she was no longer of use or after she managed to break the honeycomb stone, she was certain their betrayal was imminent. In either case, Sabanexus was still the safest place for her to hide while the Fates were on high alert, especially since they knew she had the Second Wish.

The Second Wish was encased within the clear honeycomb stone, teasing her with its presence. It was a curved platinum blade with a wavy golden hamon that travelled from the tip to a golden guard that circled above the hilt—three curved blades surrounded by a ring. The handle was braided in cloth of black and silver, and hanging from the end cap was a chain with an ornament—a small round bundle of fabric tied to look like a cute little ghost. Two slits on the head gave the impression it had two closed eyes, sleeping eternity away. Thick strands of honeycomb stone stretched from the top and bottom of the prison to hold the tip and handle of the Second Wish, while the rest of the sword suspended within empty space.

Towering above the honeycomb stone was a suit of black armor, the leviathan Wrath—icy blue leylines of energy pulsed along the surface in glowing channels. It was long since thought that Liam Whitewater, King of the Realm of Whitewater, was the last living leviathan. However, a large clan was hiding in Sabanexus waiting for their chance to strike back at the humans that tried to slaughter them all a hundred years ago. Whether Ivory had just learned of their existence or was always aware, once she exited the mist she offered her gift of power to Wrath. His instrumentation was extraordinary, giving him many powers that made him nearly invincible. Increased strength and endurance, a body that seemed impervious to the mundane, armor that devoured enchantments, and an aura that disintegrated flesh. In his recent altercation with the Moths and their leader, Elder Waylander, he had the opportunity to test his new power, and he liked it. Even with their best efforts they barely wounded him and were forced to flee and surrender the city of Lyre and the Second Wish. Though he was a terrifying presence of inescapable cataclysm, he got along very well with Fever—almost gentlemanly in her presence.

Wrath wrapped his hands around a large iron halberd and raised it high above his head. He roared as he brought it down, crashing the blade upon the fissure with enough force to crack the stone beneath his feet and send a rumble throughout the halls and corridors. The blade shattered on impact, sending shards of dark gray iron in all directions, clanging as they struck the floor. Wrath growled beneath his helmet as he raised the shaft and examined how far it had bent.

"You don't give up, do you?" a deep, rumbling voice growled behind him.

Wrath slowly turned to see Agathuxusen, the Ravenmane. Ivory's first Instrument. Despite being a massive Blademane Baku, he was still a bit shorter than Wrath, though it didn't seem to affect his arrogance. The Ravenmane wore the same black armor that seemed signature to Ivory's Instruments, but currently did not adorn the helmet, showcasing his red-tan fur, lion-esque face, and long black mane—the glint of blades woven into it clinked against his pauldrons. Born of the Blademane tribes in the Baku Sands, he was once a strong candidate for pride alpha, but with Ivory's offer of limitless power the squabbling tribes of the Baku Sands quickly seemed insignificant when there was a whole world to rule. He was vicious, ruthless, and a devout believer in the survival of the fittest. "You don't speak much, do you?"

Wrath silently turned back to the Second Wish and wedged the iron shaft into the crack, straining to lever it open.

"You're never going to break it."

"**Only weak surrender,**" Wrath replied in his guttural leviathan tongue. The language was difficult to enunciate properly without practiced throat control and almost impossible for humans to learn.

"**Only wise know when defeated,**" the Ravenmane replied.

Wrath stopped struggling with the stone. The shadows of the room nearly engulfed the Ravenmane's face, but the glimmer of his red eyes flickered with the fire. "**You speak the leviathan tongue?**"

"**Yes.**"

"**How do you know?**"

The Ravenmane crouched in the corner and watched from the distance. It didn't seem a comfortable alternative to sitting, but it stood to reason that Baku instincts disallowed them to be physically unprepared for combat. "**Baku were comrades of leviathan long ago. We are both hunted by humans.**" The leviathan tongue didn't have a word for friends.

"**If comrade, why do Baku not help when Whitewater attacks?**"

"**Baku helped leviathan in Emberwilde. We could not help in Whitewater.**"

Wrath nodded as he followed along. The leviathans of Sabanexus were a collaboration of different tribes from all over Elanta and many cliques still existed. The tribes of Whitewater rarely conversed with those of Emberwilde, so he was unaware of any Baku influence. He was inclined to believe the Ravenmane considering their language could not have been learned without immersion and assistance. The slaughter that Whitewater brought upon the leviathans was quick and unexpected, and Sabanexus now exists only because they survived. If the Baku helped them, then he owed them his respect.

"That crack," the Ravenmane began, "Fever could fit her hand."

"Sword is still attached. Sword is very powerful. Useless effort, very dangerous."

"Yes... but how dangerous?"

The Ravenmane stood and left the room, returning with an Orbweaver cultist who clearly did not seem comfortable with the summoning.

Wrath tilted his head and examined the human. "He cannot be here."

"He is my guest," the Ravenmane replied. "The smallest hands I could find."

The Orbweaver didn't like how he couldn't understand them and took a step backward, only to bump into the Ravenmane's armor.

The Baku raised his hand to gesture to the Second Wish. "Pull the sword out."

The cultist shook his head nervously. "No."

The Ravenmane lowered his palm and set it aflame with white fire. The flame roiled in slowed time and emanated heat so intense the cultist felt his skin on the verge of blistering. "Pull the sword out."

With a hard swallow the cultist stepped away from the flame and cautiously approached the honeycomb stone. There was so much oppressive energy resounding within the room he was becoming nauseous, unsure whether it was the artifact, the Instruments, or the combination. He rolled up the sleeve of his robe and looked back to the Ravenmane one last time, who watched him like a predator watches prey. With trembling fingertips he slowly slid his hand through the crack until his forearm became pinched. "I can't go any further."

"Try harder."

The Orbweaver looked back at the sword, which was almost close enough to touch. He winced as he twisted his arm back and forth, wedging it further into the stone until he was almost there. One last painful effort and his fingertips gently graced the braided handle. His body immediately seized and his head flailed backward, mouth wide open in silent agony. The tiny eyes of the ghost charm sleepily opened while the eyes of the Orbweaver rolled back into his head. His flesh began to deflate and form to the contour of his bones as wispy strands of life essence drifted from his skin and entered the blade. His arm, still pinched in the honeycomb stone, broke apart and fell to the bottom, instantly bursting into a pile of dust. The Orbweaver's legs began to crumble, causing the body to hobble backward and fall, disintegrating as it struck the floor, leaving only the heavy black robe intact. The last of the essence drained from the pile of dust and the little ghost closed its eyes once more.

Wrath knelt to the dust and examined it. **"Very dangerous."**

The Ravenmane picked up the cloak, the fine dust poured out and took to the air. **"Ivory better be as powerful as she thinks she is."**

20

BASTION NINE, AND THE PALACE OF ROILING CINDERS

The deep bellow of horns sounded as Phori approached the steps to the Palace of Roiling Cinders. From a distance, it looked magnificent, but now, as she stood at its doors it was far more than anything she could have ever imagined. Spires of ornate black glass stretched into the sky, while glowing orange flame drew patterns across its surface like streams of roiling magma. The palace was built into the side of an active volcano, so close and powerful she could hear the constant low rumble of destructive force bottled at the source—however, she did not feel the intensity of heat she expected. Instead, the air was cool, clean, and comfortable, a testament to the enchantments embedded into the obsidian walls.

One would expect the massive doors into the palace to groan with the weight, sounding something guttural to welcome one of the few people permitted within the halls, but instead there was nothing. The towering doors glided on their hinges like silk and wind, revealing the ornate architecture and shimmering glass floors of the first hall. Wispy, glowing orange essence twinkled across the lofted ceiling, casting a beautiful luminescence that sparkled across the floor and accented the glass features of the arches. It was more than enough light to see by and its nature created the feeling of warmth all the while accenting the sharper, more unforgiving features of the obsidian architecture.

In the center of the hall stood a man clad in golden garbs, with long crimson cuffs that hung nearly to the ground. Roaming the palace was forbidden for all but the Bastion Nine, the high-scholars, and the Phoenix Queen herself, and this man was clearly not a warlord.

"A high-scholar, I presume?" Phori asked. She needed to know his status before determining whether to bow.

"Yes, General Phori," the man bowed deeply with an upright palm atop a closed fist, emulating the rise of flame with his hand, "the war council is expecting you."

Phori entered the room, taking in the vast loneliness it projected. It was too large a space for so few people. "Have you been waiting long?"

"Only since you entered the outskirts, General Phori." The scholar continued to hold his head down until she gave him permission to rise.

"That was hours ago." Phori flicked her fingertips to gesture his ease.

The man smiled politely. "Your arrival to the war council was important and my being here to greet you was paramount." He held open an arm and signalled toward a corridor at the end of the room. "Please, this way."

She began to follow him, letting her eyes wander to the glorious décor that surrounded them. Golden candelabras stemmed from the pillars and walls, ornate wooden hutches with brilliant filigree held golden eggs and jewels, and tall crystal floor cases displayed various ornaments, weapons, and armors of significance. Every treasure was breathtaking.

"What is your name, high-scholar?" Phori asked.

"Thees, General Phori."

"What is your specialty, Thees?" When enlightened mortals learn to use sigils, most study a broad spectrum to become adept at a variety of useful skills. By spreading their focus across different disciplines and techniques their enchantment aptitude becomes more diverse, but their skills develop a limit. To become a high-scholar, one must choose only a single discipline and pour all their effort and skill into it, foregoing the rest.

"Abjuration, General Phori."

His formality had already become repetitive, but it would be dishonorable for her to have him stop. "A very fine choice," she said politely. "You and I may become good friends." Abjurers were the finest wardsmiths you could employ, capable of creating powerful barriers and resistances whose duration depended on the fortitude of the enlightened.

Thees brought her before a curious door, as beautiful as it was aggressive. The obsidian channels carved into it left sharp edges, where rivers of bright lava coalesced into a pool in the center. "Forgive me, General Phori, but this is as far as I am permitted to go." He pointed to the glowing pool of molten stone in the middle of the door. "The palace will devour any hand not permitted to open the War Room, including my own."

Phori slowly raised her hand to the lava and paused. She hoped she wouldn't feel the heat, but she could, and it made her nervous about plunging her hand in. She hadn't yet received the General's feather for her hair or had the ceremony honoring her new role. In fact, she hadn't met anyone of equal or higher rank since she arrived to let her know her promotion was absolute. As far as she was concerned she was still just a Brigadier General, but what mattered now was what the palace thought. She took a deep breath and steadied her nerves. Ivory was many mysterious things, but she wouldn't send her here to lose her hand on misinformation.

Phori plunged her palm into the lava. The thick fluid oozed around her hand—hot, but not enough to burn. She pushed deeper into the door and with the lava mid-way up her forearm she felt a handle and twisted it, sending a low rumble of winches and gears through the surrounding walls. The door began to slide up into the wall and she pulled her hand from the pool, the lava peeled itself from her arm and remained in the center.

As the door reached its pinnacle it revealed a large room surrounded entirely by fire. In the center was a long, low obsidian table with nine golden cushions—eight of which were occupied while the last remained empty, presumably hers. At the end of the table, set upon a dais of three stairs, sat a golden palanquin with crimson curtains, each pulled and fastened to the side to show the woman within—her headdress of red, gold, and black matched both her makeup and silk robes.

Phori met her once before when she defended the city of Akashra and earned her promotion to Brigadier General. This woman was the malikeh, the Phoenix Queen, and she was exactly as she remembered her.

The Phoenix Queen outstretched her palm, a finger ring of golden wire coiled down her index and up her thumb, glinting in the flames. "Welcome," she said with authority, "to the Bastion Nine."

Phori silently bowed and approached, taking in the details of the room. Eight generals sat upon their golden cushions and judged her, but not a single eye met her own. Though everyone was gloriously adorned in a variety of ruby half plate and golden chainmail, everyone was affixed on her vicious obsidian armor. The razor edges flickered an orange malevolence in the dance of flames surrounding them and the teardrop blades of her staff faded in and out of sight, so thin and dark it was intermittently lost to the shadows. As Phori travelled to the Palace of Roiling Cinder she was anxious about her lack of experience hindering her welcome to the Bastion Nine, but instead of being looked down upon as the green general of unearned authority, their eyes were that of reverence; their breaths were that of awe.

Behind each general was a weapon's rack, bearing their instruments of choice for all to see, and as Phori approached her seat she wondered if hers would be large enough to accommodate her double-bladed staff.

"Welcome," sung a sweet, exotic voice. A slender woman with fine cheekbones and almond eyes outstretched her hand and patted the golden cushion beside her—the golden chain of her shoulder cloak jingled as she moved. Without even seeing the woman's face Phori knew she was an Emberwilde highborn of the north. Though many argued that the accents of nobles sounded too pretentious to be pleasant, Phori loved how smooth and delicate it was compared to her rough southern tongue.

Phori walked through the entirety of the room and this woman was the first to make eye contact. Her sharper features seemed almost too unnatural to be human, leading her to believe she was using some form of subtle glamor to adopt the finer features of the Setsuhan figure. She was lightly clad in ruby scales that left her arms bare and her honorary tassels hung from the buckle of her golden chain cloak. Hanging from the weapon rack behind her was a hip and shoulder harness with two slender sheaths, each with a silver hilt and handle from the blades they let slumber. One sheath had a silver medallion and a General's feather hanging from it.

"I am Lilia," she said.

Phori bowed her head and removed her bladed staff from her harness. "Phori." She carefully leaned it against her empty rack before taking her seat. Immediately, she noticed the silver medallion fastening Lilia's cloak, a ruby insect glimmering upon it. "You're a Firefly." Her surprise almost made her feel silly, but she had never met anyone from Clan Firefly before. They were agile, elite warriors, heavily trained and educated to act as the lawful counterbalance to the assassins of the realm. Fireflies were hand chosen from only the finest; honed under extreme conditions, they operated almost entirely under cover of nightfall. As a general rule, if you were ever to meet one, it was probably too late.

"Yes, I am," Lilia replied. If she was flattered, she didn't show it, maintaining a regal composure that seemed matter-of-fact. "And you?"

A deep voice sneered from across the table. "She's a Salamander." A broad, handsome man with auburn hair leaned forward onto his elbows, lacing his hands together. He neither smiled nor blinked, an unmoveable stone that patiently awaited a reaction.

Phori looked him over. Brilliant crimson steel embellished with gold filigree and a pair of golden ram's horns that curled off his right pauldron, protecting his neck from an attack on his non-dominant side. Without even seeing his clan insignia she knew he was a Ram, stubborn and hardy guardians of Emberwilde's western cliffs. Rams were plentiful and for good reason. They were strong, disciplined, and loyal—the preferred guardians for anything the Realm deemed of value. Phori had nothing but respect for the Rams of Emberwilde and she knew not to take his gruff tone personally. If he was addressing her, it meant she was worth addressing. "Indeed, I am."

Lilia nodded. "Salamanders are clever and resilient." She spoke almost as though she were quoting a text, devoid of any personal bias. "Where a Ram possesses the forthright power and conviction of a straight line, the Salamander is much like a circle, shifting and adapting to find unity without force."

Having heard it aloud, it rung true to Phori's ears. The principles of Salamanders and Rams were completely opposite, yet somehow the contrast intrigued her.

"Why are we allowing her to sit when she doesn't yet have her feather?" the Ram stated to the masses.

Phori became immediately uncomfortable. She already felt like she didn't belong yet and the tradition of rank was something she also had a very strong opinion of. She agreed with the Ram and was content to leave until her ceremony if she was asked to.

Lilia's posture tightened. "What does it matter? Her rank was bestowed by our malikeh, the Fates have chosen her as a vassal of their will, and the Palace has allowed her entry without harm."

"Emberwilde is rich with tradition, and to enter this space is a right bestowed through the sanctity of ceremony. Anything less is dishonorable in the eyes of the Fates. She must have her pinion to mark her rank."

"To mark her rank, perhaps, yet she needs no pinion to mark her worth." Lilia lifted her hand and gracefully drew his attention to Phori's obsidian armor. "She is an Instrument of Fate, lest you forget. It is *us* who require the pinion of the General to sit in *her* presence."

The Ram crossed his arms in defiance. "Instrument or not, our capacity to honor tradition without concession is what keeps the sanctity of the Bastion Nine without fissure. We are as feared for our convictions as we are our skill."

"Stop," the Phoenix Queen commanded, her voice resonating through the hall, flickering the fire as it bowed to her. "I am curious to hear what our Salamander has to say."

Phori knew exactly how she felt about sitting in the war room with the Bastion Nine and couldn't help but wonder if the Phoenix Queen was testing her. Fortunately, her response would have been the same regardless. Phori stood and bowed, the glass beads woven in her hair rattled over her armor. "Lilia honors me with her defense, but I must agree that tradition is a cornerstone of our strength."

Lilia tilted her head and listened carefully, but it was impossible to tell if she was unhappy with Phori's position or simply emotionlessly objective. However, the Ram seemed both surprised and impressed, relaxing his shoulders and palming his chin with intrigue.

Phori continued addressing the silence of her audience, her voice growing bolder. "That being said, Emberwilde, *our* realm, is in a state of emergency. A whole city has fallen to the Overworld, thousands of people were forced from their homes, and the hour of reckoning draws closer with each wasted second. Now more than ever you need your ninth Bastion, and here I am. Do not push me away because I lack the ceremony, do not concede because I am an Instrument— embrace me, because together we are stronger and the people of Emberwilde, *our* people, are suffering."

The Phoenix Queen smiled, pleased with Phori's words and the silence they brought to the rest of the Bastion Nine. "Well spoken, Salamander, but since your summoning, a decision has already been made regarding the mist of the Overworld."

This was the part Phori had been dreading for the entirety of her journey here. When the mist funnelled down it devoured the major city of Valakut. The standard response of the realm would be to reclaim it by amassing an army and marching inward, but Ivory had explicitly instructed her to convince the Bastion Nine not to advance. She had no idea how she was going to do it. Eight of the realm's most brilliant war minds, plus the eternal wisdom of the Phoenix Queen; it was more likely she would be demoted and shunned by the realm for even suggesting it. "I see," Phori began, preparing herself for the backlash she was about to endure from her queen and her peers, "I have an opinion on the matter..."

The Phoenix Queen raised her hand, instructing Phori to stop talking. "Though I have no doubt your opinion has merit, my decision is final. Forces are to be assembled on the outskirts of Valakut to ensure the Overworld influence doesn't expand, but we will be making no attempt to reclaim the city as of yet."

Phori was at a loss for words and her surprise was obvious. Somehow, the war council had already agreed on exactly what she was there to convince them of, and as relieved as she felt, there was a deep part of her that wondered why such a decision was made in the first place. It was counterintuitive to their nature, brewing distrust within her. Something was awry. She was chosen by a Fate and bestowed with the impossible burden of creating this unified decision to do nothing in the face of war, yet the surrender came of its own volition.

There was something missing, some vital factor that contributed to such a drastic lack of action, and by the disapproval and shame she saw in many of the other Generals she wasn't alone in the dark. The strongest military in Elanta had surrendered one of their largest cities without even trying, and even though it's exactly what Ivory wanted, she had to know why.

21

PICK YOUR POISON

Sharp, acrid overtones lingered in the caverns of Sabanexus, the lair of the leviathans, as glass flasks filled with liquid bubbled atop an old oak table in a room far off the beaten path. Candlelight cast hunched shadows in the far corners of the room, where dismal moans desperately called above the gentle roil of fluid, but no one listened. No one cared.

Seated amongst the orchestration of chemistry and dancing flame was an hourglass figure, loosely cloaked in Orbweaver robes so the soft skin of her shoulders could be teased from beneath a cascade of golden curls. With a quill in hand she silently wrote on a piece of parchment, swaying her head to the dissonant cries of the downtrodden. She had listened for hours now yet the tune never seemed to lose its appeal.

With her hand, she wafted the vapors of the nearest flask to her nose, documented her thoughts, and then poured a small amount into a cup. She placed a cube of plant resin into the center, creating a thick mist that floated at the surface like oil upon water. She delicately picked it up as though it were a crystal glass filled with the finest of wines. It rested against her sultry red lips, the fluid creeping ever closer as the vapors poured over the edges and dissipated into the air. She titled the glass to consume its contents, prepared to taste the bitter essence as the concoction washed over her palate, yet she tasted nothing.

She looked down at the cup in hand—the fluid clung against the edges, refusing to move. The mist no longer roiled, the moans no longer sung, and the flasks no longer boiled. Time had stopped, freezing everything in place while the colors of the room drained into scales of gray.

"What are you doing?" Sung a glorious voice from behind her.

There was only one person she knew who could do this—the power to bleed the world of vigor, defy the laws of time, and create a calm so beautifully eerie that her skin tingled. The visitor silently crossed the room and placed a hand on her bare shoulders, fingertips gently clawing along her skin to the base of her neck. The figure leaned in and rested her head against her golden curls, the visitor's long black hair poured down across her breasts.

"My beautiful Fever," the woman whispered, her breath tingling the edge of Fever's ear.

"Hello, my Fate," Fever replied with a smile.

"Please, call me Ivory. You and I are well beyond formality." Ivory gently ran her hand down Fever's arm and wrapped it around the cup. She examined it with her gloriously blue eyes, her black spider pupils traversing the flasks upon the table. "What have we here? Poison?" The crippled subjects hunched in the corner of the room, frozen in perpetual agony, were more than enough proof. With Fever's incredible beauty and allure it was easy to forget that she was an assassin and even easier to overlook that assassins were some of the best educated in the world. "You were going to drink it?"

One would assume there was little in the world a Fate did not know, though omniscience was usually associated with Illy, not Ivory. Fever turned her head to brush the tip of her nose in Ivory's hair. "Looks like I can surprise you." An ill-advised practice, she had always used her sense of taste to test the balance of her poisons, giving her the thrill of the burn while increasing her own tolerance.

Ivory smiled and gracefully dissipated into a coil of shadow, reappearing on the edge of the table. White mist weightlessly danced at the base of her dress, continuing to conceal her feet. Her raven hair slithered across the table and coiled down its legs as though it had a mind of its own. She reached out for Fever's hand and pulled it close, placing Fever's palm against her chest. Her heart raced with excitement. "You, my beautiful Fever, are the reason I want to destroy the Weave."

Fever was intrigued. Anyone wanting to destroy anything for her commanded her full attention.

"I've known too much for too long," Ivory said, closing her eyes and losing herself in Fever's warmth. "Where once knowledge was my business, now knowledge is my pleasure." Ivory lifted her hand, coalescing shimmering energy into a strand of thread that seemed to protrude from Fever's chest.

Fever looked down at the silk, perplexed, and followed it to Ivory's palm where it wove between her fingers.

"This is your anchor. The thread of silk that connects your soul to your fatespinner." Ivory held it aloft to look at it more closely. "Origin uses them to bind, Avelie uses them to track, and Illy uses them to scry, but I use them to kill."

Fever's heart began to race, but it was not fear that filled her lungs with heavy breaths. The idea Ivory could take her life with the pluck of a thread made her feel gloriously owned, gloriously vulnerable.

"This thread keeps no secrets and gives no escape, as everything about you is manufactured, written, and ruined at the hands of people you've never met. You can be found, you can be known, you can be destroyed," Ivory lowered it and released, the silk dissipated back into the aether as if it had never existed. She leaned in toward Fever with devouring eyes. "But I want to *discover* you."

Fever bit the corner of her lip. "I might be too much, even for a Fate."

"That's just it," Ivory smiled, "You could be my greatest undoing, but how I unravel is my choice to make. Something the Fates have stolen from the world. Something I once stole from the world."

"Destroy the Weave so that people might write their own life?" Fever pouted slightly. "Sounds a little too nice for me."

"On the contrary. I am not the aspect of life—I am death itself.

I will destroy the Weave so everyone may write their own *end*." She leaned in closely, her lips gently brushing against Fever's. "And some undoings may be far more glorious than others."

Too many people died in the solace of their beds. Too many people died to needless, forgettable happenstance. Fever always vowed that would never be her, forgotten and unfortunate. Where once Ivory's plan seemed bland and uninspiring, suddenly she was thrilled with the idea of a legendary demise.

She pressed her lips to Ivory's, sinking into her destructive allure, willing to drown in the suffocating roil of silky black hair and ivory mist. Her teeth gently bit Ivory's lower lip before pulling away, looking deep into the blue of her eyes. "A good start to a glorious end."

Ivory tilted her head and watched Fever's lips with hunger. "This is just the beginning. I have far more recklessness planned." The shadows of the room began to coalesce into a roiling black portal, the darkness like living ichor, stretching out as if to grab them both and pull them in. "Are you ready?"

The cool forest air fell still as the shadows stretched from the trees, reaching ever forward to create a dark mass against the earth. As Fever stepped from it, the darkness slowly peeled from her Orbweaver cloak until she had fully exited.

The world turned bright once more and she found herself standing high upon a winding mountain path of dirt and stone, overlooking a vast stretch of cold blue water. She was in Whitewater—she knew it even without being told. The crisp air, the cool shades of blue and gray, and the massive belt of conifers that towered behind her. She hated it. She preferred the heat of Emberwilde—the sand, the sirocco, the dry warmth of red and orange hues that seemed to blanket everything. She already felt damp and pulled in the edges of her robe before looking down the cliffs to her destination, a small village nestled in a bay fringed in glorious red blossoms—Roserun.

Of course, she had heard of it. Every assassin worth her salt was privy to the fencing and smuggling hubs scattered across Elanta and despite Roserun's renown for piracy and drugs she had never desired to be so far beyond Emberwilde's borders.

Fever pulled her cowl over her head and began to descend the trail, quietly discussing Ivory's intentions amongst the voices in her mind. Something didn't seem right and most of her inner council agreed. The entirety of Ivory's original plot was to release the Second Wish from the honeycomb stone so she could gain some magnificent power. A power locked away by the Immaculate Artisan, Shiori Etrielle, millennia ago.

With great sacrifice, Fever and the leviathan Wrath stormed the bastion city of Lyre, crushing their defenses and capturing the Second Wish for Ivory. To her knowledge, Ivory had an agreement with the Chitin Kings that would give her the key to breaking the indestructible stone that encompassed the artifact, which led her to her biggest question. Why was the sword still in the stone?

Every drop of blood and sweat, every demon unleashed upon the world, all to put the artifact in Ivory's hands and bring the Weave to a crushing end, and yet here she was, cold and displeased, standing on the edge of a cliff running yet another errand. Something went wrong in Ivory's plan. Either the Chitin Kings betrayed them or the key was something she didn't have—or both. All Ivory told her was that one of the kings was seeking something and it was her job to find out what it was. Presumably as leverage. Regardless, it meant interrogating some people and that brought a little smile to every voice that chimed within her.

As she neared Roserun, the salty air began to remind her of home—a small consolation amidst the dismal blanchwood and rotting buildings. She was surprised the structures hadn't yet succumbed to the elements, but if fencers were anything, they were resilient.

The people of Roserun were filthy, drunken sorts. The kind with calloused hands, rotting teeth, and more brawn than brain—easy targets, but unlikely to know anything of value. Then, something peculiar caught her eye. A symbol of faded black ink was quickly scrawled across the door to, what seemed like, the only sturdy building left in the village.

A smile crept across her lips. It was draconian script. A complicated language that very few people knew how to read, making it a staple of communication for an educated assassin such as herself. Why it said *Freestone*, she couldn't be certain, but it meant there was a message in the undertow that someone meant to keep exclusive and the only thing she liked more than secrets was making someone tell them.

She stairs creaked as she ascended and opened the door, revealing a long counter of wood and stone with a man standing behind it. He was important. She could taste it—too proper to be a survivalist, too clean to be a pirate, and too soft to be a small fish in the black waters of Elanta's underbelly. A man like this would be torn to shreds in Roserun, so he was likely to have either formidable backing or significance.

"Good evening, miss." He smiled sweetly, but she could tell he was sizing her up as well. "My name is Jury."

She shied from his gaze, deciding vulnerability might be better for this prey. It was safe to assume he was too smart for assertion and too suspicious for seduction.

"Is there something I can help you with?" he asked.

"I'm not sure," she replied meekly. In the corner of her eye she spied the black spider brand of the Orbweaver on his wrist, a backing most fearsome these days. It certainly explained his stature, especially now that the Orbweavers were running one of the largest coups in history. "I need someone to help me find a boat to Emberwilde."

"Why, pray tell?" He leaned against the counter, ever curious to hear what brings a woman to Whitewater's most undesirable shores.

"What does it matter?" Fever carefully mixed in a tone of desperation, just enough to convey she was fearfully defensive and unfamiliar with such interrogations.

Jury continued to smile as he looked her over.

She could sense he recognized the Orbweaver cloak. "I'm a refugee from Lyre and a citizen of Emberwilde, but when I tried to flee back to my realm I was denied. My uncle is an Orbweaver and he told me to come here to be smuggled back into Emberwilde. He said someone would help me."

"Interesting," Jury replied, leaning his elbows on the counter as though being that much closer made her that much more audible. "A tragedy, what happened in Lyre. You were fortunate to have escaped before the wyrmsong ravaged it completely."

He knew about Lyre and with more detail than she imagined, considering how far apart they were. Remembering the heat of the wyrmsong flames as they melted the flesh off Lyre's army almost made her smile, but instead, she filled her eyes with tears. Enough to make them glossy and ready to burst. "It was terrifying."

"I can imagine." Jury presented a massive book from under the counter and dropped it on the surface. The loud thump of leather and bindings was startling and Fever made sure to jump a little. "What was your uncle's name?"

Fever didn't care to know any of their names, but through her training her memory had become quite impressive. "Euland Stonewoke," she replied, confident she had heard the name in passing at least once.

"Stonewoke? Let's see then." Jury placed his hand on the cover and the room quickly smelled of blood. The edges of the parchment turned sanguine and as he lifted his hand the book opened of its on volition. Countless pages covered in a chaotic spattering of dark red splotches flipped until reaching the approximate middle, where one of the splotches peeled itself from the page with a sickly crackle and floated just above. Jury smiled and slammed the book shut, the stench of blood lifted from the room while leaving the tinge of iron on their palate. "It seems your uncle's blood is in the book."

"What does that mean?" Fever asked.

Jury placed the book back under the counter. "It means I can help you."

Fever feigned relief. "Fate's be blessed."

Jury fetched a small piece of parchment and a quill. "Your passage to Emberwilde will be arranged in the morning."

Fever acted nervous. "Is it safe to stay in Roserun?"

Jury tilted his head as he thought. Roserun wasn't safe even for the battleborn, but his influence and name carried with it the full force of the Orbweaver sect. As she was indirectly affiliated with the cult she could fall under their protection if she had representation. "Go to the docks and stay at the inn. If anyone approaches you be sure to tell them you are a friend of mine."

Fever nodded. It wasn't perfect; she had hoped he would offer her a room, but she had lots of time to kill.

22

THE QUEEN'S VAULT

Phori's footsteps echoed through the massive obsidian halls, the ceiling so high it almost disappeared into the darkness. She was wandering for nearly an hour, yet the palace seemed almost entirely empty. So far, there wasn't a single door locked to her, but despite the exquisite amenities and ample space everything was ghostly silent. Just as she was beginning to admit she was irretrievably lost, the hall opened into a massive room filled with hundreds of glass display cases. Innumerable artifacts, small and large, sat solemnly in their tombs with no wondering eyes to gaze upon them.

The room was impossibly large to hold such a quantity of treasures and beneath each case was a plaque and catalog number. She leaned in closely to examine one of the pieces: a jade comb used by the very first embodiment of the Phoenix Queen. Countless priceless artifacts filled the room and she couldn't quite understand why such pieces weren't in a vault somewhere.

As she pondered the magnitude and value of the room, noticing it was organized by category, her eyes rose to the furthest wall, which was not a wall at all. A massive network of golden gears and ruby mechanisms covered the entire length of the room, sealed behind a translucent layer of honeycomb stone. Ornamental dragons carved from black stone decorated the corners. Underneath stood four armed guards, two at each end—long spears with crimson tassels held at the ready.

Phori approached the wall with a slack jaw, the closest gear nearly dwarfing her in height. "Is this a vault door?" she asked, but the guards offered no reply. If it was the entrance to a vault, it was the largest and most elaborate she had ever seen in her lifetime. She slowly reached out to touch the honeycomb stone when each guard struck the floor with the bottoms of their spears in unison, warning her that such an action was not permitted.

"Lost, Salamander?" a familiar voice asked from behind her.

Phori turned to see the Ram, his arms crossed and his jaw clenched, too stoic to tell what he was truly feeling. "What is this room?"

The Ram turned his head to span the army of glass prisons. "This was a reliquary, once. I suppose it's just a treasury now. It's shameful. Holy relics and instrumentations of the divine deserve their own sacred space. Though I can't turn my eye to the value of these treasures, I simply wish there remained a segregation between the mundane." It was subtle, but there was the smallest hint of despair in his voice.

"I admire your respect for tradition," Phori said. She turned to face the wall, knowing that if anyone understood her confusion it would be him. "Is this a vault?"

In Emberwilde, it was tradition to have one's vault on display to the public. It was a show of wealth, power, and status, inviting the world to wonder of the riches within and even dared them entry. To have such a massive and beautiful vault hidden deep within the labyrinth of the Palace of Roiling Cinder was very unusual. Even more peculiar were the guards—vaults were rarely guarded, and for such an impressive door it seemed unnecessary.

The Ram approached and stood at her side, his height became much more apparent as the horns of his pauldron came to her head. "Yes. There is reference to it in our oldest codices, but it's a language preceding our current tongue. The sages say it's called Aura-Sara, but no one really knows what it means. Some say 'chamber of life', others argue it's 'prison of the mind'. There's a big difference if you ask me. Either way, it predates the palace itself."

"Really?" Phori looked back across the room and wondered about the multitude of confusing hallways she had navigated. "All of this was built around the vault? Isn't it possible the palace wasn't meant to be a palace at all, but a gauntlet to protect the vault from infiltrators?"

"I once thought that." The palace always felt more like an elaborate fortress than a home for royalty. "I believe the vault and the palace were both created by Shiori Etrielle."

"A believer in the Immaculate Artisan? I never took you for a creationist."

The Ram shrugged. "I don't know if I believe she made the world, but this place, sure as Fate, didn't build itself. There are essence techniques embedded into this architecture we still don't understand."

Phori spied the guards once more. If it was guarded, it could be opened. "Do we have the authority to enter?"

The Ram shook his head. "Only the malikeh may enter and she has made it very clear the knowledge of its contents are exclusive." His eyes cautiously shifted as he leaned in closely, whispering softly as not to share his suspicions with the guards. "This door wasn't always guarded, though—eleven, maybe twelve years."

"Do you think someone broke in?" Phori whispered back.

He shrugged. "Can you think of any other reason?"

Another familiar voice sung around Phori, her flowing noble's accent identified her immediately, "Are you spreading rumors?"

Phori looked over her shoulder, expecting to see the sharp features of the Bastion Nine's Firefly, but only the stretch of lonesome glass and looming shadows greeted her. She was almost certain Lilia's voice was right by her ear, the heat of her breath still lingering, but there was nothing. She turned back, where Lilia's almond eyes and braided brown hair appeared before her. Phori tried not to appear startled, but her eyes betrayed her. The Ram didn't seem to flinch at all—it was possible he was used to her sneaking up on him.

"I'm simply saying it's suspicious," the Ram said sternly.

Lilia scolded him with her eyes, unimpressed and disappointed. Even her body language, all angles and curves, whispered her displeasure. "It is not our place to spread hearsay."

The tension between the two was palpable, but a certain convenience began to concern Phori. "Were both of you following me?"

The corner of the Ram's lip twitched as he crossed his arms defensively, while the Firefly was much more candid. "Yes," Lilia replied, shaking her head at the Ram, "though some of us are better at it than others."

"No one said it had to be in secret," the Ram scowled.

"My apologies," Lilia said as she bowed her head to Phori, "We were instructed by our malikeh to ensure you were not attacked before your inauguration."

"Why would I be in danger?"

The Ram remained still, a ruby sentinel in the largest treasury she'd ever seen. "We are the Bastion Nine and as the name suggests, there can only be nine generals. For you to take a seat in the war room, someone must be removed."

"I see," Phori replied. "Someone lost their position so I could have my seat."

"Yes. If you were to die after your inauguration, filling the seat would fall to the vote of the remaining members, but should you die before, then the previous general would be reinstated."

Though Phori understood the situation, she was unhappy with the secrecy. Had the Bastion Nine presented her with the concern and offered her protection she would have considered, but now she felt they didn't trust she could handle herself. "Who is the former General?"

"His name is Oba, the Jade Dragon King," Lilia said.

While the Rams had the reputation of being strong-willed sentinels, the Jade Dragons were infamous for being thugs—the two clans rarely ever got along. Despite their brash behavior, Emberwilde could not deny their incredible strength and often used them as blunt instruments when diplomacy was moot.

"Oba is an idiot," the Ram said scornfully, "Unwise to the words of his peers and too reliant on his strength to resolve his problems. We're blessed to be rid of his foolishness."

"Was he the strong?" Phori asked.

Lilia broke eye contact, while the Ram sneered. "Strength isn't everything."

That was a yes.

Phori walked through the treasury as she made her way back to the hall, her unwanted entourage in tow. She could hear the golden links of Lilia's cloak behind her and wondered how she hadn't heard her following before. A testament to the Fireflies, she supposed.

They wandered into the armory portion of the catalog, where glorious suits of armor and weapons sat on display. Many of the older pieces were archaic and worn, grievously damaged from fantastic battles but historically awe striking, made long before the modern practices of ironwork and alchemy. Even behind the glass, Phori's ability to manipulate densities was allowing her to *feel* the pieces she passed—the cold, unforgiving bronze, the supple leather bindings, and the sheepskin linings. It was inspiring to see how much they had progressed through the ages, feeling the difference between the pinnacle pieces of then and now.

As she continued along the displays, something odd beckoned her attention. A single sword stood on its tip—its red crystalline blade of hollow hexagons shimmered beautifully. Beside it laid its scabbard, a bois de rose with silver inlay, ruby accents, and silver gears. The blade looked exactly like honeycomb stone, but she could feel it was far more brittle—colored glass, perhaps. The ruby inlay on the scabbard was wrong as well and the gears seemed to be a cleverly placed decoration. Everything in the treasury was genuine thus far, but this was clearly a replica, unusual to have in the treasury unless the sages somehow hadn't noticed.

Phori stopped to examine it closer, reading the plaque below. 'The Scarlet Charm'. The bronze sheen slowly began to peel into a scale of gray and as she raised her eyes the rich crimson color of the blade began to fade. She experienced this before and knew what to expect next. She looked behind her to see the Ram and Lilia frozen in mid step, victims of Ivory's power of time suspension.

Each shadow of the room slithered across the floor like sentient rivers, joining to create a black pool of shifting void, where Ivory's figure rose from beneath. She was hunched at first, the shadows clinging to her and weighing downward like a sticky blanket, and as she stood, raising her hands in sheer authority and reverence, the shadows split along her spine, rebuked, and fell silently from her flesh. The pool in which she stood rippled outward, the hum of an aura so powerful it was its own invisible force. She was a ruler, commanding the shadows to bend to her will, and as Ivory exited the pool of liquid darkness, Phori had to remember to breathe.

"Hello, my Instrument," Ivory's sweet voice vibrated along the tines of Phori's obsidian armor. "Fighting the good fight?" Ivory turned into a wisp of smoky darkness and slithered through the air past Phori.

Phori turned to see Ivory seated atop one of the displays, the misty cloud of ghostly vapor still danced below the fraying strands of her dress, concealing her feet. She teased a spark of elation in her eyes, arching her back and leaning on her hands—breathing deep the essence of ancient relics and the power they had through reverence alone.

"I spoke to the Bastion Nine, just as you asked," Phori said.

"Don't worry, love," Ivory replied as she evaporated into a wisp of mist and reappeared before the crimson sword. Her fingertips delicately ran along the glass display. "They'll come around."

"They've surrendered the city of Valakut to the demons of the mist."

Ivory turned her head and smiled with surprise. "Well done! And with such haste too. I was right to pick you."

Phori shook her head. "The decision was made before my arrival."

Ivory's eyes quickly narrowed with suspicion. That was something she hadn't calculated, which meant someone else spoke with the Phoenix Queen regarding the situation. The only conclusion she could draw was that the Chitin Kings contacted her and made a deal, which made Ivory very uncomfortable. She gently tapped the glass while she thought. She already gleaned suspicions in Sabanexus when she noticed one of their strongest Orbweavers, Blackrock, disappeared without a trace, and worried one of the kings was conspiring. She decided to send Fever to Roserun to speak with one of the Orbweaver gatekeepers, and now worried that the events may be connected. If a Chitin King was behind this strange and sudden moral shift, it meant they had something of value to offer the Phoenix Queen—something more valuable than a whole city. "Have you seen anyone speaking with the Phoenix Queen, other than the Bastion Nine or her council?"

"No, but I haven't been here long. There was an air of dissatisfaction in the war room. I'm inclined to believe the Bastion Nine weren't privy to either the decision or the reasoning. I'll dig deeper and see what I can find."

"Good. Keeping a finger on the pulse of Emberwilde is the reason I sent you here. If anything changes in the council it's your responsibility to make sure the Generals continue to hold their forces." Ivory's tone fell serious, but she continued to admire the crimson sword beyond the sheen with a glint of amusement. "Keep an eye on the Phoenix Queen as well. If she is working with someone else, it's imperative we know who."

"Forgive me," Phori said, "but isn't this the outcome you wanted anyways? You didn't want them to move on Valakut and they aren't."

"This is the outcome *I* wanted, but if someone else wanted it too then I need to understand their agenda, just in case it affects our own."

Phori stood alongside Ivory, the cool mist seeped between the seams of her armor and crawled across her skin. "Is there anything that could stand in your way now that you have Shiori's Second Wish?"

Ivory gave a single, soft laugh, but didn't reply. Instead, she continued to revel in the presence of the honeycomb stone sword before her.

Phori was far from ignorant, though, and immediately read the silence. "You don't have it."

Ivory tilted her head and smiled. "I do, I just can't wield it. Yet." Ivory paused a moment. She hadn't yet told anyone her reason, but of all her Instruments Phori was the least likely to judge her if the plan had a setback. While the others had enough loyalty to be easily manipulated, she and the Salamander were still in the process of forging their relationship and Phori seemed to respond better to honesty.

"Here is my truth," Ivory began. She straightened her posture and folded her hands. "The Second Wish is the most powerful artifact in existence and is consequently encased in the hardest substance ever known, honeycomb stone. When I was in the Overworld, I discovered that the Chitin Kings possessed the draconian recipe for honeycomb stone—a recipe banished into the mist when the Fates declared war on the race—but they had no idea what it was. With it, not only could it be manufactured, but I could learn how to destroy it and free the Second Wish.

"I made a bargain with the kings, building them a bridge into Elanta and assembling their army of Orbweavers in exchange for the formulae, but when I finally read it I was met with a harrowing problem. Only the blood of a true dragon can destroy honeycomb stone and I dare say we murdered them all."

Phori crossed her arms. "We aren't actually working with the Orbweavers, are we?"

Ivory seemed to disapprove of her tone. "It's complicated."

"What about the Chitin Kings?"

"Temporarily, but also complicated," Ivory replied.

"You had me burdened with knowing we've sacrificed the people of Valakut for a higher cause and I chose to accept that, but now you'd have me a pawn of the continued darkness that has begun to cover the world?" Phori ground her teeth, summoning every ounce of restraint she could muster. "I strongly disapprove and I will not act against my malikeh."

"I don't meant to alarm you, outspoken one, but has it not occurred to you that perhaps your malikeh is already working with the Chitin Kings? After all, she seems to have come to a very convenient decision regarding Valakut without me or you."

"Impossible," Phori replied sharply, "the malikeh is dedicated to the sanctity of her people. She would never surrender our rights without a fight."

"And yet, she has."

A twitch took to the corner of Phori's eye. "There is a reason for Valakut's surrender, one we don't yet know. It's foolish to assume we know what it is and conspiracy to presume she is working with the enemy."

Ivory's eyes became soft, almost sad. "Phori, my dear, your faith is beautiful, but if you think her devotion is to that of the people rather than herself then you are high upon a fragile branch, destined to plummet with the weight of expectation."

"Isn't that the same faith you'd expect me to have for you?"

"I mean to sacrifice many to save the rest, your malikeh means to sacrifice many to save herself. Two evils, I assure you, but which is the lesser?"

Phori stepped into Ivory, cutting her down fearlessly, and Ivory took a step backward in momentary surprise. It was the first time a mortal had ever challenged her knowing full well who she was, and she was far too impressed and confused to be upset over it.

"My apologies," Ivory said softly, bowing her head to Phori's growing rage. "I will not speak ill of your malikeh, nor will I ask you to act in such a manner that is contrary to her ideals."

Phori nodded. She was far from calm, but Ivory's concession helped a little. If she was going to continue being an Instrument, she needed to know that she wasn't acting against her realm—better yet, she didn't want to be associated with the Orbweavers or Chitin Kings, but she was willing to trust Ivory that it was a temporary necessity for the grand scheme. She sighed, blinking long and hard while she eased the tension in her chest with each passing breath. Getting too broad a view of the intricate relationships between the malikeh, Ivory, the Orbweavers, and the Chitin Kings was confusing, frustrating, and overwhelming, and if she was going to be of any use she needed something closer to focus on. "You said we need a dragon to free the Second Wish?" It was the only thing she could think of that neither acted against her malikeh or aided the Chitin Kings.

The Dragon War cleansed Elanta entirely and any that managed to elude their fate had done so by evolving or transmuting beyond their lineage. "Are there are no dragons in hiding?"

"There is only one dragon I know of that survived the scouring—Ogra. He was a honey shrike who had his eyes torn from his head before being banished into the Overworld for crimes against humanity. Consequently, in his exile he has become one of the four Chitin Kings."

A chance to kill a Chitin king was all she needed to feel as though she was back on the side of justice once more. "Then we find Ogra." The solution seemed simple enough and she said it as though it weren't a feat. "If you're working with him, I'm sure you already know where he is."

Ivory laughed. "He is as pompous and egocentric as he is unreasonable and cannot be privy to the knowledge of the Second Wish. If he found out how much power he would be granting us he would try to claim it for himself. Taking his blood would be an act of war, negotiating for it would be folly, and even if we managed to convince him to bleed for us there is no guarantee that the chaotic nature of the mist hasn't twisted his lineage beyond use."

Phori shrugged. "He sounds like our only chance."

"Not our *only* chance."

She knew Ivory was referring to her, but she couldn't fathom the idea of breaking honeycomb stone, even with her power to control an object's density.

"Have you ever tried?" Ivory asked, gesturing to the sword behind the glass.

"Firstly, that's a fake," she interjected sternly, "and no." As certain as she was that she didn't have the strength, she hadn't actually tried yet, so there was a glimmer of possibility in the back of her mind.

Ivory gently placed her hand on Phori's shoulder. In the past, Ivory always acted alluring around her and Fever, but Phori never cared for it. This time was different. There was something genuine in the drowning blue of Ivory's eyes, something that cried with need and burdened her with necessity. "I believe in you, Phori," she said softly, placing her other hand on Phori's breastplate, just over her heart. "You possess unfathomable spirit and are bound only by the reality you choose to believe."

It doesn't matter how often you try to convince yourself that your efforts are solely for your peers, there is always a deep satisfaction in the recognition of your superiors. She would never admit it, choosing to convince herself that her devotions were to the people of Emberwilde, but there was always something that wanted to be noticed and appreciated. Recognition is the root of everything of value—the size of your vault, the number of tassels you held, the color of feather in your hair. No matter how badly she wanted to doubt her ability to manipulate honeycomb stone, the strength in Ivory's eyes resounded within her, and she began to feel unstoppable.

"I will train harder with my power. Perhaps I can grow strong enough to manipulate honeycomb stone," Phori said.

Ivory closed her eyes and smiled, dissipating into a swirl of ghostly shadow, reinvigorating the world by lifting its blanket of grays. The brilliant crimson of the honeycomb blade was almost too bright at first and she squinted as her eyes adjusted.

"That's one of my favorites," Lilia said as she stood at Phori's side and awed over the weapon. "The Scarlet Charm, one of the sharpest blades in the world. With the gears and springs built into the scabbard, the velocity of the first cut is several-fold, and in the hands of a master it's thought to be capable of cutting honeycomb stone."

Ironically, the one item in the treasury that boasted an ability to free the Second Wish wasn't even genuine. At least, *she* knew it was fake. "Only if it's real."

Lilia seemed as offended as a noble blooded assassin could be, delicately scoffing with her almond eyes and scrunching her forehead ever so slightly. "Of course it's real, it's in the treasury."

Phori nodded, the Firefly had a very good point. "Has anyone ever broken into the treasury and stolen something?"

Lilia didn't dare entertain the idea. "Absurd. None could be so foolish, nor would they succeed."

"I see," Phori replied. "Imagine our reputation if someone had."

23

THE MACABRE WALTZ

Dusk was falling upon Roserun, the grit of hazy gray light enveloped the stretch of red flowers that blanketed the stones along the shore. The working children bounded along narrow planks with woven baskets, collecting their last flowers and buds before turning the fruits of their labor in to their task masters.

The clean-cut Jury stood behind his counter and adjusted the cuffs of his shirt while opening a boar skin book. He turned to the first blank page he could find. Placing his hand upon the page, he channeled his spirit through his palm, creating a ghostly green glow. He then lifted his hand, manifesting black ink from the aether that welled up through the parchment and bled into full text. He had read this message several times before, but the contents continued to intrigue him. His informants in Emberwilde were orchestrating some form of arrangement between a Chitin King and the Phoenix Queen. There were few details, but Jury was barely able to hide the smile of elation that curled across his lips. With exclusive knowledge of the arrangement between Carver and Blackrock, he was perhaps the only man in Elanta who knew the two arrangements were connected.

A scream suddenly echoed through the bay.

Jury closed the book and made haste for the door, opening it to see Fever curled in the dirt; a small group of men surrounded her like jackals. One of the men kicked her in the stomach, sending a cringe across Jury's face as her breath left her body and she nearly vomited. He stormed down the stairs, drawing a glyph of glowing green upon his palm. He raised his hand to his mouth and drew blood as his teeth sunk into the meat. With a flick of his hand, now spattered a sickly sanguine, an array of long, fine lashes of blood snapped from his palm and cracked in the air, commanding everyone's attention. He swung the lashes above his head and snapped them to his side. The sharp clap of the many strands echoed across the bay as they tore both earth and stone, kicking free fine dust and debris in a display of menace and turpitude. The few that hadn't backed away at the very sight of him certainly began to now, quickly turning heel in retreat.

The men scattered like roaches, scurrying without compass to the nearest darkness, cowering as they watched from the safety of their filth and pestilent numbers. Once Jury was certain there was no immediate danger, the lashes of blood receded back into his hand with a nauseating *slurp*, like moist clay clenched between one's fingers. Once every last drop returned to his veins, the glyph faded, and his wound scabbed over. He carefully flexed his hand, the wound taut and angry.

Fever clambered to her knees and clutched her stomach, coughing sticky strands of saliva and bile while her forehead rested on the ground. Tears welled behind her eyes from the sickness, but the bloodshot slowly faded the more composure she collected.

Jury shook his head and looked out across the town, spectators from afar silently observed without remorse. So far as they were concerned she deserved it simply for being a woman, an outsider, or both. Jury took a knee at her side and helped her stand, draping her arm over his shoulder as he rose.

Together, they silently walked away from the cove until they arrived at a small home, crudely built but fairly kempt compared to the rest of Roserun. Bleached by the light of day, stripped to fibrous strands from the salty winds, and held together if only by the ivy that crept along the corners and sills.

Fever regained most of her strength and began to walk on her own, slowly trailing behind him as he placed his hand on the door. A sigil glowed across the surface and with a quiet click of iron the door creaked ajar. Jury bowed his head and offered her entry, where she graciously obliged.

Fever immediately examined every detail of the room—the dimensions, the nearest improvised weapons, and the number of exits. Though she couldn't see any, she was certain the home was littered with enchantments. It was one large room, with a hearth at one end and a bed at the other. There were basic amenities—tables, chairs, chests—nothing immediately unusual, though as she walked she could feel the slightest bevel beneath her feet. A false floor, perhaps.

"I thought I told you to mention my name," Jury said, taking one last look outside before closing the door behind them.

Fever wandered the house, running her hand along the stone of the hearth, admiring its rough edges. Resting atop were some clay bowls, cups, and a small strongbox. She reached for the clay cups and adjusted them curiously, being sure to press the back of her hand against the box to gauge its weight. It didn't budge and usually heavy meant valuable. She folded her hands and journeyed to the kitchen—crates of hard tack, cured meats, and a barrel of water. None of which appeared to have a false bottom, but it was difficult to know for certain without removing the contents. "I'm sorry," she replied shamefully, "I was caught by surprise and once I thought to speak, I couldn't breathe."

Jury nodded along, her curiosity and attention to detail roused a suspicion.

"It's been so long since I've been in a home," she said woefully, "a real home, that is." She took a deep breath and calmed herself, her eyes gazing sadly at everything in the room. "So much longer, still, before I return to my own in Emberwilde."

Jury quietly walked to the hearth and collected the two clay cups. It was easy to forget she was driven from Lyre and had been traveling since. "You're welcome to stay here tonight," he said, "I will not risk a repeat of today's incidents." He walked to the barrel of water and filled both cups, outstretching his hand to offer her one. Droplets fell to the floor with a hard spatter.

Fever bowed her head and accepted the offering, cradling it with both hands as though his grace were precious. "Thank you."

Jury nodded, gave her a gentle pat on the shoulder, and sat on the edge of the bed, swirling the water in his cup like the finest of wine.

Fever fought a smile, everything was falling into place, but when she tried to approach her feet would not move. Confusion crept across her face and the clay cup slid from her hands and fell to the floor. The crash of brown clay shook her senses with a quick realization—her body was frozen in place, paralyzed entirely. With great effort she could turn her head, the cartilage in her neck squeaked in her skull like a thumb on wet glass, and in the corner of her eye she caught a glimpse of a faint green light on the back of her shoulder.

"I honestly thought you'd be better," Jury said, scolding her with a gentle shake of his head.

Fever used her tongue to pad her palate, rolled back a fold and slid a small steel tine to the back of her teeth. The glint of metal peered briefly from between her lips, and with a swift blow she shot it from her mouth.

Jury's hand quickly rose, barely deflecting the tine with the cup of water. The clay shattered, spilling across his hand and pants. The shock of near death was clear upon his face and once he caught his breath and stilled his racing heart he began to laugh nervously. "Well done." He shook the liquid from his hand and pushed the shards aside with his foot. "That's the Fever I expected." He crouched down, and with the tips of his middle and index fingers he began to draw another glowing green glyph. Once completed, he placed his palm in the center. The crackle of hawthorn brambles splintered the floorboards beneath her feet and coiled around her legs like creeping ivy, the hooked spines anchoring into her flesh. "A little poison should prevent any more tricks."

Fever could feel the heat of the unusual plant in her skin—the burn of something vile coursed through her veins and gave her both sweat and smile, fighting the paralysis if only to bite her lower lip in the pleasure-pain. She assumed it would affect her coordination, or something of the sort, an assurance for Jury that she would not try to bury a steel tine in his eye again had she another, but she had yet to experience the plant's full effect.

"Do you know where you erred?" Jury asked. "One of our cardinal rules, Fever—information." He smiled cleverly, victory brewing behind his eyes.

He gave a sharp whistle and the door opened, the group of men from the street entered and surrounded her. One of the men approached Jury and handed him a small leather satchel of coin, the very bribe Fever used to convince them to assault her. She initially tried to instigate a losing fight, but somehow everyone knew Jury wanted her unharmed no matter how much she tried to deserve it. Money was the only language that seemed to catch their attention and commanded a very small degree of compliance. Jury taunted her with a jingle of its contents.

"Very convincing theatrics but, unfortunately for you, everyone in Roserun works for me." Jury shrugged his shoulders and flexed the hand he'd wounded to create his blood lash. The thugs in the room smiled foolishly, waiting for Jury to let them off their chains. "You know nothing of me, but I, I know everything about you. The infamous Fever of Emberwilde." Jury stood and approached her; stared deep into her vibrant blue eyes. Even still, she fearlessly defied him. If looks could kill. Her eyes were not those of someone willing to take a life. No, that was far too simple. These eyes would have him slit from nave to neck; hanged from his ankles to keep the blood in his brain, as not to lose consciousness. These eyes would watch anxiously, joyously, and without blinking. Devouring every last glimmer of light and hope as he journeyed from terror, to agony, to despair, and finally surrender. Her eyes unnerved him greatly, even with so many fetters upon her, so much so he took a step back just in case she knew something he didn't. "You finished your studies well before me, and in your wake you left the most amazing stories."

The corner of Fever's eyes curled, smiling. He was a student of the same assassin's guild she had trained in. Small world.

Jury wiped a bead of sweat from his brow and stepped awkwardly back, his legs brushing the foot of the bed and his eyes narrowing with pride. "You treated me like an Orbweaver, when I'm actually an assassin." His vision blurred for a moment and he stumbled, shaking his head to regain his balance.

Jury had weakened enough for the glyph on Fever's shoulder to wane and though she still couldn't move her body, she could speak. The corner of Fever's lips curled, drowning the room with joyous turpitude. "And you've treated me like an assassin, when I'm actually an Instrument."

From beneath the sleeves of her robe, a dozen serpents of roiling shadow and ichor lashed outward and wrapped around the throats of Jury's thugs, lifting them from the ground and thrusting them against their closest walls. The room rumbled as wooden beams splintered, nearly buckling, and they struggled for one hopeless moment before she crushed their necks in unison. Bone and cartilage crackled and popped, and their hands and toes twitched violently—an easy and unimaginative death that somehow shamed her to do, though the quick orchestration of broken necks was a score worth experiencing at least once.

Jury stumbled over his feet and fell backward, missing the edge of the bed and falling to the floor. He watched in horror, the eerie dangling of feet. His vision began to blur again, sweat slowly soaking into his cotton vestments. He tried to speak, but his tongue only fumbled around his mouth.

Fever continued to hold the dead men aloft, letting them shake and sway to set the tone for the slow demise she planned for him. Something much more inspired, she assured herself. "Confused, love?"

Jury shook his head to regain his focus, retracing his steps to find where he had erred. He then noticed the burning on the palm of his hand. As he looked closely, he noticed a rash had spread across his fingers and around the scab of his wound, a red scape of small bumps and broken vessels so warm they made his palm slick with sweat. Fever waited patiently for the revelation to strike him and as his eyes lazily shifted to the shards of broken clay, that's when she saw it. It made her smile, the kind of smile that grinds your teeth in intense elation.

As Jury weakened, so did the paralyzing glyph on her shoulder and she stiffly began to stretch her arms and legs. She couldn't have known which clay cup Jury would use, so as she feigned interest in the strongbox she spread poison on both. Her hands developed a faint rash as well, but she was accustomed to her own recipes and knew there would be no other adverse effects. The brambles at her feet began to wither, pulling their spines from her flesh, blood trickling from their tiny hooks onto the floorboards. She plucked one tine from the plant and ran its point along her tongue, licking clean her blood and suckling a drop of the poison within. It was acrid, pungent, and warmed to the very touch, and somehow she knew what it was meant to do. She couldn't explain how the mere taste of it imprinted on her, how it filled her with absolute assurance that it was meant to inverse its victim's physical control, turning up into down and left into right, nor could she fathom how she suddenly knew that the bramble was a chthonomantic incarnation called Bedlam Thistle.

Fever lowered one of the mangled corpses and had it approach Jury, swinging it back and forth in a macabre waltz. Its eyes had rolled into the back of its head, mouth wide open, screaming silently, frozen in a perpetual state of terror. Fever shook it like a puppet in Jury's face, its head flopping chaotically. "You should have been more careful, Jury."

A chill swept across Jury's skin and stirred him from his slumber, a simple breeze that crept along a blanket drenched in his own sweat. Somehow, he was laying in his bed. Disoriented and confused, his eyes slowly opened, the glow of a single candle cast shadows across the ceiling's beams. He licked his lips, his mouth and tongue so dry they ground in his ears like the wringing of old leather. His thirst for water was powerful, but the sudden smell of stool and urine was overwhelming. He cringed, clutching his mouth and nose with his hand and squinting into the darkness.

His home had been ravaged—broken chests, shattered stone, and splintered floorboards—torn asunder and scattered haplessly to all corners of the room. As his eyes rose, silhouettes caught his attention.

Half a dozen corpses hung by their throats from the rafters, their feet swaying in soiled trousers.

Jury was no stranger to the stench of fresh death, but the residue of Fever's poison was amplifying his senses and making him reel with nausea. He rolled to the side of his bed and vomited, heaving until he felt his lower ribs crick.

"There, there," Fever sung from the darkness, the shadows peeled themselves from her soft flesh like thick ichor as she neared the flame, the gold of her curls were the first to pierce the black of nightfall. In her hands she held a small black ledger she found in a strongbox beneath the floor. "You are as well informed as you brag, not that it's helped you any." She tapped the chapbook against her lips, the musty tones of old vellum and leather wafted beneath her nose. "You might even say that being so well informed is what's gotten you into this *glorious* mess."

With labored breaths, Jury scraped the bile from his tongue and spat to the side of the bed. The burn of her cocktail pulsed beneath his skin and groaned deep within his joints, sweat continuing to drip from his brow and throw him into a fit of chills at the slightest breeze. "Just kill me already."

Fever laughed sweetly. "Of course, love, I'm simply wondering how. It can't be too simple, you know. After all, not only are you a highly ranked Orbweaver gatekeeper, but an assassin from the same guild. Imagine my reputation if I didn't make an example of you."

Jury's eyes swam like lazy koi, coming to terms with his imminent death and weighing exactly how much pain and suffering was worth whatever it was she wanted from him.

Fever sifted through the pages of the chapbook before stopping at one and running her finger along its rough ridges. "Recently, you played messenger for an agreement between a man named Carver and one of the Chitin Kings, Ogra. On the surface, it looks like Carver paid to employ the service of one of Ogra's Orbweavers, Blackrock, but what does Ogra gain from such a transaction?"

"Carver paid a massive price for Blackrock," Jury said.

Fever tilted her head curiously, pursed her lips and closed the book with a creak of bindings. "I understand that Carver *thinks* he bought a service, but Ogra isn't from our world. I find it hard to believe he cares about something as trivial as currency." Fever rolled her sleeve back to reveal one of her black diamond bangles—each facet glimmered and danced in the candlelight and was the channel of her venomous, serpentine power since receiving her instrumentation from Ivory. The light of the room began to strain and the darkness coalesced into a slithering coil of jet shadow, two glowing eyes opened as the tip formed into the head of a snake wrapped in void. The shadow serpent stretched out from the black diamonds and slithered slowly through the air toward him, its tongue flicking with glints of roiling flame.

When Fever used the shadows to crush the necks of Jury's men, it had all happened too quickly to discern the features of each animate coil, but each serpent possessed a consciousness of its own, moving independently on the will of their master while sharing her hunger and bloodlust. He tried to lift himself from the bed as the serpent touched his leg, but he was far too weak to run. Instead, he froze in place, staring into the malevolent blaze of its eyes as it neared.

"My serpents are capable of a most magnificent venom," Fever said cheerily, "First, it destroys all your senses. The world fades into a vast emptiness, where you are enveloped in an inescapable darkness. Then, the venom makes its way to your mind, overwhelming you with claustrophobia. Suddenly, that inescapable darkness is a binding weight, wrapping itself around you, shackling you to a perceptive eternity of immobility while desperately drowning you in a need to breathe. And once you think the worst is over, it amplifies your reception to pain, making every breath feel like a razor's wind; making every heartbeat feel like a beast trying to burst from your chest."

The shadowed serpent slithered up to his shoulder and began to wrap around his throat, tickling his skin with the flick of its flaming tongue and tasting the heat from the blood that rushed to his head.

"There's a mark... I think," Jury said quickly, the pressure slowly building behind his eyes. The serpent stopped at Fever's will, loose enough he could still breath yet taut enough to turn his face purple. "The captain of the Bone Grove, Oona Kismet, he's the only man to ever break into the vault of the Phoenix Queen and escape. Carver thinks Blackrock is going to help him destroy the Bone Grove, but his true intention is probably to capture Kismet and deliver him to Emberwilde."

"Boring." Fever tapped her fingers against the cover of the chapbook—the symphony in her head beginning to play to her elation. "Why Emberwilde? And how does that benefit Ogra?"

"All I know is it's between him and the Phoenix Queen," Jury said, trembling from either fever or fear. "I only know of the arrangement from my end, and not what's being exchanged."

"Unfortunately, I believe you." She was disappointed, having hoped for just a little more resistance. "I also noticed that, shortly afterwards, you prepared an enchanted message to Liam Whitewater. Playing both sides, are we? Your fellow Orbweavers wouldn't approve, I imagine. The least of your concerns should be Ogra finding out. Especially since I believe he is positioning himself to conquer the city of Whitewater."

"No, no," he pleaded, "I was preparing a message for Kismet. He has the king's mistborn aboard his ship. He was arranging her return to Whitewater." The serpent slowly drifted back and forth, ever poised on the verge of striking.

"The king's mistborn? You mean Whisper?" Fever only knew Whisper by reputation, but what a reputation she had. Fever always felt they were one and the same, twin souls from two separate realms. Both built their reputation from the corpses in their wake, both surrendered to violence through the tragic loss of their family, and both of their names were a vexing hush on the lips of those who dared jinx their good fortune. Fever believed they were a massive imbalance on Elanta and if the Fates ever arranged their introduction, destiny itself would demand they fight to the death—there could be only one. She would never admit to it, but Whisper was the only person she ever felt apprehensive about contending. Perhaps it was because Whisper was the first person she thought she could lose to or that by killing someone so similar she would be killing a piece of herself. Either way, the thought made her heart race and brought a hush upon the symphony in her head. "So, Ogra has sent Blackrock to kidnap someone, but Whisper is also there..." Fever smiled as the vision gained clarity, "If Blackrock accepted this contract, then he obviously doesn't know."

"He doesn't, but even if he did I'm not sure he'd worry. He's truly quite terrifying," Jury replied.

"I've never heard of Blackrock, love, but I never stop hearing about Whisper. Trust me, it's mismatched."

The serpent began to tighten, little by little, enough so Jury could feel his own pulse behind his eyes. "I... told you everything."

"Oh, and it was good too," Fever winked and approached, reaching out and running her finger along his blueing lips, "But I'm missing one last thing to finish this beautiful evening." The serpent's eyes floated into view and licked the air with its blazing tongue. Fever leaned in close and whispered, the heat of her breath washed over his ear. "Scream for me."

The serpent bore its fangs and buried them deep into Jury's neck—his eyes wide to the terror he was about to experience. The serpent then slowly dissipated into the aether and Fever sat at the edge of the bed, allowing his head to fall into her arms. She cradled him dearly, cold, salty sweat dripping from his hair. She held him with the grace of a lover, closing her eyes and awaiting his voice to join her symphony of souls, but she received only his shuddered breaths and nothing more.

Fever's eyes snapped open, her brow falling, jaw clenched. She watched his eyes roll hazily in his head. Listened to the steady labor of his chest. He was far too stoic for the terror he should be experiencing and far too subdued for the pain he should be enduring. She dropped his head and rose.

"What's happening?" she roared angrily. If Jury could hear, he wasn't answering. Despite her chaotic nature she was a creature of method and when something formulaic went tragically awry it was a thing of anxiety. After all, what good was an assassin who couldn't kill when she intended. She summoned another serpent of shadow from the black diamonds of her bangle and held out her hand. The serpent lay its head in her palm, her fingers quickly wrapping around and forcing its mouth wide. Venom dripped from its long fangs and with the tip of her finger she tasted a drop—acrid, pungent, and warming to the touch. It was Bedlam Thistle, the exact same poison she just tasted from the bramble Jury summoned, and now, somehow, her serpents held it in their maw.

The confusion quickly passed, leaving behind only a delightfully morbid curiosity. She began to focus on one grand idea—that perhaps her power wasn't actually the ability to conjure many shadowed serpents capable of a single venom, but to conjure many terrible venoms, delivered by individual serpents. Her immunity was becoming more apparent, she could somehow identify a poison's properties simply by tasting it and it would seem her serpents were capable of inflicting such concoctions on her victims so long as she completely understood it.

She closed her eyes and focused on her original venom, imposing her will upon the serpent and commanding it to produce the supernatural concoction of psychological debilitation that came with her Instrumentation. She tasted the serpent's venom once more—fiery, smooth, and overwhelmingly oppressing. Just as she remembered.

A dark smile curled across her supple lips as she swayed, the bodies hanging from the rafters swayed silently in suit. It was a grand discovery indeed, one that required much more experimentation. Fortunately, Jury still owed her a scream.

24

BREAK EVERYTHING, JADE DRAGON

The Palace of Roiling Cinder had a massive courtyard, filled with lush green grass and trees—far too lush to thrive so close to the active volcano without the help of enchantment. Large, fragrant blooms swayed upon tall stalks, adding a myriad of vibrant colors and shades to the kempt expanse. Phori found herself somewhat relieved to see something that wasn't red or gold.

Stone arches stretched over winding paths, all of which led from the outermost cloisters to a round stage of black stone—glowing orange light fissured through like volcanic veins, pulsing, alive. Such a courtyard held immense reflective solitude when it was empty, but today, the day of Phori's inauguration, it was a bustling chaos. Thousands of Obsidian's feathered classes filed in, shoulder to shoulder, with nothing less than intrigue and excitement on their faces. Those with active military ranks stood closer to the center stone, donned in their armor and proudly displaying their tassels and clan insignias on the scabbards of their swords, while the common folk stood en masse behind, the white feathers woven into their hair to display their right to be there. Anyone without a feather to mark some degree of military training was not considered a valued citizen and thereby had to stand, shunned, at the very outskirts, which was impossibly far away. In a city such as Obsidian there were very few un-feathered and fewer yet were audacious enough to dare an audience to such a timeless honor, but even the forsaken loved their realm and tried in some manner to remain a small part in its history, even if just to say they were there to see an Instrument join the Bastion Nine.

Far above the courtyard, Phori and Lilia stood atop one of the palace's tallest towers and gazed down in awe at the crowds, flowing like a sentient river along the winding paths of old stone. The gentle clicking of glass beads in her hair made her realize she was shaking her head in disbelief.

"Most people have never seen an Instrument before," Lilia said, delicately folding her hands. Her posture was tall and proper, and gazing downward upon the masses with authority reminded her of the privilege she once had before becoming a Firefly. It made her proud, sad, and weak all at once. "Watching the inauguration of a new Bastion commands significant respect, but for that Bastion to also be an Instrument... a ceremony such as this is the first in history, perhaps the only. It is without wonder that people have ventured from all corners of Emberwilde to witness it."

Phori turned around to see four high-scholars, one of which was Thees. He bowed deeply. "Are you ready to use the Garda, General Phori?"

She wasn't and was certain she'd never be. The Garda was an ancient device used by Obsidian to strategically place units of soldiers when time, position, or surprise was crucial. Twenty black slabs of stone laid atop the tower and Thees gestured for her to stand on one. Phori looked at it with apprehension. She knew very little about how it worked, but enough to know it involved something exploding.

"Wait," Lilia commanded sternly, "who is this diviner?" She briskly approached one of the scholars and towered before her, a younger woman with shying eyes and passive demeanor.

"The high-scholar of divination could not be present and has sent his apprentice in his stead," Thees replied. "I assure you, she is more than qualified for the Garda procedure."

"What's happening?" Phori asked, her nerves showing through ever so slightly.

Lilia didn't appear to like the substitution. "The Garda requires four scholars to effectively operate—a diviner to scry the landing spot and supply the appropriate coordinates, a transmuter to calculate and adjust the slabs so the proper trajectory is achieved, an evoker to create a sigil that will explode with the appropriate amount of concentrated force to get you to the landing spot, and an abjurer to wrap you in a ward so you don't die on launch or impact."

Her abjurer, Thees, gave a clever smile.

The high-scholars remained silent while Lilia stewed, until she finally surrendered. "Well then, what's the worst that could happen?" She turned to Phori and shrugged. "It's not as though you're going far. Even a neonate could probably ensure we don't fire you into the crowd... or the volcano."

If the Firefly was trying to make a joke, Phori didn't find it very funny.

A procession of horns and drums began to sound down in the courtyard, signalling that the Bastion Nine and the Phoenix Queen were about to part the crowds and proceed to the center stone. Lilia gracefully turned and began to make haste for the exit, as she would be expected to walk with the other Bastions and ensure the safety of the malikeh.

"What do I do?" Phori asked.

Lilia stopped and turned, the golden chain of her shoulder cloak swayed, yet somehow made no sound. "Once we are ready, we will announce you. Then, the Garda will land you in the center for everyone to see. The high-scholars will know when to send you." She hurried to the exit once more, pulling the door open with a heavy creak.

Phori reluctantly stepped atop one of the black slabs. "Is this even safe?"

Lilia's body had all but exited, her sharp features peering from behind the door with a quaint noble's glee. "Fates no!" she replied. Once again, she was being impossible to read, likely on purpose. "This archaic contraption is a death trap, but I've heard it helps to bend your knees." With that last gem of wisdom she disappeared beyond, leaving Phori entirely speechless.

She looked to the high-scholars, pleading with her eyes for some degree of reassurance.

"It does help to bend your knees a little," Thees said.

The crowds below parted for the Bastion Nine, who marched in pairs with the queen's palanquin between them. Wispy red curtains swayed from the golden dome like feathers in the wind, giving the occasional glimpse of the royalty within. To each side of the palanquin were four shirtless bearers in fine hakama—flaring, deep pleated pants of stiffened silk. Their brawn flexed with the weight of the throne, stretching their skin to the point of bursting beneath the mass.

The sea of soldiers took to their knee for as far as the eye could see. By the time the palanquin reached the center stone, not a single spectator was left standing. It wasn't until the men lowered the palanquin and the sound of drums ceased that anyone dared rise.

Lilia carefully scoured the crowd, her sharp eyes carefully analysing every face and expression. Even when celebrations were in order she was working, perpetually on guard as a result of her training. She pulled her elbows backward slightly, bumping the hilt and scabbards of her two blades—harnessed hip and shoulder. A nervous habit, not that unlike laying a hand on your money purse in a crowded marketplace.

Two bearers knelt before the crimson stairs of the palanquin and pulled the curtains apart, revealing the malikeh in all her splendor. The glimmering radiance of her headdress, feathered extravagantly with black, red, and golden plumes, matched the flourish of paint across her eyes. She carefully descended the stairs, the weight of her ceremonial robes hung delicately yet cumbersome over her slender frame. The crowd did not cheer, it was not their custom. Instead, each and every person placed a fist upon their palm and raised it in the air—an honorable symbolism of their origins, where an open heart would humbly offer a cup of hot tea to their beloved. The malikeh, too, placed a fist upon her palm and raised it in return.

Lilia continued to watch with scrutiny, her noble posture and cold eyes made many shun from her gaze. The malikeh had begun to speak, but Lilia wasn't paying attention, instead, she began to focus on one man in the crowd whose eyes shifted both left and right before meeting hers with an aggressive shame. Two others in the crowd listened restlessly to the malikeh's speech, their jaws flexing as their teeth ground. They were dressed in plain cottons of little descript, but as one turned to scout across the crowd she noticed a small scarred brand under his ear—the circular coil of a dragon consuming its own tail.

"Jade Dragons," Lilia concluded. There was no doubt. These members weren't wearing their armor and now that she knew what she was looking for she began to spot more blending in with the crowd—two dozen, maybe more. Jade Dragons were notorious for their arrogant brawls, but they were street savvy enough to wear at least some semblance of armor. Pride was in victory, not fairness. They didn't appear to be there to fight, but rather, watch. Eventually, one accidently raised his eyes to the Garda and spoiled the plan.

Lilia immediately began to draw two round glyphs in the air, one with each hand. The lines of energy blazed silently from her fingertips in a mysterious twinkling white until she grabbed them and they faded into her hands. She flicked her wrists toward the Garda, glittering discs of translucent light flung from her fingers like blades, stopping suddenly above the crowd. She began to sprint across the discs, flicking more as she needed, making great haste for the Garda. If the Jade Dragons were here, so was their leader, Oba. If Oba was here, then Phori was in grave danger.

Atop the Garda, the high-scholars began to prepare for Phori's grand entrance. The eyes of the diviner clouded as she folded her hands and focused, and the transmuter knelt alongside the black slate with an open palm upon it. The diviner navigated weightlessly through a clouded vision, strands of gossamer swayed gently at the edges of her peripheral. The sounds of the crowd were incomprehensibly muffled and her spectrum of color bled into pastel shapes and lines that squiggled strangely. She navigated her sight to the precise spot on which she wanted Phori to land. To each side of her the Bastion Nine had marched onto the platform and behind was the malikeh's immaculate golden palanquin. The malikeh had descended the stairs and was making a speech, holding aloft a glorious golden feather with black stripes, the mark of a General.

"I'm ready. Here are your coordinates," the young diviner said before relaying a series of numbers.

The transmuter repeated the numbers under his breath, closing his eyes as he calculated the necessary angles and used his enlightenment to shift the black slab—tilting and turning in short bursts beneath Phori's feet. Once he was satisfied, he rose and placed a hand on the diviner's shoulder, pulling her back in from her trance. She shook her head as she returned to her body, the transition seeming to tax her mind.

The evoker placed a glyph at her feet and a control glyph at his own. They both glowed a ghostly orange, though she was told that when he was ready to fire he would channel energy into them and hers would blaze moderately before ignition.

"Are you worried, Brigadier General?" Thees chimed pleasantly. This wasn't his first Garda and he seemed to take an innocent pleasure in seeing Phori squirm. "You needn't. I've done this many times."

Phori took a deep breath and padded her black stone armor, ensuring that if she was about to be shot off a rooftop she would at least have everything when she landed, wherever that was. "I'm ready."

Thees gave a soft nod and placed his hand on the stomach of her armor, infusing it with a hazy blue mark that shimmered almost imperceptibly around her. "This ward will protect you from harm and create a burst of energy upon impact to soften your landing." He stepped backward and smiled, holding his hands with interlaced fingers as he continued to sustain the energy of the glyph. Then, from each side of the black slab, a transparent force erected to create a tall box to concentrate the force of the blast upward.

Phori nodded, ready for her departure, and looked up to the sky she was about to traverse when she noticed a lid began to form atop the box. "What's happening?"

Thees shook his head, confused. "I'm not sure. It's not me." He turned in time to see two men in green jade armor, dragons spiralling across the pauldrons. One was holding his hands in such a manner as to channel energy into a barrier of his own, sealing Phori within, while the other marched toward her with a massive steel gore-maul.

Phori turned to see the men, quickly realizing that if the glyph were to explode within her entombment she couldn't be sure that Thees' ward would hold against the heat and pressure.

"What's the meaning of thi—" Thees barely spoke his last word before the gore-maul tore through his head, spattering red on white bone across the stone of the Garda with a terrible crack.

Phori watched in horror as the rest of his body flew backward from the impact, and as his life force burst in a spray of red, so did the protective ward he was sustaining around her body.

The Jade Dragon spied her down the bridge of his nose, looking down upon her shock with arrogance and entitlement. Spatters dripped from his short brown hair and furry eyebrows, a smug smile across his thin lips. It was Oba, the leader of the Jade Dragons and former Bastion Nine. He didn't have to introduce himself for her to know his name and he didn't have to explain himself to know he was there to kill her before she was inducted into the Bastion Nine so that he could have his seat back.

The evoker swung with a war-fan of blazing orange fire, missing as Oba deflected it with the haft of his gore-maul. He plunged the steel into the evoker's stomach, winding him badly seconds before the gore-maul crashed down upon his head and crushed his spine in upon itself.

The transmuter and the diviner attempted to flee, nearly reaching the door to the tower before collapsing to a force that rose from the stone and clutched their ankles. The Jade Dragon holding Phori's ward had outstretched a hand and summoned the focus to ensnare the high-scholars while juggling her own capture.

Oba laughed as he slowly walked toward them, dragging his gore-maul along the stone and letting Phori watch the malice in his eyes. "Who shall I kill, Brigadier General? I'll let you decide."

"Me!" she roared, striking the barrier with all her might. Despite her incredible abilities, it seemed she was defenseless against the gossamer nature of pure enchantment.

Oba gave a sharp sneer and raised his weapon above the diviner.

The young girl cowered, throwing her arms across her eyes as though reality would halt if she didn't see it. She cried out; warm, salty tears splashed into the cracks—a cry so horrid, so terrified, that Phori would be vexed to remember, vexed to forget. Phori could barely be heard, roaring like a beast, pounding against the ward with every bit of desperation she could muster as the glint of Oba's gore-maul swung downward , and then, a miracle, as the next sound she heard amidst the bellows was that of steel on steel, then steel upon stone.

The impact on the stone was explosive, sending a cloud of dust and debris upward, breaking the Jade Dragon's line of sight and freeing the high-scholars, who immediately scrambled to the door and escaped. The dust quickly settled, and through the silence echoed the spattering of blood as Lilia stood with hands dripping, swords drawn, already injured from merely deflecting such a powerful attack. The silver handles of her swords were slick with blood, red with agony—it streamed down the wavy edges of her long, thin blades and dripped from the tip into small, trembling pools.

"You'll never be fast enough," Oba said, his hands glowing orange.

Lilia adjusted her hands, squeezing her blades as tightly as possible to wring out the blood and gain a better grip against the silver.

Oba turned and sprinted for Phori, his hands blazing a full evocation, but in a blinding burst of speed Lilia crouched weightlessly upon his pauldron and drove her narrow blade through the slit of his guard and into his shoulder.

He bellowed, grabbing her by the arm and hurling her along the stone. Her blade remained buried deep in his flesh.

Lilia tumbled well enough, but her wounds ached terribly as she slid along the Garda on her hand and feet, her other sword clutched tightly. Oba raised his hand above Phori's control glyph. Flames burst from his palm as he channelled everything he had into one massive evocation, which he swung downward upon the glyph.

Lilia knew she couldn't make it to Oba in time to stop him from creating the blast within Phori's cell and with a great arc she hurled her blade with all her might. The silver sung through the air—a blurred, glinting disc that cut through the winds like flame to cobweb.

The long, thin point of Lilia's blade slowed to its last revolution, while the blaze of Oba's flames lazily roiled over the pulsing strain of his clenched fist. Each neared, each called for blood—in the final moments both steel and flame hungered all their own.

Oba's fist struck the glyph, the flames of his rage stretched out as if to grab it before he even contacted. They hungered, they devoured, they burrowed deep into the stone, feasted on the will of desolation and destruction, and engorged themselves to such elation they prepared to burst beneath Phori's feet in a fantastic, unrelenting display of malice.

The orange light of Oba's ignition glowed along the edges of Lilia's blade—dancing up and down the wavy edge to the tip, where the light seemed to stop and hone its intent. The point slowly dropped below the Jade Dragon enchanter's chin, lightly kissing his stubble before piercing his skin. The apple of his throat bobbed and caught the edge, breaking the skin as the blade slipped through with ease. So quickly, so smooth, his body had yet to wonder whether or not to bleed. The silver continued through the soft bits of his throat and slid between the disc of his neck, sliding through the cartilage and severing the strands of his spinal cord before exiting his nape, just beneath his hairline. Such a narrow blade, thrown with such force, slipped through unhindered until the guard struck, instilling the full force of her weight and snapping him off his feet.

The ward dropped as the flames burst outward and upward, sending Oba and Lilia tumbling to opposite sides of the Garda. The explosion continued to echo thunderously against the side of the volcano and across the crowds below, where people stood in awe, unsure whether to run or watch.

Lilia's ears rung, her eyes stung, and her lungs filled with smoke and dust. Before the explosion she had managed to raise her chainmail shoulder cloak across her face and body. The chainmail prevented any debris from piercing her skin, but she took some serious brunt force that was sure to bruise badly. She braced her hands to stand, when her fingers touched a large piece of black stone, curved and vicious, like that of Phori's armor. Blood slicked the inside, still warm, dripping into the dust.

Through the smoke she heard footsteps. Heavy soles dredged through the splintered stone, until a silhouette pierced through the haze. It was Oba, wounded, but towering proudly with his gore-maul in one hand and a large piece of Phori's bloody armor in the other. He was bleeding profusely from the wound Lilia had caused and untreated he would soon suffer consequences. If she could evade him long enough, perhaps he'd just fall down and die.

She tried to stand, but her legs would not allow it. They trembled from the explosion, and even if she could muster the strength to stand she was certain she didn't have the coordination to run—the ringing in her ears created a wobbling haze like heat from a Baku dune.

Oba tossed the armor before her and clutched the haft with both hands, heaving the gore-maul above his head.

Lilia had nowhere to run and scowled at the nature of her demise. Bloodied, on her knees, in the wake of her failure. An end brought by such an unimaginative, oafish foe—it was as maddening as it was sad.

Oba swung hard, hurling downward with the bulk of his weight, but as the head of the gore-maul nearly struck Lilia between the eyes, the stone beneath his feet crumbled and he plummeted through to the floor below.

He landed hard, coughing in the dust and darkness, bowing before a silhouette in a hazy beam of light that shone through a second hole in the ceiling, one directly beneath the Garda. As the dust settled and his eyes adjusted, Phori's fearsome red gaze stilled his heart for but a beat. Her armor shattered, her flesh bloody, and her eyes furious.

He grabbed his gore-maul and swung as he stood, striking

her flat against the side of her head. The gore-maul shattered into hundreds of tiny pieces, each one dying in the light as they bounced like gravel into the shadows, yet she did not flinch. He stared at the haft, dumbfounded.

Phori lunged forward, he raised the haft to block, but her hand tore through with little effort. A paralyzing shock overtook him as her hand snapped the haft in two, crumbled the center of his breastplate, and plunged into his chest. It happened so quickly, so swiftly, that his slow body had yet to react to what his slower mind couldn't fathom.

Pressure built behind his eyes, as though the blood in his head were trying to escape, and in one fell motion she tore his heart from his chest. It hopelessly beat in the palm of her hand as she held it before him, being sure it was the last thing he saw before he died.

His eyes fell still and lifeless, and his body collapsed into the rubble. Phori placed his heart in his hand and disappeared into the darkness.

25

IVORY'S PLAN, FEVER'S APPREHENSION

Fever hummed blissfully as she sat in Jury's chair, a warm fire crackled in the large stone fireplace, flickering across the hearth. What tune she was singing no one knew, save for the voices in her head perhaps, and though it sounded sweet and harmless it was certain to have a grim undertone of some sort.

In her lap laid a large black tome, once bound with the long leather straps that hung to each side. The pages were old, written with ink and blood, adorned with sigils, glyphs, and runes, many of which she didn't understand even with her extensive education. She licked her finger and turned a page, the spine groaned a little each time—a deep, mournful groan, that regaled her of all the darkness it had seen, warning her not to delve into the next page lest she lose her soul within and be forced to groan with it. She loved it.

"What about this one?" She held the book aloft and turned it to face Jury, who lay sweaty, weak, and on the brink of death upon his bed. It was written in an unfamiliar language, but emanated gruesome ruination.

His eyes lazily rolled to the side to see the page, an invocation to turn bone to jelly. "Take a walk, wench."

Fever tilted her head, a curious 'hmm' upon her lips. She gave a charming wink, "This one's a maybe." Her fingers marked the top edge of the page with a fold and continued to the next. Her eyes brightened as she plucked only a few familiar words from the scrawl and turned the book to face him once more. "What about this one?"

"By Fates, shut your mouth you vile bi..."

"Tssss." Fever scrunched her nose as she interrupted, keeping him from saying something he'd truly regret. She set the book back in her lap, roughly interpreted the contents once more and clutched it to her breast. "Oh my. This is a good one, isn't it?"

The curls of flame slowed and the shadows narrowed and stretched until they met the furthest wall, where they coalesced into a black pool of darkness. Shifting and rippling like pitch water.

The ivory crown was the first to peel through the shadows, bone white and gleaming with intricate curves and ornate swirls. Her hair, long and black, was almost impossible to distinguish between the strands of darkness that stretched from her as she began to exit. The shadows clung to her porcelain features the least, too smooth and flawless to grip with their sticky strands. Her eyes were closed, her lips curled. The shadows peeled down her throat and wrapped around it like a choker, forming long silver stands of silk that delicately traversed her collarbone until they reached her dress—a roiling shadow so dark the more it entered the room, the more color it seemed to absorb from its surroundings, until she completely exited and all was black and white. The dress of living shadows clung to her figure, tracing her curves as it slithered down her body until it degraded into torn strands of wispy silk that listlessly waved above a cloud of white mist that concealed her feet. On her left arm sparkled a large diamond, held fast by two platinum wings that wrapped around her wrist. It was the First Wish, an artifact that could create infinite wealth and even still, it could not command such attention as when Ivory opened her eyes. The room drowned. Fever's breath pulled from her lungs and left her to tremble without even realizing. Pupils of black spiders, legs stretching into an iris so unfathomably, supernaturally, blue; black strands of silk laid within to create a web, capturing one's soul before falling into the depth.

"Hello Ivory," Fever said softly, catching her breath and loosening her grip on the tome.

"Hello, my love," Ivory replied, a rich sweetness in her voice, almost as though she hadn't noticed the bodies hanging from the rafters, or didn't care. "You've been busy."

"I've been restless." Fever turned the book so that Ivory could see and flipped between several pages. "Which technique should I practice on Jury?"

Ivory glided across the floor and leaned over the book, her hands on her thighs, her long hair climbing the chair and caressing Fever's face. "Is this a tome of chthonomancy? Assassin, chemist, and now a blood mage as well?"

Fever smiled at the touch of living hair. "I have no use for an art that requires I sacrifice my own life energy to use, but I've found some poisonous enchantments that have piqued my interest. I'm considering practicing one."

"Interesting," Ivory said, accepting the book and perusing the text. "There is great use in creating something from nothing, when circumstances arise." Many of the pages marked had a common theme, changing the blood or bone into something else entirely, like lava or centipedes. Though dramatic and nefarious it all seemed too much, even for the harbinger of death. There was something artistic in orchestrating a simple tragedy that bordered on ironic. "Perhaps we can talk about what you've found out, first."

Fever reached into the sleeve of her robe and withdrew Jury's small boar-skin ledger, holding it aloft for Ivory to take.

Ivory's hair slowly stretched out and exchanged the cthonomatic tome for the ledger and placed it in her hand. Her living hair thumbed the pages for her as she held the book so delicately, as though it could crumble through her fingers.

"One of the Chitin Kings, Ogra, is working with someone in Emberwilde. I think he's agreed to deliver a traitor of the realm in return for something." Fever crossed her legs, the robe sliding down her knee and thigh.

"The Phoenix Queen." It was a much a scowl as Ivory's elegance could muster. "That... bitch."

Fever examined her nails, certain she would get an explanation if she feigned enough disinterest. She had chipped one somehow; that was disappointing.

"I'm almost certain that's who Ogra's working with. If so, then I know exactly what he wants." Ivory flipped through the book to the newer pages. "Where is the Bone Grove?" She had never heard of it while in the Weave and she had heard of almost everything. It must have been founded after she left.

Fever shrugged. "No idea, but I wouldn't worry about it." Ivory lowered the ledger and peered at her curiously, to which Fever responded with big eyes and a smile of sheer glee, brightening with news. "Ogra and Carver don't know it, but the Whitewater mistborn, Whisper, is with the mark in the Bone Grove." There was a sparkle in Fever's eyes that shone the brief and bloody end she expected of Carver's fleet, but as she delved deeper into Ivory's blank gaze her glee began to wane. "You don't know who Whisper is?"

Ivory's brow furrowed. Illy had never mentioned someone named Whisper, but by Fever's tone she sounded important.

"Whisper is a twisted woman with incredible power. She's a mercenary, as infamous in Whitewater as I am in Emberwilde. She once beat a man to death with his own horse." Fever wondered if Whisper ever spoke of her with such admiration, but knew it wasn't likely. Whisper was too broody for such trivial things, probably opting to save her praises for those worthy of her wrath in the climax of battle.

Ivory interrupted the gloss of reverence on Fever's face. "Ogra must capture the traitor and deliver him to Emberwilde. To be certain he's working with the Phoenix Queen we have to know where he delivers him."

Fever shook her head in disbelief. "Blackrock is going to die," she said with absolute affirmation. "His soul was forfeit the moment Ogra chose to send him."

"Yes, but he is not an Instrument," Ivory sung slyly.

Fever froze, her smile quickly faded into something Ivory hadn't yet seen—nervousness. "You want me to go?"

Ivory folded her hands and said nothing, the corner of her lip raised ever so slightly. "Are you afraid of this mistborn girl?"

"I will not be just another corpse in Whisper's wake." Fever pursed her lips, realizing the voices that often conversed in her head had fallen deathly ill, not one of them knowing what else to say. "I'm unprepared for such an encounter."

"What do you need?" Ivory said as though she could snap her fingers and manifest it out of the aether, thereby quashing any further means of argument.

"Advantage. Time, study, information..." Fever's eyes betrayed she was throwing out the first words she could think of. A means of blanketing her with excuses in hopes that one would be enough.

"How about this," Ivory began, "I'll place you on the *Last Breath*, where you will observe Whisper from a distance. If it seems the mark will not be captured, you give a little nudge to ensure he does. You don't even have to fight if you don't want to. You could just snatch him while Whisper fights this Blackrock. There are many alternatives."

Fever knew she wasn't getting out of this mission and at the very least she liked the idea of being able to study Whisper. One day she would get into an altercation with her, it was the destiny she wanted for herself, and the information would be crucial in either making her the victor or ensuring her death was the kind bards wrote songs of. She nodded, trying to look as confident as possible, though awash with hesitation. "Why do I have to spend time at sea with a bunch of ingrates? Can't you just send me to the Bone Grove? I'll grab him and then you pull me back."

Ivory was pleased with Fever's surrender and it showed in the way her hips swayed in her approach. "I can't sense the Bone Grove, therefore it's either too far away or too close to the mist. However, I can sense the *Last Breath*. Well enough to place you onto it, but it will have to be soon, before it gets too far."

Fever closed the tome and tucked it under her arm, taking one last look at Jury. His weariness was inspiring, though bittersweet. She would have to kill him before she left to ensure Ogra would not be informed of her interrogation. If only there was more time. There were so many interesting experiments to perform.

'Break his neck, I like the sound.'

'Smother him, let the terror build.'

'Poison him, it's your signature.'

She tilted her head and smiled, almost tearing at the return of lovely voices. It felt as though they had been gone for so long, abandoning her to the maddening quietude, yet returning to her with so many wonderful ideas. The last thing she wanted was for any of them to be disappointed. *'Why not,'* she shrugged, *'there's time for all three.'*

26

PHILOSOPHY IN RAIN

Raindrops spattered against a swooping roof of clay tiles, converging and leaping into the dark soil that lay just beyond the pagoda's open doors. It was a large, single room with raised wooden floors, surrounded by sliding paper doors. To the furthest end, the floor dropped into a fire pit and kettle rod.

The herbalists and enchanters had come and gone before the first rain came, but Phori could smell its burgeoning presence in the air and asked that they leave a few doors open so she could experience it while she recovered. She liked to watch the rain. In ways it made her feel unique, a paradox—a woman forged in the flames of Emberwilde yet inexplicably drawn to her opposing element. There was something deep and wise within it and even though she felt the message was as hard to hold as the rain itself, it made her feel like a philosopher for trying.

She lay on her back, her neck resting on a curved wooden block, covered in a warm blanket. The cool air was welcome. Her bandages were wrapped so tightly she could barely move and when she did it only brought to light how damp her bindings were. It made her wonder if what moisture she felt was sweat or blood, but she was almost too solemn to care. She continued to watch the rainfall, letting all her questions wash away with it. *Where was she? Was this her room? Where did they find her body?*

She turned her head and caught a glimpse of the golden striped General's feather in the corner of her eye, woven into her hair while she was unconscious. She didn't know who opted for such generous symbolism, because the only one she thought capable lay unconscious next to her.

Lilia's noble features were pristine even in recovery—her head faced the rafters, her body lay perfectly straight, every hair in place. It was hard to imagine maintaining such polish could be restful, but it didn't seem the Firefly was suffering from it. With barely a stir, her eyes slowly opened and spied Phori without turning her head. Almost as though she could sense she was being watched and sprung to life to ensure wandering eyes were those of good intentions. Upon noticing it was Phori she seemed to relax, blinking long and hard to ease her mind back into her body. "You're alive," she said. She had meant to sound as composed and regal as usual, but her voice cracked with the wounds and weather; her velvet accent covered it well. "You lost too much blood to be certain."

"Thank you," Phori replied, meditative with the rain. "I know a Firefly prefers to work from the shadows. Confronting Oba head-on had to be uncomfortable."

"If a Firefly has drawn a blade in the gaze of her mark, something has certainly gone awry." Lilia attempted to rise, but cringed with the sudden ache of her ribs and rested back into her woven rice mat. "And awry it did go. In fact, I would be dead if it weren't for you."

Phori joined Lilia in staring up into the rafters. Perhaps it was just the tautness of her wraps, but she could still feel Oba's heart pulse in the palm of her hand. She expected to feel rage, anger, or maybe remorse, but instead she simply felt cold. Fed up. Broken. As indescribable as the rain was to catch, all she truly knew was that she didn't really feel like herself.

Phori needed to distract her waning mind. "It's unusual for a Firefly to wield two blades at once, isn't it?"

"Yes," Lilia replied, "one is mine, the other belonged to my brother."

"Oh," Phori's bandages felt as though they tightened a little more. She remembered the silver medallion and General's feather than hung from one of the sheaths. "I'm sorry. What happened to him?"

Lilia remained silent a moment, pondering her words carefully, until she spoke in a breath that seemed to surrender her truth. "He was once a member of the Bastion Nine, but they say he betrayed Clan Firefly, dishonored our family name, and renounced his seat." A tear seemed to hide in the corner of her eye, held back by sheer pride. "The malikeh executed him and I assumed his seat in the Bastion Nine to rebuild our broken noble name."

"It doesn't sound like you're convinced he did it."

Lilia shook her head wondering what she really believed, or if it even mattered now. All she knew was her brother's heart was far too noble and his shoes far too big for her to fill. "May I ask you something?" Lilia said softly, almost nervously.

"Of course."

"What is it like? Being an Instrument?" Maybe it was the rain talking, but there was a mournful yearning in her voice, coupled by a deep wonder in her almond eyes.

Phori thought about it a moment, struggling with words. Many people strived for such an honor—they trained diligently every day, educated themselves in every field their minds could handle, and developed their virtues at every opportunity. Proving one's worth to the Fates was a lifestyle, a massive undertaking for an even bigger exaltation, and yet she was possibly the only Instrument in history that wasn't pleased with the privilege. She didn't want to say it aloud and shatter the romanticism it held for Lilia, who was clearly saddened she was not the one in Ivory's favor. *'It's a terrible responsibility, filled with agonizing leaps of faith that test your integrity,'* was what she wanted to say. Instead, "It's an honorable role, filled with fateful challenges that hone your convictions."

"It's interesting," Lilia said, "growing up, my brother and I always imagined being Instruments. Standing high above the masses, commanding reverence through sheer influence alone. Now it seems so foolish to think power and imperviousness mean the same thing. The look in your eyes when Thees was killed, your desperate call for Oba's wrath to strike you and spare the diviner, and even when all was thought lost, you returned, soaked head to toe in your own blood, to plunge your hand straight through a breastplate and tear his sinful heart from his very chest." Lilia swallowed as she remembered watching it through the dust that stirred within the hole of the Garda, like she was peering down into a seer's stone, witnessing something too far away to be real. "It is not pristine, uncontested, nor without its scars. You took everything that was godly and everything that was human, and bestowed upon me a humbling perspective."

Phori remained silent in the Firefly's revelation.

Lilia turned her head, tears she insisted not fall lurked behind her eyes. "Thank you, Phori. Your humanity is inspiring. It defies everything I thought Instrumentation would be yet somehow it empowers me. You are unlike any Instrument I have ever read about, and you wear it best." She let a single tear escape, and as quick as it was to flee she was to capture it. "You have my blades, no matter the course."

Phori looked at her with silent affirmation, proud and thankful. A single nod to seal the deal. A close ally was comforting in this time of unrest, where she struggled with which side she was actually serving. It made her wonder if she should confide in Lilia regarding Ivory's current position and influence on the war, at the very least to let her know what she'd be getting in to by lending her sword to her cause. Where she would normally stir with the pros and cons of such a disclosure, she was so worn to Ivory's mystery that she was beginning to not care what consequences might occur. She was, after all, her own person and Ivory had said nothing about inclusion.

"I'd like to share my thoughts with you in confidence," Phori said. Though she wouldn't mention everything in great detail, there were some things she wished to vent aloud—the tragedy of her Instrumentation, the Ravenmane, Fever, her apprehension regarding Ivory's plans, and the razor's edge she walked between honoring both queen and Fate.

"One moment," Lilia replied, adjusting her neck on the wooden block and licking her lips. She gave cooing songbird's whistle, which cut through the rain into the gardens beyond.

A soft thud struck the tiles above them and the runoff at the far end of the pagoda poured red into the earth. Shortly after, a body clad in dark fabric slid off the roof, landing with a cringing splatter.

Lilia gave two sharp chirping whistles and nodded into the rain before returning her attention to Phori.

Phori lifted herself enough to see the mound of fabric, bleeding out into the beyond. "What happened?"

"An Orbweaver spy was following you ever since you arrived to Obsidian, but my Fireflies have been following him to see what he does. If you were to confide, I thought it'd be best to kill him now lest he have wind in his lungs to share your words." Lilia looked at her with such genuine loyalty. "My Fireflies have withdrawn and we are alone. Please, speak your heart."

27

LAYERS OF THE BONE GROVE

Whisper sat on her bed and held her wooden practice sword, gently waving it in the air. They had been sailing for so long, it seemed, and while the crew was showing sign of restlessness she was right at home. Isolated from the world with nothing else to do but hone her skills, it felt like she was back at the monastery in the mountains of Emberwilde.

Her hair had grown longer, though it wasn't growing as fast as when she first came back from the dead. She refused to cut it and now it hung to the dark lace of her navy corset. When the light hit her raven hair just right the shimmer of red would trick one's senses into thinking she was a cardinal. She was beginning to enjoy her new body. The clothing was a big improvement from the white robes she had worn for twenty years and without the need to hide her features she felt much freer. In the waking hours of her transformation she was wracked with fear and confusion, but even though she was weaker in this form she somehow felt stronger. Or maybe empowered, if there was a difference. Perhaps it was simply confidence, not that of a warrior with a purpose but of someone who belonged for no other reason than being human.

Yoru was curled in the blankets and lifted her head with a gaze half present. Irritated? Tired? Disinterested? Who knew, really? The talking, non-talking, cat—or rather, elantan velvetine—was as opinionated as she was fluffy.

"Am I disturbing you?" Whisper was brimming with sarcasm. Yoru's sharp yellow eyes lazily rose from beneath a furry brow, unimpressed and judgmental. It was a definite 'yes'. Their standoff was interrupted by the padding of small feet as they scurried to Whisper's room, the young Lau Lau throwing the door open in a fit of glee. "We're here!" she cried. "Come see!"

Whisper set the sword down and ruffled Yoru's fur, widening her eyes and sticking her tongue out in childish antagonism, to which Yoru simply ignored her and began to smooth down the mattes with her bristled tongue.

Lau Lau hurried through the halls ahead of Whisper, who took her time. The Bone Grove was simply an island somewhere out in Elanta. Not really something worth getting so excited over, but curiosity was often stronger than her apathy. Having been cooped up on a boat for so long she was willing to accept that, perhaps, something as boring as a lump of stone could be surprisingly refreshing.

Whisper ascended the steps to the deck and opened the door, expecting the darkness of nightfall to be illuminated by the soft white glow of sigils, as it always was in the late hours, but the sigils shone no light. Instead, the water glowed ghostly green, which gently lit the faces of Kismet and Lau Lau as they stood against the starboard rails. The young child stood on the tips of her toes so she could peer as far over the edge as possible, the captain's eyes glassy from a pipe of burning rumrose.

The *Windborn Chance* was deathly silent save for the flap of sail and creaking wood, and Whisper was careful to walk as quietly as possible across the deck, for no other reason than everyone else was. She approached the rail, the radiant glow rippled over her face as she looked down into the water—green, glowing creatures the size of house cats floated calmly beneath the surface: wispy, round, and feathery looking. The water of the Bone Grove was as clear as crystal and smooth as silk, an eerie stillness made mesmerizing with light from the deep. She had never seen such animals and with so many of them scattered throughout the water it radiated like a passage into something otherworldly, a gateway onto another plane of existence—a living sigil. She wanted so desperately to ask what they were, but the will to speak was quickly lost in the hypnosis of their movement—dozens of feathery strands waved and scooped, pulling it slowly through the water.

"They're dragon souls," Lau Lau whispered. "The current pulled them here after the war."

If Whisper hadn't been staring directly at them she would have slapped the child sane and made her read a book, but this presence was unlike anything she had ever expected or was prepared for. It made even the preposterous idea that the souls of dragons swam in ocean currents plausible. Whisper watched the closest one, flicking its wispy strands as the wake of the boat gently pushed it away.

Kismet took the pipe from his lips, closed his eyes, and took a deep breath of cool air. "Every time I draw my sword, here I am. Crystal water—more beautiful than any woman; too free to ever hold." Whisper noticed he wasn't even looking at the dragon's souls, but into the horizon of water as it stretched into the darkness, where the illumination dissipated into the dead of night. "Every time I draw my sword, here I am. Every fight feels like a dance."

Whisper shrugged. She didn't understand peace like that and wasn't losing sleep over it either. Though she was learning the art of the sword from Kismet, she had no quiet place to send her mind to make her feel like dancing, nor would she ever. Dancing was for fools and why bother learning the steps when she could change the song, tempo, and chord whenever she wanted to put an opponent on their heels. It's why she preferred to use her fists—they made every fight feel personal.

The dragon's souls floated listlessly in passing, lighting their way to something massive and encompassing. Whisper forced herself to look ahead at the encroaching darkness, where the dragon souls dared not go. Tall pillars of stone jutted from the water into the void, its sharp and unruly edges could be sensed in any light.

Djagatt stood at the helm and carefully adjusted his heading mere inches at a time. Slowly, he guided the ship into a crevice that tore through the stone. Not once did the bells on his ears jingle, his focus so still he dared not move anything but his hands, even then, not much.

"There are three trials that protect the Bone Grove. This is the outermost rim and the first trial, called *The Fear*," Kismet said quietly to Whisper, the red embers of his pipe giving his location away. The sigils of the deck began to illuminate, casting light and giving sense of how narrow the passage truly was. Merchants prodded the rock on each side with long gaffs to keep their course.

"*The Fear?*"

"Because you will need to get past it to survive."

"It's just a narrow corridor."

Djagatt began to turn the boat, fighting a rightward current and commanding the merchants to push the *Windborn Chance* to the left of an intersection. "There are many passages into the trial," his deep voice rumbled, "but only some lead through the outer rim."

"Where do the others lead?"

Kismet used the stem of his pipe to point down a shaft of darkness, holding a finger over his lips to command an attentive silence.

She could hear a rumbling in the distance. Bubbling water growled over itself in a constant stir of fury. "What is that?"

"Dragon's Breath. *The Fear* pulls you in many directions, most of which you must find the resolve to fight against. Such currents lead to Dragon's Breath, which boils the water and sinks whole ships, pulling them down into their mouths and crushing them with their teeth."

Whisper raised an eyebrow, the roaring of water faded as they floated further from it. She pictured a dragon on the bottom of the ocean floor with its head upturned, a whirlpool of water funnelled from its open maw to pull boats down into its mouth, absurd.

Djagatt carefully navigated through many more intersections, fighting the flow of water that beckoned them toward more Dragon's Breath. With each new turn the stone walls grew further apart, making it much harder for the merchants to steer with the gaffs. Each turn felt like it was supposed to be the last, opening to some still bay, but instead it was just faster water, sharper stone, and stiffer nerves. Whisper unfastened a button of her blouse to ease the feeling of being strangled by the current's intent. The air swept across her collarbone and opened her lungs, a sudden and welcome reprieve accompanied by the widening of the river's mouth. *The Fear* spat them out into open water, dark and still, the silhouette of another smaller island lay in the faint light of growing dawn.

Kismet flicked his head at Lau Lau, who quickly scurried to the bow of the ship. "This is the second trial of the Bone Grove, *The Dance*," he said, "because you need to know the steps."

Lau Lau closed her eyes and focused on the waterscape, holding her hand outstretched. Wherever she pointed, Djagatt would adjust his heading. Whisper didn't see anything in the water, but it was clear they were carefully avoiding something as they weaved without rhythm or rhyme.

Kismet took a deep breath of his pipe and focused carefully, calculating and approving of each change in direction as though he already knew it was correct and was using Lau Lau's psychic ability as reassurance. "In the coves surrounding the Bone Grove there are monsters that nest in the weeds below. They're sirens, and they are extremely territorial. All captains in my fleet are taught how to navigate them and we use Lau Lau to keep our maps current, because if we get too close to a nest the sirens will climb aboard and devour everyone without a trace." He sighed a curl of thick smoke. "Many boats in my fleet floated to shore, empty, before we got it right." No ship of Carver's had ever conquered *The Fear*, but who knew what Blackrock's demon was capable of. This time, even if Carver managed to navigate all the way he expected the Dragon's Breaths would claim at least a few ships. He wished he could see the look on Carver's face when the first siren crawls aboard. His teeth bit the stem of his pipe as he smiled.

The island ahead jutted up into the sky like a sleeping volcano. Steep edges plummeted from an open mouth, covered in veils of vibrant vegetation that skirted the mountainside, twinkling with fading fireflies in the first breath of dawn. The *Windborn Chance* approached a wide river, which appeared to lead inland toward the mountain.

A loud *thump* struck the boat, but its course did not waver.

Whisper looked over the edge to see what they had hit—there was nothing but the dark abyss of black water, though a strange sheen seemed to glimmer like clean silk, waving in the current beneath them. She squinted and leaned further over the rail, only to be pulled back onto the deck by Kismet, who shook his head. "This is the third trial, *The Shallowdeep*."

"Beneath this water, there is another world." Lau Lau had returned from the bow. If she was trying to instil fear in Whisper she wasn't doing a good job, her excitement and curiosity slipped in the tone of her voice. "The silver in the water is where the ocean ends and the other world begins. The *Windborn Chance* is light enough to float above it, but any boat whose hull sinks deep enough to touch it will fall though. Whole ships have disappeared without a trace."

"Why can't I look over the edge?"

"Anglers," she replied, making claws with her hands and a snarly face. "They live in the lower world and can't breathe our water, so they use long, spiny tongues to catch food and pull it down through the barrier. If a boat were to fall into the lower world, the anglers would snatch the crew while they swam for land."

Whisper wanted to poke her head over the ledge again. Her curiosity to see one was far stronger than her fear of getting speared through the face. She didn't though, much to her chagrin. The more she heard about the Bone Grove, the more it reminded her of everything she read about Setsuha, the forbidden realm where everything wants to kill you. Strange creatures, dangerous territories, and humans at the very bottom of the food chain. It was as though someone took her old Setsuhan tomes, scrawled out the name and replaced it. "Is there anything in the Bone Grove that won't try to kill me?"

Lau Lau thought a moment and perked spritely. "We have berries that make you warm when you're cold!"

Djagatt interrupted from the helm. "That's because they're poisonous, child."

"Oh—then no."

28

CORNBREAD AND CHANTILLY

A cornbread muffin sat lonesome on a platter of thin steel—its golden crust glistened amidst the curls of sweet steam, fresh and fragrant. The edges of its top were crisp with butter, ready to crumble upon one's palate at first bite, barely managing to stay perfect under its own weight upon the plate, but it was. The faintest scent of orange zest wrapped around the rising vapors, two likely lovers in a dissipating dance that lingered forevermore. It was an invisible story, told by either the cornbread muffin or the chantilly cream to its left. Light, fluffy, and whipped to a perfect curl, it nested in the comfort of a deep spoon while it awaited its destined union.

Salem hadn't eaten for days and food was becoming more and more poetic with every growl of his stomach. Never had he thought he'd miss being a Setsuhan—a construct of the living mountain—no hunger, no sickness. With flesh, blood, and purpose came pain, desire, and necessity. More so, the last twenty years of his emotional journey as a human now seemed only a fraction of what he now felt since losing Whisper. It was bittersweet; crimson flora with petals sharp as blades and petals sweet as honey.

He spied the cornbread muffin from the shadows of a blazing cast iron oven, deep in the galley of the *Last Breath*. The heat was almost unbearable. Sweat drenched the oil of his hair and slithered into his stinging eyes, but it was the darkest spot and therefore the safest. The second round of crew had finished their evening meal—a whirlwind of gnashing teeth and sloppy lips that left any remains entirely unidentifiable—and the cooks struggled to clean the mess. It seemed almost a worse job than emptying chamber pots, where at least the mess was confined to a single spot. Here, potatoes marked the ceiling, bone shards were stuffed in the cracks of the tables, and moist grog coated everything in a sticky film that always seemed to elude the dampest of cloth. Only one cook remained near the ovens and Salem could already feel the butter and cornmeal crumble against his cracking lips.

Deep, thunderous footsteps entered the room—the floorboards trembled beneath Salem. It was all too familiar and he knew to remain as still and quiet as possible. A broad, muscular man approached the counter, the very same who had answered the harrow shrike's calls in the hold. This was the closest they had ever gotten and with new light came many features Salem hadn't noticed the first time.

The broad man was covered head to toe in slick, rippling scars, more than he had seen in the poor light of their first encounter. The serpentine rivers of pink flesh Salem recalled were simply the most prominent it seemed, as they coiled atop the canvass of burnt flesh with wordless tales of anguish and rage. The canvass of scars were not the long, straight and tidy kind men liked as trophies to showcase their fortitude, but a veil of wet cottons scrunched in handfuls. He was clothed in it. The man was without shirt, the scars twisting every inch of flesh, yet he wore it as a loud warning. No man looked upon him in condescension, but rather a fearful respect if they stomached a look at all. Anything once vulnerable had been seared from him, leaving only salted hide and a jaw for crushing walnuts. He had fists like anvils, arms like masts, and eyes that wouldn't blink once while popping someone like a blueberry. He walked even heavier than he looked and, despite his size, the closer he neared the cornbread muffin the more Salem began to convince himself he could kill this leviathan of gnarled leather if he dared try to eat it.

"Blackrock, sir." The cook bowed, veering his eyes from the twisted mess of glossy skin. His voice shuddered faintly as he cowered, "I'll fetch your shrike's evening meal." The cook couldn't have retreated into the storage pantry any quicker.

Blackrock looked down at the muffin, so tiny next to him it almost made Salem feel disappointed. Blackrock expressed no interest in the morsel, though the idea of eating it seemed almost hilarious—his sausage fingers plucking at it like a single rogue hair, his other hand delicately spreading the chantilly without the whole thing surrendering to his presence and bursting in some strange cornbread muffin suicide.

Salem smiled. It was the little things that kept him sane next to the heat of the oven, or perhaps they were the first signs he was slipping. It was just so hot, the cook was taking so long... and he was so, so hungry. His draconian heart, filling his veins with draconian blood, was overwhelming him with draconian emotion, making it terribly hard to remain patient. Dragons eat when they command it.

Blackrock turned his head and looked directly at Salem, still with sudden suspicion. Short of willing the shadows to engulf him whole, Salem neither moved nor breathed, and Blackrock stared directly into his emerald eyes. Neither waivered nor blinked; a crack of embers threw Salem's pulse into his throat. The light faded and the distance between them seemed to close as the room oppressed Salem with heavy air and dark intentions.

The cook returned from storage and dropped a quarter boar on the counter with a smack, interrupting their standoff and setting the room back in place. The joints of the meat had begun to develop a sickly brown and green, but Salem imagined the shrike was fine with it. It was a demon after all and life couldn't always be fresh blood and virgins.

Blackrock looked at the quarter boar and then back in Salem's direction. His eyes shifted bit-by-bit, surveying the side of the oven for something he thought was once there but was no longer. Salem slowly exhaled as Blackrock's eyes failed to meet his a second time and, if the massive man continued to wonder, he certainly didn't show it, grabbing the quarter boar with his anvil hand and turning to exit. It wasn't his ship and the crew weren't his brothers. In fact, nothing about the *Last Breath* commanded his loyalty but coin, so why should he care if some unfortunate fool happened to be stowed and starving.

The cook wiped his hands on his apron, filthy with stains of brown and red, and watched silently as Blackrock ducked beneath the doorframe and exited. He exhaled sharply, relieved, and spotted the gleam of steel in the corner of his eye. The plate was empty, only a light scattering of crumbs remained from the muffin's vanquishing, and the spoon laid on its side with flecks of cream in only the deepest nooks. The cook collected the plate and turned back to the door of the hall—Blackrock had a far more delicate palate than he imagined.

Salem flopped onto the bed of his chambers, sure to claim each lingering crumb that might have been hiding in the corner of his lips. It was dark out. Too dark to see where he was, but he tried nonetheless. From his porthole the occasional ship in Carver's fleet was spotted, but they would always fall back to the wake. Salem hadn't been on deck once in his journey, as the risk was too great. Even the galley was a gamble, but with his growing hunger he had little choice. The last time routine patrol inspected his room his stomach almost gave away his hiding spot.

With his stomach temporarily satisfied his mind began to race, different rivers of thought all winding in different directions. His next excursion beyond the relative safety of his room required planning, timing, patience, and forethought. The need to navigate kept his senses restless, analysing every new scent, sound, and sight in hopes of determining where they were and where they were headed. The yearning in his chest not only ached but unwound him the closer he neared Whisper. His constant struggle with the draconian emotion kept him uncomfortably liminal, ensnared between foreign and familiar despite his persistence in picking the emotions clean with infallible logic.

He closed his eyes and clutched his head, so many sounds and thoughts—too many.

'*This is the longest you've been sober.*' Savrae-Lyth knew exactly why Salem ailed most.

'*My thoughts run too rampant and now I have emotions to consider as well.*'

'*Dare we steal some rum?*'

'*I am considering it.*' The grog had a bit of rum in it, but not enough to still his nerves. He needed a bottle of pure liquor, but the captain kept it under strict lock and key in his cabin. Only when new grog was being prepared could a bottle be taken, even then, only by the head cook.

'*Your withdrawal has reached its peak. Perhaps your need will decline now.*'

'*Convenient as that would be, I do not think the* Last Breath *is the best place for such an optimistic experiment.*'

Salem stared at the ceiling and forced himself to focus, his teeth grinding. Above his bed was a narrow slit, from a sharp blade perhaps. He squinted, channelling such desperate intent it could have burst into flame. Slow, deep breaths exited his aching chest and the world funnelled into that one, single gash in the wood. The room began to quiet his heart to a tempo he could manage and he closed his eyes. It was the only way he'd been able to sleep, that blemish burnt into his eyelids—the only thing he could see or hear. Force of will was barely working and stupid ideas were becoming more and more appealing under the guise of rationale. Perhaps a trip to the captain's quarters wasn't as difficult as he once concluded. At the very least, it was becoming worth it.

29

WIND AND WATER

With a spin of the ship's wheel, Djagatt passed a jut of forested stone and turned the *Windborn Chance* into an open bay. Six other ships were already anchored there and floated in wait for Kismet. They were the entirety of his modest fleet and were manned with a skeleton crew while the bulk of them were on leave. Half the ships appeared to be 'borrowed' from Emberwilde's fleet—redwood railings and crimson sails. They were even continuing to fly Emberwilde colors. The figureheads of winged women stretched from the bow with open arms, welcoming forth their unsuspecting prey. Along each side of the hulls were long slats where it looked as though the planks could be removed, but Whisper couldn't imagine what for.

The remaining ships were much larger and heavier, but long and narrow, with massive bows that tapered to form a blade that submerged into the water—beneath the surface the blade stretched outward in front of the boat as one grievous, hidden tine. They seemed capable of incredible speed at the cost of maneuverability. The ships had many masts, all of which had dark sails and flags with a bone white dragon's skull—Kismet's crimson honeycomb blade protruded from its mouth like a blast of inextinguishable flame. It was the first time she had seen the sigil of the Bone Grove Merchants and it was far more menacing than what she imagined.

Whisper's eyes looked beyond the towering masts and bundled sails to the forest beyond. Deep green trees blanketed the inlet from the stony drop of the water's edges to the towering peak behind. While they sailed through *The Dance* and *The Shallowdeep*, the mountain at the island's center first appeared to be a volcano—a single stretch of rigid stone that tapered as it reached up into the sky, cloaked in a canopy of leaves. The closer they floated, Whisper began to see that it wasn't a volcano at all, or if it was, it was no longer. *The Shallowdeep* took them around the cliffs, where the entire backside of the mountain was missing—a sheer drop from crest to coast that turned it into the curved face of half a monstrosity. It was as though the Fates had taken a perfectly good volcano, hollowed it dry, and tore it in half.

Lau Lau took Whisper's hand and tugged it, guiding her to the bow of the *Windborn Chance*. "Look," Lau Lau said, pointing into the water, "that one's Palindross."

Whisper squinted as they approached something white in the water. The name meant nothing to her, but it sounded inherently draconian. As the object drew closer she began to understand why. Passing beneath them was the skeleton of a dragon. Its ribs arched like spires that dared to pierce the surface of the water. Its head a hollowed relic of angled teeth and forgotten menace. Soon there was another and then another, each a more twisted petrification of the draconian tragedy than the last. Their broken claws and eel infested spines littered the seabed. Lau Lau could name every one of them.

"How did all these dragons get here?"

Lau Lau stopped naming the lost. "Wind and Water, right Kissy?"

Kismet tapped his pipe on the rails and sprinkled the ash into the water. "After the war there were so many corpses the realms didn't know what to do with them. They took their skin, some used the bones, but the rest was either toxic or tough. Kings, queens, and tribal lords threw the bodies in the ocean like some disgraceful tithe, but Wind and Water took pity on the dragons and embraced them with her currents, guiding them here so they'd always be together; then guided me, so they'd always be remembered."

"Wind and Water," Whisper repeated softly the names of the lesser gods, "I never took you for religious."

Kismet stowed his pipe into his lapel pocket. "Praising the gods for taking you as you are is religion, Whisper, but serving the gods because they make you a better person... that's true worship."

"What do I call you then? Worshiper? Priest? Avatar?"

"I'm whatever Wind and Water wishes." He spied her cautiously in the corner of his eyes as she tread on thin ice. "To you, Kismet will do just fine. *Master* is better. *Captain* would be ideal."

Whisper laughed slyly. "Careful, I might start calling you Kissy just to keep your feet on the ground." She winked at Lau Lau, who laughed nervously at the joke. Even Yoru seemed to shake her little head. Whisper smiled cleverly to herself—she thought it was hilarious—and then she saw something that wiped her face clean. The *Windborn Chance*'s figurehead, a beautiful woman in flowing robes, was casting a reflection upon the water that was entirely different. A near-luminescent figure of another woman stretched in the water— the ripples on the surface made her sway as though she were dancing in the waves. Whisper stretched to peer beneath the figurehead as best she could, but it was not crafted for such a reflection, and it was lost on her how she hadn't noticed it until now. The woman's dance hypnotized her, somehow filling her with something that left no room for ignorance.

There was only one dock and it was reserved exclusively for the *Windborn Chance*, stretching across the water like a royal carpet of wind-worn splinters. Half a dozen men waited for the lines and once the heavy mooring ropes were thrown overboard and collected they began pulling them in.

Whisper and Lau Lau disembarked first, at Djagatt's command. The Daggermouth would remain with the ship for now, overseeing the restocking of supplies and arranging the transportation of their dead. With so much business to attend, the two would just be in the way. Kismet followed them, and Yoru followed him. He stepped onto the plank and floated down the wobbles to the dock, acknowledging his men with a tip of his hat in passing.

"Come, let me show you what you will be saving," Kismet said, striding the dock with a surprising air of trepidation. His boots hit the earth of the Bone Grove and what glimmer he once had began to fade, his heart already yearning to be back on the water with the wind in his face. Earth and stone carried a tune he didn't care to dance to.

Kismet guided Whisper along a short trail that led into the trees, the scent of fresh dew still lingered with the dawn. Small speckled deer sprung through the brush in surprise, while cooing quail scurried on blurry legs with their family of tiny chicks, no bigger than a thumb—their little feathered tufts bobbed furiously as they panicked and dashed into the ferns.

Off the beaten path, Whisper spotted the speckled gray of a statue covered in rich green moss and ivy—two women with flowing hair and airy robes danced in each other's arms, the fabric of their gowns wrapped over and under to create a circle around them. At the base was a stone bowl filled with rainwater and flower petals.

"Is that a shrine?"

"It is," Kismet replied. "To Wind and Water. My one and only."

"You know there's two of them, right?"

If the intention was to trip him up, it didn't work. "Wind and Water are depicted as two maidens, but they are truly one. Wisdom and philosophy, cleverness and luck. A delicate dance between elements that create a union so pure they become one entity."

It wasn't lost on her that Kismet had referred to the Wind and Water as entities before and she recalled their likeness in the figurehead of the *Windborn Chance*—the woman of airy splendor whose reflection cast another woman dancing along the surface of the water beneath her. Whisper couldn't recall any faiths about the Wind or Water from her education at the monastery. There was a big difference between *faith* and *truth* in Elanta. The Fates, the Chitin Kings, even the Shén Shé god Sha'maielle, all were worshipped, but their existence was also proven and inarguable. These were *truths*. Whereas *faith* was belief in the absence of fact. If there was one true *faith* in Elanta, it was in Shiori Etrielle. Many believe she is the creator of the world, but without proof it could not be *truth*.

Lau Lau read Whisper's cynicism and took her hand. "Together,

Wind and Water become the spirit of the sea. They rule everything below and above the water's horizons."

"But they're not real," Whisper replied, feeling almost blasphemous as the figurehead emblazoned behind her eyelids, "are they?"

Kismet shot her a look in the corner of his eye. Lau Lau squeezed her hand tighter. "*Faith* makes things real to those who have it," the child said sweetly, "and it rewards peace and bounty to those who seek it."

"I had *faith* I could beat Kismet with a sword, yet I couldn't. Are you saying it's because his is stronger than mine?"

The young girl knew Whisper was being closed-minded and brash, looking for a soft spot to prod because she could never be content with the wisdom of silence. Lau Lau smiled softly nonetheless. Belief was an abstract dance, whose steps could only be learned by moving your feet and trusting where they land. "*Faith* isn't about making something true," the child said, "it's about finding the strength to weather truth itself."

Whisper nodded as the shrine passed from view. She wanted to argue something moot, tugging at her chains to hurt something inside or out, but she refrained. Instead, she pressed her destructive nature down into the darkest parts of her lungs, the parts you could only reach with the full breaths of enlightenment. Even she knew that something as powerful as belief shouldn't be trifled with in the company of allies, lest she become stranded on this impossibly fortified graveyard.

The trees began to open at the base of the mountain. Buildings of wood, bone, and thatch made a small village that surrounded a communal fire pit large enough to spit a dire wolf. There was a large storehouse, where merchants hauled provisions and stored their stolen wares; a forge, where a blacksmith and his apprentice took blazing red iron from a kiln and hammered it into braces and fastenings; and a mill of felled trees, where a dozen burley merchants stripped bark and sawed new rails and planks.

Carver had the largest pirate fleet in Elanta and he was quick to establish a pirate's reputation as being bloodthirsty seafarers, albeit two oars short of a rowboat. As Whisper walked the Bone Grove she was surrounded by anything but. Humble tanners tethered skins and laced leathers, their eyes and hearts calm with peace in loyalty, seeking nothing more than adventure and an excuse to master their craft in the harshest of environments. Lithe corsairs, kempt and clean, honed their blades around the fire while they sung slow shanties—the hilts gracefully floated in their hands like bows of violins, ready to create an orchestration of singing steel. Even the drunkards didn't seem to have a spec of malice in their veins, cheering and laughing while they made asses of themselves.

Whisper sized everybody, one by one, and imagined her strategy if confronted—a favored shoulder, a slight limp, a lazy eye—fissures she was a master at clasping and tearing asunder. Despite the loss of her supernatural vision, her instincts seemed sharper than normal. Since her outburst on the *Windborn Chance*, something monstrous continued to lurk within her. Sometimes it hid at the base of her neck, quick to tingle her skin whenever someone was watching her. Other times it nested in her chest, drinking her anxiety and filling her with predatory focus. She knew it was only a matter of time before whatever stirred beneath her skin showed its face once more. She could feel its hunger as it tasted the air for blood or as it spied a pack of humans and imagined who would be first to fall behind if pursued. The irony was not lost on her—a whole island of pirates and she was the madcap.

"... we take them to Shén Shé to be enchanted." Kismet's voice faded in from the aether like a bank of fog. He had been speaking the whole time, but Whisper was caught up eyeballing the toughest merchant she could spot.

"Sorry, what?" Whisper said.

"I'm hard pressed to tell if you're just daft or disrespectful."

"You brought me here to see and I'm seeing. If you wanted me to listen too, then your cat should have negotiated better."

Lau Lau politely chimed from behind. "She's an elantan velv—"

"You know I know that, right?" Whisper interrupted sharply.

Lau Lau's tone dropped as she kicked the dirt. "Yeah. I know."

Kismet began to repeat what he tried to tell her earlier. "The Bone Grove Merchants are comprised of every race in Elanta. Even the Shén Shé enchant our boats in exchange for literature. This has been our home for many years."

"What color was your feather?" Whisper asked.

Kismet stopped abruptly, his eyes lowering down to Lau Lau, who simply shrugged as she denied his silent accusations.

Whisper crossed her arms. "Relax, she didn't tell me anything."

Kismet sighed heavily. "I'm from Whitewater—"

"Nope. You have red eyes."

Kismet pulled his tricorne down a little further. "I moved to Blackthorne and worked the plum groves for my father—"

"Nope again. You're too well educated."

"I apprenticed for a merchant of coin and had my first business managing freight at the Blackthorne docks—"

Whisper shook her head. "Your gait is too refined."

"—then I learned the art of swordplay to protect myself in—"

"You're far too skilled to have learned swordplay in adulthood. Are we going to do this all day? I can't guarantee I won't lose my patience."

"Why do you suddenly care?"

Whisper tilted her neck to her shoulder with a crick. "Because I'm supposed to kill someone, who apparently wants to kill you. Understanding your history tells me more about them. The only thing I can't seem to figure is your rank before you left the military in Emberwilde and I need to know because highly ranked officials often have highly skilled enemies."

Kismet chuckled; Whisper smiled with dead eyes. His skin had a tone of northern Emberwilde. His connection to the sea probably placed him west of the orange groves. His accent had a hint of highborn noble and his swordplay was a result of rigorous training, possibly even before academic enrolment. He had finesse with his blade and footwork uncommon even to the Red Quill style—there had to be more she didn't know.

Kismet sighed and looked among his crew, his voice falling soft enough to reach only her ears as he leaned close enough to brush her cheek with the bristle of his jaw. The heat of his breath carried a stillness that stopped Whisper's heart, her eyes slowly widening as he spoke.

Whisper took a step back and fumbled with her words. "You're..." her head shook in disbelief and she ran her hand through her hair to still her thoughts. Soon, she was laughing. "By fate... you moron. How have you managed to survive this long?"

Kismet tipped his hat, a nervous and forced smile poorly feigning innocence. "Now you see me."

Lau Lau choked back a lump in her throat as she felt Whisper's aura shift into something nauseously smothering, a toxic concoction of fear and bloodlust that was both exciting and terrifying at once.

Whisper gathered her words, barely. "You're way more trouble than I need right now. Fates, you're in worse than I've ever been and I *literally* have a Fate and their Instrument hunting me. A god and her lackey, Kismet, not to mention the Orbweavers, maybe even more. If I kill Blackrock I'll have all of bloody Emberwilde nipping at my heels also." She took a deep breath, one that trickled down and awoke the destruction she had suppressed earlier. Her excitement roiled as the creature within her stalked through her veins, tingling every hair as it prowled beneath her skin, its claws setting her spirit ablaze. It was the worst idea fathomable, but now she wanted to kill Blackrock more than anything, and she was certain she wouldn't be able to contain herself. "Shit."

30

VOID, VENOM, AND STONE: FEVER VS. BLACKROCK

Carver removed his spectacles from the end of his nose and squinted with wrinkled eyes, carefully cleaning the round glass with the lapel of his charcoal suit jacket. In his cabin, the soft flicker of orange light danced from a lantern atop the table, where a map of Elanta's eastern shores laid open amidst curls of parchment and old texts. A compass box, heavy and broad, held flat the furthest edge; the compass bobbed gently with the sway of the ship. He held his glasses to the light and examined them, peering down the bridge of his nose as he evaluated with intense scrutiny. Despite his age and history of ruthlessness, his hands were as still and cold as his cunning. Some people never get used to the bloodshed, but he was born to it.

He carefully slid the spectacles back onto his face and turned toward a small cast iron stove, fat with glowing red coals that made the room nearly too uncomfortable for the three piece wool suit. A soft groan slipped his lips, giving way to his old knees as he crouched before it and stirred the coals with an iron rod. The cartilage in his fingers ground like sand as he loosened his cravat and began to unbutton his vest. He withdrew the iron rod, its tip glowing raw and angry—the heat emanated across the hard edges of his features as he looked at it closely, almost sad. "They say the eyes are the gateway to the soul," he said softly. Carver's knees rattled as he rose and gently blew on the blazing iron to peak its quiet rage.

Closest to the entrance, where the lantern light refused to reach in full, one of Carver's crewmen sat bound to a chair. His eyes fearfully narrowed as best they could through the grievous swelling of his face. The crewman's cheeks were bulbous and red, crushing inward as though his skull were trying to engulf his eyes completely. In the far corner, skirting the light and observing from the veil of shadow, Blackrock crossed his leathery arms across his chest and remained completely silent.

Carver began to approach the crewman, gently waving the rod to each side of the man's face. The heat aggravated the inflamed flesh in ways only a fit of tremors and pleas could express. "I do wonder though," Carver continued, "if I burn the eyes from your head, is your soul trapped forever?" A thin smile stretched across his face, the corners of his eyes curling with elation. "Your tongue will be taken last, so you have lots of time to tell me."

Carver placed his hand on the man's head and pried his eyelids wide. The hot glow of searing iron neared slowly. The blaze of unforgiving red grazed the eyelashes, curling the fine hairs in a death of acrid smoke. The crewman ground his teeth, all trembles and sweat and fear, when a cry sounded from beyond the doors. Carver stopped, the heat from the rod so close it may as well have been in the man's skull.

"Captain!" a voice called clearly from the main deck.

Carver looked to Blackrock and gestured with a flick of his head, to which the massive beast of twisted skin lumbered across the room and opened the door. Carver's eyes still seemed gleeful in the moments before he left, assuring the bound man of his prompt return. "Hold this," he said, plunging the searing hot iron into the man's leg and leaving it there. He turned and exited, burning flesh and bellows of agony to mark his departure.

As Carver and Blackrock stepped into the night they were quickly oppressed with a deeper darkness, shadows stretching and pooling from every source of lantern light. The midnight air turned heavy as cream and thick as smoke, obscuring the world around them in a haze of churning shadow. The darkness coalesced into a pool of deep void and peeling herself from the sticky strands of living shadow was a woman of golden curls and ocean blue eyes.

The darkness poured over Fever's curves. Her robe hung loosely over her arms and barely around her waist, baring the heat kissed Emberwilde skin of her shoulders and chest, leaving little to the imagination. Held to her breasts she clasped Jury's cthonomantic tome, the scent of old blood and leather wafted up to her nose and made her bare gleaming white teeth in a smile of something dark and otherworldly. She gently flicked her head to bounce her curls from her brow and examined the crew surrounding her—her teeth bit her bottom lip, elated with the idea of play and bloodshed.

Carver's voice cut through the darkness as the shadows began to recede. "Who are you?"

Fever's ears tingled. She recognized the tone of a sociopath when she heard one. "Who are you?"

Though rife with suspicion, Carver recognized the robes as Orbweaver attire and opted for a touch more civility in his address. Besides, otherworldly she may be, there were hundreds of them and only one of her. If she was looking for trouble she was likely to drown in it. "I am Carver, Captain of the Fleet of Sunken Links."

"Really?" Fever tilted her head curiously, "You're so old."

He chuckled politely, unsure how to react. He'd flayed men for lesser transgressions. "And who might you be?"

Fever looked around, ignorant of his question. "Where is Blackrock?"

One of Carver's six remaining mercenaries approached her with heavy steps, his long greasy hair coiled down a brow made for beating and a chin that would sooner break the fist striking it. His voice was a low rumble of menace and calculated executions, "Captain asked you a ques —"

Before he could finish, two ichor serpents lashed out from Fever's black diamond bangles and ensnared each of his legs, lifted him into the air, and ripped him in two, snapping him at the groin like a dry wishbone. Blood spattered across the crew as the mercenary wailed in pain, still tragically conscious as each piece of him was flung overboard. The serpents slithered back into the sleeves of her robe. Fever basked in the silent mortification, where not a single breath dared leave a wary lung, until a terrible thought crossed her mind and she placed her hand delicately across her red lips. "Fates, that wasn't him, was it?"

With a low rumble like distant thunder, Blackrock pushed his way through the crew—his burnt flesh a landscape of dark crevices in the light. "I'm Blackrock."

Fever eyed him up and down. His suffering brought the glint of appeal into the blue of her irises and she caught herself smiling slyly. "Of course you are." She approached him on the pads of her bare feet, silent as venom. "You certainly look the part," she said sweetly as she stepped around, evaluating him from top to bottom, "but do you know what it is you've gotten yourself into?"

"Who are you?" he rumbled.

"Can't you tell, love?" she smiled, gently dragging a fingertip along her collarbone. "Every citizen of Emberwilde should know, though I have changed a little."

Blackrock's eyes didn't move, betraying an answer he already knew, "Fever."

A wave of whispers and wide eyes washed over the crew, leaving very few who did not recognize the name. The attention tingled across Fever's skin with a soft shudder. "In the flesh."

"Did Ogra send you?"

Fever laughed. "He should have."

If Blackrock was being goaded he certainly wasn't showing it. His cold, dark eyes neither wavered nor flinched. "Then why are you here?"

"Oh, haven't you heard? I'm an Instrument now, and if I'm here it means the Fates themselves think you're going to fail. Maybe even die." Fever expected Blackrock to chuckle in hubris, as the big ones often did—he did not.

"I think I'll be just fine," he said.

"Oh love," Fever pouted, an ichor serpent glided up his body and rested on his shoulder. "You will die, make no mistake, I'm simply curious how long you'll last." The serpent struck like lightning, its fangs dripping with Bedlam Thistle, but as it struck Blackrock's skin its head burst against a spine of obsidian that tore from his flesh.

With a flex of his massive frame, razor shards of black glass rent his twisted skin until every inch of him was covered—a hulking mass of shimmering ebon blades. Even his eyes seemed to turn to slate, dull and lifeless. "As I said, I think I'll be just fine."

Fever's eyes softened as a dark smile crooked in the corner of her lips. She held the tome out to her side, let it fall to the deck with a heavy *thud*, and tucked her hands into her robe sleeves. "Come then, let's see what you've got."

Salem's ears perked to the sound of commotion, crewman hustled through the corridors to the main deck. He peered out the porthole, but there was no sign of land yet. A sudden thump rumbled above him, specs of dust sprinkling down into his hair.

"What, by fate?" he whispered, peering upward, wondering what was causing such commotion. Were they at the Bone Grove? Were they under attack? Has some creature of the deep come to claim them? There were too many questions, unanswerable from the confines of his room, leading him to a difficult decision. '*My queen,*' he called.

Savrae-Lyth's voice whispered in his head. '*Yes?*'

'*I need you to see what is happening.*'

'*Is that wise?*' she replied. '*If someone were to sense my presence we could be caught.*'

Salem was well aware of the risk, but if they were under siege it was more important to know sooner than later, before their door was kicked in or the ship was scuttled. '*We have no choice. You go above deck and see what is happening and I will sneak back to the kitchen to capitalize on the distraction.*'

Emanating outward from him like the manifestation of aura, the room filled with the electric roil of vibrant pink and white peach blossoms. The perfume of Freestone softened his senses while the tingle of electricity raced across his skin. Coalescing from the static in lightning turned flesh was the long, feathered cloak of Savrae-Lyth, cascading down her shoulders as electricity crackled across her golden plumage. The brilliant scarlet of her almond eyes flared brightly, the draconian pupils surrounded by the iconic silver blossom lacunae. *'Are you sure?'*

Salem nodded without hesitation, hunger and the vice of knowledge commanding him entirely. He strode to the door and slipped into the shadows of fallen silk to avoid any further discussion on the matter.

Savrae-Lyth raised her hand to her face as though she were placing a masque, igniting the halo of blazing blue fire that wrapped around her eyes, giving her the **All Sight** technique of her namesake. The lazy flame flicked slowly, turning over itself and letting her sense everything her aura of static could touch. She looked up, opened her arms and, with a thundering crackle only Salem could hear, her body transformed into a blast of phantom lightning that folded into itself. The web of lightning opened in the sky like an eye, high above the *Last Breath*, and Savrae-Lyth reformed in a snap of blinding light. She stood on the air as though it were solid earth, her cloak of vibrant feathers hung down past her feet in defiance of the former. It would take someone with a superior sensitivity to energy to sense her presence and it didn't appear anyone had. In fact, if anyone on the deck were capable of such a feat, they were far too distracted to notice.

Lashes of ichor serpents, dark as the void, whipped across the obsidian blades of Blackrock's body as he charged her, his footsteps thundering. The serpents bore no effect on his magnitude or momentum, shredding into strands of shadow and venom before dissipating back into the aether. Fever was far too nimble to be caught by Blackrock's bulk, easily tumbling aside. She flicked out both arms and ensnared him with a dozen more serpents, wrapping him several times over, and though he slowed for a moment he tore through the bindings with little effort and continued his assault.

Savrae-Lyth's cloak of feathers opened wide, stretching out to each side of her. From the outside, the cloak was a beautiful cascade of green, red, yellow, blue, and violet, but the inside shimmered of plain white silk. She raised her hands to her chest and entwined her fingers, summoning two blazing eyes of scarlet flame, opening on the canvas, one to each side of her—large, draconian, and burning like unquenchable wildfire, not that unlike her own. This was her master technique, the most feared in the world, and that which commanded her place as the Queen of Drakes—the *Gaze of Brittle Chains*. Many thought it was the reason the Fates decided to destroy the dragons, fearful of its power and potential. The *Gaze of Brittle Chains* allowed her to look at anyone, anything, and determine exactly how to destroy it.

The blazing scarlet eyes upon her cloak showered their gaze down upon the *Last Breath*, scouring every soul for that which would undo them best. With her **All Sight** halo she could identify both combatants by name, but with her *Gaze of Brittle Chains* she could peer directly into their souls.

Blackrock was as formidable as he seemed, bearing very few weaknesses, but an easy kill if she were still alive. However, Fever was a surprise. Though still mortal enough by all definition, with the obvious physical reinforcement all Instruments were graced with, her serpentine power seemed to emit a large field of heat sensitivity that was so innately reflexive landing any mortal wound would require a combination of distance, surprise, precision, and extreme speed. It was the only way to penetrate the lightning quick response and unfathomable awareness her power granted—a fragile body with a near perfect defense. The only other weakness Savrae-Lyth could see was that Fever had power she still hadn't realized, but as a glowing sigil began to ignite across Blackrock's chest she was certain Fever was about to learn something new.

Blackrock thrust his chest forward, sending a low thrumming blast of blazing red energy to sear the golden locks from her head. Fever's eyes dilated. Fear, elation, or both, it was all too sudden to be certain, but she knew she wasn't quick enough to avoid the beam. She raised her hands to cover her face and braced for the worst, when the ichor serpents of her black diamond bangles opened their little maws and drank. The beam of blazing light syphoned into smaller strands of churning turpitude, funneling into the void of the serpents' open mouths as they devoured the energy until there was nothing left.

Fever opened her eyes as her serpents consumed the last fleck of dancing embers and felt something strange surge throughout her body. Heat beneath her skin, fire razing through her veins. She felt powerful, invincible; brimming with an uncontrollable and intoxicating force of nature that pounded against her ribcage as it begged to be released. The blue of her eyes shimmered with orange leylines and with a flick of her open hand the serpents bore their fangs and fired the beams of searing red energy back.

The energy struck Blackrock, slid his massive frame along the deck and pressed him to the rails, the beams of light and fire flickered angrily across the sharp obsidian ridges of his chest and face. He raised his hands to block a few, the flame turning molten as it dripped and trickled through his fingers. The serpents ran dry with the last lick of fire and his body glowed shades of red, yellow, and orange, the obsidian blades angry and fierce.

Fever examined her bangles, awe glinting in her eyes. The leylines were gone, drained from her body in her last attack, leaving an emptiness she didn't realize she had and the residual burn of power that once was. She yearned for it immediately. Thirsted for it. Begged to be overwhelmed. Her sudden need filled her with intolerance and before Blackrock could regain his wits she wrapped serpents around his ankles, anchored herself to both deck and mast with strands of living void, and used every ounce of will and strength to tip him over the edge of the ship.

Blackrock plunged into the water, the cold hissed against his glow. His massive weight caused him to quickly sink and forced him to return to his human form, scrambling to the surface only to have Fever's serpents bury their fangs in his flesh and pump him full of Bedlam Thistle. He fell immediately helpless, flailing in all directions as his body revolted against him and inverted all his senses. He felt like he was falling as Fever pulled him from the water, and he thought he was being thrown into the sky as she dropped him on the deck.

Savrae-Lyth watched carefully, sizing Fever as though she were her next opponent—plotting her angle, planning her strategy. Fever was beginning to realize she could redirect energy attacks, but what she had yet to learn was that she had complete power over the chaos of the void itself, capable of manifesting replications of anything she absorbed. Fever could even devour and reproduce Blackrock's ability to turn her flesh to obsidian if her serpents were to consume some of his technique. It was fortunate she wasn't yet aware she could do that, but her instincts would guide her to the revelation eventually.

Fever smiled sweetly as her skin continued to tingle, the faint linger of fire still somewhere inside her like a forgotten word on the tip of a tongue. She gracefully walked to the tome and picked it up, clutching it to her breast. "I'll need a quiet place to work."

In a crackle of folding lightning, Savrae-Lyth teleported back inside the *Last Breath*, appearing at Salem's side as he sat in the middle of the floor, eyes wide like a child's. *'I got a whole ham!'* he thought gleefully, devouring it with voracity unbecoming of his usual refinement. Whether it was his starvation or the draconian instincts blooming in his blood, she wasn't quite sure, but he tore at it like he was dying and it was the cure.

'There is a terrible problem,' Savrae-Lyth's voice sung like a sad song. *'What happened?'*

'An altercation between two formidable powers. The man we saw in the hold with the harrow shrike, Blackrock, can cover his physical form in sharp stone and channel essence without drawing glyphs.'

'Interesting,' Salem thought, stopping for a moment as curiosity swept him. *'Can he be broken?'*

'Nothing short of honeycomb stone will do, I'm certain of it, but he isn't our biggest problem.'

Salem finished the last piece of ham, licking his fingers and sighing with complete satisfaction. The glaze of joy quickly hardened his eyes and what little indignity he once suffered disappeared completely. He straightened the high collar of his coat and adjusted his cuffs, combing his hair back as Setsuhans preened their feathers. As he once did, a feathered lifetime ago.

'There is an Instrument aboard, one I don't recognize. Her name is Fever, and she is a master of truths. I believe her to be one of Ivory's.'

Salem quickly paled. He'd definitely heard of her before and the news sat like a stone in his stomach. 'What do you mean by 'master of truths'?'

'*Truth is what is real. She can create reality from the chaos of the void.*'

'*I believe the void is called such because it is completely empty.*'

'*Humans label it the void because it lacks substance, but I assure you, it's a complex nexus of energy that is an endless source of creation for anyone able to form it.*'

'*So, Fever could be called a voidmage —*'

'*You know there's no such thing.*'

'*There are no masters of truths either. Voidmage simply sounds better.*'

Savrae-Lyth shook her head, astonished and impatient. '*You're missing the point here. We're in big trouble if she catches us.*'

'*Under normal circumstances I would be inclined to agree with you,*' Salem smiled sweetly, the emerald of his eyes gleamed their usual clever green, '*but we will be fine.*'

'*How are you so sure?*'

'*Her greatest strength has become her weakness. While Fever once acted in her own best interests, now she is thrall to a Fate. Regardless of whether or not she wishes to kill me, she will now be forced to consider Ivory's best interests, and Ivory wants us to work with her,*' he assured, reminding her of the advantage not having a fatespinner would have in a war against Fates, '*she just doesn't know it yet.*'

31

PURPOSE

Whisper stood in silence before the shrine to Wind and Water, the cool dark of night brought a dampness of mist and dew that slowly collected on the foliage around her. Though late, most of the merchants bustled in the distance, the soft glow of tall red fire illuminated above the treeline. They were preparing for the funerals of the lost and Whisper felt she was only in the way. A small part of her even felt responsible, but she was a professional at pushing those feelings down as deep as possible.

She wanted to touch the stone altar. Run her fingertips along the contour of the women's robes and sense the fluidity of their still dance beneath her hand. She didn't understand, but something inside her wanted to believe in something other than the Fates—believe in something that wasn't trying to take her life, but give it. She didn't know where to begin. Was she supposed to gift something? Kneel? Drink the water that collected in the basin? She felt stupid seeking some spiritual connection, searching for something to define her in a way that was neither blood nor vengeance.

Her heart sank with the thought of Salem. He would know what to do. Tell her whether to stand or kneel, profess aloud or speak in whispers. He'd have some grand explanation of the deities and their origins, filling her with a resolve she would pretend not to care about. She'd laugh at him, tease him for being a know-it-all, but grow a little more because of it.

She folded her hands, humbled before the altar. Too embarrassed to speak aloud she spoke in the safety of her mind, letting her thoughts ramble confused and disoriented. *'Wind and Water, or the Ocean... I'm not sure what you want to be called,'* she began awkwardly, *'I don't know what I want or why I'm talking to your altar, rock, thing, but I'm looking for something. Faith maybe? Peace?'* She looked around to make sure no one was watching her. *'I don't know what I'm looking for, but you know what I need. If you're so compelled, please guide me with the tides like you do for Kismet and I'll do everything in my power to protect your merchants.'*

A drop of water struck the still sheen of the basin, sending a cascade of ripples that bounced the light of distant fire, and Whisper's heart stilled. Was there enough dew to drip yet? Could something have fallen from the trees above or was it Wind and Water saying she was heard? The speculation of some divine act made her feel foolish and she unfolded her hands, embarrassed. In the corner of her eye was the shimmer of yellow-green—two tiny eyes watched her from the path. Pitch against the night, the shape of Yoru's black fur could be seen just enough as the velvetine bowed her little head and walked toward the docks on silent paws. Something compelled her to follow.

Whisper took one last look at the shrine, the water now still, leaving her to wonder if she imagined it entirely. With a sigh that beheld the faintest white puff of breath she turned and walked back to the path, spotted the outline of Yoru in the distance, and kept pace. The velvetine led her to a series of lit torches and a collection of merchants, all lined along the dock with Kismet, Lau Lau, and Djagatt at the very end. In their approach, the merchants gave berth to Yoru and, by proxy, Whisper.

At the end of the dock were a row of small reed baskets and in each was a metal urn sealed with the glow of sigils. The mysteriously luminous glyphs wrapped around the urns, pulsing and shifting like leylines of living energy. From this distance she couldn't tell what the symbols were or what they meant, but there was something familiar about the energy as it washed over her. It made her uneasy, built tension in her chest, churned her guts. A pungent film of ash and smoke coated her throat until her eyes began to water.

One reed basket remained empty, the last urn stood before it, lidless and hungry for the ashes of the fallen. Gentle winds danced at the mouth and the urn moaned softly. The last of the bodies was brought to the end of the dock atop a plank of iron and wood, the eerie glow of deep red light trickled beneath the corpse, wrapped tightly in sigiled cloth. The body was gently placed before the urn and the merchants bowed their heads.

Djagatt approached, near soundless for his size. The low-throated rumble of the Daggermouth dialect rolled over his jagged teeth like mist over mountain peaks, his words slowly blanketing them all with a ghostly presence. The world seemed thinner, as though she could reach out and use her fingertips to pierce through a veil into another. A deep red luminescence crawled across the body in a flicker of ghostly fire and in a sudden burst of spectral cinders the corpse arched its back and bellowed beneath the bindings.

Whisper panicked for a moment, glancing left and right to read the gathered crowd and determine if she should be worried. No one moved, but watched with something that the glint of sanguine light coerced from their eyes. Dedication. The body, bandages and all, began to dissolve into a stream of floating ash that wound through the air like a snake and began to funnel into the urn. Djagatt continued to incant beneath the noise—sputtered howls from decomposed vocal cords that cried in agony as its body and soul were devoured. There was no mistaking it now, the scent, the nausea, the blood light and living ash—this was necromancy.

Djagatt continued his incantation until the very last bit of fabric and flesh disintegrated, sealing the urn as the winding ash finished nesting within. He placed the urn into the last reed basket and he and Kismet carefully placed the baskets in the water, setting the urns adrift. The silence was deafening after such horrors, her soul bled across the gentle sound of trickling water as the urns drifted out into the draconian graveyard. The baskets eventually began to take on water and one by one the urns sunk below the surface.

"In death, merchants still serve the Bone Grove," Kismet cut through the bleeding stillness. "Wind and Water guide them, so they may guard us."

The bellows twisted in Whisper like a hot blade, and despite her better intentions amongst the grief-stricken brethren, her disapproval weighed heavily in her voice as she spoke. "Necromancy?"

She couldn't see Kismet's eyes beneath his tricorne, but the sudden glow of his pipe betrayed his irritations. He waved a hand and dismissed the masses, Djagatt among them. Lau Lau and Yoru stayed, but remained so still and silent they could have drifted into the bay as well. "You disapprove?" Kismet said sternly. His voice resonated with more power and conviction than she was used to, already putting her off balance.

"Yes." After all, necromancy was bad, right? It was against most laws of every realm, in fact, practiced only under authorization of the kings and queens, though she wasn't sure about the tribal Baku.

A puff of smoke curled over his lips and fell heavily to the surface of the water. "Merchants dedicate their souls to the Bone Grove. Their bodies may be gone, but they do not stop serving their brothers and sisters."

"Doesn't necromancy bind their spirit? Aren't they trapped in those urns forever?"

"Only until they're needed," he replied heavily, the buckles of his coat jingled as he turned, "which won't be long, now."

Kismet drifted past her. Djagatt met him at the foot of the dock and followed in tow. Lau Lau politely folded her hands in front of her and peered up to Whisper shyly. "It's a great honor, Whisper," she said softly. "A second chance to protect those you love, even in death."

Whisper looked out across the dark glass stretching into the night. She didn't like the idea of her soul being trapped, potentially forever, but there was something beautiful in the commitment it entailed. Such devotion, purpose transcending death itself. She felt something... was this envy? Did she wish she had something she loved enough to give her soul protecting? She sighed. "Is necromancy not forbidden here?"

"Where Djagatt is from, he is a shaman." Lau Lau chuckled softly at the irony. "Of all our actions as merchants, necromancy may be our only lawful act."

"This place is confusing."

"No," Lau Lau replied, "you, yourself, are confused. The Bone Grove simply makes you face it."

Whisper couldn't even find it in herself to argue and instead nodded silently.

"You have purpose, Whisper," the young girl said, "you just haven't seen it yet. A time will come when you'll find yourself choosing between yourself and something you believe in. What you do is up to you, but in that single, breathless moment you'll discover who you truly are."

Something lifted in Whisper, a weight shed from her like chains. Hearing the words, knowing that someday she would feel such an emotion was enough to give her hope. Hope to be more than what she was, more than what she imagined she deserved. "How about you?" Her voice nearly cracked as she spoke. She cleared her throat, "Is a psychic's purpose to discover purposes?"

Lau Lau looked out in the direction of Elanta. Gazed into the night as though she could see everything and anything. "There is a great sadness in Elanta. Something cries almost too quiet to hear, but I hear it. It sobs. It mourns. So lost and sad and alone." She wrapped her arms around herself, tears swelling in her big eyes. "Only I can bring it peace. Only I can stop the crying. That is my purpose."

Whisper crouched at Yoru's side, running her hand along her soft, black fur. This was the first time she had ever really pet the velvetine and the fur rung true to the name—soft as crushed velvet. "And your purpose, little one?" she said playfully, hoping the tension would be cut with the words of a magical talking cat.

"Her purpose is to serve the queen," Lau Lau said sweetly.

Whisper curled her fingers under Yoru's cheek and gave it a loving scratch, feeling the low rumble of purrs as Yoru's fuzzy little eyelids closed. "We're a little far from Emberwilde, I think."

Lau Lau turned to her and smiled, a clever glint peeked from behind her deep brown eyes. "No, Whisper. Not that queen."

32

QUEEN'S GAZE AND THE BURN OF PRIMAL BLOOD

Fever gracefully walked the lower decks of the *Last Breath* on the pads of her feet, gliding silently along halls lined with silk and sigils. In the growing distance she could hear Blackrock groan and struggle. She smiled, biting her plump red lower lip. She could easily create an antidote, but his cries were far too symphonic. Old man Carver offered to show her to a room, but she preferred to choose her own. Some poor soul would be exiled to find someplace else, or worse, be forced to stay.

She swayed with the melody of Blackrock's dissonant cries, lingering in her head well after he could no longer be heard. The tome still clutched to her breast, she wandered aimlessly to the scent of dark power. She approached a hall that called to her. Silks torn from the walls, blood and bile wafted listlessly to her senses, metallic on her tongue. She reached out and stroked the splintered boards, freshly broken and weeping ruination. Something wonderful happened here.

She approached a door, the scent of death strong enough her serpents could taste it with their flaming tongues. The hinges squealed as she opened it—an empty room, made to look kempt but clearly once the scene of some great struggle. Fever examined the room curiously. A missing drawer, splinters in the floorboards, the stringent smell of old struggles one failed scrubbing clean. Something else as well, cured meat, most suspicious. There were only a few basic pieces of furniture—the empty bedside table, a double-door wardrobe, a soft bed with crisp linens, and a strongbox with a thick iron lock. In the ceiling there was a deep cut, clean on all edges—something incredibly sharp had cut like hot iron on butter. The bed seemed undisturbed and welcoming, while the strongbox was barred shut of belongings until the captain gifted a guest with the key.

Fever walked delicately to the wardrobe, her serpents reaching out and wrapping around the handles for her. As she began to open the doors one of her serpents licked the air, peering hungrily in wait. Something had caught its attention. The other serpents flung the doors wide, but there was nothing inside. The tendrils of ichor slithered along the inner edges, tasting something they could not identify, sensing something they could not find. Though it was a curious room with the welcoming taste of lingering blood, the bile was too much for her to stand long. She was never a fan of the pungent stench and with her serpents' flaming tongues she could taste it by proxy. They returned to her bangles and she swayed as the orchestration in her head began to play once more, leaving the room with a hum of sweet discord.

Salem waited for her humming to fade down the hall, then a minute longer, before pulling the string he rigged to the strongbox lock. The iron popped open and he lifted the lid, a sigh of relief upon his lips, glad to be free of that tiny space. He stepped out of the strongbox and was immediately thrust upward by his throat, ensnared by something that suddenly coiled around his neck. His feet kicked freely, toes barely skimming the rim of the box below him, no air getting in or out.

The door opened, slowly creaking, and Fever's golden curls peeked with their air of glorious malice. The corners of her eyes curled, full eyelashes batting sweetly. She had sent a serpent down through the hole in the ceiling and waited, ready to snatch him by the throat the moment he gave up his hiding place. "Oh, little mouse," she sang "my serpents are hungry."

The coil began to tighten, his face turned deep purple, his bones ready to collapse from the weight. Blood vessels began bursting in his eyes. Red spattered and scrawled like ink on white canvas, straining the emerald sheen that desperately screamed in the confines of his mind. His eyes met hers and a flash of something powerful overtook her. She was suddenly oppressed by an invisible force of such weight and magnitude that the air itself began to tremble. It squeezed the air from her lungs, drained the blood from her face, and wrapped around her skin as if to crush her bones. She stared deep into his emerald sheen, so still and fearsome that the world literally shook around their dominance. Deep in those blood-spattered orbs of glimmering green she was paralyzed completely. In his desperation, Salem dipped into Savrae-Lyth's power and summoned a draconian eye technique, the **Queen's Gaze**—the very same technique he used to murder the Lady Rhoswan Gray in her estate. The serpent collapsed, dropping him to the floor a gasping mess. He coughed, saliva oozing from his lips, hunched on all fours, frantically trying to fill his lungs.

Serpents quickly struck from her sleeve, wrapping themselves around his limbs and thrusting him back into the wall. Though Fever couldn't move and the surprise caused the first serpent to weaken with her, the remaining quickly used their fearless independence to react and ensnare him.

Fever continued to stare into the green of his eyes, still overcome with the sudden awe of oppressive force. She had never felt such an instance before, never been overcome by a man, and the feeling of forced submission made her mouth water in a way she wasn't used to. Unfortunately, her serpents were enticed in different ways and slowly pulled at each limb, rife with intent to quarter him. Just as the pain grew unbearable and he thought his arms would surely be torn from their sockets, the serpents stopped and held him fast.

"Who..." Fever's voice trailed in her heavy breaths, "Who are you?" The tome slipped from the numbness of her arms and struck the ground loudly, but she was too distracted to notice, her arms still wrapped across herself as though it had never left her grasp. Even if she could move, she might not have thought to. "How are you doing this?"

Salem increased the ferocity in his gaze. "Release me and maybe I will tell you."

Fever wanted to laugh on the inside, but there was something about his command over her body that made her want to listen. Her serpents begged to pull him apart again, but her thirst for more made her compliant. The serpents eased off ever so slightly. She was suddenly conflicted. She wanted to make him scream, but wondered if he could do her likewise.

"I said release me."

The serpents reluctantly retreated to the black diamonds encircling her wrists. Her lips swelled as she held them between her teeth—fire suddenly lit in veins and eyes hungry for something other than blood.

Salem had never seen such a look before, but the draconian blood beneath his skin was all too familiar. His eyes narrowed, and with bared teeth he approached the woman, wrapped his hand around her throat and pushed her back against the door. His body pressed to hers, leaving no escape as he grazed her skin and consumed her with the dark of his eyes.

Fever swallowed beneath his palm, looking up at him with fealty and edges, both falling and floating simultaneously. "What are you?" she whispered, raising her hands to clutch his arm. She didn't realize the paralysis had worn off, still tingling with the sudden need to surrender. There was something primal growling beneath the surface, she could hear it rattle its cage.

'Salem,' Savrae-Lyth whispered, 'Gather yourself.'

Her words resounded in the deepest parts of his mind, echoing to what little humanity seemed to remain beneath the burn of draconian lineage. He shook his head, fighting the sudden need to consume.

'This is the blood, nothing more.'

Fever could tell he was struggling with something inside him. She took his hand and strengthened his grip on her throat, enforcing an escalation, but the aggression that once filled his eyes with ravenous intentions seemed to fade into something soft. It was a shame, but also a challenge. There was a monster rattling around in there somewhere and she was determined to let it tear itself from his chest and devour her.

Salem grew ever more conscious of himself and took a step backward. "I need to speak to Ivory."

She couldn't hide her surprise and suspicion at the mention. "Oh love, that's not how this works. See, you have to offer me something."

Salem swallowed hard, wiping a bead of sweat from his brow as he contended with the boiling in his bloodstream. He needed to say something, do something, to prove his value without letting his newfound instincts run rampant.

'The tome,' Savrae-Lyth called in his mind. 'She wants to read it but can't.'

His eyes turned to the tome on the floor and he crouched to pick it up. He knew exactly what it was. He probably even knew enough languages to translate it properly, but there were some very powerful and terrifying enchantments within. One could argue they were far too powerful to place into anyone's hands. 'Any other suggestions?' he asked.

He could feel the Queen of Drakes shrug. Fever's patience was whittling with the sharp edges of disappointment, and with a heavy heart he broke the silence. "I can translate this tome for you."

Fever pouted at the proposal, far from what she was hoping for. "What makes you think I need a translator?"

Salem opened the tome, flipping through the pages and stopping at one she had marked. It was a terrible technique and his single glance betrayed the apprehension he tried to conceal. "This is written in four languages," he said. "Sh'lay'n, ak'tonis, pra'kash'ura, and b'lay'tsu. Four different tribal Shén Shé tongues. I doubt you know all four, but I do."

Fever's interest piqued. "How is it you know these languages?"

"What matters is I do," he let his tone fall sharp as she seemed to respond well to it. It wasn't comfortable, but if he was going to see the Bone Grove he was going to have to embrace the fire of his blood. He turned and looked into her with something fierce, the tome held out beyond her reach. "The real question is what can you do for me?"

Fever smiled sharply, thinking of few things.

33

DRAGON HEART; THE HONOR IN CONSUMPTION

"This is preposterous!" Carver argued, wringing his hands. "Not on my ship. He'll be strung by his heels and skinned alive."

Salem stood at Fever's side, stoic. He smiled at Carver's helplessness with the corners of his eyes, knowing it was aggravating him even more. He hadn't thought of using prison mentality to enforce his safe passage—seeking the strongest person on the ship and metaphorically punching her in the face, yet somehow he earned Fever's good graces and protection. For now, at least.

"Aww," Fever pouted playfully, fixing the lapels of Carver's suit as she demeaned him. She preened him like a mother would a pouting child on their first day of academics. "It doesn't matter what you want." She placed a hand on her chest. "Only what I want, love."

"This is a disgrace," Carver spat, "This is my ship, my fleet. Stowaways must be made an example."

Fever took a step toward him, soft and dark, the light receding in her presence. The blue of her eyes encircled the depth of the void in her irises. "Do we need you, though?"

Carver shook his jaw with the preposterousness of it all. "What's that supposed to mean?" If it was mutiny she was hinting at he still had five good mercenaries he was willing to lose.

"This ship, it's just a boat, right? You don't sail it, you just tell it where to go and everyone else does the work. Sounds like a job anyone could do." She walked her fingers up his jacket and squeezed his cheeks together, squishing his wrinkles over his lips and giving his face a little shake. "Sounds like a job I could do."

Carver's eye spoke volumes of rage, but he said not a single word. She could see it though, feel the burn of things he might regret if they left his lips. She wiggled his face, released him, and gave his cheek a slap firmer than playful. "Words are forever, love, and when you speak you set them free. So remember who you're speaking to and watch your wrinkled mouth or I'll bind you to the figurehead and watch you die of thirst—slowly, mere feet from the water."

Carver clenched his jaw and choked back all the terrible things he wanted to say. He was outmatched and on the verge of taking the Bone Grove. A single act of hubris could ruin him. What did one stowaway really matter anyway, aside the precedence? No crewman in his fleet would blame him for surrendering to Fever over something so trivial. "Do we even know who this man is? Or why he's on my ship?"

Fever shook her head. She didn't care why he was there, only that he was. A flame was lit in the darkest part of her, awakening something she sought to explore, and if it was persuasion he needed, then persuasion she would give.

"Make him tell you!"

She spied Salem to her side and smiled. "I'm hoping he talks in his sleep."

Salem laughed awkwardly. Sleeping was the furthest thing from his mind as emotions and urges he wasn't used to churned and clawed beneath his flesh. He needed to drag out the process of translating the tome for as long as possible and pray they reached the Bone Grove before her darkness could no longer be kept at bay. Worse yet, he struggled with his own darkness as well, ever tempted to let loose the fetters he'd bound it with. He could feel its heavy breath resounding within his chest. It used his eyes to watch her lips, made his mouth water as it yearned to taste the ridges of her collarbone, and trembled his fingertips as it begged to paint her silken skin with long strokes of red. He didn't even know this woman, but he knew she was a monster, yet their urges fed one another, called in ways he knew he couldn't fight for long. He was so lost in her he didn't realize she had a serpent of ichor gently gliding across his shoulders as she spoke, tracing the heat of his veins with flicks of its flaming tongue.

"We will need some supplies and someone expendable," Fever said. "We will be testing an enchantment." She turned to Salem. "Tell the captain what you need."

Salem almost choked on the sudden reality. "We are performing it on someone?"

"Of course we are. I need to know it works properly."

"As you wish." An uncomfortable smile crawled across his lips. Some poor soul was about to suffer terribly.

Thick, fragrant curls of smoke rose from a small piece of resin set upon a coal, filling the hold of the *Last Breath* with an overtone of spring blossoms. Salem would occasionally poke the coal, moving the trivet to all four corners of a sigil he drew in chalk along the floorboards. Before him was the glow of six amber eyes, ghostly luminescent as the harrow shrike growled under its iron bindings. To his back was Fever, lounged atop a crate, letting slip her robe from the smooth skin of her thigh.

'It is ironic,' he said in his mind.

'What is?' Savrae-Lyth answered.

Salem flipped to the next page of the tome and studied the text carefully. 'That of an Instrument with power over the void, a fallen honey shrike twisted with the chaos energy of the Overworld, and a man who massacred the Blackrock prison of Emberwilde with nothing but his own flesh and bone, this one unassuming sigil of resin and chalk makes me the most dangerous person on this ship. None the wiser.'

'Is it that powerful?'

Salem laughed nervously under his breath. 'The weakness of such a ritual is two fold, requiring significant life energy and time, but once completed... a single stroke, a single spoken word, and I could claim every living soul on this vessel.'

'Have you considered, perhaps, not giving such a powerful weapon to the enemy?'

'Do not worry,' he replied, a malevolent pride prowled in his thoughts, 'I have altered the ritual by imbuing the cost with a vitus-loop, one that will cause her to overfeed temporary container sigils. Once the container sigils are full they will burst and force the excess life energy back at its source. It should overwhelm her enough to stun both her and her serpents. The window will be small, but more than enough for us to kill her.'

"How much longer must I wait?" Fever pouted, her fingers gently caressing her chest.

"This enchantment is powerfully complicated and will take time to prepare perfectly."

"I wasn't talking about the sigil." She bit her lips and devoured him with her eyes.

Salem stood and approached, something primal lurking. He leaned in. The scent of her hair intoxicated him, lips nearly brushing as his presence washed over her like wheat and wildfire. His fingers traced up the side of her neck into her hair and just as her breath betrayed the need for his mouth he clutched a handful of golden curls and pulled her head back. He smiled down upon her with ferocity, lowering himself along her throat, and grazing her ear with the heat of his breath as he spoke. "When I'm ready, you'll know." He released her and returned to his work. "Let it build," he commanded, "let it build."

A heavy breath of yearning disappointment filled her chest, yet she smiled with the want, basked in the need. "Would you prefer I beg?"

Salem smiled darkly. "Until I'm tired of pleas filling your mouth and I fill it with something better."

'You're using contractions again,' Savrae-Lyth chimed.

'I'm losing myself,' he replied as he tried to slow his pacing heart. 'What's happening? Why am I consumed with... consumption?'

Salem could feel Savrae-Lyth laugh. 'You are overwhelmed with a feeling that is very common in dragons. My blood in your veins, my very heart. They do not betray you, but open your eyes to a new perspective of companionship. *You began life as a Setsuhan, where the concept of companionship does not encompass romanticism and instead focuses on nurture and mutualism. It wasn't until you and Vaexa were carved from the same selenite that a pair of Setsuhans were literally made for one another. You were the very first mated pair in the history of the Snow Leaf, cultivating new emotions like love and adoration through the sensitivity of your stone. Even across the span of distance and time you remain connected.'*

'*I thought you crafted us of Selenite because you needed the stone's higher frequency to complete the transfer of your heart and power. Myself as the primary and Vaexa as the contingency.'*

'*That is undeniable. The intensity of companionship that resulted was a side effect I had not calculated.'* Savrae-Lyth sighed sweetly, '*But it was a most beautiful accident.'*

Salem continued to keep himself busy, thumbing pages and carefully crafting the core of the ritual. '*You said the feeling I have for Whisper is love. How can I be made for Vaexa, but love another?'*

'*Your situation is undeniably unique, Salem. Where once you were a selenite Setsuhan, mate to Vaexa, the moment you took my heart and broke free of the mountain you broke free of the emotional limitations of your race. A draconian heart beats within your chest now, primal blood races through your veins. You may be trapped in a human form, you may have Setsuhan principles, but you are a dragon now and that means you will experience draconian urges.'*

Salem envisioned two conflicting ideas of the dragons he once knew. The first was the regal nobility and pristine mannerisms of Savrae-Lyth in Setsuhan form—perfect posture and delicate tones. She was a lady like no other, a queen of exquisite nature, more graceful than any Setsuhan he'd ever known—and they walked light as feather.

The other vision was that of her natural form, the massive dragon of bellowing roars, opalescent scales, and grievous teeth. A form of such primal, unstoppable power and ferocity that she struck fear deep in the bellies of those who heard the winds howl and left mankind begging the Fates' good fortune for themselves and their flock. The sound of her devouring her prey raised the hairs on his neck—the grim symphony of crunching bone and sticky lips smacking.

'Forgive me, my queen, but what is the nature of draconian companionship exactly?'

'Honor in Consumption,' she replied. 'Dragon's honor that which they devour, both in life and love. We honor the sacrifice of our prey as we consume their flesh for sustenance. We honor our kin in death as the earth consumes them and their souls are set free of their mortal vessels. We honor the elements as they consume one another in natural balance. And we honor our mates with a passion that consumes our spirit entirely. The primal calling is complicated and all dragons learn, in time, the difference between lust and love. Your blood calls to Fever because her primal need resonates the same as yours, your mind calls to Vaexa because your spirit will always be Setsuhan, but your heart calls to Whisper because her chaotic disposition draws you to her tempests like a moth to flame.'

'What do I do?'

Savrae-Lyth shrugged in the solitude of his mind. 'They say 'follow your heart' for a reason, I suppose.'

Salem rose from his work and gazed down upon it, disappointed with its completion. The harrow shrike continued to watch him with all six eyes, the dark slits of its pupils steady with discontent, a grumble of rage in its throat.

Fever was lost in a momentary thought, tracing her fingers along the scarred flesh of her face. She knew Salem would not be able to see through the enchantment, but was suddenly worried with whether or not the flesh could still be felt through the illusory compulsion. The harrow shrike's growl eased her back into reality, pawing at her curiosity. "That demon seems especially keen on killing you, love."

Salem didn't reply, but simply glanced at her over his shoulder. The green sheen of his eyes shimmered briefly in the lantern light.

Fever sat up, crossed her silky legs and let the robe sink lower down her shoulders. "You never told me what you are. And I've asked so nicely."

"I am just a man, making an enchantment."

Fever laughed sweetly. "We both know that's a lie. Come now, love, give me a little something to sink my teeth into." A serpent slithered up his back and across his chest. "Shall I explore you for clues?"

Salem remained silent as the serpent coiled down his arm.

Fever hummed as she pondered. "Orbweaver?" A tongue flicked across his forearm, tasting for ink, patchouli, or blood.

"Instrument?" The ichor slithered beneath his coat along his skin, licking his flesh for a taste of the spider brand.

The serpent tried to slide into Salem's trousers. Fever licked her lips and smiled sharply. "Half leviathan, perhaps?"

Salem snatched the serpent and tossed it aside. Fever was growing bolder and he needed to maintain his authority over her until they reached the Bone Grove. Her curiosity could be a weapon best wielded, distracting her from her lust with the sustenance of a lineage of interest. At this point he had nothing to lose. "I was born of Setsuha," he said.

She raised an eyebrow, dumbfounded, as though she wanted to laugh at him for the audacity and lash him for the insolence all at once. "You mark me a fool if you think I'd believe you're one of those fragile bird people."

Salem let loose his draconian aura of static and smothered the hold with the tingle of electricity—clawed along her skin with an invisible elemental monstrosity. The harrow shrike roared gutturally as it wrestled its bindings—fear or rage, Fever wasn't sure. The air shook in his presence, turned her breath thick as cream in her lungs, choked her without him raising a finger. "I said I was *born* of Setsuha. I am a dragon." A floodgate opened within him as the words left his lips, releasing a wave of emotion held back only by his denial. Admitting what he was unleashed something deep, dark, and passionately monstrous. As he stared into the unforgiving oceans of her eyes he ground his teeth to fight the sudden urge to meet her lips.

She could see his need, feel his desire, taste his urges. Her eyes watered with the need to breathe and instead of forcing what little air she could muster from her throat to speak, instead she smiled sharply, her lip between her teeth.

34

INNOCENCE

Fever caressed her thigh, nails tingling her skin in the aftermath of Salem's static aura. He had since released her from the glorious oppression of his power, leaving her to quake numbly as the slow return of feeling saddened her soul. The harrow shrike had fallen silent, only heavy breaths over heavy bindings. The voices in Fever's head clustered and crowed, arguing over a variety of things they thought priority.

'He's lying, all the dragons are dead. Let's kill him and be done.'

'We should take him to Ivory. A dragon would make a good ally.'

'Never! He's ours. No one can have him.'

'Tear his clothes from him. Let's see how beastly he truly is.'

Fever hummed softly, unable to determine which voice was truly her own anymore. They all seemed fine ideas, though some were more compelling than others. However, she found herself doing something none of the voices recommended. She waited. She summoned no serpents, she spoke no words, and breathlessly waited for Salem to make up her mind for her.

Salem recognized the look. The confusion of self, begetting stillness that only intoxication could deliver. It made him smile, perhaps more cleverly than he intended, "Let us finish our business with the ritual."

It was not what Fever had hoped for or expected. Her eyes betrayed her with disappointment. "Is that what you truly want?"

Salem approached her, gazed deeply into her, through her. "You spared my life in return for this ritual, thereby placing me in the palm of your hand. The sooner I complete my end of the bargain, the sooner I can place you into the palm of mine."

An acceptable answer at best. In truth she benefited either way and her curiosity with the ritual was growing evermore in the back of her mind. "You'd better hurry then," she said, eyes filled with allure.

Salem flicked a short nod and turned around. Any apprehensions he had about testing the ritual on a living soul vanished as his inquisitive nature mixed with a brewing aggression that only seemed fair to exact upon someone who deserved a reckoning. "Everything is complete. You will simply channel your energy into—"

"Not mine, love. Yours."

The words twisted in Salem's stomach like a hot blade.

"Chthonomancy uses life energy. I have no intention of using my own in a test." A serpent slithered into the darkness and began to drag a crewman from the shadows. His eyes dilated, his expression helpless, trapped within a body that would not allow him to move. "*You* will perform the ritual on this swine and I will absorb the poison so I may replicate it in the future."

Savrae-Lyth had led Salem to believe that Fever wasn't aware she could create reality from the chaos energies of the void, but it seemed she knew she could recreate poison, at the very least. Salem looked down to the sprawl of ornate runes and glyphs he had created. He'd made five temporary sigils for his vitus-loop trap—an excessive number when one or two would do, but he wanted to be certain he'd stun an Instrument. To change them now would be suspect, to suffer them would be crippling.

Fever dragged the body into the space before the runes, trivet embers glowed across the sweat of the man's skin. He was conscious, eyes swimming in his head, well aware he was about to be subjected to something awful. She chose not to remove the Bedlam Thistle that immobilized him. There was something exciting in the helpless terror of his gaze, where impending doom prowled upon a body that betrayed itself.

"My performance of the ritual was not part of our agreement," Salem said. "I have no desire to give my own life energy."

"Well, you say you're a dragon, therefore you have more life energy than anyone else on this ship. A drop in the bucket, truly."

"I won't do it. Find someone else."

Fever looked as though she was about to strongly object, but quickly surrendered with a sneer of petty dissatisfaction, her nose upturned. "Fine." She closed the robe across her legs and stepped down from the crate, making for the exit in a whirlwind of huff and haste.

'Will this be a problem?' Savrae-Lyth asked.

'Absolutely,' Salem replied. There were many enchanters aboard and he didn't have enough time to even consider altering the sigils to function properly.

Fever returned before he could finish his thought, her next unwilling victim in tow—he was presumably enlightened and snuggly coiled in inky shadows. He writhed at his capture, even tearing at the serpents with his teeth like a feral animal snared for death. The man knew he was in danger and as Fever threw him to the ground before the runes and set him free he quickly concluded his situation would be much worse were he not to comply.

"I demand one thing from you and one thing only," she said harshly, "empower this ritual and slay your comrade."

Salem fought the urge to point out that was, in fact, two things.

The man looked to his crewmate, drool pooling beneath the man's cheek as his mouth fluttered like a fish's out of water. "That's all? Then I'm free to go?"

Fever tried to ease him with a smile as she nodded, but her reputation was traveling the ship like a plague. He knew in the sickness of his stomach that a smile upon her lips was a conjuring of something he would not share in enthusiasm. Yet, trapped there in the darkness of the hold what little choice did he truly have? Perform and perhaps be murdered for sport or refuse and certainly be murdered for punishment?

Salem crossed his arms and eyed the exit. His mind raced with escape options, all of which were futile in the middle of the ocean. One vitus-loop would be enough to stun a man, two loops for an enlightened. He had no idea what to expect from five except it would be dramatic. There was also a very large risk Fever would recognize something was awry. He clenched his jaw as he watched the man kneel before the sigils, briefly noticing he could tell there was something incorrect about the ritual, but not understanding what it was.

The man placed his hands upon the leylines, the black of splintered charcoal smeared onto his palms and turned them shades darker than the filth they were already coated in. With a straining focus that forced beads of sweat from his brow, the sigils began to illuminate—the symbols flickered and turned in a phantom dance that filled the room with the strangest feeling. It wasn't fear that poured over their skin, or sickness, or power, but a sense of nostalgia with no root to anchor it; no memory with which to bestow meaning.

The resin of floral tones immersed their senses in that of summer grass and spring's first blooms, and with a hiss from the trivet the incense began to spew a cloud of pink vapor. The puffy gas floated without weight, coalesced thick as syrup, and obscured like ink as it engulfed its victim whole. Only the babbling of a man gone mad gave hint of something within the opaque—until it was replaced with something far more unusual.

A hand breached the cloud and clutched the floorboards—wrinkles and scars receding into his own flesh as his skin turned lush with vitality. The man crawled from the vapor on all fours. The hair on his head was transforming before their eyes, developing a healthy shine and luxurious waves.

Salem and Fever watched in breathless awe as the man's flesh and bone was growing younger before their eyes. In a matter of moments, he had gone from a fully-fledged adult to strapping youth, regressing still further, until his clothes began to droop over his body and the cries of muffled infancy resounded from the mass beneath the bundle of fabric.

Fever outstretched her palms and half a dozen serpents slithered to the mass. Two burrowed into the fabric and withdrew a young child, who cried in fit and terror. The other serpents opened their maws and began to inhale the vapor, funneling it into the chaos void of their dimensional gullets. Like a flash of brilliance, she immediately knew everything about the supernatural poison—she knew how long it lasted, understood how it primarily reversed the age of the spirit, the physical reversion being a secondary effect, and she knew to call it Innocence.

Fever's serpents held the child aloft, dangling him upside down by his chubby pink ankles as it squirmed and squealed. She placed the child before the enlightened crewman, his eyes affixed, unblinking. "I believe you have yet to kill your crewmate," she sung.

He snapped back into reality with the song most sinister. "Please, don't make me—"

"Wait," Salem interrupted, "We should keep the child safe, so we might know how long the effect of reversion lasts before he returns to his true age."

With a flash of blinding green light, the five vitus-loop sigils burst. The enlightened crewman's body went stiff as iron—bone and cartilage cracked and popped as his muscles clenched so tightly they began to snap at the tendons. Saliva foamed at his lips, his body convulsed, and with a mouth wide open and ready to bellow in agony his eyes rolled back and he collapsed. His body struck the floor like a bundle of hide leather, stiff and loud, his limbs and appendages still curled and seized in place.

Salem didn't need to check the man's pulse to know he was dead—the surge likely caused his own heart to crush itself. Salem prepared to feign ignorance and surprise in the crewman's sudden and 'unexpected' demise, but Fever chuckled with an air of knowing.

"Oh Salem," she said sweetly, dropping the child onto the pile of clothing less than gently, "your assumptions have bested you this day."

"What do you mean?" Why not feign ignorance? He had nothing to lose at this point and if he could pass the transgression off as unintentional, a trap built into the text of the tome perhaps, he could absolve himself.

"I couldn't read the tome," she said, "but assuming I had no knowledge of enchantment whatsoever was a costly oversight. A vitus-loop, no less." She shook her head in disappointment. "Any novice could spot such simple utilitarian sigil-work."

"How foolish of me," Salem bowed, "You must have certainly seen the others then." He wove his fingers together, palm to palm, and pushed the tiniest trace of energy through his feet into the floorboards, just enough to trigger the delayed sixth and seventh sigils he had carefully hidden beneath the coals and resin.

Fever looked down, the sudden glow of green from beneath the lazy blaze of coals stopped her heart and the trivet burst into a cluster of sharp iron, noxious black ash, and searing hot globs of resin. She stumbled backward and raised her sleeve across her face. Her eyes stung with the blast, filled her lungs with fumes, and split her skin with shards of metal. Resin spattered across her chest and shoulders like liquid wax, hardening on contact but continuing to burn the flesh beneath.

Salem sprinted for the exit, vaulting the obstacles that laid in the shortest distance, but as the relative safety of the egress grew close enough to convince him he'd made it, his feet were torn from beneath him and he was hurled across the hold. The wall struck the wind from his chest, and as he fell to the floor he was swept up by Fever's serpents and slammed into the wall a second time. Arms, legs, shoulders, hips, throat—she spared no serpent at her calling to hold him in place.

"I like you more and more, little dragon," she said as she approached. Thin droplets of blood pooled at the tips of her fingers—she licked them clean, her eyes rejoicing in a turpitude unleashed. "You're clever, you're powerful, a little rough around the edges. A little breaking and you'd make a good pet."

"I'm terrible company, ask anyone." The shadow around his throat spied him with its glowing eyes—the void kept it hungry, Fever kept it poised.

"Now, now, I wouldn't say that. I've enjoyed myself so far." She gently placed her hands together and gazed upon him with a cruel mercy. "I think Ivory will certainly want to meet you, we'll just need to make sure you don't have the energy for recklessness until this situation with the Bone Grove is resolved. Then, love, I'll have all the time in the world to break your spirit." Her serpents opened their maws and began to spew pink gas, engulfing and obscuring him. Like strands of spider's silk, she could feel his struggle through her ichor serpents as he regressed in age. The tremors through the serpents' bodies of shadow and void allowed her to sense everything—his fear, his waning years, his thirst for plum wine, his... her—?

The air shook as a wave of distortion rippled to Fever's chest and burst in a cacophony of thunder; her body tumbled head over heel as she soared across the hold and crashed in a fantastic burst of splinters and dust.

The pink smoke of Innocence slowly dispersed; peeled from the glint of golden plumes, kissed by jagged arcs of electric blue—scarlet eyes and silver blossomed lacuna pierced the darkness like a lightning strike. A voice then sung like a song of beautiful tragedy, melodic and disheartening. "Flee, little serpent. A storm calls to the iron in your blood."

35

DEEP SHADOWS, BLINDING LIGHTS: FEVER VERSUS SAVRAE-LYTH

The translucent explosion of air forced the cloud of poisonous vapor to disperse and curl heavily from Salem's selenite body. The soft stone, fragile and statuesque, stood lifeless and vulnerable—doubly blind with his blank stone eyes. White striations and ridges along his body flickered in the sigil light, highlighting the multitude of weaknesses that would cause him to crumble into shards if he were struck with any force.

Fever roared as her serpents hurled the debris from her body and propped her back to her feet. The call of the void raged within her blue eyes as they darkened into storm caste ocean waters, keen on drowning everyone with crushing resolve. She peered across the shadowed stretch of the hold and saw the shimmer of Salem's body, glimpsing someone kneeling before him only as she began to stand.

The light glinted across the golden plumage of the strange woman's head and raced like lightning along the blue, red, green, yellow, and violet feathers of a cloak that spread far beyond her feet. Reality began to tremble before her—that familiar, breath-taking static weighing the air once more. "Uh oh, regressed his soul a touch too far, I think," the woman's words calmly cut the dark. The room began to flicker as lightning crackled in the palms of her hands, licking sharply at the air and arcing in snaps of sharp blue lines.

Fever flicked her golden locks from her shoulder, "And just who are—"

The Queen of Drakes burst into a bolt of blue lighting.

A single step; she spanned the distance of the hold.

Half a heartbeat; she reappeared.

A fist buried deep in Fever's stomach.

The air rippled on impact. Fever crumpled, hurled backward with a roar of thunder and ringing ears as she crashed through the next two adjacent rooms, finally stopping in the ruins of an ironbound chest and side stand. Her vision blurred as her head reeled and the voices all sounded in unison, each more confused than the other.

Three men barged into the hold, cutlasses drawn. Before they could speak a word, the feathered woman outstretched her palm and they were engulfed in arcs of searing blue that leapt between their bodies. Acrid smoke billowed as hair burned from their heads and they dropped to the floor as smoldering husks of charred flesh their own mothers wouldn't recognize.

A single step.

Half a heartbeat.

A palm firm to Fever's forehead.

Fever's vision finally centered, only to be blinded once more as Savrae-Lyth appeared above her in a crackling flash and stuck her downward , right between the eyes. The air rippled again, Fever's head snapped back, and she exploded through the floor down into the chamber below. The wind rushed from her lungs as she hit a massive beam, cracking the iron holds that kept the ship's structure intact. Salt water trickled in. Had she hit any harder she could have punctured the hull of the ship completely.

Serpents lashed outward and upward, nearly taking Savrae-Lyth's head as she peeked down through the hole. In two graceful steps, the Queen of Drakes glided backward, striking the serpents from the air with her palms. The ichor spattered and dissipated as she tore their little heads from the spindly shadows of their bodies, answered by almost a dozen more that swirled in a chaotic mass up from the hole. She tried to stride backward again, but a serpent slipped through the floorboards and wrapped tightly around her leg. The writhing mass of black fangs and flaming green tongues raced toward her—their heads weaved and tangled unpredictably.

Savrae-Lyth could not move her feet and the hunger of the void could be felt against her skin as they neared enough for her to see the slits of their eyes. She raised her hand to her lips, touched her index finger and thumb together, and gave a quick puff of breath between them—thin streams of jagged lightning snapped outward like glowing blue roots, creating a dense barrage of electric lines the serpents couldn't hope to weave through. Unprepared to suck the energy into the void they took the strike in full force, heads popping open and splattering everywhere.

Fever vaulted through the hole with the help of her shadows and outstretched her palms, releasing another relentless onslaught. Blood trickled down her brow; the concussion wrapped her brain in fuzzy madness.

Savrae-Lyth crushed the serpent at her leg and with a flurry of clawing strikes she tore through the shadows with a spinning grace that almost seemed a dance. She snatched a serpent by its lower jaw, clutched the upper with her other hand, and ripped it in two before a corona of lightning sheathed her body and she vanished in a flash of blue light once more.

Another single step.

Another half a heartbeat.

A knee buried deep in Fever's stomach.

The strike lifted Fever clean off her feet, legs kicking outward before buckling in from the pain. Seconds passed like minutes as Fever stared down at the sprawling cloak of vibrant feathers—weightless, breathless, and on the verge of vomiting.

Savrae-Lyth opened her palm and electric air danced and distorted in her hand, forming a swirling tempest of crackling rage. As Fever's body floated at the pinnacle of her ascent, the Queen of Drakes thrust the howling wrath upward into Fever's guts. An eruption of wind and thunder exploded in all directions, hurling Fever through the ceilings of every floor until she broke through the deck and soared high in the open air of night. Her body twirled past the crow's nest and slowed. The specs of lantern and sigil light from atop the *Last Breath* and Carver's trailing armada spun maniacally as she began her freefall.

Fever's vision shifted in all directions, her eyes begged to roll back into her skull and go to sleep. Whoever this adversary was, she was too fast for her serpents to track and too quick to effectively defend against. She was outmatched in every way possible. She couldn't fathom how reverting Salem's age had unleashed this feathered slip upon her. Her eyes caught the spark of blue in the pitch of night; fortunately, her serpents saw it first.

Savrae-Lyth looked up at her airborne prey, held her hand to her lips once more, and took a deep breath. Upon exhale, a massive array of lightning sprawled in a beam of brilliant luminescence. All Fever's serpents coiled from the diamond bangles and opened their maws to the void, inhaling the electricity and absorbing it into the chaos within their throats.

One last step.

One last half a heartbeat.

A heel on the back of Fever's skull.

Focused on eating the lightning from below, the only warning Fever received was the flash of light at her back when the feathered woman materialized behind her, right before a strike to her head rung her so badly the world itself bled with shades of gray and floating spots. Her body plummeted to the deck, buckling the boards and sending her crashing back into the hold. The low grumble of the harrow shrike her only proof she was still among the living.

Savrae-Lyth landed atop her and stared deep into the bloodshot blue as they ebbed and flowed like the tides. Dark clouds churned high above them, blacker than the night was dark, visible to the naked eye despite the impossibility. The Queen of Drakes stood over the Instrument, calm dominance and killer instincts shimmered in her silver lacunae. She raised a hand to the sky. A massive lightning bolt cracked from the clouds into her palm, where it continued to roil and raise the hairs on their skin.

Fever hazily gazed into the sparkling blue light, eyes wide, smile creeping. She outstretched her arms, basking in the static that numbed her skin, welcoming the feathered waif's final blow. A laugh filled her lungs, quiet at first, but louder as her insanity consumed her.

Savrae-Lyth roared and hurled her palm of lightning straight down into Fever's bloodied face, but the psychopath continued to laugh. Savrae-Lyth's whole palm phased through Fever's skull like aether, and when raised her hands she noticed their ghostly translucence. The crewman first subjected to Innocence was still a child, bawling in the bundle of clothing. Savrae-Lyth had no idea how long the Innocence was supposed to last for, but the crewman should have reverted before she had. Then, she noticed the trickle of blood around her ankle—two tiny punctures from where the serpent ensnared her leg earlier.

Fever choked on her own blood as it slipped between her lips, rolling to her side in a fit of laughter and bloody coughs. A clever gleam hinted in her watery eyes, her only regret was that the Innocence antidote she'd pumped into the woman's veins hadn't worked a little faster. Fever watched the feathered woman's confusion and disappointment as her body slowly faded and Salem's selenite form began to return to flesh and bone.

"You were fast, love, but for all your power, strength, and speed you lack something crucial," Fever sung sharply, "Time. And now, Salem will suffer dearly for your shortcomings."

36

SLOW BURN

Beads of sweat rolled down Salem's brow and dripped from the tip of his nose. His head drooped heavily, aloft only by the bindings of his arms to his seat as his body begged to fall and curl on the floor. Sticky strands of blood, saliva, and bile oozed between teeth clenched with agony and stretched slowly from his chin to his vomit-covered lap.

Fever stood at the other end of the room and examined herself in a sheet of polished silver, tending her wounds with bundles of white cotton and a bottle of the highest proof she could get her hands on. Most of her external injuries were from Salem's trick with the trivet, shallow and inconsequential, but in her physical altercation she sustained a significant amount of internal damage, the extent of which she still wasn't certain. She opened her robe and examined her hourglass figure—massive splotches of yellowing green and purple sprawled her stomach and rib cage like a sickness. It hurt to breathe, her ribs certainly broken. "Feathered bitch," she growled, wrapping herself as tightly as the pain would allow and then a little tighter.

"Envied Emerald," Salem wheezed with rolling eyes.

Fever spied his belongings. She had spread them on the bed to examine; a filthy book of gibberish with the title *Envied Emerald to the East* caught her eye. In her malevolence, she'd subjected him to every poison she could think of, all at once. In his delirium he revealed many things, most of which was nonsense, but she did discover who her assailant was—Savrae-Lyth, the Queen of Drakes. Muttered in reverence from his splitting lips. It would have been the most intriguing he'd uttered were it not for the slip of another name— Shiori Etrielle. Fever marked down his words and sent Ivory a short, enchanted message of her findings. With any luck, Ivory would tell her they had no need for him and she would be free to take his life when ready. Worst case, she had to keep him alive a little longer, until his usefulness could be determined by her Fate.

She kept him on the verge of death for over an hour in hopes he would reveal more, injecting him with just enough poison and antivenin to keep him conscious, and in as much pain as possible. Occasionally, she had to give him a little 'motivation' to keep his heart from failing—slowing breaths notified her of such a need.

A serpent slithered through the air and opened its jaws. Blue arcs of lightning jumped between its fangs. It buried them in Salem's shoulder and his body shook and shuttered as he bellowed in pain, eyes wide open. Fever laughed sweetly. She could still feel the lightning she absorbed from Savrae-Lyth somewhere inside her. More than enough to keep giving Salem a taste of his own medicine for a long, long while.

Carver burst through the door, two mercenaries at his back. For an elderly gentleman of classy wools and silks his expression raged like that of the Baku barbarians. "What, by fate, have you done to my ship!"

Fever paid them no mind and continued to tend her wounds as an array of ichor serpents wrapped around a mercenary and crushed him where he stood—crackling drowned only by the sickly spatter of organs forced from his frame.

Carver and the other mercenary stood appalled.

"Don't mistake wounds for weakness," Fever sung softly as she placed a sheet of cotton between her teeth and used both hands to tighten the bindings on her chest.

Carver masked no tone and roared back at her. "You bloody harlot! I expect absolute compensation for the—"

The serpents wrapped around the second mercenary and crushed him as well, dropping the body like a fluid filled sack that wetly slapped the deck. "Don't mistake silence for patience, either."

"Absolutely unacceptable!" Carver stomped loudly, face turning red.

Fever's serpents quickly wrapped around his throat and pulled him toward her. Lifted from the ground, his face flushed, feet kicked. Fever closed her robe and slid her hands into the sleeves. "Your ship has a few holes, but she floats. The real question isn't about who is going to fix her, but who is her captain." She made her snakes squeeze a little tighter, the discs of his neck strained to remain connected. "What will it be, Carver? Play Captain or shall I find someone else?"

Carver kicked and squirmed. Even if he wanted to speak there was no room for air in his throat, but when his eyes began to roll backward she dropped him to the ground. He trembled and coughed, fearful to move his neck at all.

Fever wanted to crouch before him, curl her fingers beneath his chin and belittle him into submission, but she was in far too much discomfort to even consider it, opting to tower over him and gaze downward in dominating disapproval. "Are we done here?"

Carver worried something in his neck would crack at the slightest provocation, yet chanced a nod nonetheless.

"Good," she replied. "Then get out of my sight."

The elderly man shakily rose to his feet and clambered to the door, only to be stopped by her sudden interjection.

"Take your garbage with you."

Carver looked down at the boneless sacs of expensive flesh. "I will send someone—"

"No," she interrupted sharply. "You will take them now, and you'll bear your burden alone or I will break both your legs in the same manner."

Carver had become many things in his old age—wise, cunning, ruthless, but also weak. His knees rattled as he bent down to grab their arms. They squished in his fingers like butter and sheep's bladders. With a slow, dreadful sloshing he heaved them along the boards and through the door, a smeared trail of blood and gore in his wake.

"Useless ass," she muttered. Salem's breath was becoming quiet and shallow once more. She gave him another jolt of electricity.

Savrae-Lyth spoke in the back of his mind, a distant whisper almost inaudible in the haze of his thoughts. *'I've failed you, Salem,'* she said. *'I'm so sorry.'*

Though he could hear the words they rolled from his mind like noise, foreign and without meaning. He could recognize the voice, knew what it meant when it would speak to him, but all other message or context was lost in the delirium of his fever. Occasionally a word or two would make their way to his lips, a compulsion rooted deep within something he could feel with Savrae-Lyth's aura.

"Bone Grove," he mumbled.

Fever barely paid him mind, but did notice through the porthole that the Fleet of Sunken Links had converged and slowed. She walked to the round glass, unscrewed the heavy brass latch that sealed it shut and opened it inward—it was surprisingly heavy. The salty wind ruffled through her golden curls as she poked her head out, the light of dawn illuminated a volcano in the near distance, the sound of crewman hollering from crow's nests took the air. "Interesting," she smiled, unsure as to how he knew. Despite the fact Salem deserved to suffer for his transgressions against her, the Bone Grove was likely hazardous and he would be of no use to either her or Ivory if they died. With much chagrin, she willed a serpent across the floor and pierced his skin with an antidote for each of the many poisons tearing him apart from the inside out.

A crewman approached the door and bowed fearfully. "Apologies. We will be moving to another ship, please gather your belongings."

Fever could barely restrain herself from crushing him. "Why is that?"

"The *Last Breath* is too large to navigate the Bone Grove," he replied. "We will be boarding a smaller ship."

At least it made sense. If Carver was moving her on precedent she would have a thing or two to say. "Fine," she said, trying to be sweet but hinting her intolerance. Far too weak to walk unassisted, her serpents snapped Salem's bindings, curled around his body, and dragged him from the chair. She collected the chthonomantic tome, her only belonging, and exited the room. Salem's body dragged along the floor behind.

37

THE FEAR

Even though Fever spent some time on the *Last Breath*, time she knew she wasn't getting back, the true magnitude of the ship couldn't be appreciated until one stood next to it. She and Salem boarded a smaller ship, the *Cross Ire*, which was dwarfed beside the modified frigate. Even as they departed and the distance between the flagship and her escorts grew, she still looked glorious on the horizon—a floating fortress for her coward of a captain, who remained behind until the dangers of the Bone Grove were neutralized.

Salem was regaining his strength and could finally stand on his own, though the irons clasped around his wrists and ankles still made moving a chore. He shuffled to a bucket of water and splashed it on his face, scrubbing himself clean of the crusty mix of blood and bile that smeared his lips. He felt disgusting. A blight of the man he once was, preened and proper. He looked down at his soiled clothing and died inside at the idea of anyone seeing him in such a state. He caught himself pleading with the gods and Fates that, through some tragedy, his body would have a chance to enter the water. Unshackled, preferably. He was sure to focus on that detail explicitly—gods can be comically, tragically literal at times.

The Fleet of Sunken Links spanned the coast of the Bone Grove's outermost boundary, breaking into smaller fleets and entering the channels one by one. The *Cross Ire* was not the leader of her fleet and brought up the rear as the ships ahead of her slipped between the crevices. While they waited their turn to enter, most of the crew clung to the rails and gazed upon the glow of the water. Among the bustle of talk and awe the term 'dragon soul' was spoken more than once, piquing the curiosity of both Fever and Salem.

"Dragon souls, hmm?" Fever smiled at Salem. "Anyone you know?"

Salem's chains rattled as he looked over the rail. Floating balls of wispy glowing feathers waved and flicked at the water, lazily pulling them along. "A sailor's myth," he said, "they are not dragon souls. They are comatulida."

"You sure know how to ruin a moment," she said.

"I wish I could say this was the first time hearing that," Salem sighed before shrugging nervously. "They may not be dragon souls, a symbol of a threat since lost, but they do warn of a threat yet to come."

"Is that so?" Fever's slow dance was returning.

"These are particularly large for their species and the first I have seen with luminescence. They may simply be a species I am unfamiliar with, but we have been sailing very far east. There is a great chance we are close to Setsuha. If so, the energy may have turned them into monstrosities."

Serpents emerged from Fever's bangles and entered the water, plucking one of the creatures and bringing it close. The feathery tendrils flopped down with the weight of the water like a head of hair in spring rains—too light and fragile to move itself without being submerged.

"Seems harmless," Fever said sadly.

"Monstrosity is simply a malformation of normalcy, harmfulness is not implied. Octopi with seven arms or runt kittens of a litter are monstrosities compared to their kin. In fact, you and I are as much monstrosities of humanity as the direwolves are to dogs."

Fever was an assassin made Instrument, but, no matter what light the world saw her in, she was scholar at heart. The chemistry and alchemy of toxins were her way of combining her appreciations with her role, and though the assassin in her wanted to slit Salem's throat, the scholar in her wanted to hear more. She threw the creature back into the water. The impact and splash seemed to shock it, taking minutes before the feathery strands began to move again. "How is it that these are signs of threats to come?"

Salem looked down the dark water of the channel. "They may be harmless, but not everything is. One must ask what else the waters of Setsuha may have turned monstrous."

The sails were hoisted, the oars deployed, and they began to move. Fever watched the ships ahead as they scraped the sides of the cliffs, but Salem continued to watch the water curiously, noticing the feathery creatures continuously fought the currents inward. Perhaps they were feeding, using the current to funnel in smaller organisms for food, or maybe they were conscious enough to know that the current could throw their fragile bodies against the rocks. There were many speculations, yet no answers, only that they refused to enter the channel.

A screech echoed from behind them and a dark figure approached on a beast of broad leathery wings, its six amber eyes glowing. It was the harrow shrike, and it opened its mouth and bellowed across the water once more. Its long, lithe body was matte black, absorbing the light with scales that seemed to devour. Red and tan lines made chaotic patterns along its wings and created a vortex of demonism that warned onlookers of its ferocity—though given its appearance one could argue it wasn't quite necessary. Four legs hung lazily as it soared; claws made for rending could be seen even from the distance.

Atop its back rode Blackrock, who had recovered from his recent contest with Fever and was ready to shed some blood. His dark eyes sunk beneath the sharp ridge of his brow, furrowed and focused, tasting the iron in the air already. He and his mount soared overhead and cleared the first cliffs of *The Fear*. Perching on the sharp spires of stone further ahead, he directed the first ship to the left of the first intersection and flew off to assist the other ships through the labyrinth.

"Can we trust him?" Salem asked.

"Of course not, love," Fever replied. "That's what makes it

exciting."

The ships maneuvered through the twists and turns, hulls occasionally catching the stone face and grinding in the silence. They carefully wove through the fissures of stone at Blackrock's direction; anxiety turned minutes into hours. The crew of the *Cross Ire*, for all their skill, made little sound as tensions wound, but breaths were snatched from their lungs as commotion suddenly rustled ahead. One of the smaller ships in the middle of the line was caught in the current and missed a turn, deviating from their fleet with panic and fear in the whites of their eyes. Their ship disappeared and only their cries for help could be heard echoing beyond the stone.

Fever looked up the sheet of cliff curiously; her shoulders fell and relaxed at the distant sound of despair. Her serpents stretched out from her sleeves, burrowed into the face of the stone, and hoisted her up, scaling it like a monstrous spider until she disappeared over the top.

Fever looked out across the maze. Much to her dismay, they were only in an outer ring to the Bone Grove and not the island itself. She wondered if Carver knew before he sent everyone in. The cries of the forlorn grew louder and more desperate—she couldn't help but investigate with anticipation. Her serpents carried her across the peaks until she could see the lost boat, which was quickly sinking in a pool of roiling water. By the time she arrived, the water had consumed almost the entire ship and crew, pulling wood, iron, and flesh down without bias. It consumed everything without trace until there was nothing left. The water continued to churn as though it was boiling, but nothing floated at the surface. Fever returned to the *Cross Ire* and explained her findings to the crew.

Fear and confusion washed over every face, but the captain fought to keep everyone focused, reminding them of how important a burden they were bearing. Whispers consumed the deck like fire and speculations of a creature lurking beneath the waves became the only explanation.

Fever stood at the rail and basked in the discord. "In the academy, we learned the phenomenon was called Dragon's Breath," she said softly to Salem.

"Yes," he replied, "a steady ventilation of gas from the ocean floor that lowers the density of the water and removes buoyancy."

"My, my," Fever wooed, "and here I thought I was about to teach you something."

"You have taught me much," Salem said tastelessly, "I had no idea there were so many different types of pain one could endure without dying."

Fever winked.

38

THE DANCE

With guidance from Blackrock the *Cross Ire* successfully navigated *The Fear*, but many distant cries could be heard from those that deviated with the current. As the stony channels began to widen at the mouth, releasing them onto the glassy waters of the Bone Grove's second trial, the captains ran a tally on how many ships remained in the Sunken Links' armada. Surprisingly, only a few ships got caught and succumbed to the Dragon's Breath, leaving just over two dozen ships to sail silently across *The Dance*.

An ominous fog lingered above the surface of the water, growing thicker the further in they travelled. Barely a sound was heard in the stillness of the mist, where limited visibility and high tensions made men imagine monsters peeling from the obscure. The ships cut through the water slowly. The gentle lapping of water against the hull was barely audible and Salem adjusted his bindings if only to hear the rattle of chains.

Fever was the only crew he could now see as the fog became denser by the moment—a moist weight that enriched the air. Visibility continued to close and soon Fever became only a silhouette. With it came the scent of dawn, the taste of dew, the silence after rainfall. Salem's head bobbed with the urge to close his eyes and surrender to the visage of crystal water on mossy stone, and even the tempestuous Fever began to sway in the absence of despair.

'*Behind you,*' Savrae-Lyth said.

Salem woke from his haze and turned to the blanket of mist at his back. The deck stretched out into the fog and disappeared, leaving nothing to the senses but the low groan of the mast.

'*To your right,*' she said again.

He quickly spun, but there was nothing. The iron links of his shackles rattled; his heart thrummed in his ribs. Something quick shifted in the corner of his eye—soft as shadow, silent as air—a phantom that tricked the senses, leaving Salem to wonder if he'd imagined it. A muffled splash was barely heard, followed by another, and then another. He peered over the edge of the rail, but saw only the gentle ripples of their wake.

"Hello, love," Fever said.

The hair on Salem's skin pricked at the surprise, his heart nearly in his throat. He turned to address her, when he noticed she wasn't speaking to him at all. Fever longingly gazed into the mist with arms open, releasing the chthonomantic tome from her grasp and letting it fall to the deck. He carefully shuffled to her side and peered into the slow roiling white, where the silhouette of a person approached. With each silent step the shape grew darker, but the haze refused to grace them with anything more.

The figure continued to encroach upon them and Fever smiled, her eyes black as night. "You're a sight for sore eyes," she sung sweetly.

A long, spindly leg reached out from the mist and silently padded the ground—brown chitin tubes covered in thick, bristly hairs. Salem took a step back as another leg quietly appeared, and then another, until the seemingly human shadow neared enough to show the bristled ridges of an abdomen raised high in the air. A massive spider—eight dark eyes, bushy fangs, and a dark brown body covered in coarse filaments—crawled to Fever and wrapped its forelegs across her shoulders.

Salem could barely shudder before the spider buried its fangs in Fever's chest. Without a moment's hesitation he spun around and shuffled into the mist as quickly as he could. Shapes of crewman with open arms lingered silently in his peripheral, surreal against the unwoven nature of indiscernibility. The spiders claimed their prey as he passed. Shapes consumed shapes. Forms merged into mass. Even Salem's sharp senses couldn't tell where humanity ended and monstrosity began. The spiders gingerly lowered the bodies to the deck as not to make any sound and the rigid crew, quietly pulled by their ankles into the unknown, made only a muffled splash soon thereafter.

Salem hurried in the direction of the cabin doors, noticing fewer and fewer crewmen until there was nothing but the stretch of endless deck and consuming mist. He froze, breathless—a large figure prowled ahead. To his left, a shadow lurked. To his right, the rails. There was nowhere to run. The spider ahead crawled closer and its dark eyes breached the haze while its mouth pawed in anticipation. Salem's took in everything he could, analyzed every possibility, but with the shackles at his wrists and ankles his options were severely limited.

The spider's body quivered, its legs crouched, and it prepared to pounce on him, when it suddenly stopped. The monstrous vermin stared at him curiously; its abdomen bobbed, tapping the deck softly. In the corners of his vision, more monstrous figures approached until he was surrounded. Each looked ready to leap on him at any moment, but none did. Instead, they each dabbed their abdomens against the wood in what could be nothing less than conversation.

One of Salem's links jingled as he moved, which seemed to startle them. He quickly froze and chose to breathe only when necessary, letting the gentle *thump thump* of their bodies run up his feet. They suddenly stiffened as a gush permeated the stillness from beyond sight.

"Filthy beast!" Fever roared. There was a spatter of fluid that splashed across the deck and the sound of something heavy rattled the boards.

The spiders surrounding Salem scurried away, pushing him to the ground. He lay on the boards but a moment before one clutched his ankles and dragged him to the edge of the boat. He frantically tried to grab the rail, his fingers slipping along the wood moments before plunging. As the water engulfed him, dragging him ever downward where the light dared not reach, he couldn't help but recall he did plea the gods for this.

Fever staunched the puncture wounds on her chest with the sleeve of her robe. Coursing through her veins was the numbing cold of two new poisons, both potent enough that it took her longer to burn them out than normal. Though identifying poisons was an innate skill associated with her Instrumentation, knowledge of both poisons came to her in a language she didn't know. Setsuhan.

The first poison was called nue'lian, which meant 'to catch with nothing'—a vaporized fluid that creates compelling illusions in those that breathe it. The second was rhas'elarin, which she somehow knew meant 'temple of stone'—a powerful paralytic that traps consciousness within the husk of the mortal body. Both poisons were now at her infinite disposal and if it weren't for the monstrous spider mere inches from her face when she woke she might have smiled about it.

The arachnid corpse, torn in two, lay oozing to each side of her. She picked her tome from the deck and held it to her chest, the slick of blue blood smeared along the cover and stained into the edges of the pages. The air was thinning, the mist burning itself away little by little until the stern of the boat ahead could be seen off the bow. One-by-one the dark silhouettes of the Sunken Link armada began to show themselves, drifting lazily across the open water of *The Dance*'s outskirts. Whole ships emerged empty, veering off course and hopelessly making wake to the stony shores of the Bone Grove's inner cloister. Others were manned only by those that found refuge or were fortunate enough to be below deck when the vaporous poison first struck.

The doors to the cabin of the *Cross Ire* creaked open and a handful of men cautiously peeked out—their eyes wide with awe as they spied the corpse of husk, viscera, and spindled legs that twitched unnervingly every time they tried to look away. "Sirens," the only whispered word to leave their lips.

Above them, the dark wings of the harrow shrike neared as Blackrock counted the survivors. The shrike opened its wings wide and thrummed the air, slowing itself at the stern and landing atop the helm. The ship shook and sunk a little further with the weight.

Fever called to him from the bow. The idea of approaching Blackrock felt like a submission of power and she would rather yell than look up to him on his mount. "How many survivors?"

"A handful," he yelled back. His voice a deep hum she felt in the tips of her toes.

"And how many is that?"

With a kick of his heels the harrow shrike roared and beat its wings, lifting its massive body clumsily into the sky. "Much less than what we started with."

Salem awoke with a gasp, coughing fluid from his lungs as he buckled. In the absolute darkness he could feel the shackles still wrapped around his wrists and ankles, but noticed the sound of their iron chains seemed dull to his ears. The air was stale and weighed heavily with moisture, much like a cave, making it difficult to breath. He rattled at his bindings, disoriented. It almost felt as though he was standing, but he could feel something soft and damp at his back. The more he struggled to gain his bearings, the smaller the space seemed to become. Walls he couldn't see began to squeeze his chest. Air he couldn't breathe began to drown him. His heart pounded in his ears, until something made it stop entirely. Something bristly shifted beside him, scratching his skin as it moved.

'My queen,' he called in his mind, 'please lend me your sight.'

Savrae-Lyth's static aura spread as far as she could reach, flooding his senses with shapes, figures, and objects in an electric map behind his eyelids.

'Oh fates—,' he thought, 'this is no cave.'

Deep below the surface of the water, attached to the ocean floor by a net of fine silk, he was trapped within a large bubble of air. He could sense dozens more around him tethered at different heights—each with a victim, each with a spider feeding. He could sense the crewmen's heartbeats as they were liquified alive; feel their consciousness, taste their terror. Beside him was a massive spider, its head breached the bubble while its body floated outside, but it made no attempt to eat him. In fact, Salem was the only one not poisoned, with the only spider not feeding.

'What's happening?' Savrae-Lyth sung curiously. 'It's just... staring.'

'I have a theory,' Salem replied, swallowing hard. 'I think they may be diving bell spiders, warped by the energy of Setsuha.'

Savrae-Lyth remained silent, but Salem could feel her thinking and wondering.

'Diving bell spiders are usually very small and live almost entirely underwater. They spin waterproof threads that pull air from the water, creating bubbles from which they live and hunt.'

'Why doesn't it want to eat you?'

'For the same reason I was able to access Setsuha for dremaera without being killed by fenwights—they sense your spirit within me. These spiders were made monstrous by the energies of Setsuha and that energy connects the spirit of all living things. You are the ruler of the mountain and are thereby the queen of all living things bound in that web of life.'

'Excellent,' she replied, 'let's use it to get to shore.'

Salem chuckled nervously, shaking his head. 'Oh... um, no.'

'Why not?'

'I know you see it, don't pretend you can't.'

'Salem, get on the damned spider.'

He shook his head and crossed his arms. 'Not a chance. I choose sweet death, thank you.'

'What would Whisper think of you right now?'

'We'll never know, because you and I are going to die down here.'

Savrae-Lyth's tone raced through his veins. 'Ivory wants Elanta, Elanta needs Whisper, and Whisper needs her inheritance. Without it, she cannot defeat a Fate and she cannot free Shiori Etrielle. Get on the stupid spider and ride it to shore. As your queen I command it.'

Salem grimaced, the corner of his lip curling at the thought. With great hesitation, he slowly reached out to the monstrous creature. It flinched at first, causing Salem to flinch in return, but allowed him to place his palms atop it. The coarse hairs pricked his skin and the carapace rubbed like rough velvet at his fingertips, sending a shiver up his spine and a gag in the back of his throat. His ankles still bound, he lay atop its body and draped his legs down its abdomen, cursing under his breath in every language he knew—many of the words even Savrae-Lyth hadn't heard before. The hairs poked at his stomach and chest and he reluctantly wiggled his fingers into a groove at the top of its exoskeleton. A pair of eyes were dangerously close to his cheek. The cursing continued as he got as comfortable and secure as possible, but the spider did not move.

'Okay, okay,' Salem said in stiff, shortened breaths, 'I'm ready.'

There was a quiet pause.

'Make it... do stuff,' he whimpered.

'I thought maybe you'd know how to command it,' she chimed.

Salem nearly choked. 'Damned if I know!'

In the dark silence of the bubble both he and the spider refused to move—equally confused. Salem regretted sprawling atop its back and, presumably, the spider was perplexed something had crawled onto it. His only reprieve was imagining the creature was as revolted as he was, paralyzed in fear and disbelief as it wished it could bat him off and scurry away in disgust.

'This was a stupid idea.'

39

THE SHALLOWDEEP

Of the fleet that first entered the Bone Grove, there was now barely enough crew to fill a dozen boats. The survivors rallied and boarded their best vessels, arduously abandoning the rest. Without knowledge of what was yet to come it seemed a better idea to have twelve fully functional ships than two dozen with a skeleton crew.

Fever tapped her nails against the bindings of her tome, a subtle twitch in the corner of her eye. She couldn't find Salem anywhere and she wasn't done with him yet. The slimy devil got lucky, as he was destined a fate much worse than what he received. Her irritation robbed her of any awe she might have felt as they neared the magnitude of the volcano, but its magnificence was not lost on the rest of the crew.

The *Cross Ire* navigated into the inner cloister of the Bone Grove, careful to avoid the mossy stones that stretched out from the land. In the distance the mouth of the channel could be seen, the heart of the Bone Grove nearing evermore, but the pungent scent of smoldering wood quickly robbed them of any illusion of success. Crewmen cried out from below deck, and if Fever's joy for despair wasn't enough to encourage her to inspect, the unusual alchemic familiarity in the air would.

Fever descended the stairs to the hold but stopped at the bottom as fluid seeped up through the boards below. The wood began to smoke as the edges burned and at the far end of the hall two crewmen bellowed in agony as the liquid melted through their leather boots and began to dissolve their feet. They fell to their hands and knees, which promptly began to smolder as well, but they continued to crawl desperately for the stairwell. One fell flat and surrendered to the rising acid that flooded the lower deck, but the other almost made it, though Fever knew he would bleed out. As she pondered the audacity of putting him out of his misery, a gangly creature with a wide mouth of narrow fangs burst from beneath him, clutched his throat with its jaws, and plunged him beneath. The stubs of his limbs flailed for only a moment.

Fever calmly strode back up the steps to the bustling terror and commotion of the top deck, arriving just in time to see a crewman peer over the rails and become speared through the chest with a dripping tine of barbs and sinew. It pulled him off his feet and hauled him down into the water.

The ship to their starboard had dissolved almost entirely, but the ship to their port seemed fine. She walked across the deck past screaming sailors who scrambled to connect the boarding plank to the surviving boat, and used her serpents to stretch across the gap and place her safely on the other ship.

With the boarding plank secured but the *Cross Ire* nearly sunk, the angle was sharp and many crewmen fell into the water as they tried to scramble across. They tread water for only moments before being pulled beneath the waves.

Fever smiled in fascination. It was an acidic undercurrent that devoured boats with hulls deep enough to reach it, but also seemed to have its own ecology of living things that could survive within. Most acids would have a violent reaction in contact with water and she wished she had a glass flask to collect a sample, if only to better understand how the two liquids could remain separate. She watched as the *Cross Ire* sunk entirely beneath the waves, only the crow's nest with a poor soul still standing within stretched up from the water. He cried loudly for help and Fever wondered if perhaps her serpents were long enough to reach, but quickly bored with the idea of rescuing him and gleefully prepared to watch him submerge. He floated at the surface longer than she expected, but a barbed spine soon pierced his chest and turned the water red as it ripped him from sight. Glorious.

Salem's head breached the surface of the water and he gasped for breath, held aloft by the coarse velvet sheen of the spider's carapace. The water was shallow at the outer shores of the inner cloister, but the spider's physique was designed for submersion and would not support even its own weight on land for long. Salem couldn't dismount quickly enough, hopping through the stony shallows until his feet hit damp moss and dry earth. He thrashed violently to rid himself of the arachnid's presence against his skin and fell to his knees, exhausted.

'You did it!' Savrae-Lyth praised. 'How?'

'Honestly,' he began, his shoulders still squirming to shake his discomfort—the eyes were **so** close to his face, 'I just waited on it until it wanted to get rid of me.'

'That was a good plan.'

'Yeah... plan.'

The volcanic cliffs, vine ridden and jagged, towered into the sky. A trickle of mist coiled at the top and cascaded down mid way before dissipating. Before him was uneven stone and overgrowth, but he had little time to spare. Shackles or not, he was almost to the Bone Grove, and he needed to make haste. He hobbled and hopped into the foliage, struggling through the vegetation until the cries and calls of Carver's fleet whispered at his ear. In the distance he could see eight of twelve ships smoldering, thick gray plumes of smoke spewing up out of their bellies.

'Only four ships remain,' Savrae-Lyth said, almost mournfully. She had no remorse for Carver and his pirates, but there was a weight to only a fraction of the fleet arriving safely.

'We do not yet know if it is over,' Salem replied, finally calmer since his adventure underwater. It appeared the four ships survived their warpath to the heart of the Bone Grove, but so long as their feet were not yet on land he was hesitant to assume all four boats were victorious. Just as his thought concluded, an explosion washed a ship in glowing red, setting the sails aflame and hurling burning bodies into the water.

40

SERVITUDE IN DEATH, THE HEART OF THE BONE GROVE

The crew of Fever's new boat scrambled aimlessly. Their determination suffered at *The Fear*, their moral in tatters from *The Dance*, and their integrity in ruins from *The Shallowdeep*. All that remained was their loyalty and now everyone was murdering their brothers for a seat on a longboat. Each of the remaining ships only had one, setting loose the inner beasts of mankind that wreak havoc in the face of certain death.

Though Fever loved to watch them kill each other to save themselves, she pried herself from the carnage and swayed her way below deck. When the first boat burst into flame there was no plausible explanation, but when the second set fire she noticed that both began within the hull, and that was a pattern. As she investigated, what few oar-men remained rowed with all their vigor. The hope of hitting the shore as quickly as possible was a brimming motivation given the circumstance.

A rumble echoed through the hull as another ship exploded. She stepped into an empty oaring row and peered out across the water. Draconian bones shone an ominous white from beneath them, a graveyard of monsters. The faint glow of green light rippled beneath their wake as something neared. A canister of sort, sealed with a sigil.

With the refraction it was difficult to interpret, but at the tip of her tongue she tasted a tingling death in the air that rose from the ocean floor—necromancy.

With a hollow *thud*, the object clung to the hull beneath her; it looked like an urn. A low sizzle like cured meat and hot oil sounded as a small circle of glowing red began to burn through the wood. She stepped back, hearing several more attach around her. The circle of red burnt away, but no water poured in—just a dark hole and heavy breaths. The oar-men stopped rowing. Anticipation clutched at their throats, wondering what would come of the strange hole. A hand of ash burst forth and clung to the floor, nearly too big to fit within the urn itself, sparking a flood of quick breaths. Crawling from it was a figure of shifting ash and cinder, bellowing in pain, or rage, as an orange glow flickered from its eyes and throat. It drifted to its feet and floated, spying Fever with a menace she immediately recognized.

Fever's serpents snapped forth and ripped through the specter. Ash burst as the shadows tore it to ribbons, but cinder-by-cinder it reformed. The glow where its eyes belonged burned brighter and it roared as it burst toward her. She leapt aside and the ashes struck the oar-man behind her. They forced themselves down his throat and filled his lungs. His face turned red, then purple, then blue as he struggled to breathe and eventually collapsed. The dead man's mouth opened and the arm of ash stretched out from it, the specter dragging itself from the husk.

It was tragic. Violent. Even beautiful. Fever was entranced as she watched its body reform—a ghost of ashes, a demon of unfinished business. Indestructible by design, murderous by nature. It was the perfect killer. She couldn't help but stop and appreciate it, but as more glowing circles began burning through the hull she was forced to withdraw.

Specters formed in greater numbers, chasing her while they bellowed with arms outstretched, consuming all breath in their wake. Floor-by-floor they pursued, forcing their ashen forms into the lungs of the unsuspecting and prying themselves free from their purple lips. Even with their path of ruination they were quicker than expected, killing and gliding after her until she was nearly smothered, but suddenly stopped. The glow of their throats flared as their animated forms began to expire, flexing and shifting in what looked like agony. The specters roared in tandem, their bodies merging together to form a single roiling shape of black and orange. The ashen skin began to surge, tremble even. It brimmed with power, flame fissured like cracked earth, and it pulsed and writhed as it was barely able to contain itself any longer. Red light tore through the ash and it exploded in a searing ball of blazing flame and rippling air.

The heat washed over Fever's face and aggravated the scar none could see, but before the flame could kiss her flesh, her ichor serpents opened their maws to the void and began drinking the power. A glow of orange and red trickled down their throats and disappeared into her bangles, which shimmered a little more with the warmth of newfound power. The explosion died, flames consumed, and the inner halls groaned with splinters from the sudden change in pressure. The sharp stench of burning hair filled the halls.

Fever walked back to the main deck, where crewmen continued to bicker and fight over the longboat. With a flick of her wrist her serpents tore six in half and threw any others she could overboard. The remaining men quickly backed away. The sound of more urns striking below could be felt underfoot and she cut loose the longboat with merely a thought. One crewman raised his voice to plea and was quickly silenced as a serpent sprayed a stream of flame down his open throat. Without further word, her shadows lowered her to the longboat and pushed her toward shore.

Her cheeks flexed as her jaw clenched. There had been so much excitement getting into the Bone Grove, but the amount of work and effort was exhausting her spirit. She examined her nails and then peered down at her chest to check her wounds from the spider. The pain ached enough to be enjoyable still, but she found herself growing bored. To keep herself interested she began to imagine what Whisper would be like and tried convincing herself that today could be the day the mistborn dies by her hand—should the opportunity present itself.

An explosion erupted behind her. The heat tingled her shoulders, the shock gently rocked her boat, and the cries moments prior curled a smile across her lips. Her boat drifted ashore, the only to arrive, and she stepped onto the stony earth. She hadn't thought she'd miss solid land, but after so much time confined at sea it was truly welcome. A deep breath filled her lungs—eyes closed, smile wide, until something occurred to her. She snapped her head around to look out into the cove, but other than the black smoke of sails afire the only other ship was the *Windborn Chance*, moored at the dock. The Bone Grove was barren. No fleet to intercept them in the cove, no pirates to ambush her at the forest's edge. Just an empty flagship and silent shoreline to strand the one and only survivor of Carver's once great armada.

41

WHITEWATER: A FLOURISHING NATURE; A WITHERING COUNCIL

Silence befell the forest outskirts of Whitewater, bramble and vine receding to the trackless presence of Howlpack Shade. Since being tricked by Salem Eventide outside of Blackthorne he was careful to scour every acre for signs of the Voice's arrival, but had found nothing. There was no doubt in his mind that Eventide diverted from the path to Whitewater, but without days of backtracking he couldn't be certain where he'd gone. The scorn of his Fate, Howlpack Sentinel Avelie, was enough motivation to continue his journey to rendezvous with Elder Waylander in the capital, but he didn't like it. He was meant for the voracity of nature, not the politics of man. However, the spiraling vortex of mist that funneled from the lower districts into the overworld piqued his interest more than enough.

With a single stride he leapt atop a boulder and peered into the sky. A shift of his gaze, a tilt of his head, a sniff of the wind—something was awry, but he couldn't place it. The city of Whitewater sprawled a few hours west. From his vantage the military dotted the land like fleas, but Whitewater could wait. It seemed they were not yet under siege and were well prepared in the event favor shifted in his absence. He turned his nose north, slid down the rockface, and crept into the denser brush.

He travelled north nearly an hour, unsure of what he was searching for but knowing it was close. The plants bowed, the earth shifted, and the wildlife cowered, until the forest obeyed him no more. He stood, for the first time in decades, waist deep in tall grass.

Shade searched his surroundings, crouching into the cover and using his hands to part the blades. It wasn't long before he came across a somewhat familiar plant, visinnia. Popular among herbalists and healers, visinnia was a small, leafy plant used as a numbing agent. This plant was at least twice as large as normal; easily the largest he'd seen. Shade plucked a leaf from the base and stood, rubbing it gently between his fingers and smelling the aroma. By all standards it was exactly the plant he expected.

A raven cawed above him. The bird flicked its beak, gesturing upward. Shade carefully trekked to the tree and removed the bow of warped wood and antler from his back, leaning it against the trunk. A single, powerful leap and he entered the crown, perching on a branch with perfect balance. The tree was massive—far larger than others he'd seen—with leaves the size of his head. He climbed to the top with ease and parted the foliage to look out across the forest. For miles, as far as his keen eyes could see, the supernatural overgrowth of nature wound like a river. A hundred feet wide, perhaps, stretching from the capital of Whitewater toward the towering peaks of Setsuha.

Shade caught a scent in the wind and turned north toward the former city of Lyre. The winds told him of small groups and caravans traveling south to Whitewater—refugees from the devastation, where a whole city crumbled into diamond sand. This scent was different and familiar all at once. Well worth investigating.

King Liam Whitewater, better known as the Whitewater Leviathan, towered over the four seats of his high council as he sat upon his throne. His hands wrung the black onyx orbs at the end of each rest. Three of the seats at the base of the dias were tragically empty. He frowned upon them and leaned forward to rest his chin on closed fists.

Though he was old by standard, his muscular frame flexed as the sleeveless leathers of his fur trimmed vestments groaned to keep the bulk of him contained. Even while seated he was taller than the tallest of his soldiers and broader than any two side by side. Looked upon with fear and respect that softened only with the wisdom that radiated in his long white hair, he was the last known leviathan in Elanta, a race of giants that were scoured from the lowlands and mountains long before the Dragon War. While none had been seen since, rumors from the refugees of Lyre were making him wonder if he was no longer alone. With no confirmed reports on Lyre's demise from ranking officials, the tales of armored monsters and shadowy snakes remained just that—tales—but a tragedy was certain. Whitewater was slow to point a finger or draw a conclusion until more reliable sources were found, but he was sure word would arrive shortly.

Today was a day he hoped to never see and the longer he stared at the empty seats before him, the more his eyes cooled from compassion to severity.

The first seat belonged to Salem Eventide, Voice of the King, whose last whereabouts was Freestone but hadn't been heard from since his journey there. The second seat belonged to Alexander Tybalt, the former Judiciar of Whitewater, who was recently judged for crimes of murder and treason and was currently imprisoned beneath the great hall until the day of his execution. The third seat belonged to the former chancellor, Vaughn Cross, who was just recently murdered—hanged and burned beyond recognition when an Orbweaver cultist invaded his home and set it ablaze.

In the high council's last seat was the treasurer, Victor Fairchild, who quietly waited with hands folded. He was a man who liked to show the vastness of his wealth, adorning his figure, well fed, with the finest of silks and gemstones. On both hands, soft and unblemished from his pampered lifestyle, he wore several heavy gold rings. He twirled them along his fingers to steady his mind during the most boresome of trivialities. It was well known he was pompous and uncooperative, but none could argue his language of coin. He pulled a cloth from his sleeve and gently padded the sweat that formed atop his hairless head. "Your Grace, we should begin."

The leviathan slowly turned his gaze, but said nothing.

Fairchild cleared his throat awkwardly. "A great tragedy has befallen us in such a short time, but if we falter now the Orbweaver cultists will get the leverage they want."

Whitewater took a deep breath and focused. "Still no word from Eventide?"

Fairchild sighed and shook his head. "No, your Grace, but there has been a report that his ward, Whisper, was slain."

"I've heard no such thing."

"I pay very well for prompt information. I received the message just prior to our meeting."

Whitewater was aware of Fairchild's connections. Were he not a genius with coin and deserving of the role of treasurer, Fairchild would have been given a title simply for his love of distant whispers. "Tell me everything you know."

"A cyclone of energy is drawing down a funnel of mist in Freestone, exactly like what vexes us here. They were attacked by demons on the first night, but no subsequent attacks have happened yet. After the phenomenon, huntsmen in dire wolf pelts were spotted. Whisper was confronted in the groves, but she is presumed dead."

The king ran his fingers along his chin and pondered. "They sound like Howlpack." He couldn't imagine many things capable of killing his mistborn, but the Howlpack were more than cunning enough.

The realms' rulers and dignitaries were aware of the Howlpack's presence, but the woodsmen rarely emerged from the forests unless ordered by their alpha. Even then, they posed no threat to the throne, seeming to target monstrous beasts or criminals on the lam. If they were spotted in Freestone, they were probably hunting.

"I'm not sure if this bodes well for us or not," Fairchild said, "but, if the Howlpack follow the will of the Fates, then perhaps they are hunting Orbweavers."

"Are you implying Whisper was an Orbweaver?"

Fairchild played with one of the rings on his hand and thought. "There are many possibilities. It's probable that Whisper simply provoked them in some way, but it would be foolish to dismiss the idea that she was, in fact, their target."

Whitewater clearly didn't like the idea. Whisper had been in his employ for years and despite her aggression she proved herself nothing less than loyal to his cause.

"It's not as unlikely as we would like to believe," Fairchild continued, "she is a mistborn, after all. She is literally imbued with demonic energy from the mist itself. Even if the demonic influences of the Overworld don't call to her nature, she is still just a mercenary to be bought. Her powerful hybrid form seems exactly the company Orbweavers would want in their fold and they seem at no loss for resources as of late."

"That's enough about Whisper." He refused to think she was capable of such treason, but chaos was in her blood. In the few years he'd come to know her he'd grown fond of her character, possibly because she was the same reckless and undisciplined rogue he was in his youth. The world called leviathans monsters once, and behind his back he was sure they still did. He was in no position to vilify a mistborn for being different. However, as much as he hated the idea that she could embrace the destructive calling of the Orbweavers, he knew destruction ran through her veins. His only hope was that her loyalty was enough to quench her thirst for blood and cataclysm, and that if she died in Freestone, it was an honorable death. "If Salem is still alive he will find a way to return."

"Your Grace, there is more. The Lady Rhoswan is confirmed dead."

The king grew solemn, sighing deeply. Rhoswan Gray was greatly respected, especially amongst the higher echelons. Her death was a huge loss to the realm of Whitewater.

"She drowned in her bath. There were no signs of struggle, but I've made sure the incident is thoroughly investigated."

Whitewater nodded. "My kingdom is falling to pieces, Fairchild."

Fairchild looked over the empty seats. "These do us no good empty and coins have only so much influence. It may be too soon to replace Eventide with the air of uncertainty, but we should find a new chancellor and judiciar."

Whitewater leaned back into his throne. "A chancellor can wait until we've dealt with the mist in the city, but a judiciar is imperative." His head tilted as though he were recalling something. A whisper in the back of his mind, an invisible breath along his lobe.

"Do you have someone in mind?"

"I do," Whitewater said strangely, as though he knew of whom he wanted but was suspicious of his reasoning. An inexplicable feeling; a confidence he knew with nothing but guts and intuition. "I want Elder Waylander to assume the role."

Fairchild froze and even stopped twirling his rings a moment. "Waylander, from Lyre? The leader of the Moths?" He tried to make it sound less preposterous than he did, but it was remarkably unusual to bestow the title to a non-military official. Especially one from an annexed city with no true bloodline tied to the capital.

"Yes," Whitewater replied. "He and I have been in contact regarding the duke's treason and I trust his experience and dedication to the realm."

"The man betrayed an oath to his duke."

"To serve an oath to his king."

Fairchild rubbed the bridge of his nose. "If I may be so bold, you have never even met Elder Waylander, or any of the Moths for that matter. If you let one in, you let them all. They're assassins, not soldiers. Their lives were sworn to the Duke of Lyre, a traitor, and they only owe you fealty because your father conquered their fathers well before your reign. Are we certain we can trust such a privileged position to someone of such history when there is so much to lose?"

Whitewater weighed Fairchild's words carefully, but the confidence in his eyes did not waver. "My city is falling to the blights of the mist and my ranks are contaminated with Orbweavers we cannot seem to identify. At this very moment I'm certain their spies lurk the castle halls. I need someone with combat experience who isn't from the capital, someone with no affiliations to alter his objectivity. The Waylanders have generations of loyalty and in my recent conversations with him I have grown to understand his honor runs deep. I trust his devotion is untainted and in these particular times, where no one's motives can be trusted, I think he is exactly what we need."

Fairchild had clear reservations over the decision, but it was not his to make. "I will send a message to Lyre, then."

"Good," Whitewater began, "but I have a strange feeling he's already on his way."

42

BLACKROCK'S MISSION

Whisper leaned against the blacksmith's forge, still warm from the iron works. She held a blade in her hand and admired the purity of virgin steel. Upon their arrival to the Bone Grove, Kismet ordered the smith to create a sword for her. There were many cutlasses and rapiers available, but none were sturdy enough to handle her supernatural strength should it return, so the blacksmith forged a cleaver. The blade widened from hilt to tip, like holding a long triangle, and it was heavy. Too heavy to parry, too heavy to be parried.

"All those lessons, finesse and the like," she said to Kismet, who was anxiously watching the sky and listening to the explosions in the cove, "the weight of this blade makes them worthless."

"You're better with your fists anyways."

"Why give me a sword at all? A blind crone could dodge a blade this heavy." She strapped the steel to her back with a leather harness crafted exclusively for its unusual shape.

"Are you certain? Have you fought many blind crones?"

"Just one." Whisper tightened her straps, adjusted her corset, and placed her tricorne on her head.

Kismet spied her cautiously in the corner of his eye. "You're not serious."

Whisper lounged with her elbows back and turned away sharply. "Crones can be asses too. Being blind doesn't make them invincible."

He gently shook his head. "You may need the weight of the blade for Blackrock." Removing the hat from his head he ruffled his hand through his hair. His fingertips firmly massaged his scalp, a nervous sigh seeping from between his lips. "I wouldn't worry about missing. I hear he's not the dodging type anymore."

"What's your story anyways?"

"I told you—"

"Yeah, yeah," Whisper flapped her hand, "queen's vault and blah-blah-blah. Who's this Blackrock guy?"

Kismet took a breath. "He was my partner."

"Saucy."

"Not like that, you cretin." Kismet couldn't find his rumrose quickly enough. "He helped me break into the Phoenix Queen's vault. We first met in the academy when we were young and met again when we were stationed at the Palace of Roiling Cinder. Together we investigated a way into the vault for years, until we finally succeeded."

"It sounds like you two had a very special relationship."

Kismet lit his pipe and took as deep a breath as his lungs could handle. His red-kissed eyes to the sky, he saw the leathery wings of a demonic creature soaring overhead. "Thank Wind and Water," he said as he placed his tricorne back on his head, "Never thought I'd hope for impending death to end a conversation."

Kismet walked out into the open and watched the creature near. His coat hung heavily on his shoulders, buckles gently swaying in the breeze. One hand rested carefully on the Scarlet Charm, teasing the trigger on the sheath, while the other pulled the pipe from his lips and raised it to welcome his guest.

Whisper prowled in behind on soft feet, adjusting the cuffs of her coat and cracking her knuckles. The creature within her crawled up the base of her neck and breathed across her collarbone, winding every muscle in her body until it felt like she could snap with impossible speed. Air turned to honey in her lungs, blood turned to molten iron, and every hair tingled like a lightning strike.

The flying demon brushed the treetops and swooped into the

clearing before them. Every beat of its wings filled the air with dust and dirt, and Whisper and Kismet tilted their hats to shield their eyes. The harrow shrike landed, four legs raking the ground with long talons, six citron eyes cutting through the haze of settling debris. Its barbed tail flicked behind and its wings bent at the joint and braced into the earth like arms. Its scales were mottled black with coarse, irregular edges that looked like broken feathers, and it was covered in bony spines that curved from its skull and shoulders. Standing atop it with two of the shrike's horns in hand was Blackrock—all scar, skin, and muscle.

"Oona Kismet," Blackrock said, his voice thrumming deeper than the shrike's throaty growl. He jumped down from its back and hit the earth with a rumble far heavier than he looked, "It's been a while."

"It has," Kismet replied. "You're looking... I want to say... *puffy.*"

Blackrock laughed deeply and rubbed his hand on the scars of his head. "I look a bit different than when we last saw each other. A little less hair, I think."

"And about two hundred more pounds."

Blackrock smiled at Whisper and pointed a thumb at Kismet. "Would you believe he used to be the muscle?"

"Really?" Her head tilted gleefully to Kismet, who clearly wasn't enjoying himself as much as she suddenly was.

Blackrock's eyes lingered on her a moment longer. "Is this your girl?"

Whisper spoke before Kismet could say anything, entirely capable of introducing herself. "Fates no. Kismet, here, was worried you were coming to kill him, so his cat hired me to kill you first."

The towering man of weathered leather seemed unsure whether or not to laugh. "Oona," he said, shaking his head and crossing his arms. His smile slowly faded. "You deserve death, make no mistake, and I'd love to be the one to give it, but I didn't come all this way for you."

"See," Whisper perked, "you're still friends."

Blackrock scowled. "I just said I wanted to kill him."

"That's kind of what it's like to be his friend," she jested.

The harrow shrike's gullet flexed as it sniffed the air in sweeping breaths, opening its mouth to taste with its narrow tongue. It then gave a low, guttural chirp and seemed suddenly anxious.

"Wait," Kismet barked, "you're not here for me?"

"Not at all," Blackrock replied, "I'm here for the treasure you stole from the vault. The very same you deemed more valuable than my life. It seems the Phoenix Queen wants it back now more than ever. She says it should be ripe for harvesting."

Whisper's brow furrowed as she looked at the Scarlet Charm. "How can a sword be harvested?"

Blackrock chuckled darkly as Kismet's eyes fell desperate. "The sword was never in the vault. I'm talking about the child."

Whisper looked to Kismet, lowering her head to catch his eyes, hidden beneath the brim of his hat. "Wait, Lau Lau? Lau Lau was in the vault?"

"Is that what you named it? You shouldn't have. It'll hurt so much more to lose now." Blackrock grabbed a spine on the shrike's shoulder and pulled himself onto its back. "Seems only fitting though. You took my life and made me suffer, now I get to do the same to you. Honestly, I almost prefer this to burying you myself."

"No!" Kismet roared. "Fight me, you coward!"

"You're sounding desperate, Oona. You shouldn't have gotten attached."

"Let's settle this, just you and me. I'm all you've got here, because you'll never find her."

"See, that's where you're wrong, I've already found her. My shrike just needed to catch her scen—"

Whisper rushed him, bounding off the wing of the shrike and bringing her cleaver straight down onto his forehead. The steel struck as hard as she could muster, but black shards of glassy stone pierced his skin and warped the blade. The shock vibrated painfully through her wrists up into her shoulders, numbing her hands and aching her frame. She kicked off his chest and bounded back to the dirt, tilting the cleaver to examine the damage. It was like she'd struck the horn of an anvil, contorting the steel and blemishing the edge. It was brand new, too. She couldn't have nice things.

"I see why he hired you," Blackrock said as the shrike began to flap its wings, "You swing a sword harder than he ever could." The shrike and its rider took to the sky and disappeared over the trees, headed for the cove.

Kismet sprinted past her and raced down the path, but Whisper simply stared into the fissured steel. For all her mortal strength she couldn't scratch him. How was she supposed to defeat him if she couldn't reach her inner power? How as she supposed to defend Lau Lau when she was so weak? She missed her mistborn flesh—the strength, the assurance, the safety. She missed having eyes that could see the wings on a fly and claws that could shred steel like cloth. There was nothing inherently special about being human and now more than ever she hated it. What good was fitting in? What good was acceptance or normalcy if you didn't have the power to keep what you have?

She missed the simplicity of having all the tools she needed. Now she had a head that ached when struck, a reckless power that surfaced only when it wanted to, and a beauty she only wished to share with one person. She sunk with the loneliness, grew anxious with the weakness, and feared the fact that she could die, again.

"Excuse me."

She spun around to see a man and struck him across the eye, sending him flat on his back. Shackles around his ankles and wrists jingled as he winced at the pain, but there was something unusual about the strike—it was almost as though he'd flinched backward quickly enough to minimize the impact.

"Always the face," he grimaced. The light hit his hair, casting a violet sheen that took the breath from her lungs. His watering eyes met hers, stopping her heart with the endless depth of emerald green. The sword slipped from her fingertips and landed in the dirt.

"Salem?" Her voice faded as she spoke, distant even to her own ears.

He squinted up at her, entranced by the crimson hue of her hair as it played tricks in the light. Lost in her round cobalt blues, awestruck by her milky skin. It couldn't be, could it? Where once opalescent scales shimmered across her flesh, now pale skin of silk graced her cheekbones, and what was once a monstrous arm of claws and jagged armor shamefully hidden beneath her robes was now a slender normalcy that matched her seemingly delicate frame. If it weren't for the electricity he felt surging across his chest he would have thought this was another woman, but he knew better. His search was over. All the turmoil, all the hardship. It seemed trivial now compared to how difficult it suddenly was to speak. Wordless and dumbfounded, Salem lost his inner poetry and conjured the only words he'd committed to reflex—the only words he'd spoken every single day to remain hopeful, "My dear Whisper."

"How?" Her knees began to buckle as she leaned toward him.

Salem sat up. "Oh my, where to begin. I tracked you to Blackthorne, snuck aboard the Sunken Link flagship, turned to stone for a while, was poisoned at least a dozen times, rode a giant spider—" Whisper wrapped her arms around him and embraced the most vulnerable feeling she'd ever felt. Salem's voice trailed into a breath of relief, closing his eyes and becoming still for the first time. His head fell into the crook of her neck and all he felt was peace.

Whisper abruptly pushed him away, urgency in her eyes. "I'm sorry, I have to go." She rose and prepared to dash away.

"Wait!" Salem held out his shackled wrists, almost offended.

"Right," she winced, her mind a mess of priority and emotion. She pulled him to his feet and helped him to the forge. "What does a chain breaker look like? I've never needed one before."

Salem pointed to a cast iron handle with three tapered spines and a flat back. "Has your strength gone?"

"It returns when it pleases," she said, hurried by the pressing need to save a child from an indestructible man and his flying demon.

"Your bloodline has awoken and your lineage has caused your body to become a chrysalis."

"Why am I not surprised you seem to know what's going on?" She placed the chain breaker between the links and struck it with a hammer, snapping them open. "How do I get my power back?"

"Your body is in the process of preparing itself to handle the full extent of your strength, but the best way would be to trigger your most basic, primal instincts."

"Hunger, fear, sex? Stuff like that?"

Salem bobbed his head and briefly trailed in thought at the mention of sex. "Or survival. The best way to bring a survival instinct to surface is to place yourself in need thereof."

Whisper broke the chains at his feet, dropped the hammer, and began to sprint for the cove. All she had to do was throw herself into the face of danger? Easy.

Something heavy landed on the deck of the *Windborn Chance*. Lau Lau could feel the boat shake from the dark confines of the smuggler's hold, hidden beneath the floorboards of the captain's cabin. She looked up at the light that seeped through the cracks—the illusion of luminous cascades flickered and waved as fine dust floated by the slats. The space was small and played with her breath, forcing her to keep her wits and not allow the panic of claustrophobia to settle in, but the sudden sense of hunger and rage twisted her stomach into knots. The evil aura choked her, so near its talons could be heard scraping against the wood as it walked.

"Be still, little one," Djagatt whispered as softly as he could, his voice still a growl even when he was trying to be gentle.

She could see the occasional stripe through the slits above her as he armed himself with his bladed gauntlets. The bells on his ears jingled softly.

"Come hide with me, Djagatt," she whispered, quiet and small, almost pleading.

"Do you know why I wear bells on my ears, child?"

"Of course I do." Baku shamans believed the ringing of bells connects the mind to the body whenever the spirit journeys too far. They keep their head clear when working with necromancy and ensures they cannot be influenced by the whispers of the dead.

"But do you know why Baku Warriors wear bells? To alert their enemies of their presence, so they may find honor in confrontation head on."

"I'm scared, Djagatt, please don't leave me." Tears began to swell in her eyes as her words trembled from her lips. "You're not a Baku

Warrior. There's no shame in hiding."

"I am what you need me to be," he said as he flexed his claws.

"I need you to hide."

Djagatt crouched at the hidden floorboards and looked through. She was small, scared, and silently bawling. "It will be okay, Lau Lau," he growled softly, "Be strong. You're a Daggermouth now, remember."

43

WAYLANDER

In the darkness of closed eyes the sound of gravel and wood crept, distant at first, growing closer, until it woke him from his slumber. Blinding light blurred through a single teary eye and he slowly regained consciousness. He felt like he was opening both eyes, but could only see through one. He couldn't remember why, but it didn't feel right.

"Casamir..."

He could hear a name. His name? It sounded right, but his head rung so badly he wasn't sure. He felt separated from his body, like he was seeing the world through a form unfamiliar. From the painlessness of slumber crept discomfort, teasing his muscles and bones with a hint of what agony awaited him. Sharp pain, numbness, a brow soaked in sweat but a throat dry as sand—his body didn't know what to feel, overwhelmed with a little of everything.

"Wake up, Casamir," the soft, familiar voice coerced him. It was his sister, Katya—he'd always recognize it, even if he couldn't yet recognize her. "Bastet. Venetta," she called. Her voice softened as she turned away from him, speaking to someone else. "He's waking up."

The sound of gravel became clearer as he started to become aware of his body, briskly rocking back and forth. Was he in a cart? He had to be. The cool forest air of Whitewater's mountainous mid-north was rejuvenating and gave him the energy to attempt moving. With sore, trembling hands he raised his fingertips to his face and felt the bandages that stretched across his brow and eye. The memories of Lyre began to creep through his foggy mind—the armored leviathan that stormed the gates, the city that turned into diamond sand during their escape, and the searing pain as the lovely psychopath tore his eye from his face with a serpent made of shadows.

He turned his head to see the loving hazel eyes of his sister, who knelt at his side and tended over him with worry and relief. Her face was badly bruised, and thread bound shut a long cut along her jaw, but in her gaze shone a strength of spirit that seemed indestructible.

He felt pitiful. Those big eyes reminded him she was far more fit to carry the honor of the Waylander name and tradition than he was. Casamir wet his lips and swallowed hard, struggling with the dryness of his palate.

"Katya..." he mustered coarsely, "what happened?"

Her sweet smile was a deep relief in such a time of treachery and travesty. "We escaped Lyre," she said as tears swelled in her eyes. "You saved us, brother. You got us to the duke's low road before the sand consumed everything."

"I, saved us?" The words didn't sound right. He should have smiled, but instead he fought the urge to weep. Casamir took a long blink and turned his head to gather his bearings. Light shone through the canopy of green leaves above him. It hurt to move, the pain surging greater through the numbness, spreading from his feet upward. The pain kept him from crying, or perhaps excused it, so he ground his teeth and propped himself onto his elbows. Katya paced an arm beneath his shoulders to help.

"Be careful, you're badly injured."

It was hard to breathe and the pull of skin and thread stung along his collarbone. He carefully pulled down his doeskin blanket—a terrible gash was stitched close and bindings were wrapped around his ribs so tightly he was amazed he could move at all.

At the head of the cart, pulling them along with his bare hands, was a man clad in a dark cloak and leathers. A heavy, gold trimmed, scarf hung over his neck and shoulders, pinned with a moth of brushed steel and sapphire—the uniform of Lyre's elite operatives, the Moths. The man looked over his shoulder, his tanned skin and red eyes were easy to recognize. Rowan Bastet, the only Moth with Emberwilde lineage and a close family friend of the Waylanders.

"A relief to see you, Bastet," Casamir wheezed.

Bastet gave a sad smile and short nod. In his last moments with the children's father, Elder Waylander, Bastet was ordered to ensure the safety of Casamir and Katya. In his mind he had only partially succeeded.

"You should have something to eat and drink now that you're awake," a woman's voice surprised him, his blind spot much larger than it used to be.

Casamir strained turning his head and caught a glimpse of the Moth walking beside them before he lay back down. He'd met her before, though she rarely ever spoke. Her hair shaped around dark eyes and cascaded over her scarf and leathers, black as raven quills and braided in tight rows only along the right side of her head. Though he couldn't see it in his momentary glance, he remembered a tattoo—a black vine and sigil—that coiled and stretched from the corner of her left eye to her temple. Harnessed to her back was a sword as tall as she, the handle angled out past her shoulder, the tip nearly grazed the earth. She walked weightlessly. No sheath or harness could ever hold such a blade, so it was wrapped and fastened to her back with white silks that glowed luminous violet sigils.

"See Casamir, Venetta is here too," Katya said. She did well to sound sincere. "They found us on the low road."

Of all the Moths they could have had in their company, there was no combination that could have eased his spirit more than Louda Bastet and Venetta Valentina, preferring them even over his own father. Bastet was a father figure without the expectation, and someone he could trust in both word and sword. Venetta was, arguably, the strongest of all the Moths in their father's command. The people of Lyre had come to call her battle-mad, because even though she wore a 'patience' as still and cold as the glacial peaks of the north, her resolve was a multitude more paralyzing. She was the kind of woman who would raze an entire village without hesitation if she thought it would benefit the realm. Casamir genuinely wondered if she would leave him behind if he didn't regain his strength soon.

Casamir turned his head away from Katya and nearly jumped out of his skin as he caught a glimpse of an unusual creature beside him. Laid alongside and wrapped in loose cloth was the lithe and slender body of a Shén Shé—a serpent humanoid from the jungles of the far east. The light glistened across her black scales and sharpened the tribal designs of coral that stretched from her eyes over her head.

"Calm yourself," Venetta commanded, "We needn't make more noise."

"It's a..." He gathered his composure and slowed his breathing. "I've never seen a Shén Shé before."

Bastet addressed them without turning. "She is a very powerful enchantress from the east. A pureblood of her kind. It's a miracle she survived, but I suppose her anatomy differs from ours."

"What was she doing in Lyre in the first place? Isn't it too cold for her kind?"

"Shén Shé have remarkable control over their energy and metabolism, and have learned to use both to regulate their core temperature when necessary. She and her bodyguards were commissioned by Duke Eywin, but it seems only she made it out alive."

"What did I just say about making noise?" Venetta scolded Bastet.

Casamir looked closer. Though startling at first, her humanoid features added some familiarity that made her easier to comprehend. In texts, he read about the purebloods and how they were far more humanoid than the abomination malison they used as warriors and bodyguards. "We're bringing her to Whitewater?"

"Yes," Venetta replied. "The king will wish to consult her expertise. Also, if other Moths survived Lyre, then the capital is where we will find them."

Casamir remembered fleeing his home as everything eroded into the twinkle of diamond sand. Perhaps the Shén Shé could help explain what happened. "Is our father in Whitewater?"

"We haven't heard from him," Venetta's objective detachment

made her lack of empathy clear. "If he survived, he'll be there."

Katya and Casamir exchanged a worrisome look, interrupted by a surge of pain that radiated up his body. He winced and groaned through clenched teeth. Presumably, he had many more wounds and the numb of visinnia was beginning to wear off. The pain surged again, burning from his knees.

Katya quickly opened a torn satchel and rummaged through the contents; glass vials jingled within. It was her apothecary pouch from the academy, filled with all the medical supplies she used while studying the enchanted healing arts. She withdrew an amber bottle and removed the cork with a squeak.

"Bastet, Venetta," she said urgently.

The cart stopped, and Bastet and Venetta each grabbed Casamir's arms, holding him down.

The searing pain grew more intense, coupled with the fear of what demanded such urgency as binding. Casamir tried to flail, but was far too weak to contend, even with the surge of adrenaline.

"Brother," Katya was trying to sound brave, which made him worry even more, "you lost more than your eye during the fall of Lyre." She pulled the doeskin blanket from his body.

Two stumps, wrapped in bloody cloth where his knees once were. Both legs were gone, though the phantom pain surged from toes he no longer had. Casamir stopped struggling and simply stared, forgetting to breathe. It was a dream. It had to be a dream. To stare down one's own body and see whole limbs missing. His mouth moved to speak, but no words left.

Venetta turned her attention to the forest ahead. She could sense something watching. It was startled that she noticed, and then it disappeared.

A low, thunderous rumble echoed through the Great Hall in Whitewater as the large wooden doors of abalone and alabaster swung wide open. The light from the outer cloister cast four shadows that stretched across pristine white marble floors set with ocean blue hexagons of honeycomb stone. A canopy of ivy crept down the walls behind the towering throne of the Whitewater Leviathan, who was conversing with Fairchild when interrupted.

In the doorway stood four figures clad in hooded gray cloaks, two seemed badly injured and were assisted by the others. From behind them a cloister guard quickly approached the dias and bowed. "Your Grace, forgive me. You said you did not want to be interrupted, but this seemed urgent."

The king adjusted his posture and tipped his head curiously at his new guests. "Come."

The four cloaked figures staggered forward. As they neared, the blue glint of sapphires sparkled within the wings of the brushed steel moths pinned to their scarves.

Liam recognized the symbol and rose to welcome them, concern weighed in his eyes. "Fetch the healers immediately," he commanded. The cloister guard bowed and hurried from the hall.

Fairchild turned to watch them with more intrigue than concern. Moths traveling from Lyre to Whitewater was very unusual and it concerned him that he was not made aware in advance. It was no secret something tragic happened in Lyre, but the rumors were almost too outrageous to give weight. Being on the verge of details had Fairchild salivating.

"Tell me what happened." Liam descended the dias and approached the Moths. He towered over them and gestured for them to ease their injured into the empty seats of the council. So far as he could tell they were in very rough shape, barely able to stand on their own.

The two uninjured Moths set down their comrades and took a knee before the king, pulling back their hoods to reveal their faces. The first was a beautiful woman—long, wavy brown hair with a circlet of twisted silver brambles across her forehead. The second was a man of strong, broad features, with short sandy hair and a hint of blue steel beneath his collar.

The male was the first to speak. "My king," he began regally, "I am Azel Katmin, loyal servant to his majesty, Liam Whitewater, and swordsong to the Moths of Lyre."

Fairchild slowly spun the rings on his fingers, painted with delight. Swordsong was a title given to a master of dual blades and there weren't many. He also noticed the swordsong had impeccable taste in jewelry as two brilliant sapphires glinted in the eyes of a wolf's head ring of white gold; his finger through its open maw.

Azel raised a hand to present the woman at his side, but continued to affix his eyes to the ground. "This is Diana Laurellen. Loyal servant to his majesty. Geomantic soothsayer to the Moths of Lyre."

"A soothsayer," Liam said, surprised. "How was I not made aware that I had a clairvoyant in my employ?"

Fairchild's eyes grew darker as a clever smile crept across his lips. Information was wonderful, but information before it happens—he fought to contain his elation.

"My apologies," Diana said, her voice graceful and unassuming. "I see many things across many potential futures, but I was unaware the Duke of Lyre was hiding me from you."

In light of the duke's most recent treachery—finding Shiori's Second Wish and attempting to keep it for himself—he could only be so surprised that there was more leverage he wasn't made aware of.

"It was not your responsibility," the king said, "You will bear no consequences to the actions of your former duke. He will be judged for the full extent of his crimes."

"Thank you, your Grace," she replied, "but Lyre has fallen entirely and the duke is dead."

It was a confirmation Liam dreaded, but was ready to hear.

"The attack was very sudden," Azel explained. "We were struck with such strength and ferocity there was no time to rally for reinforcements from the realm." He turned to Diana and gestured. She reached into her sleeve and withdrew a satchel.

She opened the top and poured glittering diamond sand into her palm. "The whole city has been reduced to this." She held her hand aloft for the king to see. "Flesh and stone alike, nothing still stands."

Whitewater held out his palm, dwarfing hers, and allowed her to pour the sand into it. "The whole city?"

"Yes," she replied. "The Moths were divided and only a fraction of the population escaped. Most of the refugees should be here soon."

Lyre had more soldiers than anywhere in the realm, the capital included. The idea something could have caused so much destruction was harrowing and all he could think of was the threat of swirling mist that funneled at his gates. "Is this the work of the Overworld?"

Diana seemed uneasy in his presence. "I don't believe so. I had a vision right before the city fell, your Grace. A powerful woman with a white crown and spiders for eyes, commanding two warriors. I believe she is a Fate."

"The two who attacked us, we believe them to be Instruments," Azel said. "They were much too powerful to be enlightened and one..." he hesitated at the near absurdity of what he was about to say, "...one was a leviathan."

The king folded his arms and delved deep into thoughts that tumbled over one another. It was a struggle, the possibility his kin might still exist after nearly fifty years of extinction. If there was another, the bad blood certainly ran deep enough to elicit such a vicious attack.

"How can you be sure?" Fairchild chimed in playful disbelief. "No one has seen another leviathan in decades and they aren't exactly inconspicuous."

"It was big. Even bigger than you, your Grace. We don't know where it came from."

Fairchild scoffed. "We're to trust this testimony? Make no mistake, the fall of Lyre is inarguable, but leviathans, Instruments, and Fates? It's nothing but speculation."

"I saw him," a weak and raspy voice spoke from beneath the hood of one of the injured Moths. "I saw his face, I witnessed his mark. He was definitely a leviathan and he had the brand of an Instrument on his arm."

"The Moths were wards of a traitor and guardians to a city they let fall," Fairchild said sharply, "Forgive me if I find the word of a Moth contestable without proof."

The man strained to pull his hood back; dark brown locks kissed blistered skin and framed a bloodied face. "I'm not just any Moth. I am Elder Waylander, commander of Lyre's Elite. And if that isn't enough..." He groaned and winced as he shrugged the cloak from his shoulders. He was missing his right arm at the shoulder—flesh burnt, tattered, and bloody along the side of his body, wounds cauterized by flame. He turned and revealed a black spider brand that stretched across his ribs beneath strips of burnt vestments, "...I am also an Instrument."

Howlpack Shade exited the unusual overgrowth, setting foot amidst a glen of ferns that rolled back their leaves for him. He traveled north through the fiddleheads, tracking the subtle scent of something that did not belong and stopping at the base of a large tree. According to the winds, though the source of the scent was still far away, it was likely close enough that he could glean more information from the trees.

Shade placed his hand against the bark—coarse to the touch, wise to the senses. Unknown to mankind entirely, all vegetation had the ability to communicate with one another through mycelial channels—sprawling nets of thin fungal threads that connect the roots in a communicative community. Plants provide the fungi with food and the fungi protect the roots and share information.

Shade closed his eyes and focused. His innate connection to the wild, augmented by his Instrumentation, gave him a rudimentary understanding of the language. He would never be able to glean anything more than when and where plants were being tread upon, eaten, or were thriving, but he was hoping a quick look would produce results. His senses were overwhelmed at first, a rattling in his mind from every leaf being eaten by an insect, every weed that choked a root, and every plant that bowed to his presence, but with determination he narrowed down something useful. A series of continuous vibrations in the earth and a strong concentration of visinnia.

Shade opened his eyes and removed his hand from the tree. A cart traveled the road from Lyre, pulled by something much lighter than a horse. A man, perhaps. The concentration of visinnia had to be refined, meaning they were traveling with someone wounded. He did not see anything to confirm his suspicions, but he was certain he could smell a Shén Shé in the midst. They were far from home if it were true, and that was most peculiar.

He knew where they were now and it was only a matter of closing the distance and seeing with his own eyes. Long strides, near silent, he raced through the trees until he found a vantage point. Shade crouched low, commanding the brush to circle and conceal him. Woody stems of blackberry curled before him, leaving his eyes unobstructed.

In the distance, through the trees, he could see a caravan of five. One seemed to be in terrible shock, held down by two as a woman poured a bottle of visinnia extract on the stubs of his legs. There was a shimmer of black and coral scales in the cart—a Shén Shé no doubt. It looked too small to be a malison, which was reassuring. A lone malison beyond the borders of Shén Shé could have been a very bad omen, but a pureblood had more diplomatic potential.

Shade squinted, sizing up the two warriors. Both were garbed in Moth attire, which meant Elder Waylander couldn't be far off. The man's olive skin betrayed him as a denizen of Emberwilde. His robe concealed any weapons he was likely carrying. However, the woman was far more conspicuous. She was tall and slender, six feet perhaps; the sword on her back had to be just as tall as she. The woman turned to look at him. Shade didn't move, their eyes seemingly locked over the distance. He hadn't imagined it possible for anyone's senses to be as keen as his, but with so many specializations in enlightenment he was open to being mistaken. The woman's eyes shifted slightly, no longer affixed but focused in the general direction. It confirmed that the keen of her senses were not physical, but spiritual—unable to see him, but sense him.

44

GOSSAMER THREADS

The harrow shrike took deep breaths of the Bone Grove air, lifting its narrow snout to the sky to determine where the lost treasure of the Phoenix Queen was hidden. Its talons scratched the deck of the *Windborn Chance* and the wood groaned with the weight, tapering slightly toward the hole Whisper made. New boards were fitted to the space, but only a basic foundation had been laid so far.

Blackrock thunderously dismounted, looking around the ship but knowing his eyes would never find what he was looking for. He patiently waited for the shrike to chirp with an answer, folding his arms and watching the forest for any sign of Kismet's pursuit. A sound caught his ears and he raised a hand, signaling the shrike to stop.

At the stern, the doors to the captain's cabin swung open and the jingle of bells played pleasantly in the air. Djagatt stepped out; the light made his brown stripes shimmer against the off-white of his fur. The Baku lumbered out, its claws flexed in grievous bladed gauntlets.

It was Emberwilde nature to vilify the Baku. The two races had been at odds with one another for generations, fighting for territory and spilling blood on the borders of Emberwilde and the Baku Sands.

Blackrock was filled with immediate discrimination and wasted no time with words or showmanship. Shards of obsidian burst through his flesh, his eyes turned to stone, and once he was completely covered he charged.

The deck rumbled beneath Blackrock's heavy steps and he tilted his shoulder forward to gore the Baku with the jagged points. Djagatt clasped his hands together with the sanguine glow of necromantic essence and thrust his palms into the deck. The ghostly red burst across the wood between them like phantom fire and the boards quickly rotted. They buckled with the weight and Blackrock plunged through to the lower decks with a crash.

The harrow shrike scowled through its narrow teeth, rising onto its hind legs as Djagatt dashed toward it. They collided in a gnashing whirl of talons, teeth, and claws. The Baku sunk his gauntlets into the shrike's chest, the shrike raked its claws along the Baku's back, both roared in ferocity and pain.

Djagatt pushed his claws in deeper, feeling them slip between the ribs, and pulled himself up to bury his teeth into its throat. The shrike thrashed, thrust the barbs of its tail into Djagatt's side, and hurled him to the ground. Blood spattered from his back and side, turning his fur sanguine. The shrike pounced atop him and tried to snap its maw around his head, but Djagatt caught its teeth in his sword breakers and snapped them in its mouth. The demon cried loudly, staggering back and shaking its head.

Blackrock's broad armored frame tore a trail of flinders through the narrow stairwell as he burst up from the lower deck in full rush. He charged past the flailing shrike, leapt in the air, and hurled his stony fist down at Djagatt.

The Baku rolled to stand, razor edges lightly grazed the tufts of his ear before smashing through the deck, but as he landed on his feet Blackrock had already recovered and thrown a second strike. Djagatt had little time to react and forced a mass of necromantic essence into his hands. He struck Blackrock in the chest with both palms, straining to hold them there.

Blackrock's body froze, a fist of jagged shards inches from Djagatt's face. The air blurred and Blackrock's spirit was forced out his back, hanging still and ghostly, falling in slow motion, wrapped in phantom strands of life energy that connected him to his body. Djagatt struggled with the technique. Forcing the spirit from the body was costly and it fatigued him to hold while he repositioned his feet to better evade once he released. He removed his hands and spun, narrowly avoiding the fist. They both staggered dizzily, but Djagatt had a shadow looming over him. He turned to see the harrow shrike bearing down upon him with malice and bone, talons raining.

A thrum took the air, whistling a song as the Scarlet Charm was fired from Kismet's sheath, spinning in a crimson blur of deep red crystalline facets that buried themselves in the shrike's arm and forced its strike to miss. Kismet slid on his knees through the blood as it cried, grabbed the handle, and twisted, severing its forearm clean. The shrike bellowed, spread its wings and burst into the sky, retreating to the safety of the forest.

"Are you alright, Djagatt?" Kismet rose, watching the claw of the shrike twitch and curl. Somehow the pipe still rested between his teeth as he panted, catching his breath from the run. Beads of sweat trickled down the sides of his face and splashed on his coat.

"Just flesh wounds, Captain."

Kismet looked at the blood that poured from Djagatt's back and side, staining his fur pink and red. "Looks a little worse than that."

"Well," he panted, recovering from the surge of energy he'd expended, "there's a lot of flesh wounded."

"You're getting old," Kismet teased, trying to get Djagatt's mind off the intensity of his wounds. "I watched you flay a Baku alpha with his own mane of blades once."

Blackrock staggered slightly, shaking loose the last of his disorientation. The forceful separation of body and mind was surreal, a shaman technique used in triage when physicians needed to tend to flailing soldiers. With proper preparations the effects would last longer and take less a toll on the body, but the sudden, unfiltered surge was big and wasteful.

"It's nice to see you're still keeping good company," Blackrock said, "There were big shoes to fill."

"I tried to save you," Kismet said, "I spent every resource, squeezed every contact. I couldn't find a way in or out of the Blackrock prison."

"Why not give the girl back, hmm?"

"You know I couldn't do that. She was the whole reason we broke we went to the trouble."

Blackrock scoffed. "The plan didn't even work in the long run! One girl, Oona. There were many before her, there've been many since. It changed nothing. Why does saving this one matter so much?"

"Because..." Kismet took a deep breath, "I had to give up three lives for her."

Blackrock's big stony head bobbed slowly. "I understand."

Kismet finally exhaled. "Do you?"

"Of course. Getting in and out of the vault with the child was the plan and your choice was simply business. After the plan failed, you needed to justify what it was you sacrificed by putting everything you had left into raising the child." He crossed his massive arms. "I don't blame you for leaving me behind. I would have done the same thing, for a different treasure perhaps. I don't even blame you for leaving your own life behind, you had more pressure on your shoulders than anyone. But, I *am* surprised you chose the child over your own sister."

"My life as a brother was over the moment you and I were caught in that vault. Returning Lau Lau wouldn't have changed anything. She's better off without me," he replied sharply.

"Are you sure? How can you be certain?"

Kismet refused to answer. He was ashamed to admit it, but when he felt alone or unsure of his choices in life, he would ask Lau Lau to report on his sister's health and whereabouts. An insecurity he'd never tell his enemy.

Djagatt coughed blood into his mouth and spit it aside. "He's stalling, Captain. Waiting for me to bleed out. We should attack him now, while we still have the numbers."

Blackrock smiled a sharp obsidian grin. "Caught me."

Kismet nodded and pointed his blade. "Please, don't make me do this."

"It's just business, Oona," Blackrock replied, punching his fist into his palm. Between the stones of his chest blazed a flaming red sigil that flowed like magma. "You should know that better than anyone."

Kismet moved to dash, but was forced to evade as a blast of searing light burst from Blackrock's chest—narrowly missing but turning the tail of his coat to ashes. Djagatt used the opportunity to rush in and raked his claws along Blackrock's stone skin, and while they sparked brilliantly, they gave not a single scratch. Blackrock snatched the Baku by his throat and lifted him from the ground, the flaming sigil burning brighter. Djagatt continued to drag his claws along the obsidian to no avail, and as the sigil prepared to wash him in flame it suddenly dispersed as Kismet leapt on Blackrock's back and thrust the Scarlet Charm into his collarbone.

Blackrock continued to choke Djagatt as he wailed in pain and reached behind with his free hand. He grabbed Kismet by the leathers and hurled him across the boat. Kismet barely recovered into a tumble as he rolled and struck the rails, knocking the pipe from his lips.

"Weak!" Blackrock roared, pulling the crimson honeycomb stone blade free and thrusting it under the Baku's ribs.

Djagatt's eyes narrowed. The blade cut so clean it almost didn't hurt at first, but pain and realization quickly enveloped him. He dangled, barely fighting back as his strength waned, staring into the black stone eyes. He then felt weightless, soaring through the air as the world turned over itself, cast aside and left to die. Djagatt hit the water with a splash, his vision engulfed by a haze that grew ever darker. As he sunk, he watched the wisps of red that drifted from his wounds, like gossamer threads undoing his existence. The Scarlet Charm was still in his stomach.

'Captain will need his sword,' he thought strangely, as though he could give it back. As the light began to fade, gazing up to the rippling mirror, his mind flooded with memories: Lau Lau, Kismet, the *Windborn Chance*; even Whisper, whose sass appealed to his more playful nature. He imagined Lau Lau in his absence, the tears she would cry, the heartbreak she would suffer. He suddenly regretted not learning the art of abjuration, to better ward himself. Instead, he'd chosen the life of a shaman, a necromancer—the ferryman of souls, the link between body and spirit—but who ferries the ferryman? The scarlet strands continued to unweave him. So much life energy, what a waste.

45

BURN THE BLOOD

From the confines of the smuggler's hold, Lau Lau curled into a tiny ball and wept as quietly as she could. She could feel everyone's pain, taste their despair, and hear their resolve. Yoru sat at her face and gave a fuzzy headbutt, purring lightly to cheer her spirit, but it didn't seem to be working.

She was inside the queen's vault, yet she never knew. This was the secret Kismet had been hiding from her for so long. The truth he bargained with her never to glean from his mind. She could tell why he'd hidden it from her. A child, kidnapped from the Phoenix Queen herself. It was no wonder the realm hunted him so. Despite it all, she knew Kismet to be a good man and an even better father. There had to be a reason she was locked away and there had to be a reason he took her.

Yoru nuzzled her furry brow into Lau Lau's face and was pulled in as the child quickly wrapped her arms around her. Suddenly the velvetine didn't want to be held, such was the feline mentality, but Lau Lau squeezed anyways. She could feel Djagatt dying, wrapped in breathless cold.

"You're all I have left," she whispered between sobs.

The velvetine purred and surrendered to the embrace.

"But Kissy stole me," she replied.

Yoru's yellow-green eyes half closed, glinting in what little light seeped through the cracks.

"I suppose, but now I'm losing people I love." She broke into a fit of sobs once more and slowly began propping herself up.

Yoru seemed displaced as she was pushed aside.

"Blackrock won't kill me, and if I surrender he won't kill Kissy either. I have to." Lau Lau lifted the boards to the secret hold and crawled out. She took one last look at the cabin—she'd never see it again. Through the rippled glass of the door she could see the hulking frame of midnight stone lumber toward Kismet, who was leaning against the rails and staring heartbroken into the cove. She could feel his spirit dying, pleading, begging for Djagatt to break the surface of the water with a little fight left.

"You're not so tough without that fancy sword," Blackrock said as he crouched before the fallen captain. He strained to look at the wound the Scarlet Charm left on his collar. Any mortal man would have died, but he was no mortal. It was certainly painful and he'd lost a lot of blood, but the wound eventually sealed with a scar of red stone that briefly blazed with the flames of the sigil on his chest.

Kismet said nothing, an admission of defeat. Without a sword, a swordsman was just a philosopher. "Please," he said softly, "you've taken my best friend. Don't take my daughter as well."

"You're living a dream, Oona. Borrowed time. You had to know this day would come."

Kismet looked at him, something deep and dark and desperate glowed in the red of his eyes. "Please, take me to the queen. Let her judge me for my treason, but give the child her freedom."

Blackrock pondered. The idea of locking Kismet away in The Blackrock prison had its appeal. He sighed. "I'll bring you both." He thrust a stony fist into Kismet's stomach, careful to hold back enough to pierce the skin but not rupture anything important.

"Stop!" a young voice cried.

He turned to see the child with her hands balled at her chest, her eyes bloodshot and cheeks flushed. Behind her, glowing from the darkness were two small yellow-green eyes and a silhouette of fur.

He chuckled deeply, looking back and forth between her and Kismet. "You two are precious." He grabbed Kismet by the leg and began to drag him toward Lau Lau. "Come with me chi—"

Whisper vaulted the edge of the boat, snatched a belaying pin, and leapt onto Blackrock's chest, shoving the wooden stake into his mouth and striking it down his throat as far as she could get it. As he wretched on the pin and tried to swing, she flipped backward and landed on the deck, grabbing the nearest object she could find to crack over his head—a heavy wooden capstan bar. It didn't work. Blackrock coughed the belaying pin from his throat, oblivious to the flinders of the bar as it shattered across his head.

Salem leapt aboard the *Windborn Chance* and dashed toward Lau Lau, scooping her in his arms and leaping back into the captain's quarters as Whisper's body was thrown through the door, shattering glass everywhere.

"Are you alright, little one?" Salem said softly.

Lau Lau sniffled and wiped her face with her sleeve. "You're two people."

"That is... very astute."

Whisper clambered to her feet and rushed back out onto the deck, only to be hurled back into the cabin through the wall. She groaned, pushing the debris from her body as she rose. The creature was in her, she could feel it, but it wasn't yet ready to show its face. "Any suggestions?"

"Go for its vulnerable points?" Salem shrugged.

"It's a damned rock, Salem!" She rushed back out into the fray and spotted Kismet's pipe, giving her an idea.

Blackrock swung wide and she tumbled under, snatching the mast lantern and smashing it across his chest. He reached out, snagged her by the coat, and lifted her off her feet. A sharp fist wound backward as he readied to throw everything he had, when she feinted the pipe into view—snatched when she tumbled, and now placed between her lips. She exhaled sharply; orange cinders splashed across the lantern oil and Blackrock burst into flame, but much to her dismay he seemed gravely unaffected.

"Not even inconvenienced?" she said as she let her body hang from his grasp as dead weight. Now he was indestructible *and* on fire—somehow she'd just made her situation worse. She needed her power to show itself, and fast. "Any chance you could punch me in the face, but not hard enough that I'll explode?"

Blackrock wound up again, with much more lethality than Whisper would be able to handle. She struggled to free herself but he was too strong, and as the desperation began to stir, so did the hunger within her. He roared as he swung and stood awestruck as Whisper stopped his fist with both hands, inches from her face.

She placed both feet on his hips—the roil of oil set aflame didn't seem to bother her—and grabbed each wrist with her hands. In a contest of sheer strength, she pried his grasp from her coat and slowly began to pull his arms open. Her cobalt blue eyes formed a blossom of silver lacunae, her hair began to change hue in the blazing red light, and the corona of an impending storm tickled the senses. She leaned back as far as she could and thrust her head into his, buckling the boards beneath them and dropping him to a knee. She planted both feet on the ground, wound up, and thrust her head into his again, releasing his arms and letting him tumble backward.

As dazed as he was, she reeled herself. Thin streams of blood trickled down her brow from the edges of stone. Only a few stones had actually cut her skin, but they weren't too deep.

Blackrock stood and began swinging wildly, and while Whisper raised her arms to block his strikes they were beginning to hurt very quickly. A single flinch of pain and she allowed a fist to slip through, striking her in the stomach and taking her off her feet. Blood trickled from her arms and hands as she clutched her stomach and dropped to the deck in a fit of coughs.

Blackrock pulled her up by her hair and drove a stony knee into her chest; she buckled, spewing blood between her teeth.

'*She doesn't know how to use her power properly,*' Savrae-Lyth said in the back of Salem's mind. '*I thought you said she was ready?*'

'*I said nothing of the sort,*' he replied.

'*Her body is still in chrysalis. She hasn't even fully awoken yet.*'

'*Can I help?*' Lau Lau's voice interrupted.

Salem turned to look at her with an air of surprise. Just what he needed, another voice in his head. Fever would be proud.

The boat began to rock and everyone stopped to look out into the cove. The water began churning white caps and bubbles rose from the ocean floor like Dragon's Breath. Blackrock released Whisper, who flopped to the deck a bloody mess, barely conscious. Something stirred beneath the waves and the closer he watched, the more he noticed the hint of eerie red necromantic light that neared the surface. Suddenly, bursting through the crests was a massive draconian skeleton, its eyes glowed a phantom sanguine flame.

'Palindross,' Savrae-Lyth sung.

'How did you know his name?' Lau Lau replied.

'I know the name of every dragon, it's my privilege as a queen. Palindross was most honorable. His death was a terrible tragedy, one of many to fall to Howlpack Shade during the war.'

Standing inside the skull was Djagatt, his body blazed in necromantic essence as he burned his blood in exchange for power. He pulled the Scarlet Charm from his stomach, the blood sizzled into wisps of life force, and he threw the blade to Kismet. It landed near his feet and slid to the far end of the deck. Djagatt's body slowly withered before their eyes as he sacrificed every last drop of blood to sustain the undead summoning, mummifying himself alive. The massive jaws snapped down on Blackrock, tore him from the deck, and plunged him into the water. He, Djagatt, and the dragon's bones disappeared into the endless dark below.

46

CHORUS OF SKULLS: BLACKROCK VS. PALINDROSS

Salem rushed to Whisper's side and turned her onto her back. She had been beaten senseless, eyes rolling back and lazily swimming like the feathered dragon's souls. He reached into his lapel to fetch his set of medical needles, quickly remembering that Fever had disarmed him of all his belonging and left them on the *Last Breath*. For a moment he panicked, unsure of what to do to stop the gushing wounds that poured onto the deck.

Kismet watched Salem carefully, unsure of who he was or where he'd suddenly come from. It was clear he knew Whisper, but something else seemed even clearer. He watched Salem cradle her head and desperately staunch her wounds with his hands. The heartbreak in his eyes—like staring into his own reflection. It was how he imagined he'd look if Lau Lau had been injured. It's how he felt knowing Djagatt was sacrificing everything he had to protect them and here he was, swordless and pathetic. Barely able to find the energy to crawl to his blade and sheath it. He was ruining more lives with his actions and whether he fought or surrendered, the people he cared about would continue to suffer. Blackrock, his sister, and now Lau Lau, Whisper, and Djagatt. When would it end? Could it?

Lau Lau walked out on trembling legs, overwhelmed with the

aura of despair. She could feel Djagatt bellowing in agony beneath the waves, Blackrock raging as he fought for a single breath of the surface, Kismet's mournful defeat, Salem's desperation, and Whisper's fading moments wordlessly wanting to say something. Yoru followed beside her.

The electric roil of Freestone's peach blossoms took to the air and Savrae-Lyth appeared at their side, sadness in her eyes. Even the scent of spring wasn't enough to cover the metallic tinge of blood soaked air. Lau Lau and Yoru approached her and bowed, to which the Queen of Drakes was surprised.

Salem noticed both the cat and child acknowledge her. This child seemed to have some form of enlightenment or a heightened sensitivity perhaps.

"What are you, little one?" he asked.

Lau Lau sniffled and tried to hold back her tears long enough to reply. "I'm Lau Lau and this is Yoru. I'm a psychic and she is an elantan velvetine."

Salem was struck with a revelation—eyes wide, smiling hopefully. "By fate," he said, "you just might save us all."

Far beneath the ocean's surface, Blackrock and Djagatt struggled in the consuming dark. The ghostly sanguine flames that consumed the Baku's body illuminated Blackrock's desperation as he pried open the massive draconian jaws. Free for but a moment, Blackrock dismissed his stone skin and swam for the surface, breaking the water long enough to gasp for air before Palindross towered over him and crashed down with jaws wide.

Palindross was large enough that he could keep his hind legs on the ocean floor and reach the surface by standing, so Blackrock knew he had little chance of escaping his reach. He turned his body back to stone before the dragon's teeth bore down and pushed him under, stuck in the maw of bone. Blackrock was aware of the strategy—the dragon didn't have the strength to crush him in this form, but if it could keep him under water long enough he could drown. He wasn't familiar with blood magic or necromancy, but it didn't seem like the Baku was breathing at all, just a dead vessel being consumed as fuel. If Blackrock was going to survive, he had to outlast the consumption or at least reach the shore.

Palindross plunged him into the silt and dragged him along the ocean floor.

Blackrock firmly placed both feet on the lower jaw and pushed up with his shoulders, forcing open the creature's mouth. He strained with its strength, and its flailing made it even harder to keep his grip. With absolute force of will he pushed the jaws as far as he could, unsure of what to do next. With the maw wide he could see Djagatt clearly; the sanguine flame blazed brighter, hundreds of skulls faded and flickered within. The skulls affixed their sightless eyes on him and unhinged their jaws, screaming beneath the waves with a shock that made his ears bleed. The sigil of Blackrock's chest flared, the skulls of Djagatt's aura blazed, and the two released a beam that collided into a swirling burst of water that exploded deafeningly.

Blackrock spun through the water, broke the surface, and skipped twice before hitting the stone of shore. Water spilled from his lungs as he wretched on his back. He'd made it to land, regaining his combat advantage.

Palindross surged from the water and struck him with its massive claws, forcing him down into the ground. The skulls screamed again and without the water to buffer the sound it was far more painful than he imagined. Blackrock grimaced and ground his stony teeth—his armor was useless if the Baku could melt his brain. He charged his sigil once more and with a steady burst he blasted through the dragon's claws.

Palindross staggered on three limbs as it fought to gain its balance from the force, but Blackrock capitalized on the moment of weakness and released a second ray of blazing flame that pierced through the skull like a spearhead. The orange flames struck Djagatt, seared the remainder of his flesh from his bones, and turned him to ashes. The sanguine light faded from the bones of Palindross and the skeleton collapsed, sinking back into the ocean.

'Projection,' Salem thought, 'the child is filled with psychic energy and might act as a medium.'

'Will this work?' Savrae-Lyth asked. She'd never heard of it before.

'I have no idea, but if Lau Lau can put a part of herself into my mind, perhaps she can put a part of you into Whisper's. It will be temporary, of course, but you will gain control of her power, and no one can use it more effectively than you.'

'Okay,' she replied, 'but if this works, you will need to retreat to safe distance. I'll have to heal her before anything else and you could be injured.'

Salem grabbed Lau Lau's hand and together he placed them on Whisper's chest. Savrae-Lyth closed her eyes, took a deep breath, and the electric blossoms of Freestone faded from their senses. Salem's mind fell suddenly quiet and the hairs on their arms began to rise. A static corona took the air, an invisible force that crawled across their skin as dark clouds began to churn high above. He quickly stood and pulled Lau Lau off her feet, fleeing as fast as he could to the captain's quarters and making it only moments before a bolt of lightning pierced the clouds and struck Whisper. The light was blinding, the thunder was deafening, and the force threw them from their feet with ringing disorientation.

Whisper's hair turned from crimson to blond and her eyes burst open—electricity arcing between the lacunae of her cobalt blues. Lightning continued to surge over her body, mending her wounds and filling her with power. Whisper lay there, enraged, conscious of her overwhelming strength, yet unsure of where it came from. Then, a soft voice sung in the back of her mind.

'You don't know how to use your power,' it said, 'Let me show you.'

47

THE TOUCH OF EVIL

The guest chambers in the castle of Whitewater were not as Elder Waylander expected. There was a grand expectation that came with being the ruler of a realm. One would have thought that each room was exquisitely decorated and furnished with only the finest or that each hall would have its adornment of murals and silk tapestries depicting the many victories of the leviathan king and his predecessors. Instead, the halls and rooms were barren white marble and blue honeycomb stone, and while beautiful, it was simple by royal standard.

Waylander was bandaged by the king's best healers and enchanters and was feeling much better considering he would always be missing an arm. Much to the merit of the menders, the residual burns he'd suffered were cared for so well they were likely not to scar badly, but a little was expected. He sat himself up in bed and looked over the room. The frame had tall canopy posts with no curtains, a large fireplace, a wardrobe, and a single window that looked out from the tower upon the main keep.

There was an appreciation that came with the practicality. Whitewater equalitarian rule, which was the idea that a ruler should reign as closely with his people as possible, was not popular in Lyre.

The duke lived in decadence. Every night was a feast, every day was a tribute to his name, and while a portion of the taxes went to the necessities of Lyre, it largely supported the duke's lifestyle. Here, it seemed that Liam Whitewater kept very little and poured almost everything back into the city.

It didn't feel like Waylander had been in the castle for very long, but he was almost always asleep—one loses all sense of time. For all he knew, the season was past and the war was over. The few hours he was awake, he'd noticed there was hardly a servant in the king's employ. Perhaps a cook or two roamed the halls or the occasional groundskeeper. Only once did he see a maid. He stopped every one of them to talk and was surprised to learn each of them were once homeless. It seemed the king had a system, where he would give the homeless a room and food and educate them as cooks, housekeepers, healers, or squires in exchange for their services. After a few years of experience, those new professionals would train new homeless, retire their position, and move back into the city to start a new life with new skills—and so the cycle went. Shopkeeps were hard pressed to turn down the help of someone trained in the castle, regardless of their past.

Each meal, the king brought food to his bed ridden guests himself. It was a hospitality that was almost uncomfortable to a Moth, who lived lives of servitude. It had always been the duty of a Waylander to serve his king, not the other way around, and though it was greatly appreciated, he couldn't help but feel ashamed.

There was a knock at the door and a man entered, clad in blue steel armor with a silver wolf's head protruding from the breastplate. To each side of him was a harnessed blade—the beautiful silver sweepings of a rapier on his left and a simple trident dagger on his right. The man strode in with purpose, acknowledging Waylander and walking to the window.

"Fates, Azel," Waylander said, "we're guests in the king's home and you're in armor."

"All due respect, commander, these are dark times. A battle could happen at any moment and I'd like to be prepared." Azel ran a hand through his sandy locks and tapped his wolf's head ring on the pommel of his trident dagger. "I'm not feeling terribly welcome either."

"We're the wards of a traitor," Waylander replied as he swung his legs over the side of the bed and carefully stood. "It was on our watch that a city fell. We're blessed to be welcome at all."

"Maybe." Azel looked out the window upon the Great Hall. A magnificent white and blue, with a canopy of ivy and a spire that held a massive ruby in the sky. A dragon of platinum encircled the gemstone. "How big do you think that is?"

Waylander shuffled to the window to gaze upon the ruby. "Ten feet tall, at least, maybe more."

"Looks smaller from here."

The door to the room opened and Diana quietly entered. Brown hair framed her delicate face, adorned with her circlet of silver brambles. She was neither armed nor armored, though she never was. "Am I interrupting?"

Waylander gestured for her to sit. If Diana had come to visit, it was likely she had news.

"I've seen the arrival of your children," she said, "they are with the Shén Shé pureblood and escorted by Bastet and Venetta. I have also foreseen the arrival of someone you know, but whose name eludes my senses. A tracker, come to find you from Freestone."

He tried to maintain his composure, but there was no hiding his relief. To hear his family was safe, the Moths were still intact, and the potential arrival of an Instrument ally, Howlpack Shade, was excellent news. He couldn't help but notice an air of concern lingered around her still. "What else? Is Jeren alright?"

Jeren was wounded in the altercation with Wrath in Lyre and was carried to Whitewater with them, but his injuries were substantial even compared to Waylander's.

"His health is failing, but he's holding on for now. I have been doing everything I can to mend his wounds, but the cuts and burns run deep. There's a good chance he will not make it to week's end." Diana folded her hands and scratched at a drop of dried blood she'd noticed on her thumb from changing Jeren's bandages. "There is something else, commander. It's about your son, Casamir."

Waylander felt a hot coal in his stomach; he knew what it meant. "How bad are his injuries?"

"Bad," she replied, "he will live, but he will never recover."

A scream echoed the halls. Azel immediately drew both blades, the trident dagger snapped open into three, and gave Waylander a look. "Good thing one of us is armed."

Azel dashed into the hall and pursued the source. Diana helped Waylander follow as best they could, but she stopped in the middle of the hall and watched Azel turn the corner.

Waylander looked around, wondering why she'd halted so suddenly. "What do you see?"

Diana quickly turned her head to look behind them, but there was nothing. The hall whispered from the darkness, twisting before her, slowly, barely enough to notice. She felt a warm breath on her face, the stench of death and carrion.

Waylander turned, but could see nothing, feel nothing.

Sweat formed at her silver brambles and as quickly as the feeling came, it vanished.

Azel called from further down the hall and Waylander shook Diana gently.

"There is a great evil here," she said, "It's all around us, moving quickly."

Azel had the swords, so with him they'd be safest. Waylander urged her onward, and together they cautiously turned the corner. The maid stood outside Jeren's door with her hands on her face, terror painted across her eyes. Azel exited the room and looked at them, shaking his head in warning.

"It's not good, commander," he said.

Diana and Waylander entered Jeren's room, their faces suddenly pale with sickness. There was blood everywhere—the bed, the walls, the ceiling. White marble stained red and from the ceiling a sickly *drip drip* that beat like a heart on the floor. Jeren's ribs stretched upward like temple spires, revealing the soft viscera beneath. His eyes were still open, frozen in agony and terror.

Blood continued to spatter darkly on the canvas of white; his heart was missing entirely.

48

A KISS OF LIGHTNING: WHISPER VS. BLACKROCK

Fever watched from the trees, teeth on her lip as the carnage unfolded. She teased the idea of stepping in and joining the onslaught, but instead chose to wait until she knew exactly the situation. Seeing the Baku sparked a memory within her—the death of her family during a Baku raid and her very first kill. Her village was massacred by Blademanes, mostly, and this Baku looked nothing like them. It was no surprise she wasn't overcome with the urge to kill it like she did with the Ravenmane.

The harrow shrike cried as it lost its arm to the man in the tricorne, presumably the mark, Oona Kismet. He didn't look that tough, so she couldn't imagine needing to intervene to secure his capture. The only one missing was Whisper—the whole reason she agreed to go on this stupid mission.

The harrow shrike fled the *Windborn Chance* and flew above, taking refuge in the woods to tend its wound. Despite the entertainment before her, the shrike was beginning to look like her only way back. With Carver's crew lost there was no one to man any of the remaining boats, and even if she used her serpents to do the work of twelve, she had no idea how to navigate. With great reluctance, she turned and disappeared into the foliage.

A serpent of ichor emerged from her bangle and silently slithered along the forest floor, tasting the air with its flaming green tongue as it searched for the shrike. Fever stopped as footsteps raced down the path twenty paces beside her. A woman with beautiful raven hair and cobalt blue eyes dashed by, her milky skin flushing red. Was this Whisper? The mistborn looked different than the stories told. There were no opalescent scales or demonic appendages of grievous claws and armored spines. She supposed it was possible they were all folk stories or exaggerations, which led her to wonder how much of her exploits were falsified as well. This woman certainly didn't look the type to kill a man with his own horse. Shortly after the woman's departure, the jingle of shackles neared and Salem quickly ran by with broken chains fastened to his wrists and ankles.

'Still alive, I see,' she smiled sharply, 'I suppose there's still some fun yet to have.'

The serpent caught a taste of demonic blood and urged her forward. Salem and Whisper could wait, first she needed to secure her escape. She trekked through lush green ferns until she saw the mottled black scales and citron eyes. It also saw her coming and bared its teeth for her arrival.

"Hello lovely," she said sweetly, unaffected by its attempt to intimidate. She lifted her hand and released six shadowy serpents, which lashed around its wings and throat and forced it into submission. "Don't let the serpents fool you, I'm not one for animal affinity."

The shrike fought the bindings, but she only squeezed tighter in the struggle. When the shrike would stop, she'd release slightly. Eventually, it seemed to understand that if it wanted to breathe it had to remain still.

Fever looked over the creature. The voices in her head resounded with a variety of opinions, ranging from 'kill it' to 'pet it'. One voice in particular asked a very important question. 'How will we control it?' To which Fever's true voice replied, 'The same as any living creature. Control the head, the body will follow.'

Suddenly, the sky grew dark and thunder roared through the canopy.

Whisper bellowed through the cacophony of lightning that surged through her body. At first it sounded like pain, but quickly turned into rage. The arcs of blue brilliance coursed her body, filled her blood, and sealed her wounds, leaving only the tease of soft, pale skin through the corset of blue and silver lace. Her eyes flared with the energy, lingering and snapping long after the lightning strike ended. She kicked to her feet, and buckled over—the surge of raw power filled her muscles to the point of bursting. Her blond hair hung down her face as she collected herself.

"Why does her hair keep changing color?" Lau Lau asked as she climbed to her feet. She shielded her eyes from the blinding brilliance, but peeked just enough to see the transformation.

"It is a sign of her power internalizing itself," Salem replied, "The destructive nature of energy has two forms, introversion and extroversion. When the energy within Whisper radiates, her hair turns red. It is especially good for combat against multiple, weaker foes. However, when her power focuses inward, her hair turns blonde. This hones her destructive energy into precision and is devastating against single opponents."

"Is that why the lightning healed her?"

"In a way, yes. Each dragon has an affinity to at least one element. Whisper is a halo drake, like her mother. In her wyrmling state she breathes fire and creates lashing winds, but fire and wind are only her secondary elements. Her truest nature is the combination of both, lightning."

"That's why she didn't die when she fought Howlpack Shade," Lau Lau said with glee.

This was the first he'd heard of the conflict's resolution and had wondered what happened that caused her to suddenly go into her chrysalis state. If Howlpack Shade had struck her with lightning, she would have appeared to be dead because her body wasn't yet ready to harness the power, but the ability to heal from it would still be in her blood. Such a massive surge of her primary element must have forced her blood born lineage to internalize her power, heal from the lightning, and prepare her form to handle such a quantity of energy in the future. Shade couldn't know it yet, but he inadvertently helped the heiress of house Eiliona leap toward her rightful throne as the Queen of Drakes and essentially prepared her to receive her inheritance from her mother.

Salem noticed the black ball of fur that sat peacefully beside him, its little eyes squinting in the light as it watched. "That is the bravest cat I have ever seen."

"Yoru isn't a cat. She's an elantan velvetine."

"Oh right, you had mentioned. Velvetines are increasingly rare." Salem crouched down and pet it, running his hand down its back to the tip of its tail, where the last bone formed a tiny crook. "Fascinating."

Whisper rose and looked out at Blackrock, who spotted her from the grave of dragon bones. Her telescopic vision had returned and she could see him smile and gesture a challenge. With Djagatt and Palindross defeated, his adrenaline beckoned for a worthy foe. He crossed his arms and waited for her to approach.

'This is how it's done,' Savrae-Lyth chimed.

Whisper's body flashed into a bolt of blue lightning.

A single step.

A half a heartbeat.

A palm against the back of Blackrock's head.

The thunder was deafening, reverberating to his core, and in a flash of blue light he was suddenly struck face first into the gray stone of the shoreline. His body tumbled thrice over, tearing up the earth as he spun out of control. He finally stopped, embedded nearly a foot into the mossy stone beneath, and rose to a knee.

Another single step.

Another half a heartbeat.

A heel atop his crown.

Her leg led high, she dropped it on his head and thrust him into the ground. The earth fissured under him as he buckled straight down, the stone shattering outward and spraying debris into the sky. He was several feet beneath the surface now, salt water trickled in through the cracks that reached the ocean. He leapt up and out, landing before Whisper and swinging as hard as he could.

Whisper raised a hand and grabbed his fist, stopping it dead. He swung with the other and she stopped it as well. Blackrock reeled back and thrust his stony head into hers, snapping her head back slightly. She was surprised it didn't hurt and smiled knowing she wouldn't have to endure another headache. She reeled back and returned the strike—a ripple of air burst thunderously and hurled him head over heels across the Bone Grove.

Whisper's rage was taking over, pushing Savrae-Lyth out.

'You won't defeat him with strength,' Savrae-Lyth said.

'Shut up.'

Savrae-Lyth forced herself back in and took over Whisper's body while she still could. Whisper raised a hand to her face as though placing a mask and a halo of blue flames encircled her head, concealing her eyes behind the blaze. She waved her arm as though casting something aside and a flutter of vibrant feathers began to form into her glorious cloak. The fabric waved in the wind and opened to reveal the white silk lining and blaze of scarlet eyes—the **Gaze of Brittle Chains**. Suddenly, she could see. She knew she didn't have the power to crack Blackrock's shell, but she now realized another way to defeat him.

'Do you see?' Savrae-Lyth said.

'Fine. Now let me do it.'

She felt the foreign presence bow and withdraw from her psyche; with it went the halo and cloak. Finally, she was free to fight the way she wanted.

Before Blackrock could stand, Whisper already clasped her hand around his throat and lifted him from the ground. She looked deep into the slate eyes and smiled sharply. It was good to have her power back—she'd missed it so. Whisper turned, hurled Blackrock straight down into the stone and, with every ounce of pent up aggression she could muster, drove her heel into the center of his face. The earth cracked, but his neck did not, which was as unfortunate as it was expected.

Whisper stood over him and struck repeatedly. Inch by inch his body sank further, fissures spread from the crater like a spider's web with each earthshaking connection. The crater crept wide enough to comb the shore and salt water began to pour into it. Whisper roared with each drop of her fist, sending water and stone up into the air, raining back down upon them. Blackrock tried to shield his face but her ruthlessness knew no bounds, standing on his chest and hammering through his guard without remorse. The water would burst upward with each strike, shimmering and sparkling blue as lightning arced between the droplets, and as the water rushed back into the hole it would flush down Blackrock's nose and throat. He began coughing between each strike, which was music to Whisper's ears.

With the *Gaze of Brittle Chains* there was one thing she gleaned. Though Blackrock's skin was nearly impenetrable, his organs were still soft and squishy. She needed to get a lightning strike inside of him and few things conduct electricity better than salt water.

The water rushed in and submerged him again. He gasped for air and struggled to defend himself as it filled his lungs. Whisper raised her fist to the sky. Clouds darkened and swirled above and a strike of brilliant blue lightning surged down and coursed across her knuckles. With a roar, she hurled her fist into him, a burst of lightning kissed air and mist exploded outward with a rumble that rocked the *Windborn Chance*. Blackrock's body tightened and convulsed as the water turned to steam and rose from his mouth and nose.

The lightning strike dissipated, the water rushed back into the crater, and Whisper stood on his chest with teeth ground. Blackrock did not move and any living creature unfortunate enough to be near the shore now floated at the surface. She clenched her fists, breathing heavily, and then collapsed to her knees, clutching her head and raging. A massive roiling aura of lashing wind and opalescent flame began to encircle her, gnashing at the earth.

What little victory Salem had felt quickly faded.

49

OMENS

The pristine marble halls of Whitewater's castle were barely noticeable in the dark—empty, vast, and seemingly endless. Diana stood in a corridor that melted like candle wax before her. Shadow on shadow, the walls dripped black ichor down the hazy glow of white. There was no sound, just the slow beating of her heart in her chest.

A whisper touched her ear and she spun, gazing deeply into the darkness. She felt a hunger, her own perhaps, a low rumble from stomach to throat that had her eyes carefully searching around her. The sigils of light that once illuminated the halls of the castle betrayed her and while she couldn't see, she knew each step.

A feeling washed over her. Heavy, like a summer heat. Empty, like an executioner's eyes. It crept across her flesh and urged her forward, where a warm breeze carried the scent of blood not yet spilled. She licked her lips, pressing forward through the bleeding dark until she reached a door.

She was deathly silent, opening the door and slipping into the room with none the wiser. The smell was stronger and now she could hear it too—the beat of a heart not hers. Barefoot and soundless she crept across the room, feeling the honeycomb stone grooves under the pads of her feet. Before her was a bed, wherein slept Elder Waylander. Before his slumber she gave him vissinia for his wounds and serpent's poppy for his insomnia.

Diana gazed down at him and listened to his heart beat. She could nearly see the heat rise from his veins, nearly taste the iron on her tongue. Her fingers flexed eagerly and in the still silence of midnight she clasped his throat with one hand and thrust her fingers into the center of his chest with the other.

Waylander awoke in agony as her hand wrapped around his breastbone, ribs crooked in the webs of her fingers, and she squeezed any cry for help from his windpipe. The warmth of his blood flowed over her hand and with a swift pull she tore his sternum from his chest. His ribcage snapped open and the whites of his eyes burst bloody vessels. He tried to wriggle free, but even with the vissinia he was paralyzed with the pain and her grasp was too strong. She was a silhouette against the darkness, shadow upon shadow, and he watched as her hand reached into his chest, clutched his heart, and ripped it from his body.

A sudden gasp and Diana abruptly woke from her slumber, snapping up to sit. Her heart beat furiously, sweat dripped from her brow, and she threw her salt-soaked blankets aside. Barefooted, her feet touched the marble with a chill and she raced through the dark of nightfall. The midnight air cooled her damp nightgown as she hurried through the halls, illuminating sigils of light along the way and trying not to let the cold slow her joints.

She burst through the door of Elder Waylander's room, where the outline of something monstrous distorted reality like mirage on Baku sand. It towered over him—its hunger made her dizzy with nausea, its bloodlust an acid behind her eyes—but she had the sense to cry out.

Waylander's eyes opened to see her collapse to her knees, clutching her hair in fistfuls as she fought the overwhelming oppression of psychic turpitude. He tried to rise from his bed when something grabbed his throat and he was thrust back down. His eyes had yet to focus fully, but whatever held him fast had scales that chafed his neck and claws that scratched the surface of his skin. Waylander couldn't comprehend what towered over him, but the strange shimmer of hot air seemed to move like a stalking sirocco. As his eyes blurred beneath its grasp and Diana collapsed, he saw the figure raise an arm above his chest. Then, the spatter of warm blood.

The creature released Waylander's throat and staggered backward, where it was struck a second time. Two arrows stretched from the shimmer of air, where the distortion of reality began to shift into something more comprehendible. The illusion surged across the creature's flesh, pulsing through different colors and shades before fixing on a pale translucence. Its face had no features save for a single slit that stretched along its jaw like a grievous smile, which opened and unhinged into a gaping maw of needles. Its long tongue whipped the air, hissing from its throat until a third arrow whistled and pierced it. The creature gurgled as it reeled, collapsed into the corner, and scowled its last.

Diana gasped for air as though she'd been drowning and pushed herself to her knees with trembling hands. The deep blue of honeycomb stone began to affix in her sight as the psychic weight of pure malice and hunger unraveled from her neck like a hangman's noose. In the corner of her eye she saw an antler outstretched before her, and as she grabbed it to assist her to her feet she saw the man from her visions. She knew he'd come to see Waylander and his timing couldn't have been any better.

The creature's pale body was taken to the apothecary, far beneath the castle halls, where the frigid air played with their breath until the fires began to roar in their hearths. A table was cleared of mortars and vials, and the body was placed on it. Wood cracked and split at the lick of flame, slowly building rage. Diana sat in a chair with her bramble circlet in her hands, thumbs gently rolling over the points of silver thorns. In the corner, Shade crouched at the hearth and warmed his hands, while Waylander stood over the unusual creature. He could feel his neck bruising from its grasp.

The door swung open and Whitewater, Fairchild, and Azel

entered—urgency painted in their eyes, but none more than Fairchild, whose usually pale complexion was now deathly.

They each gazed at the creature in horror. It was covered in rigid translucent scales, firm as cured leather but edges like thistle. Its head had no features, but its mouth could peel back nearly half its face to reveal an array of pointed teeth. Long, thin arms had terrible claws of green-tinged bone and the legs, inverted at the knee, seemed soundless as it walked despite its gangly structure.

The leviathan immediately noticed an unfamiliar face at the hearth. "Who is this?"

Shade wasn't one for politics or royal hierarchy, and though he was a denizen of the realm he bowed only to Howlpack Sentinel Avelie. He spied the king in the corner of his eye, but made no effort to pay a respect.

"A friend," Waylander said. "He is Shade, Alpha of the Howlpack."

"I see. You did a great service to the realm in the Dragon War," Whitewater replied. If the Howlpack were in Whitewater, their situation was even more dire than previously thought. "You're welcome within these walls."

"I don't serve the realm, I serve Fate itself," Shade replied, "and walls are simply prisons of our choosing."

Whitewater was kingly enough to recognize an ally through common enemy, but leviathan enough to imagine crushing his skull with his bare hands. "What do we know of the creature?"

"We know everything was fine until the Moths arrived," Fairchild snapped.

Diana and Waylander bit their tongues, but Azel was much less understanding. His hands eagerly rested on the handles of his blades, tapping the pommel with his ring and pacing sharply—ready for battle no matter the opponent. "Are you implying we're responsible for this creature?" he said. Azel approached Fairchild closely enough the wolf's head on his blue-steel breastplate brushed the treasurer's robes. For all his anger, armor and skill, Fairchild didn't waver a moment.

"Once a traitor, always a traitor," Fairchild smirked.

The blades nearly slid free of their sheaths when Waylander

commanded him to stop. Azel slowly slipped the steel back and snarled.

Fairchild played with the rings on his hand. "You don't need to listen to him," he said, "Draw your blades if you wish, it only proves my point. Shall I turn my back first? Would that be more familiar?"

"You fat piece of—"

"Azel!" Waylander barked, "Stand down."

Shade poked at the fire with an iron rod and pretended not to care, but Diana could sense him chuckling inside. Waiting for the swordsong to let loose singing steel. Unfortunately, he didn't.

"Seems you have your orders," Fairchild smiled.

"At least I know my place," Azel replied.

"I'm a dignitary of the—"

"I meant on the food chain, swine."

Whitewater's patience was thin to begin with and while he first wanted to hear if anything damning came of the altercation his tolerance was now spent entirely. "Fairchild," he growled, "we have enough problems already. Mind your tongue, as my patience with you wanes."

Azel backed away slowly and removed his hands from his blades. "You're lucky I have the will to walk away. If Venetta were here she would have slit you neck to nub, consequences be damned." He disengaged completely and stood on the other end of the table, directing his attention to the creature.

Whitewater walked to the corpse and grabbed its head with his massive hand, tilting it left and right to get a better look. "Is it a demon?"

"I'm almost certain," Waylander replied, "however, this creature was not summoned."

"How do you know?"

"Each Instrument is graced with special abilities when they are chosen. My ability is called *Sigilsmith*. I can learn and understand any enchantment I see once, across any discipline, and manifest sigils without having to draw them. I can also rearrange the energy of existing sigils to create new ones. When a demon is summoned from the Overworld there is an energy residue that binds the creature to the mortal realm. When the residue degrades, the demon is sent back—thus, the duration imposed on chthonomantic summoning. This creature has no such energy."

Fairchild shook his head. "So, you mean to say that we have a demon running loose in our castle and you are capable of such a manifestation?"

"I told you this demon wasn't summoned," Waylander replied. "It must have come directly from the funnel of mist."

"Says one who could have summoned it. Convenient we would require insight from a man of suspect."

Waylander couldn't argue because Fairchild was right. To his knowledge, he was the only man capable of summoning this demon within the castle walls, so his support in the investigation would, even should, be questioned.

Fairchild would never understand it, but Liam knew he could trust Waylander. It was a constant whisper in the back of his mind, a persistent reassurance that kept his nerves calm.

Diana began to draw tiny sigils along her circlet, which glowed a soft golden light before melting into the silver. "This creature is capable of exuding incredible psychic energy," she said as she finished the last one and placed it back on her head. "I must take precautions to shield my mind in case we encounter another."

"What is its discipline?" Waylander asked.

Diana noticed the king's head tilt curiously as he furrowed his brow. "No two psychics are exactly the same," she said. "Just like the varying disciplines of enchantment, psychics also have specializations. As you are aware, I am a soothsayer. I open my mind to the lingering essence of the Weave and experience insights into the future. The Weave produces a very subtle signal, so my discipline is incredibly sensitive to such energy as time and emotion."

"Psychics are very rare," the king said, "Are you saying this creature is one as well?"

"Yes, but I sense we may no longer be as rare as once thought."

Waylander gave her a look of concern, urging her quietly to reconsider what she was about to say, but he could see in her eyes she had no intentions of hiding the truth.

"Psychics become such only by exposure to the energy of the Overworld while in the womb. We are essentially mistborn, demon-touched, but instead of reshaping our bodies the energy reshapes our minds."

Fairchild rolled his eyes. "Excellent, more demon half-bloods to worry about."

"Whisper was a powerful ally," Whitewater replied sharply.

"And a liability, Your Grace. The very reason you sent her to Freestone with Salem. Every Moth here is a liability." Fairchild's pale face flushed red as he flustered, "No mistborn can be trusted."

"The problem is not the mistborns," Diana said softly. "What I mean to say is that the energy of the Overworld is psychic in nature, so we can expect many of the demons to possess psychic traits of some discipline."

Fairchild silenced. That prospect was much worse.

Diana stood and approached the corpse. "This creature is the opposite of me. Where I absorb energy, it exudes it. With such intensity as well, I cannot help but feel it was communicating over great range."

The king shifted uncomfortably and crossed his massive arms. "What are you saying?"

"I'm saying I believe this creature was a scout, mapping the castle and reporting on our defenses. The first stage before an attack."

50

AWAKE, THE SLUMBERING BLOOD

Lau Lau's eyes swelled with tears as she watched the shore, divided between Whisper's overwhelming rage and Djagatt's ashes amidst Palindross. Her fingernails marked her palms as her body tensed. Blackrock was finally dead, but the air still weighed heavily. There were no breaths of freedom, no sighs of relief. The souls of the fallen cried out and resounded behind her eyes in a chorus of agony and dismay.

"Come, Lau Lau," Kismet said softly. He placed a hand on her shoulder and guided her to the cabin. Yoru and Salem followed behind.

"I am not certain we are safe here," Salem said as he watched Whisper's aura of gnashing wind grow more vicious.

"What's happening to her?"

Whisper hunched over and clutched at her chest, roaring as her spine began to stretch against her skin and sprout six large, leathery wings. The light hit them, shimmering a fantastic opalescence that traced down her body.

"Her draconian blood has awoken. She has lost control and is assuming her true form to accommodate the energy she now holds. Dragons have incredible power in their true forms, but when they assume their alternate shapes the power condenses into a much smaller space. By going into chrysalis, their body reforms to hold the higher concentration of power, but because Whisper has not completed her chrysalis state yet, she is incapable of retaining her human shape under the current conditions. Her instincts are forcing her into her draconian body."

"The heiress of house Eiliona," Kismet said under his breath, "The last halo drake."

Whisper's coat of black boar-skin tore at the seams as her shoulders bulged. She ripped her sleeves to shreds as her arms and hands turned into powerful draconian limbs and claws. Opalescent scales shimmered across the distance, greater the larger her form grew.

Kismet pulled Lau Lau further into the cabin where she couldn't see Whisper's transformation, though he knew she still knew what was happening. "I need you to listen to me—"

"Why didn't you tell me?" she sobbed, punching him in the chest with her little fists. Kismet buckled more than she expected, but he deserved it.

Kismet sighed and took a knee before her, removing his hat and placing it against his chest. His dark brown waves framed the flame kissed eyes he tried to hide so well, brimming with apology and sorrow. "I wanted to protect you."

"That's stupid," she cried. "We've always been in danger. We've always been running. Lying to me doesn't protect me, it only protects yourself."

Kismet's head bowed. "I didn't want to burden you with the choices I'd made. The life I left behind. I wanted a clean slate. A new life, with new adventures."

"People are dying, Kissy. People I love. You have to take me back." Kismet shook his head. "I can't do that."

"Why?"

"Because," he said, placing a hand on her shoulder, "the Phoenix Queen is not what she seems. If I take you back, she will kill you." He pulled her in tightly and held her close. She sobbed into his shoulder, warm tears smeared his cheek, her little arms slowly wrapping around him to hold him in return. "I love you, Lau Lau, and so long as I breathe I'll never—"

Her fingertips bruised on the seams of his coat as his body was torn through the stern windows with a crash. His hat fell to her feet, his boots disappeared from the wreckage, and suddenly she was alone again.

Lau Lau screamed and cautiously hurried to the broken glass, cutting her feet through the soft leather soles of her shoes and smearing small strokes of red. Salem appeared beside her and plucked her from the shards.

'There, to the left,' Savrae-Lyth said urgently.

Salem shuffled back to the doors and looked out. Just above the tree line was the dark stretch of the harrow shrike's wings. Atop it stood Fever with serpents wrapped around the creature's head and throat, and beneath hung Kismet, dangling in a tangle of ichor and shadow.

Whisper caught the scent and roared, but it was not the usual anguish of human lungs. Her roar was deep, loud, and shook Salem and Lau Lau to their very core, like the cacophony of nearing thunder. Her jaw unhinged as her face stretched out into the maw of a massive dragon, and in the blinding flashes of a barrage of lightning strikes that engulfed the shoreline she emerged in full form. From snout to barbed tail she was easily the length of the *Windborn Chance* and all six wings stretched as wide as she was long. Jagged scales and thorny ridges sang with the light, creating a symphony of red, yellow, blue, green, and violet hues across her pearl sheen. The air shook as her wings thrummed and lifted her from the ground; lightning crackled from her jaws and arced between wing-beats. Once airborne, she turned toward the half-volcano and pursued the harrow shrike with increasing speed.

"We have to stop her!" Lau Lau cried. "She'll kill Kissy too!"

'The child is right,' Savrae-Lyth replied, 'but I'm not sure there's anything we can do now.'

Salem put Lau Lau down and ran his hands through his hair, almost pulling it out. "I'm open to suggestions."

'The confrontation is in Whisper's hands now. We must have faith she will gain control and come to her senses.'

Salem looked like he'd been slapped. '*Do you even know Whisper?*'

"Please!" Lau Lau tugged at Salem's wrist. "You have to help Kissy!"

"I—" Salem looked into the child's eyes and drowned—swollen and red from endless heartbreak. He looked back out across the forest. Whisper wasn't fast enough to overrun the shrike, so she landed on the cliff sheer. Her massive claws scarred the stone and she opened her jaws; thunder roiled and lightning sparked along her wings and gullet, bright enough to see from the distance—she was preparing to breathe. With a single blast of concentrated lightning she could easily turn her prey to ash.

'*My queen,*' he said in his mind, '*lend me the power of* **Single Step**.'

'*Absolutely not. You may be able to use some techniques, but your body isn't designed to teleport. The strain would be immense and could easily kill you.*'

'*I'll be fine. Give me the power.*'

'*You're no good to our cause dead, Salem.*'

'*And Whisper will never be ready for her inheritance with the burden of remorse and fear of her power. Give me* **Single Step**.'

'*You can't even make it there in one step. You'd have to make several. Assuming the technique doesn't tear you to pieces, the pain would have lasting psychological effects. You could damage your brain, Salem, lose your intellect. Is it really worth it? Trying to save Kismet.*'

"I'm trying to save Whisper!"

A silence drew, stretching seconds into hours as they watched a ball of brilliant blue lightning form in Whisper's jaws, tearing at the stone and cracking the cliff face.

'*I'm sorry queen,*' Lau Lau's voice chimed in his head. She touched her hand to Salem's chest and washed him over with uncontested access to Savrae-Lyth's power. '*Get her, Salem,*' she said, '*but be careful. It's going to hur—*'

A single step, his skin felt aflame.

Another, blood trickled from his eyes and ears.

Another, his flesh began to split.

In the blinding flash of light from his last step he materialized above Whisper. The eye of the storm was a single, massive corona of energy that instantly numbed the senses. She was preparing to exhale the pulsing surge of crackling ruination that brewed in her maw with such virulence electricity arced between every scale on her body, but at the moment of release she was violently forced from the cliff face.

Salem opened his arms wide and clasped his hands together—recreating the queen's *Noble Admonition* technique—striking Whisper with a thunderous ripple of air that boomed across *The Dance* and shattered her stony perch. Whisper was torn from the rock, her head arced as she fell, and she breathed—a pillar of brilliant crackling blue light speared the mountain and sheared the top clean, raining boulders down upon the Bone Grove village.

Whisper and Salem both tumbled through the air as they plummeted toward the earth, and as she neared impact her wings caught the wind and she slowed her descent. Salem had no such advantage, and as he approached Whisper in freefall he clapped his hands together and used *Noble Admonition* once more, hurling her into the earth and slowing his fall with the burst of air. Whisper hit the ground and shook the stone, shattering it beneath her. Salem broke his fall on her wings and tumbled into the fissures.

Her heavy, monstrous breaths rumbled and her form began to revert back to human. Opalescent scales turned to pale pink flesh; grievous horns folded into raven hair. Her eyes closed as she curled into the dirt and stone, naked and exhausted, on the brink of unconsciousness.

Blood trickled down Salem's face and his vision blurred. Sharp pain surged through his body and the dull throb of agony swelled in his head. Tears in his skin ran jagged down his body, like crimson lightning immortalized in his flesh, and they bled him slowly. He turned his head to see Whisper asleep in the wreckage, coiled into a ball like a child. There was a vulnerable innocence to her he'd never expected to see, and he closed his eyes, smiling.

'Well, I hope you're happy,' Savrae-Lyth scolded.

'Happiness?' he thought, 'Is that what this is?' He took a deep breath and winced, the smile quickly returning to his lips as he surrendered to the dark and let his body fall. 'It feels different than I remember. Better.'

Fever watched in awe as the mountaintop crumbled behind her. She had incredible faith in her abilities, but even she wasn't sure if her serpents could have eaten the blast in full. The wind blew through her golden curls as they soared past *The Fear* and over the open ocean, and she felt Kismet stop struggling beneath her mount. A shame, she liked his desperation.

"What do you want with me?" he called up.

"You've been a bad boy, it seems," she replied sweetly, "and your Blackrock friend couldn't finish what he started." It occurred to her she actually had no idea where they were going, but the harrow shrike seemed to fly with conviction. Either to Sabanexus or the Palace of Roiling Cinders in all likelihood, but without knowing exactly who struck a deal with Ogra there was no sense in steering.

Kismet watched the Bone Grove grow smaller in the distance. He knew it was Lau Lau they were after, but by some stroke of luck a misunderstanding landed him in the clutches of the enemy instead. He knew where he was headed—a fated reunion with the Phoenix Queen. He had been running for so long that a small part of him believed he and Lau Lau might actually escape the queen's clutches. He pondered his destiny now. The queen would certainly kill him, but how quickly was debatable. Most of Emberwilde already thought he was dead—hierarchal propaganda to protect the illusion that justice was as swift as it was absolute. Were Emberwilde to discover the queen's vault was infiltrated, a treasure stolen, and the culprit evaded capture for twelve years the queen and Bastion Nine would lose significant face.

They flew over the *Last Breath*. Carver's gray suit could be seen on the deck. He and Kismet both locked eyes and smiled at one another. Carver didn't yet know his fleet was destroyed and he certainly didn't expect what was going to happen next.

Lau Lau sniffled at the rails of the *Windborn Chance* as she watched the flashes of blue in the distance, but the tears in her eyes kept blurring her vision. She was alone now. Kismet had been taken away, Djagatt had been killed, Whisper turned into a dragon, and Salem had gone to stop her. There was nothing left—

—Yoru pressed her furry head against Lau Lau's leg; green eyes, sharp as the night was black, looked up at her with sad reassurance.

Lau Lau bent down and scooped the velvetine in her arms; Yoru's little legs dangled. She held the talking, not-talking, cat, not-cat, against her chest and stepped off the boat onto the dock. Tears slid down her cheeks and landed on Yoru's head, but through the velvetine's half-gaze it seemed she was more unimpressed with the method of carry.

"I don't want to put you down, though," she said.

Yoru's hind quarters bobbed with every step.

"But if I hold you then I can't lose you too."

Yoru flicked her tail.

"What if I hold your bum up?" Lau Lau stopped to slide a hand under the velvetine's hind and lifted her into a cradle. "Is that better?"

A slow, long blink, preceded the tiniest of purrs.

Lau Lau's feet touched earth and stone as the dock ended and she shuffled to the remains of Palindross. The massive dragon's skull lay on its side with its jaw broken open—an ominous gateway to the pile of ashes that was once her best friend. Her shuffle slowed to a crawl as she placed Yoru on the ground and inched her way closer. There was nothing left—no flesh, no fur, no bone—but the matte gleam of black steel bells and hoops that once adorned Djagatt's ears.

The tears swelled again, blinding her as she sifted through the ash and collected anything that jingled in the palms of her hands. Eventually, she had them all. Ten steel hoops, ten black bells, clutched in her hands while her tears mixed with the ash. She dropped her face to her hands and held the bells to her forehead.

Lau Lau bawled, curled in the dragon's maw, and the velvetine hung its head in silence.

51

ALWAYS ROLL IN THE LEMONGRASS

Salem's awakening was like a sip of dremaera—bitter on the tongue, with the fuzzy separation of body and spirit. A soft haze that made him feel in two places at once. His body lay in a firm bed of fine silk and goose down covers, but his spirit felt inches above, looking down upon himself with dismay. Daylight shone through rippled glass and cool ocean air filled his senses. He didn't feel real, trapped in the aether, cradled in gossamer.

The pain began to creep across his body and the space between reality started to close. His skin felt tight, groaning like worn leather as he tried to move. Dried blood crusted in the fissured tears of his recent strain, stretching across his body like dark crimson rivers on a landscape of pale, bruised skin. His mouth was dry, scraping against his palate like a horse brush. He'd lost so much blood; the fact he'd woken at all was a blessing.

"Well, look at you."

His heart turned beneath his ribs.

'Now's your chance.'

Salem squinted and focused his eyes on the figure that approached his bedside. Her cobalt blue eyes pierced the haze like beacons long before raven hair framed her porcelain skin.

"I leave you alone for a few moments and look what happens," she said.

Salem felt his lips crack as he smiled. "You know me. Always a step ahead, no matter how it looks."

Whisper looked him over and nodded, irritation laced in her voice. "All part of your plan, hmm?"

"There may have been some improvisation."

'Tell her.'

Whisper slung an old coat over her shoulders. Her clothing was destroyed in the transformation, so Lau Lau had given her some of Kismet's. None of it fit very well on her slender frame, but there were enough belts and buckles to keep her pants up at least. Only her tricorne had survived and she donned it with pride.

"My dear Whisper," Salem said, swallowing hard, "there's something I need to tell you."

She adjusted her cuffs, rolling them up to free her hands. All she'd wanted was to see him again, but since feeling the familiar static presence thrum in her veins from Salem's touch, and seeing him leap through arcs of lightning to strike her down with a burst of thunder, an anger slowly dragged her joy to the shadows and choked it. She'd always assumed he knew more than he was saying, but this was almost a betrayal.

'Tell her you love her, Salem.'

"You've traveled a long way," she said sharply, "must be important." For a moment her eyes softened—sad, almost hopeful. She curled her hair over her ear.

"I... do not know how to say it."

'Tell her.'

Salem curled his fingers into fists beneath the covers. "I was there when your mother died."

'You idiot.'

Whisper's gaze turned cold as her defenses went up; she crossed her arms so she wouldn't be tempted to throttle him right then and there. "How am I surprised?" She remembered the static she felt that day, the numbing power that smothered her as an infant—the aura of the man that murdered her parents. "Tell me, Salem. Did you kill her?"

"No," he replied woefully. "Your mother sacrificed herself to protect you from the onslaught of the Dragon War."

"Horse shit," she snapped.

"Truth, I assure you." He took a deep breath and winced. "Your mother was as powerful as she was brave, and she tore her heart from her own chest to place her power within me. I have been watching over you for two decades, waiting for the day you were strong enough to accept your inheritance and assume your rightful place."

"That is the most ridiculous—" It suddenly occurred to her she'd heard the story before. The tearing of the heart, the ending of the Dragon War. "You expect me to believe—"

"You met her," he said, "your mother. She was the spirit that overcame you right before you took your true form."

Whisper opened her mouth to speak, but nothing came out. The transformation, the creature in her veins, the voice in her head. Strange pieces with indefinable edges seemed to be coming together in inexplicable ways.

"You are Whisper Eiliona, heiress of House Eiliona. Your mother is Savrae-Lyth, the Queen of Drakes. Your father is Me'landris Eiliona."

"I'm a dragon," she said under her breath. The words aloud suddenly made it real despite having become one.

"Yes, a halo drake. Your mother was the only one before you."

"What is my inheritance?"

"Her power—all of it. Combined with your own inherent capabilities you will become one of the most fearsome entities to have ever existed."

"Why are you only telling me now? I spent my whole life thinking I was an abomination. I was an exile. An outcast. A monster. You watched me, with your own two eyes, as I tore myself apart over my family's death, and you said nothing. I could have had purpose, Salem, instead you let me waste my life chasing a resolve that didn't exist."

"I wanted to tell you," he said, "but if the Fates discovered Savrae-Lyth and Me'landris had a child they would have done everything they could to kill you. I had to keep your presence a secret until you were strong enough to withstand their judgement."

"Fat lot that did!" Whisper's urge to smother Salem grew stronger and there was a pillow within reach. It'd be so easy. "Shade tried to kill me anyways."

"The Fates did not know who you were. The attacks by Shade and Rhoswan were because you and I have no fatespinners. If they knew your lineage, Howlpack Sentinel Avelie would have come down and handled you herself. Chance favored us that day."

"Chan—I died! Wait..." she spied him carefully, "Rhoswan attacked you?"

Salem's disposition grew even more dismal. "Yes, and she forced my hand."

"Fates, Salem, she was your friend. Probably your only one." Whisper rested her hands on her hips and sighed.

"Our secret is no longer safe," he said through his teeth as he tried to sit up. His cuts opened a little, speckling his body with fresh red. "The woman who took Kismet is an Instrument. Soon, Ivory will know the dragons are not dead. Fortunately, Ivory is an exile of the Weave and may choose not to inform the others. However, there is still a chance she may, because you threaten their very existence. A common enemy."

"How so?"

Salem finally sat all the way up and took a moment to catch his breath. "Once you have your mother's power, you need to free Shiori Etrielle. Only you can do it. She is the rightful ruler of Elanta and the Fate's greatest threat. They will do anything to prevent that from happening, but only once Shiori is released will you truly be safe." A brisk breeze blew in from a broken window and Salem saw the Bone Grove in the distance. He was in Kismet's bed on the *Windborn Chance* and they were at sea.

Whisper rolled her shoulders and cracked her neck as she walked to the cabin doors.

"Are we sailing?" he asked, brow furrowed.

"Kismet had his crew hide in the smuggler's hold on the lower decks. When Blackrock was dead, Lau Lau told them and they navigated us out of the Bone Grove."

"Where are we going?"

Whisper opened the door, the bustle of bodies in hard sail could be heard. "The war isn't over yet," she said, "but it's about to be. Don't go anywhere, our conversation isn't finished." She stepped out onto the deck and closed the door behind her.

'Why?' Savrae-Lyth asked sadly.

'She needed to know the truth before anything else,' Salem replied.

'I suppose that makes sense. Once the air is cleared then?'

Salem hung his head and sighed. 'I do not know.'

'How come? She deserves to know how you feel.'

'But does she deserve to suffer for it? Your power is the only thing keeping me alive and I have to give it up soon. With her inheritance I lose my life. The need to say the words seems selfish when there is no prospect for a future. All we could possibly get is pain, and while mine will end shortly hers could last forever.'

'Salem, I understand your logic, but one could argue that it is better to feel woe than regret. There is affirmation in losing what you know you have and there is an everlasting anguish in uncertainty. The only path to resolution is knowledge, whereas keeping your feelings secret can create a suffering that cannot be reconciled. Whisper doesn't need you to protect her.'

'I am not just trying to protect her. I, too, have never felt this way before. I am overwhelmed with something I cannot describe, but I recognize that living these fantastic ideologies is not the future I am given. I must make due with what time I know I have, and the best thing for me is to accept that if I am to break a heart, I wish it only to be my own.'

The mist in the Setsuhan sky was a blank slate of gray. Tall blades of soft grass stretched upward, and when laid in it's the tunnel's end; the organic frame of uncertainty. Here, the grass grew greener and reached higher and further than anywhere else, eventually bending at the stalk from the weight of its ambition. The scent of lemon drifted lazily through the air as the soft blades tickled like feathers, appealing to every sense. A gentle breeze lifted, an invisible caress.

The scent was stronger now. With it came memories, with memories came sadness, and with sadness came nothing. Staring ever-upward, lost somewhere between the cold of the earth and the dismal gray of the Overworld, there she was—lost in lemongrass that once meant something greater.

'Always roll in the lemongrass,' Selva had told her right before he died.

She'd tried, but it was never the same. Nothing was.

52

THE SUNKEN LINK—THE MERCHANT WAY

Whisper walked to the bow and stood behind Lau Lau, who was perched on the rails precariously. In her hands she held a rope to keep her balance, but it still seemed reckless even by Whisper's standards. Far ahead was Carver's *Last Breath* and his two escorts, one to each side. Whisper pulled her tricorne down and noticed the reflection of the figurehead gazing back up at her. A woman danced and swayed with the rippling water, while its figurehead counterpart met the wind with eyes closed and smile wide. If she didn't believe in Wind and Water as lesser gods yet, she had no reason not to now.

"Wind and Water have chosen to help us," Lau Lau said. "They love Kismet and Djagatt, and they don't like Carver."

"Okay. So..." Whisper noticed they were the only Merchants, and on a collision course with ships four times their size, "Kismet had a plan, right? For how to take the flagship?"

"No," Lau Lau replied. In her hand she held Djagatt's bells, fastened at the rings with a small piece of rope. "But Djagatt did." She held the bells high and began to shake them, filling the air with a resonance that cascaded into a cacophony even Carver could hear.

"This is for you, Djagatt," she whispered, "Wind and Water guide us."

Carver was washing his spectacles on the lapel of his suit when he first heard the bells. It started softly, filling the wind in all directions, teasing the senses with something that may or may not exist. He placed the glasses back on the bridge of his nose and peered out across the bow—the *Windborn Chance* was coming straight at them. He chuckled, crows-feet curled at his eyes, wrinkles framed his cheekbones, all-the-while the ringing grew louder. He'd seen Kismet carried away by the shrike and the head on assault of the Bone Grove's smallest ship seemed a desperate last effort.

He walked to the bow and folded his hands behind his back. "What is that sound?" he asked; two of his three remaining mercenaries stood to each side of him.

"A battle cry of sort, maybe?" one replied with a smile. "We needn't even move. Let them sink their ship on the hull."

Carver smiled sharply and bared his teeth, when he was abruptly interrupted.

"Captain!" the crow's nest cried, "Two ships, port and starboard!"

In the distance, closing quickly, a thick bank of fog arose from the water and peeling from it were two massive, slender ships. The Bone Grove crest waved on their flags as they gained tremendous speed, their sails filled with gusting winds Carver could not feel, flexing the masts with a strain the crew fought hard to endure.

Carver squinted and noticed a faint wake set before one of the boats. "Dressers!" he called to each ship in his escort. "Brace! Brace!" The ships were coming in fast and hard, and beneath the surface of the water was a stretch of solid wood and iron that formed a spine. That was the difference between naval rams and dressers. Rams were blunt and meant for brute smashing, but dressers were narrower and turned the whole bow into a crescent shaped blade— this curved blade was their namesake, as they looked like the curved blades hunters use to field dress their kills. Not only were they faster because they cut through the water, but instead of smashing hulls they would cut boats open—sometimes in half. The wound from a dresser was cleaner than a ram's and would take on less water if the ships remained pressed together. This gave pirates more time to loot before the vessels sank.

A crewman called from one of the escorts. "There's no wind to maneuver, Captain. We're dead in the water."

Carver knew the dressers were meant for him and without the ability to turn head on to narrow themselves as targets he only had one option. He was at a tactical disadvantage, forced to keep his escorts on each side to protect the flagship.

"Captain!" the crow's nest called again, "Bow!"

"What now?" Carver turned to look. The *Windborn Chance* continued to close the distance, but the water grew shades darker to each side of it. Four large ships burst through the surface in a spray of brine and white caps, sails already full. His eyes were playing tricks on him—it almost seemed as though the wakes formed a pair of hands that lifted the ships to the surface. A powerful wind pushed the Merchant sails faster than any their size should be capable of. The four ships had open slits on each side of the hull and in a sudden gleam of shimmering steel a row of large bladed hooks snapped out of them and locked into place.

"Chum-hooks, shit!" Carver waved his hands frantically to the escorts. "Heave sail! Oars! Anything!"

The Merchant chum-hooks raced to the sides of the escorts and buried their curved blades into the hulls. Splinters took to the air and danced in the swirl of torrential winds that filled the sails—a woman of white wind stood in each sail blowing an endless gust. Waves formed in the chum-hook's wakes and continued to thrust them forward, pulling Carver's escorts with them.

Carver watched, enraged, as the Merchants towed his ships away, and when the chum-hook's dark sails cleared his line of sight he saw the Merchant dressers in full wind, now with a clear path of charge to the *Last Breath*'s vulnerable broadside.

"BRACE! BR—"

The two dressers struck the *Last Breath* simultaneously, creating a pincer of incredible force that severed the lower decks. A massive fissure stretched up through the middle of the flagship, nearly splitting it in half, and was now afloat only so long as the dressers didn't reverse. The Merchant dressers snared the rails with grappling hooks and tethered them down tightly. If the rams didn't row backward the *Last Breath* would not take enough water to sink, and so long as there were riches worth pillaging she had value afloat.

Bone Grove Merchants, armed in dark leathers, red sashes, and glinting blades, poured onto the deck of the *Last Breath* in droves—jumping, climbing, and swinging aboard to clash with Carver's crew. The roars of war echoed across the water to Whisper's ears. The flashes of steel on steel beckoned her to join the fray and the moment the *Windborn Chance* neared she vaulted the rails, leapt from the bow, and scaled the side of the ship.

Carver's three remaining mercenaries formed a triad around him, slaying Merchants as they cleared a path to the captain's quarters at the stern. Two of them entered the room with Carver while the last remained at the door.

Whisper's eyes smiled something dark as she leaned forward and pumped her legs into full sprint. By the time the mercenary saw her clear the mob of clanging steel she was already upon him—mid-air, a knee buried into his chest. His sternum crackled as the rib-heads slid from their sockets and his body flew from his feet, crashing through the door—removing it from its hinges entirely.

She felt strong, as though some of her former strength had remained since the transformation. The second mercenary attacked with a falchion and she stopped his swing with a single hand. Confusion washed across his face in the half-second before she flipped him onto the war table. Papers burst out from under him as he crushed the compass box. She thrust her head down into his, cracking the solid oak and dazing him badly—a cut along his brow now bled profusely across his face and through his hair. She turned to the cast iron pot-bellied stove, clutched it by the handle, and tore it from the chimney of brick and mortar, heaving it in an arc over her head and smashing it into his chest, splitting the table in two.

She pried the stove from his ribcage, now dripping with blood as old coals and ash spilled from within, and turned to face the third mercenary. Wide eyed and terrified, he dropped his sword and immediately surrendered only to find himself hurled through rippled glass and wood into the ocean below.

Carver cowered before her and she dropped the stove with a satisfying *thud* that rumbled the floorboards. She was beginning to feel like herself again, which was bad news for, well, everyone.

Shortly after Carver's capture, and with the pile of bodies at Whisper's feet growing bigger, what dwindling crew remained of the *Last Breath* laid down their arms and surrendered. Carver hadn't anticipated the Merchants would leave the Bone Grove and meet him head on, and with the full force of the rival fleet on all sides he was greatly undermanned. The *Last Breath* had begun taking some water from the dressers, but there was more than enough time for him to watch as everything he owned was carried away.

One-by-one Whisper shackled them to the mast, leaving Carver for last. Chests of gold medallions, boxes of jewels, crates of silks and spices—each passing Merchant took a piece of Carver with him. He watched from his knees, wringing his hands through irons.

"You're aware this is a loss for both of us," he said looking clever over cracked spectacles.

"You look like the loser to me," Whisper replied.

Carver smiled—a darkness she knew all too well. "With me dies the reign of Sunken Links, but with Oona dies the Bone Grove."

Whisper rattled the chains at his wrist to ensure they were secure, and bound his legs to a crewman's hands, completing the chain the Sunken Links were feared for. "Kismet isn't dead," she laughed.

"Perhaps, not yet, but he isn't here either. Neither is his Daggermouth. Without command the Merchants will fall apart."

Whisper looked out over the pirates she knew as smiths, tradesmen, shipwrights, and sailors. She remembered their loyalty to the cause, their dedication to their home, and their continued service after death itself. Her eyes met Lau Lau's, now fierce and unafraid, as she stood at the helm of the *Windborn Chance*. Whisper smiled. "We have a leader until we get Kismet back."

"Ha! She's just a child."

"You noticed she's taking your stuff, right?"

Carver scoffed.

Djagatt's bells rung as Lau Lau shook them from below, signaling them it was time to go. Whisper gently pat Carver's wrinkled face with playful slaps.

"You did well," she said. "From one insane person to another, you pissed off a lot of people, including a few lesser gods. That tickles me." She tipped her hat to him and vaulted the rails, landing with perfect balance on the rails of the *Windborn Chance*, surprising herself with how easy it felt.

The Merchants aboard the dressers cut loose the tethers and deployed their oars. With each stroke, the hull of the *Last Breath* cracked and groaned, quickly taking on water. Before long, the once mighty frigate was almost entirely consumed and shackled Links scrambled to free themselves. They bobbed in the water as the towering masts grew smaller and filled the air with pleas for mercy—words they'd surely heard before. One-by-one the ocean took them, their heads gasping one final breath before disappearing.

Whisper wondered a moment if it was cruel. She had no qualm with crushing the skull of an adversary in combat, but these men had surrendered. Regardless of their history, did they deserve to be executed after they had nothing left? Despite her affinity for chaos she had always lived in a society that had judicial structure—the Monastery of the Eternity Ring, the city of Whitewater.

"This is our way," Lau Lau said, nearly startling Whisper. Dragons weren't known for their hearing and her little feet were so small.

"Punishment should reflect the crime?"

Lau Lau nodded sadly. In her hands she still clutched Djagatt's bells. "We spent our lives taking from others. Loss is my penance."

"I disagree," Whisper replied. Only a few heads remained at the surface. "These men chose this life in defiance of Elanta's standards. They made the decision to drown innocent people knowing it was wrong, but you were born to these rules. Can you really be doing something wrong if you were raised to think it was normal? Can you really let the rules of mankind tell you what you do and do not deserve?" Partly through her sentence she realized she was talking about herself.

Lau Lau made sure she didn't blink as Carver's head went under. "This is our way," she said, "That makes the judgement real to us."

Whisper was glad Salem was safely tucked away in the captain's quarters. He would have had some long-winded explanation of how different cultural expectations were—epistemes, regimes of truth, and blah blah blah. The idea of it made her glad to be free of the monastery, where she'd learned all this once before. Life at sea seemed simpler and more to her liking.

"You say 'us' and 'our' a lot," Whisper teased, nudging the child with her elbow, "almost like I'm one of you."

"You are," Lau Lau replied quietly, "if you want to be."

"Well, I am fond of a life of independence, violence, and adventure, but I also—"

"Be my first mate," the child said spritely.

"First mate? Maybe I want to be captain?"

"Can you sail?"

Whisper pursed her lips. "Fine, but why do you get to be captain?"

"I was Kismet's first mate, which makes me acting captain now."

Whisper looked around, where it didn't seem a single crewman would disagree. Child or not, she was a psychic, a founding member of the fleet, and held the longest record of service to the Bone Grove. She could read and write, sense the weather, hear sunken treasure, and be aware of every inch of the ship. There was no one more qualified to lead in Kismet's place and everyone knew it. She suddenly realized they weren't having a laugh, they were having a conversation.

"Is this a serious offer?" Whisper asked, jests aside.

"It is. You've proven yourself a friend and ally. We'd be blessed to be your family."

"Family?" The word hit her hard.

Lau Lau reached out and placed her hand on Whisper's arm, nodding sweetly.

"I accept," she said, softer than she meant to. "What does a first mate do?"

"Well, normally I'd say your top priority would be to keep me safe, but you were also the Ward of the Voice and I've seen the shape

Salem's in. For now, you'll man the helm."

Whisper's eyes gleamed sharply for a moment—low blows were her style and she'd met her match.

"I see. Too short to see over the rails? Or just too weak to steer?"

"Too smart to do it myself."

Whisper turned and walked to the stern, ascended the stairs to the helm and placed her hands on the wheel. "Shall we rescue Kismet?"

"Yes," she replied, "but there's somewhere else we need to be first."

53

HARBINGERS, A NEW SPECK APPROACHES

Waylander could see the caravan from his window high aloft the guest tower, though he only knew to look because Shade could smell Casamir's wounds at the gates and Diana predicted the hour of their arrival. She warned him that his son wouldn't recover from his injuries, but hadn't told him exactly what the injuries were.

Waylander was regaining his strength and could now dress himself—a seemingly trivial victory to some, but monumental to one who lost his arm. He slung his heavy cloak over his shoulders and pinned his scarf with his Moth. He considered foregoing any armaments, but at the last moment fastened his sword and dagger to his belt. Azel would be proud. While Diana and Shade assured they could neither smell nor sense another demon within the walls, one couldn't be too careful now. In light of Waylander's quick recovery the king mentioned the role of Judiciar was yet to be filled. The insinuation was that he would fill it, but he needed time to think. He would be the target of anyone disgruntled with the idea of being led by a Moth—namely everyone, Fairchild made it seem.

Shade and the three Moths stood before the doors of abalone and alabaster waiting for their kin and comrades. Waylander felt a strange tingle along his skin, the faintest breeze of a struggling sigil—something only a sigilsmith could ever feel. He followed it to the arch of white marble and ocean-blue honeycomb stone that framed the massive doors to the Great Hall.

"What is it?" Diana asked.

"There is a sigil here somewhere. Broken, but not gone. Can you find it?" Waylander placed his hand on the wall and traced the hexagons. He was getting closer, he could feel it.

Diana focused on the arch above them, but found nothing. Since enchanting her bramble with a defense to the demon's psychic extroversion her sensitivity wasn't as sharp—an exchange of necessity.

"Here," Waylander said. His hand stopped on a slab of marble and as he pulled his fingers from it the faint glow of luminous white marks rose to the surface.

"What is it?" Azel asked, tapping his wolf's head ring on his pommel.

"It's a harbinger mark," Waylander replied. With a touch of focus the mark glowed brightly and sparked at his fingertips. "There, fixed."

Azel rolled his eyes. "Ugh, harbingers are annoying. They probably disabled it on purpose." He walked through the archway to the doors, where the honeycomb stone pulsed with light and gave a gentle chime.

A beautiful voice echoed through the hall. *"Announcing Azel Katmin, Moth of Lyre, Blue Wolf Swordsong."*

"Even knows my guild title," Azel chuckled. Since attaining the title of Moth no one referred to him as Blue Wolf anymore.

Shade sneered quietly. No one knew wolves better, and Azel was a stray at best.

Diana stepped through the arch with a smile, the chime sounding with the soft blue light once more.

"Announcing Diana Laurellen, Moth of Lyre, Geomantic Soothsayer, Lady of Thorns, Lady of Closed Eyes, Silver Sail Haruspex..." The voice continued to list titles.

"How do you have so many?"

Waylander smiled, "Azel has title-envy."

"People think psychics are tools to be used and so we are given names to show we are owned. Not all people of power are as polite as Liam Whitewater. Psychics are often property, not people, and before breaking free of those bonds and becoming a Moth I had many owners." The list finally ended. "All those titles are old now. I'm surprised it knows them. Moth and soothsayer are all that matter now, because those I chose myself."

"Wait. You're a haruspex too?" Azel tried to hide an undertone of nervous surprise. "Sacrificing things, pulling out their guts and reading the future in their entrails?" He tapped his ring faster.

Diana smiled sweetly, but didn't answer. Those days were as dark as they were old.

A sliver of light cut through the center of the massive doors as they began to open, echoing the halls until silenced against the canopy of ivy that cascaded behind the throne. Bursting through was Katya, arms wide, as she leapt onto her father.

"Announcing..."

What pain he suffered he hid with the tears that swelled behind his eyes, clutching her tightly. Soon thereafter Bastet arrived with Casamir in his arms, Venetta and Ashissa steps behind.

"Announcing..."

"Announcing..."

"Announcing..."

"Announcing..."

Azel smiled awkwardly, certain the harbinger mark had been removed for sake of sanity. He noticed that Venetta's titles also continued. "Why does everyone have more titles than me?"

"It's not a contest," Venetta replied sharply, her cold eyes cutting him down, "but if it is, I'm winning." Even when joking she wouldn't smile.

"... The Great Divider ..."

"I cut a man clean in half once. The name stuck."

"... Bone Breaker ..."

"I've broken a lot of bones. Not mine."

The harbinger began speaking in different dialects.

"There's a name for me in every language."

Azel stepped back. "Fates, Venetta."

"That's a good one too," she said, cold as tombstone.

Waylander released Katya and saw Casamir in Bastet's arms. Bloody bandages wrapped around the stumps of his knees. Casamir hung his head low, afraid to make eye contact, and Waylander stormed toward him.

Casamir prepared for the worst—disappointment, pity, regret— any or all of them. If only he'd been faster or better trained. If he'd spent less time building contraptions and more time searching his soul for enlightenment he might still have his legs. If he'd stopped trying to be something he wasn't maybe he'd still have his eye. He was a failure as a student, a failure as a son, and a failure as a Waylander. Whatever his father had to say, he deserved.

Waylander marched with purpose and threw his arm around him, clutching him tightly. "Welcome back, son. I'm proud of you."

The winds at the top of Setsuha were colder than usual and strongest at the mouth of the chasm that plunged straight downward into complete darkness. Vaexa stood at the edge and peered into the endless pit; it howled back up at her in long drawls that ruffled the black and gold feathers of her head. She remembered almost falling into it when the mist first blanketed them, saved only by a static energy that came and went when it pleased. It felt wonderfully familiar, but always left her empty when it disappeared.

Since then, the mist had lifted. Far, far in the distance, creatures with sharper eyes than hers would tell her of towering spouts of energy and mist that stretched upward, connecting Elanta to the mist above. At first it seemed that Setsuha would be no different, but shortly after the phenomena occurred the mist withdrew. No one knew why it had fallen in the first place, but the mountain had been suffering since.

Souls weren't reincarnating like they used to and one-by-one her people were turning back into stone with no warning. Each day was beginning to feel hopeless, waiting and wondering whose turn it was to die next. She and Nuith were the only elders left. The Setsuhans looked up to them for hope and reason, but the days grew colder every time one of them turned to stone. Now, none of them talk about it anymore. They just wait.

Vaexa wanted to give up. If not for Selva's dying words she may have, but morale was in ruins. Each week she would travel the mountain on a pilgrimage, placing sacred marks on the statues of the fallen. The marks were made of blessed ink and used to act as an anchor for the soul when they created new bodies. The mountain would fill the stone vessel with life and thus a Setsuhan was born. But now the stone statues just reminded her the mountain spirit was gone and soon they would be too.

Soft leathers and leaves waved in the wind, blanketed over a delicate frame that could blow away at any moment. She gently ran her fingertips along a Setsuhan carving that had been created at the peak decades ago. They called it the 'last heart'. It was an empty vessel they tried to fill, but weren't certain they even could.

She traced its almond shaped eyes and feathered features. It had been around so long they had lots of time to give it more detail than the others, back when they had the time and spirit. Since the mist fell she almost stopped visiting, but instead saved it for the end of each week's journey. It reminded her of how things used to be—the hope she and the elders once had.

The pit moaned as the wind picked up and she wrapped her arms around her body to keep warm. Nightfall was upon her. It would be prudent to make haste homeward, but she caught herself dragging her heels through the shale. Death was coming anyways.

She looked out across the forest—magistrates would have dared the Setsuhan wilds for such a glimpse—and noticed something she hadn't seen in her lifetime, perhaps not even in her last lifetime either. Far past the trees, far past the mountain, a tiny speck sat on the ocean's horizon. She'd been captive to the mountain for millennia, never allowed to leave lest she turn to stone at the mountains border. She recognized a new speck when she saw one.

Fever had so many voices in her head she hadn't thought it was possible to reach her wits end, but all her voices were beginning to object in unison. She forced the harrow shrike into a hard flight by pumping it full of adrenaline, taking refuge in the cold Whitewater coastal forests when sleep and food were absolutely necessary.

Amidst the cries in her head Ivory's soft voice would occasionally intervene with sweet assurances and praise, but it was getting old quickly. Ivory would keep her company long enough to glean information from the journey, expressing great interest in Salem, his embodiment of Savrae-Lyth, and his mention of Shiori Etrielle. While it was a shame he couldn't be captured, it seemed what few words he shared were enough to paint a picture for the forlorn Fate.

Finally, the mountain ridges of Emberwilde were passing beneath them. Even from such height the orange groves sprawled like an ocean of deep green. She never thought the trees blanketed the mountains and now that she had seen them she was already bored.

Throughout the journey, she hadn't been steering the shrike, presuming it knew where it was supposed to go, but for all she knew it was just pissing around. It looked as though they were headed toward Obsidian, where the Phoenix Queen resided in her Palace of Roiling Cinders.

Kismet hadn't fought Fever's bindings once, seemingly content to dangle precariously and admire the view. It was deeply aggravating, and had she thought she could control the shrike well enough to keep his flailing body from striking the earth she would have played a little game of 'catch and release' to pass the time. He didn't say a single word, ate what he was given, slept when he was told, and freely surrendered to the serpents when it was time to fly. She even left his fancy sword at his hip in hopes he'd try something reckless, but he never did.

In the distance, rising into the sky like a massive black pike of volcanic glass, was the palace. It seemed close, but was likely a day away at least. To the far west she could see the funnel of swirling mist that engulfed the city of Valakut. Even at such a distance it was impossible to miss. She wondered how far the evacuation went. Surely the whole city wasn't immersed, but would people still dare to sleep in their own beds?

The voices began to argue about the evacuation. She smiled, relieved. So long as they were in discord she felt normal, it was when they were all in agreement she began to fear the clutches of sanity.

54

REUNION—SENTENCE AND SELENITE

The *Windborn Chance* anchored off the coast of Setsuha. The full intensity of the mountain rained down upon the crew as their necks cranked backward just to take in a portion of the scale. Lush green trees lined the ridge of the cliffs ahead and long vines with vibrant red blossoms draped down the face toward the water. A ring of cloud encircled the higher peaks and wisps of ice crystals swirled against the sky.

Whisper was placing some supplies into the longboat as she, Lau Lau, Yoru, and Salem prepared to disembark. The shores were far too rocky to bring the *Windborn Chance* any closer and almost too dangerous to chance the longboat, but Salem and Lau Lau both assured them this was where they were meant to be.

Salem sat in the longboat and waited, acknowledging Whisper awkwardly while thumbing through Grove's last ledger, *Envied Emerald to the East*. She was still upset with him over the secrets he'd kept but he wanted to share more when they reached their destination. Until then, he took the time to heal as best he could and peruse the ledger, even though the pages still made no sense. However, now that there was a psychic in his presence it couldn't hurt to ask what she thought.

Whisper and Lau Lau began addressing the crew, preparing them for their absence. In her little hands, Lau Lau held an old map of worn vellum, folded and bound with soft leather braids.

She carefully placed it in the hands of one of the crewman. "I've marked the location of a sunken merchant ship and two Emberwilde galleons off the coast of Shén Shé. Take the diving bells, divide the fleet into pairs, and get the treasure. When you're finished, send the fleet back to the Bone Grove and take the *Windborn Chance* to Fool's Cove. Have her repaired and once she's finished have an enchanter send me a message."

The crewman nodded and began to relay commands with newfound authority.

Lau Lau scooped Yoru into her arms and looked to Whisper. "I'm ready."

Whisper nodded and helped them into the longboat. It swayed precariously above the waves as it dangled from its ropes. She lowered it into the water, took the oars in hand, and began to row for shore.

Lau Lau sighed as she watched the crimson junk sails of the *Windborn Chance* open, catching the wind and pulling away. Things weren't the same anymore.

"Excuse me, Captain," Salem said politely. His wounds had healed a little since their departure from the Bone Grove, but not much. He cringed as he lifted the cloth-bound book of mottled green. "I was wondering if you would look this over." She took it from his hands and he withdrew the soft selenite crystal he kept in his sleeve, quietly admiring the striations while she flipped through the pages.

She crouched in the boat, bringing her knees up to her chest and hunching over the text like a little gargoyle. Despite its nonsense she seemed emphatically perplexed by it. "There is great sorrow in this book," she said.

"Someone wrote it while they were held captive," Salem replied. "I believe there is an enchantment on it, but I cannot determine the key."

"The key is you," she replied sweetly. "There's a powerful bond in this book, made of words rooted in your friendship."

"You can sense that?"

"No, but the spirit of the book is telling me."

"Interesting." He knew it probably required a certain word or phrase to activate. Knowing it wasn't simply random but something familiar to their friendship was a welcome clue, but he was still far from guessing what it was.

"I'm sorry I don't know more. Even the spirit doesn't remember its name anymore, but it knows it's not *Envied Emerald to the East*." She raised the book to hand it back and noticed the selenite in his hands. "Oh!" she cried, "I love rocks!"

Salem chuckled. "Well, it is not *just* a rock." He held the stone aloft to her eager hands, but as she grabbed it her eyes rolled back into her head.

A heartbeat that wasn't a heartbeat. A breathless stillness filled with the fragrance of green and red, as though colors had a smell. Her vision was sharp, peering with such intuition that she could see beneath the earth at her feet. A cliff edge against the ocean, straight and razor sharp, creating its own horizon despite the endless stretch of blue below, but the blue wasn't all blue. There was red, too. A small spot of it, ruffled sails on a ship in disrepair. She approached the edge and looked down, hundreds of feet but fearless to the core. There, fighting the stones that littered the shores like teeth, was a boat. In that boat she saw herself.

Lau Lau's head snapped back and she pulled her hand from the stone. What she felt was too concrete to be a vision. She looked up to the cliff edge. There, hundreds of feet above the ocean, was a woman of fragile features standing at the base of a blossom ridden veil of green.

Salem looked up to see her and his heart weighed like a stone in bittersweet symphony.

"You know her," Lau Lau said, "and she knows you too, but not you, you."

Whisper chanced a look to the cliffs as she maneuvered through the jutting stones that lined the shore. Her telescopic vision was improving, though it still wasn't what it used to be. There was a time she could see the lacuna of the woman's eyes, but for now she had to settle for the ruffling of the fine black and gold feathers adorning her head.

Salem nodded slowly and slid the heart back up his sleeve.

As the harrow shrike neared the Palace of Roiling Cinders, Fever and Kismet both expected an onslaught of fire and prepared for the worst, but with each muscular flap that rotated the world beneath them it seemed the guards simply watched. It became clear at the gates, when the outer cloisters of Obsidian hadn't launched an aerial assault, that their presence was expected—or at least permitted, unusual as it was.

The shrike soared to the tallest tower of the palace, where stood a woman in flowing orange, red, and yellow silks. Atop her head was an ornate headdress of ruby, gold, and obsidian, and lacing each hand was a delicate weave of golden wire. It was the malikeh, the Phoenix Queen, with not a single soldier at her side.

She and Kismet locked eyes and her expression turned from sour to an elated malevolence. She was expecting Lau Lau to arrive in the harrow shrike's clutches and Fever was not the rider she hoped would infiltrate her city's walls, but Kismet was certainly a prize worth smiling for.

Fever set Kismet on the tower, keeping him bound in shadowed serpents, and dismounted the beast. The shrike landed loudly, growling with every tired breath as it rested from the strain of its journey.

The Phoenix Queen pried her gleeful eyes from Kismet and spied Fever carefully. While fragile in frame, there was something dark and calculated in her eyes that made the hair on Fever's neck rise. "Where is Blackrock?" Her voice was powerful and squeezed a little air from their lungs with every word.

Fever had the strangest compulsion to bow in her presence and immediately attributed it to an enchantment hidden somewhere on her person. "Blackrock is dead," she replied, "but lucky for you I was in a helping spirit."

The queen tilted her head curiously. "You're Fever, are you not?"

Fever couldn't hide her smile. Her infamy had earned the recognition of the Phoenix Queen. "The one and only, love, and the closest you'll ever get to catching."

The queen chuckled sweetly and affixed her gaze on Fever's ocean blues while she approached Kismet. She unfastened the Scarlet Charm from his hip and held it in her hand, not once breaking eye contact.

Fever loved it, lost somewhere between adoration and arrogance. The queen held such composure she couldn't tell whether she was friend or foe.

"Do you presume I wish to capture you?" the queen asked. She gently graced the handle of the Scarlet Charm, but continued to stand tall and regal.

"Are you implying I'm not worth catching?"

"I'm implying your sentence is execution." The queen began walking toward Fever, slow and graceful—patience in her form, invincibility in her eyes.

Fever laughed and released Kismet, who took a big step backward. He peered over the edge at the sheer drop to the gardens—there was no escaping even if he wanted. He'd excused many opportunities on their journey already, there was no sense in trying now.

"Oh love," Fever sang as she clutched the tome close to her chest and released all her serpents from her bangles, "don't tempt me."

The queen continued forward, her fiery silks trailed behind her. One of Fever's serpents struck, snapping at her with incredible speed and sinking its fangs into her throat. The queen neither flinched nor blinked, but continued to slowly close the distance despite the burning venom filling her veins.

The smile on Fever's lips began to fade. Her Bedlam Thistle seemed to have no effect and, in a sudden flash of crimson honeycomb stone, the blade burst from the sheath. Fever's serpent coiled around the queen's throat and pulled her back just enough—the Scarlet Charm slid through the chthonomantic tome and sheared it in two, the papers scattered as Fever dropped them in surprise. With a quick snap, the serpent acted on impulse and broke the queen's neck with a nauseating crack.

Fever's mind went silent, each voice wondering the consequence of such actions. One finally cut the silence and spoke of the infamy, another warned of Ivory's reaction, while another chimed sweetly of the sound of cracking bone.

A glimmer of crimson stone flashed and severed her serpent before disappearing back into the sheath. The queen's neck cracked back into place and she lunged at Fever once more. The serpents reacted, tearing through her flesh, but in a swift swing of her blade she cut them clean and nearly took Fever's head, carving the stone behind as she evaded.

Fever regained her footing and watched as the queen's wounds healed almost instantly. 'The rumors are true,' she thought—the Phoenix queen was indestructible. Fever's serpents formed before her, opened their maws, and released the remainder of Savrae-Lyth's lightning in a beam of brilliant crackling blue and white.

The queen daintily outstretched her palm and explosively dispersed the blast in a roar of thunder that shook the stone on which they stood. Now it was only a matter of time before the Bastion Nine arrived.

Fever felt something she wasn't familiar with—concern. She was trapped in one of Elanta's most dangerous places with one of Elanta's most dangerous people. She slid her foot back and felt something grab her, inching its way across her skin like mud. Engulfing her feet were ichor shadows that pooled beneath her and pulled her in. The sticky strands of void stretched up and ensnared her, dragging her beneath the surface. She recognized the sensation as one of Ivory's portals and surrendered, allowing it to consume her whole.

The collusion of shadows dispersed, leaving the queen surprisingly placid. She turned her gaze to Kismet, who slowly raised his hands in non-confrontation. She examined the Scarlet Charm, gently caressing the ruby inlay.

"Twelve years, Oona," she said softly. "I have my sword back, but where's my psychic?"

"Dead," he replied, dropping his head to feign mourning, "Blackrock was too aggressive in his attempt to capture her and she was mortally wounded. She bled internally and died hours after."

"I'm to believe this when you have that Baku shaman of yours?"

"He lost his life defending her—defending me." He clenched his fists with the thought, burrowing his fingernails into his palms until he imagined they bled. "I have no reason to run from your judgement any longer. Everything I had is gone."

The queen gracefully approached him. "As much as I'd love to believe that, I've been fooled by you before."

The tower door burst open and the Ram charged through, a golden horn cestus on each hand and a unit of men at his back. "My queen," he called.

She raised a hand to ease them.

The Ram looked at Kismet and a strange ringing clouded his thoughts. He seemed familiar somehow, but his mind wouldn't allow him to place it. "Who is this?"

"A criminal of the Realm," she said.

Kismet could tell she wanted to execute him right there, but then a clever idea gleamed across her eyes. It made him terribly uncomfortable.

"Lock him up with double guard," she commanded, "and ready a cell in the Blackrock prison by morning. I want him in the center of the volcano for as long as his flesh will hold."

55

BROKEN STONE

Vaexa scaled the cliff-side paths down to the base of the mountain where Whisper was dragging the longboat ashore. She watched in awe at the spectacle. She'd never seen a human female before and certainly didn't think they possessed such strength. The feather-light avian frame and hollow bones of the Setsuhan race lent little to strength, but their dexterity had little contest to anything in Elanta.

Salem was the only human she'd known in this lifetime. He made a habit of venturing from the neighboring realm of Whitewater in search of dremaera. In exchange for the exotic fruit exclusive to the soil of the Snow Leaf he would utilize the proceeds from the sale of dremaera wine to purchase land surrounding the mountain. This prevented any idea of expansion eastward and thereby kept Setsuha safe from explorers and ambitious conquerors.

Whisper caught the frail young thing looking at her. Just as the Setsuhan had never seen a human female before, she'd never seen a Setsuhan. In the monastery she'd read about them, though there wasn't much information. She heard they were skillfully crafted from stone and given life through the will of the mountain spirit, but this woman didn't seem very stone-like. In fact, it was much the opposite. She looked delicate, like she'd collapse under a scowl or catch the wind and flutter to the earth like paper if thrown.

"What are you looking at?" Whisper scoffed, testing the Setsuhan's mettle.

Vaexa turned her eyes downward and bowed her head. "My apologies. I'm marveled by your strength." Grace was Setsuhan nature and as an elder she had plenty of it. The Setsuhan community had enjoyed peace and attunement with nature for millennia. It was unlikely she'd understand any of Whisper's candor, but the way Whisper spoke was as fascinating as it was foreign.

Vaexa turned to Salem and attempted to greet him in formal Setsuhan fashion before remembering he had explicitly requested she never did. It was generally unceremonious to deny a formal greeting, which was to touch one's fingertips to the other's forehead—a tactile reinforcement of good intentions—but as he was a respected guest from Whitewater the elders chose to acknowledge his request. Somehow, he was the only person to survive the journey through the Setsuhan wilds—namely the fenwights, the massive wolf guardians of the mountain—and if they approved of his presence she had little reason not to trust him as well. She was sensitive to feeling memories in people she touched, and she presumed that as the Voice of the King he was required to keep them in his head. While most Setsuhan were carved from hard stone, her predecessor decided to carve her new form out of soft selenite. The result made her more fragile than the others, but honed her senses several-fold. She was certain Salem knew this.

Salem bowed his head. "Vaexa est'alara celys."

It felt so long since someone referred to her by her full name and title. Selva and Rhys used to, back when they were alive. It was a nostalgia that saddened her almond eyes. "Thank you," she replied, "but much has changed since you were last here."

Salem swallowed hard. He wasn't sure how the burst of energy from Lyre would have affected the Snow Leaf, but he could see in her eyes that she had suffered. "What happened?"

"Come," she gestured, "I'll show you."

Llaesynd, the sky cradle, was a series of bulbs that hung from the trees like ornaments. They varied in size from single nests and homes to full sanctuaries suspended between canopies. Each bulb was crafted from woven plant fiber and connected by thin bridges of braided vine, suspended high above the ground. While Setsuhans were light and dexterous enough to travel the vines with ease, a fall from such a height would be tragic.

While the hanging city was breathtaking, the devastation beneath was hard to draw away from. Dozens of statues laid beneath Llaesynd—Setsuhan vessels that lost their souls and reverted back to stone—frozen in poses of perpetual agony. Many were broken, having reverted in the trees and fallen.

Lau Lau clasped her hands over her heart as she walked through the graveyard. Each statue was a tombstone. Each face was the bitter regret of an early end. She could hear the statues weep in passing, the soft sobs of hopeless spirits lost in limbo.

"It began after the light struck us and the mist descended," Vaexa said quietly. A few Setsuhans peered cautiously from their nests at the visitors, but none ventured out to greet them. "Since then, the mountain has been taking life back."

"I presume the rituals are not working?" Salem asked.

"No. The mountain will not breathe life any longer, no matter how many blessed marks I leave. It's not just the Setsuhan people that are suffering either. The creatures of the mountain are dwindling as well. Fenwights are getting weaker and the kin'nyi are thinning."

They arrived beneath a massive woven orb suspended with a multitude of braided vines. This was Llaeilyer, the heart of the sky, and it served as a reliquary. When each Setsuhan is crafted, a piece of stone is kept to represent their connection to their earthly form. This stone is called a heart and each Setsuhan heart is kept in a nest within the reliquary.

Salem had been in it several times before. It was a sanctuary for the elders and where they held their conversations regarding the diplomatic relations of the two realms. It was also where he'd see the empty nest of the 'last heart'.

"Are the elders within?" he asked.

Vaexa fell solemn even more so. "Nuith is resting, but Rhys and Luseca have been claimed."

"Rhys and Luseca are gone?" Salem's heart nearly stopped in his chest. Half their elders had turned to stone. If it was devastating to him, he couldn't fathom how the Setsuhans were feeling. The elders were the cornerstones of knowledge, history, and culture for as long as the mountain was breathing life.

Salem sighed at the devastation. "Vaexa, I must speak with you in private."

Whisper's head cocked slightly.

"Certainly, would you like to go into Llaeilyer?" Vaexa replied. "Nuith would be pleased to see you and hear of news from the other realms."

"No," he replied, "I know a place." He turned to Whisper and bowed his head slightly—a twinge of pain flicked the corner of his eye. "My dear Whisper, please watch Lau Lau. We will return shortly."

"I'm your ward," Whisper objected, "I should be going with you."

"You are Lau Lau's ward also," he said, "Stay here with her. I require a private moment."

She crossed her arms and spied the Setsuhan sharply. "I'm sure you do."

He noticed as she scoured Vaexa head to toe and mischief sparked in his eyes. "Are you jealous?"

"I'm checking if she's armed, you cretin."

Salem caught Lau Lau gently shaking her head and he chuckled. He turned, spying her slyly in the corner of his eye and began to walk away. Vaexa followed close behind. "I will return shortly, I promise."

'Nnnhnn,' she hummed, unimpressed and agitated.

Lau Lau seemed somewhat frightened among the statues. Their eerie cries and hopeless eyes, doubly blind. Whisper held out her hand and the little girl squeezed it tightly.

"You still got those bells, little Daggermouth?" Whisper said.

Lau Lau nodded with a frown.

"I have an idea, if you're—"

"I am," Lau Lau replied, already knowing. She was fond of the idea as soon as she felt Whisper think of it—helix piercing her ears with Djagatt's bells. The piercing of ears was a common practice in pirate culture. Seafarers were often very superstitious and despite their love for the sea they had too much respect for the afterlife not to dread the idea of having their bodies thrown into the ocean if they died at sail. So, the practice of piercing ears became standard to pirate culture. They would fashion rings of pure gold and gemstone from their spoils and put them in their ears, so that if they were to die the crew could pay for a proper burial.

"We will do it when we get to Whitewater," Whisper said. "I'm not sure we have any of the materials to do it here."

"It's going to hurt, isn't it?"

Whisper looked out at the trees where Salem had disappeared with Vaexa and listened to her heart pound in her chest. "Supposedly pain makes us stronger."

Salem brushed aside a veil of wispy green branches and waded into the soft, fragrant blades of lemongrass. Here, the grass thrived to the edge of a drop that overlooked the rich green canopy of Shén Shé's jungles.

Vaexa had been here before, and often. She gazed out across the canyon of ivy and watched the distant mist of a waterfall. If one dared approach the edge they could see a beautiful turquoise lagoon far below.

Salem sighed, "Always roll in the lemongrass."

The sadness in Vaexa's eyes suddenly dispersed. "Where did you hear that?"

"It means 'always find time to do the things that make you feel free'." He ran his hand along the blades. "Selva told me this once. Actually, he told us."

"What do you mean?" She'd never been here with Salem before, she would have remembered, and she was certain he'd never met Selva. Fenwights only communicated with Setsuhan elders.

He reached into his sleeve and withdrew the selenite crystal. She immediately recognized it as a Setsuhan heart, not unlike her own, though hers was hanging in the reliquary.

"Where did you get that?" she asked.

"The heart you have in the reliquary is not yours," he replied as he approached, "it is mine. I gave it to you and you gave me yours." He gently raised his hand, a precursor to a Setsuhan formal greeting, and gestured for her to do the same. "Vaexa est'alara celys, it is time you know the truth." He reached out and placed his fingertips on her forehead, she did the same, and her mind burst with long lost memories.

He was not Salem Eventide, he was the Setsuhan poet Delris, carved from the same selenite as she—they were the only two in history. She remembered how the sensitive nature of the stone gave them emotions new to the Setsuha. The flutter in her stomach when they embraced, the spark in his eyes when they met. They were two pieces that formed one, two spirits crafted for one another. He was their fifth elder, the 'last heart', the missing Setsuhan they couldn't remember, and the lost soul they began to wonder never existed.

Her eyes welled with tears and she threw her arms around him, squeezing him tighter than she thought her delicate arms could. He slid his hands to the small of her back and held her close, daring to close his eyes and fully succumb to the embrace.

Her mind was flooded with questions. "Why did you leave us?"

"I had to," he said softly, "I was given a mission from the queen that involved leaving Setsuha."

"But how?" She pulled away with bright eyes, elated at the idea there was a way to escape the mountain's influence.

"The queen gave me her heart and power, thereby breaking me free from the mountain. However, Setsuhans share their life energy in a perpetual circle of life and death. We did not know it at the time, but by removing my spirit from the cycle it also removed my presence in perceptive time. While I did exist here with you for millennia across different forms, you could not remember me and you could not replace me."

"And now you've returned!" she said joyously. "A hope we truly needed. Another elder, one with experience outside the realm would be—"

"I cannot stay," he said, his own heart retching in his chest. "My mission for the queen is not yet complete and when it is, I will be gone forever."

Vaexa's heart could be seen breaking in her eyes. The world seemed to be crushing her people's spirits with every passing day and this was just the hope they were looking for. An ideal beyond the borders of the Snow Leaf or at least the return of a Setsuhan when so many were mysteriously disappearing.

"Please, no," she plead, "we need you here. I need you here. Our world is dying." She embraced him once more, refusing to let him go. "Don't leave me again, Delris."

Salem felt heavy in her arms and dreaded the words he knew to follow. "I am not Delris anymore," he said sadly, "I am not even a Setsuhan. I have draconian blood in my veins and with it come new feelings, emotions, and convictions. I am oathbound to the Queen of Drakes and though I love the Snow Leaf, I discovered I love Elanta more.

I chose to give my life and everything in it for an ideal twenty years ago and that has not changed today. I will die, Vaexa, but it will be with great purpose."

She said nothing. Just one more disappointment she was helpless to fight. Instead, she cried on his shoulder in the silence of sweet wind, where through sharp eyes Whisper watched the embrace from the veil of weeping branches, heart twisting.

56

DEAR SALEM EVENTIDE

Fever delicately sifted through a chest of riches and trinkets she 'convinced' some of the Orbweavers to grace her with, in exchange for their lives of course—or at least their sanity. She was biding her time in Ivory's diamond chamber, separating the jewelry from other objects and holding them up to the light. Luminescent glyphs shone eerily beneath the diamond walls, creating a mesmerizing glimmer that made even the mundane look enchanted. Her fingertips toyed with a veil of silver chains—either a fancy necklace or a belt trinket, she wasn't sure. As she adjusted it in the light she could hear someone enter the room behind her. She sweetly turned her head, still deciding whether to welcome or destroy her guest. A smile met her lips as she saw the leviathan Wrath, crouching to squeeze his heavy obsidian armor through the diamond arches. "Oh love, you are a sight for sore eyes."

Following behind him was the Ravenmane Baku, Agathuxusen, carrying his helmet under his arm. Though he, too, was large, his struggle to enter the room was far less obvious.

Fever's smile faded with eyes of growing cold. "You, I could do without."

The Ravenmane chuckled cockily and made no retort. He wasn't one to waste words on the weak.

Fever held the trinket of dangling chains across the left side of her face, as though it were a circlet veil, concealing her scars with a cascade of glistening silver. "What do you think, love?"

Wrath watched as she addressed him, but didn't reply.

"Still the strong, silent type?" She tilted her head back and forth to see how the jewelry felt. The chains whipped around a little, but were long and heavy enough that they didn't bother her scarred eye—she couldn't see out of it anyways. Ivory's illusion simply made it look normal.

"He doesn't speak your language, human," the Ravenmane sneered.

She fiddled with the clasps and adjusted the length behind her head to fit her better. Somehow, she was less irritated with his offense to her humanity rather than her sex. "There's more to communication than just words, simple Baku." She shared a sweet look in the corner of her eye with the quiet leviathan.

The Ravenmane laughed and turned to Wrath, addressing him in the leviathan's guttural tongue. **"She thinks you understand her."**

Wrath silently watched her preen to conceal her scar. He was present when she received it at the battle of Lyre and knew the Ravenmane was not aware. It was their secret and he could see her desperately trying to find the strength to bury it. **"I understand,"** he replied.

Though Fever didn't understand the language she was shocked to hear him speak and stopped what she was doing. Their eyes met through the slit in his helmet and somewhere beneath the power of Instrumentation and killer instincts there was something vulnerable—a trust forged in innocence long since forgotten.

"I understand well," Wrath said again.

The Ravenmane paused awkwardly, rolling his eyes and distancing himself from the conversation. There was something here he didn't understand and didn't care to.

Moments later, Ivory entered the room, drawing all attention to the vibrant blue of her webbed eyes. "Hello, my Instruments."

Fever returned to her trinket while the others gave their full attention.

Ivory sighed. She had already told her shameful secret regarding the Second Wish to Phori and now it was time to inform the others.

"There has been a setback," she said. It was unusual to hear defeat in Ivory's voice. "Though I have bargained for the key to destroying the honeycomb stone that imprisons the Second Wish, it turns out it may be almost impossible to do."

As she spoke, the Ravenmane quietly translated to Wrath.

"As you know, the dragons developed the formula for honeycomb stone and in doing so they manufactured a secret weakness so that their creations could never be used against them. That weakness, it seems, is the blood of a true dragon." Ivory was excellent at maintaining her composure, but it was clear her shoulders were tensing up. "There is something within a true dragon's blood that will break the honeycomb stone resin."

"We find dragon, then," Wrath replied.

The Ravenmane rested his helmet on the ground and chuckled. He understood Ivory's ordeal. **"The leviathans have been in hiding for too long,"** he said, **"The dragons have been dead for twenty years."**

Fever could see the confusion in Wrath's eyes.

Ivory shook her head in dismay. **"The Fates killed them. I killed them,"** she said in the leviathan tongue. The irony was palpable, eradicating the one thing she needed to attain the incredible power now just beyond her grasp.

"I assume we're telling him the dragons are dead," Fever interrupted, being the only one in the room who didn't speak the language.

Wrath was unsure how he felt about the new information. Though the leviathans rarely ever associated with the dragons directly, their strength and majesty were highly revered, sometimes even worshipped. The idea that the Fates were responsible for destroying something so sacred stirred something distrustful within him. Why would they perform such a travesty? What right did they have to judge such a glorious creature? Were the Fates responsible for the scouring of his people as well? Since meeting Ivory and becoming her Instrument, he had served her with unwavering, unquestioned loyalty, but Ivory's new light illuminated fissures in his conviction—cracks only real answers stood a chance at mending. **"All dragons? You murdered all dragons?"**

Ivory pursed at the word 'murder', which made it sound as though the dragons were helpless, innocent victims. **"Yes,"** she replied. Ivory began to speak the common tongue and trusted the Ravenmane would continue to translate for Wrath. "All hope is not yet lost, however."

"There are no purebloods left," the Ravenmane said. "What few 'dragons' still roam are either lesser forms or abominations of the Overworld."

"In Fever's journey she discovered a Setsuhan who could transform into the Queen of Drakes when poisoned with a chthonomantic venom called Innocence, but Savrae-Lyth is incredibly powerful. While she is an option, there is at least one other true dragon left," Ivory replied, "or at least, there may be." Ivory sighed. She clearly didn't like what she was about to suggest. "Ogra."

The Ravenmane laughed. "That's the better option?"

"The Chitin King?" Fever chimed, interested enough to draw her attention from her project. "Even if the Overworld hasn't twisted his blood, making him bleed seems... reckless. Even for me."

The Ravenmane would never have said he agreed with Fever, but it was clear he thought the option of Ogra was a facile one. "If the mist twisted the harrow shrikes, why would Ogra's blood work?"

"Ogra is no ordinary dragon," Ivory replied. "He is the strongest of his species and once held a seat in the draconian court. His bloodline is not only pure, it's royal, hopefully making it harder to twist."

"His larger size would slow the effect," Fever said, "but a lot of time has passed, it's likely he no longer has the lineage in his veins. He's probably more demon than anything now." Fever cared very little for Ivory's ideal to begin with and chose not to contribute ideas over facts. So far as she was concerned the Second Wish didn't involve her, she was just there to kill marks and wreak havoc.

"What's our plan then?" the Ravenmane asked. "Assault Ogra?"

"Certainly not," Ivory quickly made clear. "Ogra made a deal with the Phoenix Queen for something, which means he can be bargained with. He will surely discover soon, if he doesn't know already, that his mission was a failure. That gives us an advantage." Ivory folded her hands and floated across the room. Fever took it as divine pacing. "Ogra aside, our best chance is with Phori."

The Ravenmane sneered, while Fever rolled her eyes. Wrath was the only one who clearly had no opinion, though he was the only one who hadn't yet met her.

"Phori informed me that there exists a sword capable of cutting honeycomb stone, and by Fever's description it may now be in the hands of the Phoenix Queen. Also, Phori's ability to adjust density could grow powerful enough to affect honeycomb stone, but her power is far too underdeveloped to know for certain. Whether you like her or not, protecting her and honing her skill is one of our top priorities now."

Fever scowled. "In case you hadn't noticed, Phori is in Obsidian." She gestured across the room to Ivory's other instruments. "We have a leviathan, a creature the Bastion Nine helped push from the face of Elanta; a Baku, a race they *still* try to push from the face of Elanta; and myself, a notorious criminal wanted as far east as Setsuha, which is pretty much the whole world. If you think any of us are getting into Emberwilde as allies to the Phoenix Queen you're more insane than I am. I had feet in the palace all of sixty seconds and almost lost my head."

"We can approach Ogra and make a deal," Ivory said, "but the odds aren't good he would do anything that would allow us to become more powerful. Even conspiring about it puts us at risk of him turning his hordes against us."

"I'd sooner put my faith in Ogra than Phori," Fever replied.

"The main concerns are the Orbweavers and Chitin Kings. If we express need they will take it as vulnerability, if we strike one down they will mark us as traitors, and if they find out how much power the Second Wish will truly give us they will immediately kill us and claim it for themselves."

"Wait," Wrath interjected, "Chitin Kings are enemies, not allies?"

"Yes," Ivory replied softly. "They are evil—a necessary, albeit temporary one. Only of use until they are not."

Wrath's discomfort regarding the death of the dragons stacked with the idea of betraying his kin, who were currently allied with the Chitin Kings. Betrayal after betrayal, the deceit was scratching at the back of his mind.

Fever perked at the idea of subterfuge and espionage.

"It isn't ideal, but we will speak with Ogra," Ivory said, "Meet me on the stone bridge to his temporary domain in an hour and be prepared for the worst."

In heavy silence, Salem pressed through the lush green landscape of Setsuha, Vaexa only a few steps behind. With nightfall quickly approaching they would be safest in the nests of Llaesynd. Setsuhans turned to stone in death but that made them no less prey in the dark of night. While their swift and dexterous nature made them challenging to catch, it also made them fun to chase.

Vaexa walked with her arms wrapped around her, closed off and distant. "Why would you tell me?"

"What do you mean?"

"After everything that's happened to me and our people, why would you further worsen our spirits?"

A large plant slowly reached for him and he brushed it away briskly—everything here was carnivorous. Lichen crept up their ankles if they stood in one place too long and even the lemongrass lured insects with its sweet scent and snared them with tiny fibers on their stalks, but they were of no harm to the thicker skinned.

"I thought it was important for you to know what we suffer for," Salem said.

"What *you* suffer for. We're dying because the mountain has forsaken us. You're dying because you've forsaken the mountain. There's a difference."

"Do not speak ill of Savrae-Lyth. Her vision for Elanta is greater than we could imagine."

Vaexa scoffed. "The queen is dead, Salem. Though I loved her, any ideal she once had was silenced by the Fates."

"It has not. Savrae-Lyth and Me'landris had a child."

"True, but I remember only now that my memories have returned. And it doesn't change what we're suffering through." She struggled to find joy in the words. "Is it Whisper?"

"Yes," he replied, "and I believe she has the strength to finish what we started."

"You mean free Shiori Etrielle?"

Salem nodded. It was always a foolhardy plan, but it was one worth pursuing.

Vaexa didn't like it, she didn't like any of it, but she was just a leaf in the current. She always was. She was never truly free her whole life—caged in the Snow Leaf, bound to the will of the mountain. Nothing she could say or do led her to believe she could influence the outcome of her people. They'd always be birds in the world's largest cage.

"Why did you call Whisper a 'deer'?" she asked. When she and Salem exchanged memories, she caught a glimpse of an emotion similar to kinship but stronger between the two.

"I called her 'dear'," he replied. Setsuhans were created and though they were capable of feeling companionship they were unfamiliar with endearment. "It is a term of affection."

Twenty years ago, after he left the Snow Leaf, it wasn't until he met the enchanter Grove that he learned there was so much more to human language. Grove was one of his first friends, who taught him much of what he knew now, but always teased him for having the emotional experience of a child. Salem was always too serious to pay it any mind, though he was curious as to what affection might feel really like. Grove always told him that an emotion can be perceived as one thing, but when we truly feel, it redefines itself into something fantastically new. Salem was frequently warned that someday he would know the right moment to use the word 'dear' and, when what he knew as 'affection' changed into that new and amazing feeling, he shouldn't miss the opportunity. When Salem first introduced himself to Whisper the word just flew from his lips, and now he knew why. In fact, he rarely called her name without it preceding since. He liked to believe Grove would be prou— "Wait..."

Salem withdrew Grove's ledger and examined the cover, carefully running his fingertips along the letters.

"Do you have affections for Whisper?" Vaexa asked.

"I..." he allowed himself to become more distracted with the book than necessary, and then it struck him. *Envied Emerald to the East* was not about the jungles of Shén Shé at all, but a fantastically long anagram encompassing all three capitalized words. Each letter could be perfectly rearranged to make an entirely new phrase—in this case, "Dear Salem Eventide."

The book suddenly opened and the pages flipped blindingly without end, fluttering to create an image that shifted with each turn of parchment. It was a map of Elanta, and within the map were long, winding roots that stretched from various points and converged at Setsuha. He recognized that many of the roots stretched to familiar places. One went to Whitewater, one to Freestone, and one to Valakut, while there were others that seemed to go where no cities were at all—the Baku Sands, Shén Shé, and to the northern ice fields of Whitewater.

"They look like rivers," Vaexa said, peering enchantedly. She'd never seen such tricks before.

"They certainly wind like rivers, but I do not recognize them," he replied. There were no bodies of water that ran inland from Setsuha. "Perhaps they are geomantic leylines? The natural flow of earthly energy."

"They almost make a draconian symbol, don't they?"

Salem tilted his head. "I think you may be right. Each spot I recognize is where the Orbweavers used their blood crystals to summon the mist downward." He pointed to three separate points. "There are spirals of mist in all three of these locations, funneling energy down into them. However, it would seem there is no syphon of energy here or in Shén Shé. I cannot speak for the Baku Sands."

Vaexa recalled the kris daggers Selva and the other fenwights were collecting from cloaked humans that kept dying at the face of the mountain. "I think they've been trying to create one here, but none have been successful." She hovered her finger and traced a pattern in the flurry of pages. "Portions of the symbol look familiar, but I'm not sure what it means."

'It is Vruk'moraea' Savrae-Lyth said in the confines of his mind, 'a glyph of planar shifting, but those are not natural leylines.'

Salem looked at it more closely when he remembered the overgrowth of forest outside of Blackthorne. "They are rivers," he said, "Underground."

Vaexa's eyes went wide. Rivers? Under the earth? It was preposterously magical to her.

"Water is one of the most fascinating substances in Elanta and any geomancer worth his salt could make an underground channel with enough time and effort," Salem said wondrously, "Inexplicably, water is capable of adopting the frequency of external energy influences, thereby acting as a natural medium."

"What does that mean?"

"It means the Orbweavers have created a massive sigil, one that spans Elanta, and they are charging it with energy from the Overworld. If they complete it by performing their rituals in Setsuha and Shén Shé..." He pondered what it could mean, "...then all of Elanta would shift planes to... somewhere else."

57

DEMONIC COLLUSION

The darkest depth of Sabanexus held creatures the light feared most. Hundreds of leviathans armored themselves in hide and steel, while cultists tamed demons with sigils and rode upon their backs. A massive funnel of swirling mist churned through the ceiling of the largest cave where everyone could marvel. The armies were a sprawling darkness from the stone bridges that connected the cave systems above.

Since the arrival of the Chitin Kings the armies had amassed and segregated into four groups. Ivory was watching them very carefully, and now that all her Instruments were present she was ready to confront Ogra regarding his secret plan with the Phoenix Queen.

Down below, a unit of Orbweaver enchanters were working on a glyph to increase the armor plating on their mounts. Many groups of demons lingered in their presence. They amassed in groups of their own kind, teasing invisible boundaries of bias that separated them.

From her journey through the Overworld Ivory knew that, while the four Chitin Kings were working together to destroy Elanta, they were rivals in their home world. They were constantly battling over territory and hated one another more than anything else. The four Chitin Kings were going to amass their armies at different energy funnels before assaulting Elanta, but met here at Sabanexus first while they argued a division of the spoils. Eventually they would reach an agreement and part ways, but until then the mix of rivals in one space was a disaster on the brink of realization. Elanta's war could be won simply from the enemy tearing themselves to shreds.

Concern lingered in Ivory's eyes. She did not wish chaos upon Elanta, but freedom. However, this chaos was the only way to counter the supreme order of the Fates hiding in the Weave—undesired, but entirely necessary in the grand scheme.

"Come," Ivory said sternly to her Instruments, "We have work to do before the madness starts."

Fever, Ravenmane, and Wrath followed close behind as she left the main cave and traveled the darker tunnels into the deepest parts. The caves became wider the further down they walked, illuminated only by Ravenmane's glowing flames. Eventually they came upon the mouth of the passage, where it opened into a massive cavern— hundreds of amber eyes glinted as they took in the Ravenmane's flame. Ahead of them, a growl rumbled as shifting stone and dozens of leather wings flapped along a huge silhouette.

"Ogra," Ivory called with assertion, the only way one could truly be respected in the presence of a demon king, "a word?"

The silhouette rustled and growled a low menace as its monstrous head caught the light and cast shadows over its spiny contours. It brought its long snout and toothy maw into the flame-light, dwarfing them with his size. Dozens of harrow shrikes shuffled on his back as they clung to his body. Unlike his smaller kind, he had no glimmering amber orbs to gaze with. Instead, his eyes remained shut and crusted—blind since the day Savrae-Lyth judged him for his crimes against Elanta and pried his eyes from his skull.

"You dare disturb me?"

"Blackrock is dead," Ivory replied.

Ogra sneered, his nostrils pulled the stale air past their shoulders and swayed Ivory's living hair. "I don't know what you're talking about."

"I'm not a fool, Ogra," she scolded, "Your deal with the Phoenix Queen has failed, but it doesn't have to." She expected Ogra to roar, but instead he spoke very deeply and with great control, which was almost more terrifying.

"Are you accusing me of acting outside of my treaty with the other Chitin Kings?"

"Yes," she replied, "and now I offer you an agreement for my silence."

"Or I could just kill you now. Devour your flesh and add your bones to the others. None would care, your usefulness has exhausted." Ogra bared his monstrous teeth in a menacing grin.

"You could kill me, but then you would not get what you sought. You don't even have to tell me what it is."

Ogra seemed to calm his hunger for ruination enough to continue the conversation. "I'm listening."

"I will retrieve your prize from the Phoenix Queen in return for a bottle of your blood."

Ogra paused, sightlessly examining her unusual offer. "Why do you want my blood?"

"It's none of your business. Do we have a deal or not?"

Guttural rumbles roiled across his throat and the harrow shrikes stirred restlessly. He slowly lifted his head and towered over them, poised to strike at any moment. "I accept, but she will not exchange it without the psychic child."

Ivory bowed slightly, not once taking her eyes from him. Despite his cooperation he was not to be trusted; bemusement whipped in his tail. "I may have something else she'll want."

EPILOGUE

THE WOLVES OF WHITEWATER

Light didn't shine the same within the mist. It was a pale haze that suffocated like ashen air, blurring one's vision and inducing hallucinations when overexposed. The borders around the funnel of mist that churned slowly in the lower district of Whitewater were heavily guarded, but that didn't stop him from sneaking in.

There was something about the air that immediately snuffed flame, though he heard a rumor an explosion occurred once in Freestone. Instead, he held a small glowing glyph of light in his palm, casting an eerie halo of emanation about his wrist. Light danced from the ring he gently twirled on his finger.

A chittering of hundreds of tiny legs scraped the stone as something approached, something that sounded larger as it neared. In the glow of light, teasing its furthest reaches and playing shapes in the cloudy darkness was a long, spiny figure. Its many legs could be seen trailing down its slender body as it curved itself upward like a large centipede and glared down at him—mandibles the size of axes were a silhouette almost indiscernible.

"What happened to my U'shuun?" the creature rasped. Its voice scratchy and harsh.

"Your damned scout got itself caught," he said.

"U'shuun are masters of stealth."

"It was detected by the soothsayer," he replied. "You're going to need to send more."

The creature chattered its jaws. "U'shuun are too useful to waste. I need assurances."

"Look," he said sharply, clenching his fist about his ring until it hurt, "you'll never take the city with the Moths and two Instruments protecting it. You need at least one U'shuun for each of them and they need to strike at the same time."

The creature flitted its legs and clicked in frustration. "Deliver me the soothsayer," it scratched, "then you may have all the U'shuun you want."

He sighed, gently bobbing his head in apprehension. "Shouldn't be a problem," he said as he began tapping his ring on the pommel of his dagger, the muffled glint of the silver wolf and sapphire eyes shone strangely in the mist, "she trusts me."

In the late hours, Whitewater's Great Hall was dark. The ivy could be seen in the ambient glow of sigil light every thirty feet, hanging like a woven tapestry against the castle walls. Fairchild just finished the night's duties and held in his palm a steaming cup of tea—the aromatics of orange and gooseberry tingled his senses. The tea was a rare and expensive import.

He climbed the steps to the large doors of alabaster and abalone, blowing at the steam to cool his first few sips. He lifted his golden robes with his free hand as not to trip and released them when he reached the top.

Fairchild took a moment to sip the tea, scalding his tongue. He was growing impatient, wishing it to be ready sooner, and pushed open the door in frustration.

The large door groaned, casting a single beam of light into the hall. It was empty, dark, and deathly quiet—not a sigil lit, not a soul in sight. He peered into the vast shadows and listened to the silence, but nothing stirred. The hall's sigils should have lit when the door opened, but all remained dark. He took a breath and stepped into the room.

"Announcing..." a soft voice sounded, raising his hackles, "*Vaughn Cross, Chancellor of Whitewater.*"

Fairchild scoured the room with absolute scrutiny, not moving until he was certain no one heard the harbinger. He raised a hand to the arch and pulled the harbinger glyph to surface, examining it suspiciously. Someone fixed it. He was lucky no one was present when he arrived. He clutched his hand shut, broke the glyph entirely, and shuffled into the dark—orange and gooseberry lingering.

BARGAINS AND BLOODLINES

The prisons of Obsidian were separate from the Palace of Roiling Cinder, buried at the base of the volcano. The heat from the magma churning within radiated through the structure, making it incredibly uncomfortable.

Kismet sat in the corner of his cell and awaited his fate. He was sweltering. Soaking through his shirt from both heat and withdrawal, wishing he had his rumrose to numb everything just a little. He could see his coat at the other end of the room, though he imagined his drugs had been confiscated. Even if they hadn't, his pipe was gone.

Heat does strange things. It makes you want to sleep and fills your head with illusions. He slouched with a small clay bottle in his hand and day-dreamt. The guards were gracious enough to give him water to survive, but he knew it was only because the queen wanted him in the Blackrock prison alive.

He tried to imagine Djagatt in a better place or Lau Lau safe with Whisper. The idea soothed him, if only a little, dreaming his sacrifice somehow resulted in something good. It wasn't that he'd given up or that he didn't want to live. He wanted to live more than anything. Wanted to feel the ocean breeze on his face, see Lau Lau at the bow of his ship, embrace the joy of lost treasure slipping between his fingers. What he would have given to see Carver's stupid face when their plan took sail or chain him to the mast of the *Last Breath* himself.

He took a sip of the water, almost gone, when he heard someone enter the guard post. Sweat dripped into his eyes and it took him a moment to focus before he could see an Emberwilde woman standing before his cell. She had the black-striped golden feather of a General woven into her hair along with an array of colorful glass beads. At her back was a vicious obsidian double-bladed staff. Fastened to her side was a sword and from it dangled an impressive number of honorary tassels and a crest of Clan Salamander.

He drank the last of the water and flicked the bottle from his hands, letting it break on the stone.

"Do you have an appointment?" Kismet asked drearily, "I'm truly quite busy."

"My name is Phori," she said. "Are you Oona Kismet?"

"What's it matter to you?"

Phori crossed her arms. "Despite my research, I can't seem to find what merits your sentence to the Blackrock. I have a theory though."

"Please," he opened his arms and bowed his head, "regale me."

"When the demon flew you above the palace I sensed a honeycomb blade on you. One I believe matches a fake I've seen in the queen's displays. I've checked your paperwork to confirm but no such blade was documented, which only raised my suspicions further. When I asked other Bastions about you their minds clouded. I believe any knowledge of your crime was shrouded by powerful enchantment."

A smile of intrigue crept along his lips.

"I believe you stole the Scarlet Charm and escaped. To save face, the queen had a replacement made to conceal the theft, and created an enchantment to haze the memory of anyone who may have known."

"Hah!" he laughed loudly, "You think the queen lied to her people and hunted me for twelve years to cover up the theft a mere sword?"

It did seem unusual. After all, the sword wasn't under much protection.

Kismet leaned forward and gleamed slyly. "I broke into the queen's vault."

"Good." She reached out, grasped the lock with her fingers and shattered it like glass. The iron shards struck the floor in an orchestration of tiny jingles and clangs. "You're going to do it again."

Kismet clambered to his feet. An escape seemed too good to be true and he half wondered if this was a trap by the queen to give him a moment's hope before dragging him off.

"Why are you so interested in the vault?" he asked. After he broke in the first time it was likely the queen took measures and made it several times harder to infiltrate.

"The queen is conspiring with the enemy," Phori replied.

"To even consider entering the vault is treason and as a Bastion your punishment will be severe."

"I am an Instrument and a servant to the people of Emberwilde first. Even the queen is not beyond my judgement." Phori opened the prison door and gestured for him to exit. "Choose your ending."

Kismet took a deep breath. It was suicide to try to get into the vault a second time, but he was hard pressed to think of a better partner than an Instrument. "What's the deal here? I get you into the vault and I go free?"

"Yes."

It wasn't going to get better than that—the Blackrock the only alternative. Besides, he'd get to tell the world he broke into the vault not once, but twice. If he survived. "Just you and me against the Phoenix Queen and her Bastions?"

"Not all of her Bastions."

From the shadows stepped a lithe woman in ruby scale and a golden cloak fastened with a silver Firefly medallion. Tears struggled behind her sharp almond eyes as she held her second sword in her hands—the narrow, wavy blade rested peacefully within its sheath. The silver hilt caught the light and shimmered something both alluring and familiar as she held it out to him. Hanging from it was a silver medallion of Clan Firefly and the black banded General's feather.

Kismet's heart skipped.

"Oona?" the Firefly asked softly, her voice rich with northern nobility.

He bowed his head in shame, unable to meet her eyes, and accepted the return of his blade. "Hello sister."

In the Phoenix Queen's chambers, curtains of red and gold lace cascaded down from high obsidian ceilings. To the furthest end of her chamber was a large bed of only the finest silk and goose-down. In the center of the room was a circular sitting pool warmed by the heat of the volcano.

The queen relaxed in the water, curls of steam wafted past closed eyes while the occasional drop of water would fall from a stalactite above, filling the room with tranquility. Beside the pool laid the Scarlet Charm; her fingers gently traced the scabbard's ruby accents and silver inlay while she relaxed.

She slowly opened her eyes to a stretching of shadows that coalesced and formed a pool of ichor against the doors to her chambers. It was silent—a soundless brew of darkness that beckoned forth something from within. A figure pushed through and as the shadows peeled from her porcelain features the room's color bled into shades of gray.

The crown was the first she noticed, bone gleaming a most brilliant white against the black of her long, living hair. The woman floated out on a cloud of mist and tattered silk, threads waving behind from her dress of clinging darkness. Bright blue eyes devoured the last of the room's color until the world seemed foreign.

"I'm sorry to disturb you," the crowned woman of shadows sung sweetly. "I am Ivory."

The Phoenix Queen was a woman of immense composure, and if she was nervous about the sudden interruption she wasn't showing it. Instead, she lounged deeper into the water and closed her eyes once more, waiting for the next droplet from above. "This must be important to disturb me in my private hours." No drop struck the water. She peeked with one eye to see a single bead frozen in time, mid-freefall, inches above the surface.

"I understand you had a bargain with Ogra, the Chitin King, that was unsuccessful," Ivory said, the pool of shadows continued to turn behind her.

"It was a failure, yes, but I received... consolation." She gently tapped the gears of the Scarlet Charm's scabbard.

Ivory spotted the sword and curled a sweet smile. "I was hoping you could tell me what Ogra would gain from such an agreement and what he was supposed to deliver to you in the first place?"

"Why such interest?"

"Because I may wish to bargain for what he sought." Ivory delicately folded her hands and waited, silently sensing the Phoenix

Queen's anchor as she held the invisible fatespinner thread between her fingertips. It was as she thought, the queen was indestructible, even with her power over death—cutting her anchor would be impossible.

"I'm interested," she replied, "As a Fate I can imagine you have much to offer." She rose from the pool. Water trickled down her smooth skin, freezing in time the moment it dripped from her body. Ivory was one of few modesties and admired her form from afar, until she was concealed with the draping of red cloth. "What Ogra wanted from me was a phylactery," she said. "A vessel in which to place his soul so his body could be indestructible."

Ivory's eyes gleamed. She had no idea Ogra was close to attaining something so powerful and now she had a potential opportunity to take it for herself. "A phylactery requires a significant amount of life-force to create and just as much to sustain. Was recharging his phylactery a part of the bargain?"

The queen chuckled, "Certainly not. It would last long enough for his war, but I think he presumed it was permanent. I didn't find it necessary to correct his misconceptions." She tied a sash around her waist to seal her robe shut. "In exchange, I wanted the return of one of my daughters. She was taken from me as an infant."

Ivory was unaware the queen ever had a daughter. "Might I make a proposition then?" She opened her palms and the pool of ichor and shadow fluxed. Soon after, the leviathan Wrath peeled from the darkness with Shiori's Second Wish, still sealed within the block of clear honeycomb stone.

The Phoenix Queen's eyes smiled, her first expression since Ivory's arrival. "Is that what I think it is?"

"The Second Wish," Ivory said, outstretching her hand to present the gold and platinum blade sealed within. Wrath carefully placed the honeycomb stone down and stepped back. "I must admit, I have had trouble releasing it, but if you are willing, I would trade you the phenomenal power of the Second Wish for the immortality of a phylactery. You needn't charge it more than once, but I must insist you tell me how I can do it myself."

The Scarlet Charm was carefully lifted into the queen's hands. "I accept your bargain," she said. With a snap of her fingers a flicker of sparks swirled before her chest, and as the sparks fell they revealed a deep red gemstone that radiated like embers. It floated into the palm of her hand where she outstretched it to the forlorn Fate. "You must commune with it to create a haven for your soul, and so long as the phylactery is not destroyed your body will be invincible. If the phylactery is ever broken, your soul will have nowhere to hide and your mortality will return."

Elation in Ivory's eyes couldn't be contained as she accepted the gemstone—a curl of mist from her platinum bangle enveloped it and shaped a glorious choker of thin platinum chains. She already knew it would be foolish to give it to Ogra. If the Phoenix Queen could free the Second Wish, Ivory had a chance at both treasures, and if not, then she would have to trust that Phori could grow strong enough to take it. "How do I charge it?" she asked as her hair took the amulet and fastened it to her throat.

The queen placed her hand on the honeycomb stone surrounding the Second Wish and spied Ivory in the corner of her eyes. "That which preserves life must consume life in turn. The stronger the soul you allow it to consume, the longer the effect will last."

"I see." Ivory touched the gem at her throat, suddenly wondering. She was the taker of lives, but this almost seemed contrary to her moral stance. Sacrificing the few for the many was the foundation of her conviction, but harvesting souls almost felt monstrous. Her only justifications were to slay her enemies and use them as fuel—the Chitin Kings, the Fates, and their Instruments. Theirs would surely be powerful enough to last her a while. Once her mission to destroy The Weave was over, she would stop her consumption and allow her mortality to return.

With a blinding flash of crimson stone the Scarlet Charm was released from its sheath and sliced through the top of the Second Wish's prison at an angle. The blade melted through the stone with ease and the corner of the prison slid to the floor with a *thud*, chipping the obsidian.

Ivory couldn't believe how easily it cut and now the Second Wish was within reach. The power could be felt radiating from the platinum blade's wavy golden edge, and the black and silver wrapped handle beckoned for someone to wield it. The balled fabric charm hanging from the hilt looked like a little ghost, slumbering in wait.

The Phoenix Queen licked her lips and basked in the radiance, dropping the Scarlet Charm like a trinket and slowly reaching for the Second Wish. "Infinite lives and ultimate power," she sung, drunk with new ideologies for a regime that spanned more than just Emberwilde.

She wrapped her fingers around the sword's handle and the eyes of the little ghost charm began to open.

TELL HER

Vaexa and Salem arrived back at Llaesynd to find Lau Lau curled in front of a statue with her face buried in Yoru's fur. The velvetine purred in surrender.

He took a knee beside her and placed his hand on her back. "Where has Whisper gone?"

Lau Lau sniffled. "She left. They always leave."

He tried to sound as calm as possible even though he knew she knew he was panicking inside. "Where?"

She pointed into the woods, toward the shores where they'd landed the longboat.

"Please watch her," he said to Vaexa. She nodded and he briskly exited into the brush.

The fading light played with the branches, casting illusions of eyes and limbs everywhere. Carelessness in the dark could be his undoing, but his impatience was a hard beast to tame. As he neared the edge of the forest he could hear the crash of waves from the ocean beyond, and through the canopy of hanging branches he could see Whisper standing at the cliff's edge.

He slowed his pace and brushed aside the last branch, where she turned to greet him with sad and distant eyes.

"What do you want?" she asked, turning back to the water. The wind ruffled her raven hair and she did her best to hook it behind her ears.

"Are you alright?" he asked. He approached and stood at her side, the sudden drop to the dark water below was almost dizzying to look at.

She crossed her arms. "I don't know. I thought I was fine, I've always been fine, but now I'm just... not."

'Tell her.'

Salem only nodded. He wasn't fine either and he had yet to find the words as well.

"I don't know who I am anymore," she said. "I was used to being a mistborn and now I'm apparently some dragon queen. I have all these powers and feelings I can't explain or control and I'm scared that, if I let myself get used to them, everything could change again and I'd be lost once more."

"I understand," he replied, "I was once a Setsuhan, you know."

She watched him, curiously confused.

"I was once an elder, like Vaexa, but when your mother tore her heart from her chest to end the war and prepare your inheritance I was separated. My mountain forgot me, my people forgot me, and life was suddenly strange and new. I walked into Whitewater educated, but naïve, still without the experience of wisdom. I spent years rebuilding a new life for myself, preparing for when you grew strong enough to leave the monastery so I could help guide you to your kingdom. Then life changed again."

"What happened?"

He turned, emerald eyes suffering something beautiful. "You came into my life." He shifted awkwardly. "Setsuhans do not experience emotions like humans or dragons do, and when we travelled to Freestone together it awoke something I could not understand. Everything I knew changed again, and I am still trying to understand it."

Whisper took a nervous breath. "I think I feel the same. It's hard to talk about. I'm not great with words or feelings. How can something that's supposed to be amazing feel so confused?"

"I have been holding back, keeping something from you," he replied. "Your inheritance, your mother's power, is the only thing keeping me alive. I've been creating distance between you and me because I know that, when I give you your power, I will die."

Whisper was quick to respond. "Then keep it. I don't need it."

"You do need it, my dear Whisper. It is the only way to make you strong enough to free Shiori Etrielle and defeat the Fates. If you do not, then you will either die or spend your life running."

Whisper rapped her fingers on her arm as the anxiety settled in. "I don't care, I won't accept it. I've had power my whole life and now

I finally want something different."

"A life on the edge is not what you deserve. It is not what your mother gave her life for. She would want you to—*I* want you to live. Even if it means my death."

"I'm a queen now, remember. All that matters is what I want." She laughed a rare laugh and Salem realized he loved it.

He hung his head in thought. She was ready for her power, but maybe he didn't need to give it yet. Perhaps they could travel to Whitewater and explore their feelings further, saving the inheritance as a last resort when needed. She was certainly strong enough to defend herself against most foes without it.

'Tell her.'

Whisper reached out and timidly laced her fingers into his hand. The world faded into the sound of ocean waves. He turned to her, heart pounding in his chest, and leaned in, pressing his lips to hers. He lost himself in the softness, reeled in the scent. His hand slid up her neck and into her hair, gently tugging it in fistfuls. She pressed into him, held him close, and there on cliffs in the falling dark they left Elanta behind.

They slowly pulled apart and gazed into one another's eyes, finally found. The noise of the world quieted into the heartbeats between kisses.

'Tell her.'

"My dear Whisper," he said softly, "you have changed my life." He took a breath and swallowed his fears. In his eyes there was a sad softness, tearing him apart.

A brilliant blue light and crackling corona lit the cliffside and raised the hair on Whisper's neck as he placed his hand on his chest, withdrew an orb of swirling essence, and thrust it into her stomach. The power overwhelmed her as it absorbed into her body, shaking the air and seizing her muscles as electricity surged across her frame. The silver blossom lacunae in her eyes flared open as her hair shifted blond and a phantom cloak of vibrant feathers pulsed with each electric spasm. The green of Salem's eyes had already begun to fade, but he smiled at her with all the love he could.

He expected her to roar in pain or swear in rage, but instead her eyes filled with tears, shock, and denial. "I don't want it!" she cried, "Take it back!"

"I love you, my dear Whisper," he said, "That is why you must live." He staggered backward and fell from the cliff edge.

The physical pain was agonizing, but nothing compared to the breaking of a heart. Mustering everything she could, she leapt from the edge in pursuit, her phantom cloak of feathers trailed down the cliff face behind her. He struck the waves and moments later she was engulfed in the bitter cold. The crackle of blue light pulsed under her skin and flashed across her eyes, squeezing her body into a desperate fit of convulsions.

There, below her, illuminated by the flicker of power that surged through her, Salem was slowly engulfed by the darkness. His hand stretched up toward her in his descent, skin turning pale crystal the further he sank. She tried to reach for him, begging with her eyes and roaring in a fit of bubbles, but the life in his eyes faded doubly-blind and the depths of Setsuha swallowed him whole.

Death can be a sinking stone—cold, lonesome, and hopelessly heavy.

ABOUT THE AUTHOR

S.K. AETHERPHOXX

S.K. Aetherphoxx is an author, poet, and small business owner with a passion for providing beautiful, exciting, and dynamic reading experiences.

He can be studied in his natural habitat, a Kelowna coffee shop, where he uses caffeine to replace the basic necessities of human life—namely sleep.

When his cat gives him permission, he travels western Canada's Expo circuit, educating aspiring writers and motivating them to share their words with the world.